THE Family

KIMBERLEY CHAMBERS

THE Family Man

HarperCollins*Publishers*

HarperCollins*Publishers* Ltd
1 London Bridge Street,
London SE1 9GF

www.harpercollins.co.uk

HarperCollins*Publishers*
1st Floor, Watermarque Building, Ringsend Road
Dublin 4, Ireland

First published by HarperCollins*Publishers* 2021
This paperback edition 2022
1

A catalogue record for this book is available from the British Library

ISBN: 978-0-00-836603-2

Typeset in Sabon LT Std by
Palimpsest Book Production Ltd, Falkirk, Stirlingshire

Printed and bound in the UK using 100% renewable electricity
at CPI Group (UK) Ltd

MIX
Paper from
responsible sources
FSC
www.fsc.org   FSC™ C007454

In memory of my very own Bond family,
Nanny Daisy, Aunt Doll, Uncle Cliff, Lily, John,
Betty, Charles, Lilian, Violet, Rose, Percy, Reggie,
Maurice and Vera.
Love and miss you all xxx

ACKNOWLEDGEMENTS

Big love to the amazing team at HarperCollins. So very grateful for the support myself and my books are given. You always do me proud!

Kimberley Young, who I totally adore working with. Not only are you a brilliant editor, you've been so patient on giving me extra time on this book. Very much appreciated.

Special mentions to my blinding agent, Tim Bates, my wonderful publicist Felicity Denham. Sarah Shea and Katie Lumsden, who are both a joy to work with. Also, Charlotte Brabbin, Charlie Redmayne and Laura Meyer, who all have my back.

Love also to Rosie de Courcy, the legendary Sue Cox, Pat Fletcher (second mum), and me bestie, Sharon Borthwick.

Shal, I dunno what I'd have done without you during the lockdowns. I know I've driven you doolally, but at least I've repaid you by giving you a major part in this book as Kenny Bond's old woman. We're even now, girlie. Even though there is a good chance I might kill you off in the sequel!

And last but certainly not least, I want to thank my readers. It's been such a mad time with all this Covid lark. I've struggled mentally and I'm sure many of you have struggled in all different ways. Yet, whenever I put a post up on social media, you're always there to cheer me up. I honestly can't thank you all enough for that.

God bless and let's hope for better times ahead xxx

PART ONE

'In family life, love is the oil that eases friction, the cement the binds closer together, and the music that brings harmony.'

Friedrich Nietzsche

PROLOGUE

I was born in 1943, in Stratford, East London. A war baby, I was my mother's first child and would turn out to be her only.

I never had a dad, but I had lots of different uncles who'd visit. Some were nicer to me than others.

Then Uncle Pete turned up on the scene and, unlike all the others, he didn't disappear. Quite the opposite, he moved in with us.

Even though I was only six, I could tell Uncle Pete couldn't stand the sight of me. I tried to be a good boy, keep out of his way so I didn't antagonize him. That didn't stop the beatings though, especially if he'd been down the boozer. He'd just stroll into my bedroom and start on me for no valid reason.

One day, after being whipped on my bare arse with Uncle Pete's leather belt, I caught two buses and managed to find my grandparents' home in Canning Town. I was in agony, had to stand up throughout the journey as it was too bloody painful to sit down.

Me granddad went ballistic, shot straight out the house.

My nan comforted me, bathed my sores and made me numerous cups of sweet tea.

I never lived with my mum again after that. I moved in with me nan and granddad. I was much happier there.

Life was good for a while. Nan and Granddad never seemed to be poor like a lot of people. Granddad didn't have a normal job, but sometimes he'd come home with lots of money and give me some. I recall asking him how he earned his money once. I was about nine at the time and I'll never forget his words to me. He looked me in the eyes and said, 'Kenny, one day when you're old enough, I'll teach you all about my world. I promise.' After that I was always intrigued about Granddad's world. Sometimes he'd go missing for almost a week, but Nan never seemed too concerned when I asked if Granddad was OK. 'Your Granddad's fine, boy. He's on a bit of work,' she'd chuckle.

Tragedy struck first just after my tenth birthday. Nan went off to Rathbone Street market one day, came home complaining of terrible stomach pains, spent the night on the sofa, and me and Granddad woke up to find her dead the following morning.

Granddad was never the same after Nan's death. He lost his sparkle, seemed to give up on life and earning money. He rarely ate and started hitting the whisky. Would sit in his favourite armchair and drink a whole bottle before lunchtime. So I was packed off to live with me mum's sister, Aunt Nelly.

Aunt Nelly was nice, lived in Bow. She'd never married, had no kids, but she felt warmer to me than my real mum ever had. She would praise me, show me love by hugging me. Affection, I wasn't used to that. Only my nan had ever hugged me in the past. Not once do I remember my

4

own mother doing so. She never even stepped in when Uncle Pete smashed the living daylights out of me.

I was still worried about my granddad, would regularly visit him, urging him to teach me about his world, like he'd once promised to. Unfortunately, by that time he was unable to piece together a coherent sentence. I was gutted. Even as an eleven-year-old, I sensed Granddad's world was destined to be a mystery to me, and that would always haunt me.

Then fate struck. Me grandfather got rushed into the London Hospital one day. It was Aunt Nelly who sat me down and wiped away my tears as she told me he was dying. His liver had packed up on him.

I begged Aunt Nelly to let me see Granddad one last time. She was reluctant, but even she could see I wasn't exactly your average twelve-year-old boy by that point. Not after what I'd been through in life. I was a proper little man.

Granddad had the same colour eyes as me: a bright, piercing blue. As I greeted him, I saw his eyes light up like they used to for the first time in years. He grabbed my arm and clung to it. 'Kenny,' he croaked. 'Nell, leave me and the boy alone for a minute,' he added, even though he was struggling to breathe.

Aunt Nelly left the ward, then Granddad smiled. That cheeky smile that I remembered and hadn't seen for ages. 'I never told you how I stole a living, did I, boy?'

'No. Please tell me. I'm old enough now,' I pleaded.

Granddad held my hand, clasped it like he never wanted to let it go. 'You are my prodigy, Kenny. I want you to carry on the Bond name.'

'Go on, Granddad. I will, I swear. I owe you and Nan everything.'

5

'Never be a dogsbody. Only work for yourself.' Granddad paused to catch his breath. 'You earn money any way you can. That's what I did. Banks, security vans – I've held up lorries carrying quality loads. You never thieve off your average man on the street, though. House burglars are vermin. Ya never rob your own, either.'

'Yeah. But how? I wouldn't know where to start.'

'You'll find ways. You plan. Always be cautious. That's why me and Nan were never poor like every other bastard. I walked the walk and talked the talk. You can be the next me, Kenny. I can see it in you. The right road is boring. The wrong road is much more fun.'

'OK,' I replied. Granddad was taking ages to get a sentence out now, but I got the gist of what he was saying, and I was desperate to make him proud and carry on the Bond name.

'Marry a good woman like I did. But stay away from the booze. It's the devil's work, that. And never forget what I taught ya. The stories, the sayings, they've all got meanings, boy,' Granddad panted. I could see he was finding it harder to breathe, his grip on my hand was loosening.

'I will, Granddad. I promise I'll do all you say.'

Seconds later, me grandfather shut his eyes and died right in front of me. He had a half-smile on his face that I'll never forget.

Later that evening, I picked up a pen and pad and wrote down every single quote and saying I remembered Granddad telling me. It was only then I began to understand the meaning of life and what carrying on the Bond name truly meant . . .

CHAPTER ONE

Spring 1975

Kenny Bond lay on his bunk, hands behind his head, savouring the peace. Five whole days now he'd had the cell to himself and it was absolute bliss. It felt more like Butlins than Wormwood bloody Scrubs.

Glancing at the photo on the wall of his beloved wife and their kids, Kenny allowed himself a wry smile. Today was visiting day and not once had his Sharon ever let him down. She was his soulmate, and today he had something important to ask her.

Kenny's daydreaming about what his wife's reply would be was cut short by a jangling of keys, his cell being unlocked, then Perky's fat face appearing.

'Good morning, Bond,' Perky said, a supercilious smile on his piggy chops. 'Meet your new cellmate, Tamplin. Okey doke, I'll leave you two to get acquainted,' he chuckled, before slamming the metal door and locking it.

Kenny eyed his new cellmate with suspicion. He always got lumped up with a wrong un, knew the governor ordered that purposely. Usually, it stood out like a sore thumb at first glance what was wrong with each and every one of them. He'd had a lovely combination of druggies, alkies, notrights and nonces. Not this geezer though. For once, he had a cellmate who looked half normal.

Tamplin grinned. 'All right, Mush? What you in 'ere for then?'

Kenny sighed deeply. There was no mistaking that accent. A gypsy one.

Sharon Bond shuddered as she listened to the news. That serial rapist had struck in Cambridgeshire again. A twenty-two-year-old this time, the rapist's sixth victim in six months. How she missed having Kenny at home with her. He'd always made her feel safe and secure since the night she'd first met him.

Sixteen, Sharon had been when she'd met Kenny. He was seventeen, but already a man in comparison to other lads who'd asked her on dates. Kenny was mature, good-looking, oozed confidence, and within a few dates, Sharon had fallen head over heels for him. Luckily for her, Kenny felt the same and the following year they got married.

Sharon turned the volume up on the radio. She adored Minnie Ripperton's voice and the song 'Lovin' You' was currently storming up the charts. The words were beautiful, could have been written for her and Kenny. As soon as the song finished, Sharon turned the radio off. She usually looked forward to her prison visits, but not today. She had something to tell her husband and it wasn't good news. It was really bad.

Kenny Bond grinned as his blonde bombshell of a wife walked towards him. Shal was only five foot one, but whenever she visited him, she looked taller because she always wore high heels. She knew he got off on a pair of stilettos, had worn them in the bedroom while stark-bollock naked before he'd had the misfortune of getting a long stretch.

Kenny wrapped his arms around Sharon and kissed her. He could sense Percy was glaring at him, so gave him a cheeky wink as he pulled away. With her pretty face, cheeky smile, infectious laugh and personality, there wasn't a single man in this joint that wouldn't fancy his Shal, and no way did Percy have a woman indoors. The miserable bastard looked like he'd fallen out of the ugly tree and hit every branch on the way down.

'Tea and a Marathon?' asked Sharon.

'Yeah. Go on then. Don't take those shoes off though. I wanna watch you walk in 'em.'

'Three times I've nearly stacked it since I got out the car, Ken. Stilettos and flares seriously don't work. No way am I falling arse over tit in front of your fellow inmates and the screws. I'll be a bleedin' laughing stock.'

Kenny chuckled. 'Hurry up then. I got something import-ant to ask ya, like I told you on the blower.' He focused on her backside as she walked away. It looked almost edible in those jeans. Then again, she'd always had a great arse. Plump, with a bit of meat around it.

Sharon was filled with dread as she stood in the short queue. She wasn't prepared to ruin the whole visit, knew Kenny would lose the plot, so she'd tell him the bad news towards the end.

Kenny stared at this wife's breasts as she returned. Big and bouncy, especially in that skin-tight white T-shirt. They'd had such a good sex life on the outside, even when she was pregnant. That's what kept him going at times.

Reliving every moment they'd shared. The passion, the love, the togetherness.

'What you grinning at?' Sharon asked as she plonked the coffees on the table.

'Your tits. What else?' Kenny winked.

Sharon squeezed Kenny's hand. 'So, what's this important thing you want to ask me?'

'You remember that first night we met at that party in Canning Town? And your mate Sheila said, "You can't date him. He's got ginger hair and you don't want ginger kids!"' Kenny had planned this speech carefully, had too much time on his hands not to.

Sharon smiled. 'Yeah. You told Sheila your hair weren't bleedin' ginger, it was a coppery bronze, and you weren't hitting on me 'cause you preferred blondes.' Sharon's hair had been her natural colour at the time, a dullish brown.

'Well, I was right, weren't I, girl? We had a brown-haired son and a coppery bronze-haired daughter.'

'Yeah. And?'

'I want us to bang out another kid, Shal, when I get released. Aside from the fact I've missed watching Donny and Sherry grow up, I wanna see if the next one pops out ginger,' chuckled Kenny. 'We're still gonna be young enough, ain't we? Whaddya reckon?'

'Erm, yeah. I don't see why not.' By the time Kenny was released, Sharon would be too old to want any more kids. But she didn't want to rain on his parade.

'Good girl,' grinned Kenny. 'That'll be all I need to get through the rest of me sentence, that. I'm gonna need something to take me mind off things, 'cause I've been lumbered with a new cellmate today and he's grating on me already. A fucking pikey they've forced on me this time! They know how much I hate 'em, and that accent is doing me nut in already. He keeps singing an' all, the irritating prick. He'll get a clump before long if he keeps it up, I'm telling ya.'

'Don't go to town on him, Ken. You don't wanna get yourself put in solitary again. I couldn't visit you the last time.'

'I won't. I'll just give him a gentle dig. It's the Old Bill telling Pinky to make my life a misery. Pinky's right in with the filth.' Kenny had nicknamed the governor Pinky and his least favourite screw Perky. The gov had a pinky-red complexion, probably because he was an alkie. You could smell it on his rancid breath. As for Perky, he had a little turned-up snout and looked ready to be chopped up in rashers.

'Just try not to rile anyone up too much. I know what you're bleedin' well like.'

Kenny winked. 'It's me mum's birthday on Thursday. She wrote to me the other day, probably just to remind me. Full of the joys of spring, as always.' Kenny rolled his eyes. His mum still lived in Stratford and their relationship was a difficult one. The anger she obviously felt towards his dad, she tended to take out on him. She never had a good word to say about her only son. Or his father. She'd never disclosed his old man's name, but bitched about him all the time, saying what a wrong un he was and how he'd left her in the lurch.

'I always remember your mum's birthday. I got her a nice present from us. I'll give her a bell and arrange to take the kids over to visit her sometime this week.'

'Thanks, Shal. Leave her some dosh an' all, to waste on the bingo and the slot machines. Give her fifty quid – and while you're at it, pop in and see Aunt Nelly. Give

11

her the same and take her some flowers from me. I wrote to her yesterday and I'll pen a letter to me muvver later today.'

The rest of the visit was mainly spent nattering about the kids and family. Kenny could sense Sharon was on edge though. Nobody knew her better than he did. 'Come on, spit it out, Shal. You got something on your mind? What's a matter?'

Sharon took a deep breath. After being hounded out of two previous addresses over the years, she'd finally felt settled at her latest. Until now, that was.

'There's no easy way to say this, Kenny, but it's started again. I had crap posted through the letterbox, then the usual graffiti appeared.'

Kenny's jaw began to twitch, a trait of his when worried, angry or both. 'You need to get out, Shal, and I mean tonight. This time it won't be just the car they set fire to, it might be the fucking house with you and the kids in it.'

'But where will we go? I can't leave tonight, Ken. The kids'll be hungry and tired when I get home and—'

Sharon's words were cut short by Kenny banging his fist down on the table. 'I want yous out that fucking house, immediately. Go to your parents if you have to!'

'But we need to pack our belongings.'

Eyes blazing, Kenny stood up. Furious he was stuck inside here while his family were at risk, he picked up his chair and threw it against the wall in frustration. 'For fuck's sake Shal, just do as I say—'

Seconds later, half a dozen screws came piling in and he was pinned to the floor.

'Ooh, Kenny! "Fancy Pants",' squealed twelve-year-old Sherry Bond. She had loads of posters of her pop idol, who shared the same name as her father, on her bedroom wall. She'd been besotted with him since 'The Bump' was released last year.

'Sit down, will ya? I can't see,' complained fourteen-year-old Donny Bond. *Top of the Pops* was the highlight of a Thursday evening, yet every week his selfish sister would spoil his viewing by chucking herself about in front of the TV, her unruly mop of curly copper-coloured hair obscuring his view. 'I mean it, Shel. Move. Now.'

Sherry turned around. 'Make me,' she taunted, before turning her attention back to Kenny.

Donny leapt off the sofa and tried, as gently as he could, to physically move her.

'Mum. Mum! Donny's hurting my arm,' lied Sherry.

Sharon Bond slung the chopped-up potatoes in the frying pan and wiped her hands on the tea towel. 'If you two don't stop arguing, you'll be going to bed with no sodding dinner. I've had a stressful enough day as it is.'

'How long 'til dinner?' asked Donny. 'I'm starving.'

Sharon poured the baked beans into a saucepan. 'Ten minutes, if that.' The journey back from the prison today had been a cowson. Roads were gridlocked thanks to a bad accident, hence the late meal. That was the least of Sharon's problems, mind. Today wasn't the first time Kenny had lost his rag during a visit and she doubted it would be the last. She would have to move sooner rather than later. She knew how Kenny worried about her and the kids, would hate him to take that out on another inmate and get an extension on his sentence.

'Oh, not again! Mum, tell her to sit her arse down,' bellowed Donny.

Singing along with the Bay City Rollers' 'Bye Bye Baby', Sherry let out a deafening scream as the front room window shattered and an object hit her bang on the shoulder.

Donny leapt off the sofa. His sister's hair was on fire. He grabbed the round rug and clumped the bottom of it against the right side of his sister's head.

Usually calm in a crisis, Sharon Bond screamed before kneeling next to her daughter. The stench of burnt hair and skin filled the front room, but thanks to her son's quick thinking, Sherry no longer seemed to be on fire.

Donny yanked open the front door. There wasn't a soul in sight.

'Ring an ambulance, boy. Tell 'em to come quickly,' shrieked Sharon. Thankfully, her daughter's face had been spared, but her neck and shoulder were burned. To see her in so much pain was heartbreaking. Sharon had never felt so helpless in her lifetime.

'I looked outside but I couldn't see nobody. The ambulance is on its way.' Donny kneeled next to his mother. His sister was writhing and screaming in agony. He squeezed her hand. 'It's all right, Shel. You're gonna be fine, ain't she, Mum?'

Unable to bear the pain one second longer, Sherry Bond passed out.

'Slow down, Charlie, for Christ's sake,' ordered forty-nine-year-old Maggie Saunders. She'd very nearly taken a tumble while trying to keep up with her husband in her high-heeled wedges.

'When I find out who's responsible for this, I'll give 'em fucking fire,' ranted Charlie. 'I'll personally cremate 'em, and that is a promise.' At five foot eight, Charlie Saunders wasn't the tallest of men, but what he lacked in height he made up for in brains and brawn. A keen weightlifter

14

in his spare time, Charlie had converted a room in his house into a gym, and was as sturdy as a bull.

Maggie had no doubt that her husband would carry out his threat. He wasn't one to be messed with, her Charlie. He'd been far too clever for the police over the years, had earned their fortune from high-profile robberies before retiring from a life of crime and going straight. 'Go easy on Shal, love. She's bound to be in a right old state. Don't be ranting on with "I told you so" like you have all the way 'ere. That's not gonna help no one, especially poor little Sherry.'

'But I did bleedin' well tell her so. After she had that agg last time, I told her to move right away, near to us. Why didn't she listen to me, eh?'

'Because she's as obstinate as you bloody well are,' sighed Maggie. She'd been at a Tupperware party round her mate Pauline's when Charlie had dashed in and broken the awful news. They'd only been blessed with one child and Sharon and their two grandkids were their world. 'I mean it, Chas. Don't you dare start pointing the finger.'

Knowing his wife only ever referred to him as Chas when she was about to lose her temper with him, Charlie pushed open the door of St Helier hospital and turned to face his wife. They'd met when he was sixteen and Maggie fifteen. Two years later they were married with a child. 'OK. I'll go easy on her. But believe me, love, she ain't going back to that house and neither are those kids. They're coming home with us. End of conversation.'

Sharon Bond thanked the doctor, then stared at her sleeping beauty. Sherry was going to hate it when she looked in the mirror and realized half of her hair had been shaved off. She was at that age where she was into fashion and conscious about her appearance. She'd been bullied as a youngster for being ginger, even though she wasn't. That was until she'd bitten two of the bullies, punched another and got herself suspended at the tender age of eight. Sherry not only had the same hair colour as her father, she'd also inherited his fiery temperament. The bullying stopped on her return to school. Kenny had loved that story, described his daughter as a 'chip off the old block'.

Sharon sighed. Dr Matthews said Sherry had a second-degree burn to the side of the neck and deeper second-degree burns to the arm and shoulder. He was very upbeat about her recovery, but couldn't rule out long-term scarring. Obviously, a petrol bomb being slung through the window wasn't her fault, but Sharon couldn't help feeling partly to blame. If only she'd taken Kenny's advice, put the kids in her car and driven straight to her parents'.

It had been just over a week ago when Sharon had been woken in the early hours of the morning by a noise. She'd always been a light sleeper, especially since she and the kids had been hounded out of two of their previous homes. On investigation, Sharon found dog muck had been posted through the letterbox. It must have been a big dog as there was quite a lot of shit, but when she looked outside she couldn't see anybody. Not wanting to unsettle herself or her children, she decided to clear up the mess and tell nobody. Sharon knew what worriers her parents were when it came to her and their grandchildren, and Kenny had enough on his plate doing a long sentence. She would hate to think of him lying awake in his cell thinking she and the kids were being hounded again.

Over the next couple of days she was constantly on the lookout for graffiti nearby, like there'd been the other times. When none appeared, Sharon convinced herself the shit through the letterbox must have been teenagers messing around. Hardly the work of the heavy mob. But then things took a turn for the worse. First, she spotted graffiti spray-painted on a wall nearby, exactly the same wording as they'd used the last time:

JUSTICE FOR HARRY HARRISON

The following day, the dreaded letter arrived. Same as before, they'd cut out letters from a newspaper and glued them in a skew-whiff fashion on plain white paper:

MOVE OR FUCKING DIE!

Sharon put her weary head in her hands. They'd been living in Croydon when the last threatening letter arrived. A week later her car had been set alight in the middle of the night.

She'd thought her whole world had fallen apart back in 1971 when Kenny had been sentenced to a fifteen-year stretch. Eleven years for manslaughter and four years for possession of a Section One firearm. Though having already served four years, Kenny could apply for parole as early as 1979, providing he kept his nose clean. So far he had, but Sharon knew this latest incident was liable to tip him over the edge. He had the temper of all tempers when riled. Kenny adored Sherry, he'd so upset over what had happened that it would send him off his rocker.

Donny's return snapped Sharon out of her anxious thoughts. Her son's pale blue denim flares were soaked down the front. 'What you done? Wet yourself?'

'Don't be so daft. I bought you, Nan and Granddad

cups of tea, but I couldn't carry 'em properly and ended up dropping the lot. I burnt me balls, Mum. Didn't 'arf hurt.'

'Not you an' all. Come sit next to me, boy. We need to talk.'

'What's up? Shel's gonna be all right, ain't she? Where's Nan and Granddad gone?'

Sharon rubbed her son's unbrushed hair; his cheeky smile and big brown eyes were the spit of her. 'I spoke to the doctor and he assured me Sherry will make a full recovery. She might have to stay in hospital for a while because they don't want to risk her burns becoming infected. But other than a bit of scarring, which should fade in time, she'll be as right as ninepence.'

'That's good news, Mum.'

'Because of what's happened, there has to be some changes made. Nan and Granddad have gone to our house to collect some of our belongings. We're going to move in with them.'

'What, for a couple of weeks? Until we find another house to move to like the last time?'

'No, love. It's not safe for us to live in South London after this. Nan and Granddad have plenty of room for us at their place. We'll move in with them until your dad comes out of prison.'

Donny's eyes widened in alarm. 'But what about school and all me mates?'

Sharon stroked his cheek. He was a good boy, her Donny; kind, funny and helpful, and it looked as though he was growing up to be a handsome man. 'We'll find you a new school and you'll soon meet new friends.'

'But I like the ones I got.'

'I'm sorry, son. But when I visited your dad he told me

we must move – and that was before what happened to your sister. You two are me and your dad's world. It's our duty as parents to make sure you're safe. Nobody will get past Bonnie and Clyde, will they?' Sharon forced a smile. Bonnie and Clyde were her father's guard dogs, two slobbery Rottweilers who scared the life out of her, if she were honest.

'Why was the petrol bomb thrown, Mum? Was it 'cause of what Dad did?'

Sharon had never tried to wrap her children in cotton wool, but she'd played things down. Donny was now fourteen, the same age she'd been when her parents had sat her down and explained about her father's past after she'd heard disturbing rumours about him at school. 'You're not a little boy anymore, Donny, so I'm gonna be straight with you from now on. Don't be saying anything to your sister, though. At twelve, she's still a baby. Well, my baby, anyway.' She laid her hand on his. 'Yes, that petrol bomb can only be to do with Dad's mistake. We don't have any other enemies. That's why we have to move out the area. For good, this time.' Sharon sighed. She was a South London girl through and through. All her friends lived there. But Kenny had made the ultimate sacrifice after they'd wed by moving out of his beloved East End. Now the time had come for her to make a sacrifice too.

Digesting this information, Donny squeezed his mother's hand. 'I understand. It's nice where Nan and Granddad live anyway. Don't worry about me. I'll be fine.'

As soon as his mother excused herself to use the toilet, Donny's false smile faded. The mistake his father had made wasn't just any old mistake. He'd fired eight times at a big hedge in their driveway believing an intruder was

19

on their old property in Purley and all their lives were in danger.

Turned out it wasn't any old intruder his dad had killed stone dead. It was DS Harry Harrison. A popular, married police officer with three young children.

Kenny paced up and down his cell, mind working overtime. Sharon hadn't answered the blower when he'd rung her this evening. He'd then phoned her parents and there was no answer there either. Had Charlie and Maggie driven over to Shal and helped her pack some belongings? Because if anything had happened to his wife and kids, Kenny knew he would lose the plot completely. He was a family man. Shal and the kids were his everything.

Kenny got down on the floor, began doing press-ups and thought back to that fateful night. They'd been living in a drum on a posh estate in Purley at the time. Kenny had been a successful armed robber for a good few years, which was how he'd bought the gaff outright in the first place.

The driveway was massive, surrounded by big bushes, trees and shrubs. Kenny had been on a paranoid one for a couple of months beforehand. He'd had a bad tear-up in a boozer with a geezer called Micky Walsh. Walsh was out of Millwall and unbeknown to Kenny on the night of the fight, Walsh was an out-an-out lunatic who dealt with grudges in an extremely violent manner. He had previous for GBH, attempted murder and had got away with a lot as his victims were too scared to snitch on him.

Walsh had spent weeks in hospital with his broken jaw wired up, drinking through a straw. The rumours had circulated soon after that Walsh was planning some form of retribution when Kenny least expected it.

On the evening in question, Kenny was looking out of the front room window for signs of intruders. Instinct told him that Walsh had no morals and wouldn't bat an eyelid about involving Shal and the kids in his quest for revenge.

It was the light in between two bushes that made the hairs on the back of his neck stand up. He ordered Shal and the kids to hide upstairs, then ripped up the loose floorboard and grabbed hold of his gun.

'I know you're 'ere, Walshy. No fucker comes onto my property to threaten me,' he bellowed, storming towards the bushes in question. Having taken so many beatings as a child off Uncle Pete, Kenny was fearful of no man.

As he neared the bush, Kenny smelled cigarette smoke. 'Get out those bushes and face me like a man,' he'd ordered, his jaw twitching with anger. No villain he knew would turn up on another's property to try to do him in while his wife and kids were present. Immoral, that was. The underworld had certain rules.

Hearing a rustle, Kenny lost the plot. He fired numerous bullets at both bushes and was amazed when a geezer fell out of one, towards him, dressed in camouflage – and it wasn't Micky Walsh.

Kenny's reminiscing was ended by his cell being unlocked and the return of the singing gypsy.

'All right?' grinned Freddie Tamplin. 'I had to see a doctor. Had a terrible pain in the head. Thought I was a goner.'

'It weren't verbal diarrhoea then,' mocked Kenny.

'You're a miserable fucker, you are,' retaliated Tamplin.

Kenny grabbed hold of Tamplin by the throat and smashed his back against the wall. 'Sick of your endless rabbiting. Shut your bastard cakehole, else me and you shall fall out big time.' Kenny grabbed hold of Tamplin's nuts, twisted them, released the grip on his neck, then smirked as he sank to the floor in agony.

Holding onto his private parts for dear life, Tamplin glared at Kenny. 'You're gonna regret you did that. My brother Bobby is king of the gypsies. He's a prize-fighting champ, yer mug.'

Kenny looked down at the tosser. 'I couldn't give a flying fuck if your brother is Henry Cooper. Just ignore me and I'll ignore you. Oh, and no more singing country and western songs. Not unless you want your tongue cut out.'

CHAPTER TWO

'Right, we'd better make a move, go and visit your nan, Donny.' Sharon glanced at her watch. When she'd rung Kenny's mum to tell her she and the kids would be visiting on her actual birthday, Vera had told her in no uncertain terms that she had a very busy day planned. First she was going shopping down Roman Road market and having lunch with friends. Then she was going bingo early evening. 'Don't get to mine before three, Sharon, and I want you gone by five,' Vera replied curtly, as though she was doing Sharon and her grandchildren a massive favour by allowing them to visit her at all.

'Thanks so much for the bread pudding and tea, Aunt Nell.' Sharon hugged the woman who'd helped raise her Kenny and shown him love like his mother never had. 'We'll visit you again soon, I promise.'

Aunt Nell stuffed the money Sharon had given her back into her handbag. 'I can't take that. You and the kids need it more than me, darlin'. The flowers are enough. Beautiful, they are.'

Unlike Kenny's mum, who dressed a bit too young for her age, was thin and dyed her hair blonde, Aunt Nell was the opposite. So much so, it was hard to believe they were sisters. A large woman with short curly grey hair, a huge smile and heart, Nelly could not be more different to Vera. Nell was always happy, Vera always miserable. Sharon took the notes out of her pocket and shoved them back into Nelly's hand. 'Kenny will be so insulted if you don't take it,' she insisted. 'You know what he's like. Me and the kids are fine. We aren't short of readies.' That was actually true. Their house in Purley had been worth a lot of money. Kenny had told her to sell it and rent and spend sensibly until his release. Sharon had done as asked. She had always been the brain behind Kenny's brawn, especially when it came to over-spending. Not only did she still have plenty of dosh in the bank, but her parents were wealthy too. If the money ever ran out, her dad would see to it that she and the kids went without nothing. He was that kind of man.

Nelly reluctantly took the money back. Fifty quid was a fortune to her, would enable her to treat herself to some-thing nice. She worked full-time in a local cafe. There was little left over from her wages once she'd paid her rent, bills and a bit of shopping. 'I'll write to Kenny and thank him later. So kind to me, you and him are. 'Ere, Donny. Take this. Buy yourself some sweets,' Nelly said, giving him a pound note. 'Give your sister fifty pence, eh?'

'Thanks, Aunt Nell.' Donny hugged the woman. 'I'll split it with Sherry.'

'Have a nice time with madam. Hopefully 'cause it's her birthday she'll be in a more cheerful mood,' chuckled Nelly.

'We should be so lucky.' Sharon grinned. It used to really rile her the way Vera put Kenny down all the time, but now she just took it with a pinch of salt. Too long in the tooth to change now was Vera.

24

The journey from Canning Town to Bow was only a short one. Sharon thought about her daughter. She hadn't wanted to worry Aunt Nell, so told her Sherry couldn't visit as she had chickenpox. She'd tell Vera the same story too. Vera would only blame Kenny if she told her the truth. If there was a bad thunderstorm, Vera would find a way to blame Kenny for it.

Sherry was still in hospital but would hopefully be discharged soon. Sharon had spent most of the week at her daughter's bedside, trying to lift her spirits, but Sherry couldn't stop crying. She was more distraught about her lack of hair than her actual burns. It was a long journey to St Helier hospital and back, now that she was living at her parent's house in Ongar, but either her mum would accompany her or Donny.

'I wonder if Nan'll give me ten p and a Jamboree bag?'

Sharon laughed. It was a standing joke between herself and the kids that whenever they visited Vera, that's what she'd give them. Even Sherry was too bloody old now for Jamboree bags. As for Donny, he was fifteen this coming weekend. 'Bound to. Don't say nothing to upset her, for Christ's sake. Just thank her. Don't put your foot in it about Sherry either. She'll go on one of her rants about your father if you do.'

Donny chuckled. 'I know Nan's an old cow, but she is a funny one.'

Vera greeted her daughter-in-law and grandson with a hug and a smile. 'Cor blimey. You seem to grow a foot every time I see you, boy. Look, he towers over me now, Sharon. What you been feeding him – bowls full of growing seeds?'

Sharon chuckled. 'He certainly bleedin' towers over me, I know that much. Takes after his father height wise.'

Vera pursed her lips. 'Hmmm. Let's hope he don't take after his father in any other way. Fancy a cuppa?'

'Please, Nan. Happy birthday.'

As Vera busied herself making a brew, Sharon nudged Donny and gestured to him to clock the length of his nan's tight-fitting skirt. It was a good couple of inches above the knee. Vera was fifty-two today, no spring chicken. Although she seemed to think she was. Her sandals had to be four inches high.

Donny nudged his mother back. 'Any men friends on the scene, Nan?'

'No there bleedin' well ain't!'

'What happened to Hackney Harry?' enquired Sharon.

'Oh, I dumped that tight bleeder. Took him up the bingo, he paid for his own books and not mine. Sod that! Better off with me mates. Had a lovely time with them today and an 'andsome bit of pie and mash in Kelly's. Who needs poxy men? Arseholes, the lot of 'em.'

'Until the next one comes along,' Sharon whispered in her son's ear.

Donny giggled.

His nan loved music, always had her cassette player on in the kitchen. 'They don't make songs like this anymore,' Vera said wistfully as she carried the tea tray into her front room.

'Who is it?' enquired Donny.

'Brenda Lee. Great singer.'

'Your hair looks nice. You had it set?' asked Sharon. Vera's bouffant was also a standing joke between herself and the kids. Ever since Sharon had met the woman, she'd sported a bouffant, but every year it seemed to get another inch or two higher.

'Yes. I have it set every week, you know I do. Right

– enough about me. How's that rogue of a son of mine? Wrote to him last week. Heard sod all back, but that doesn't surprise me. Not even as much as a birthday card. Me mates couldn't believe it when I told 'em he never even bothered to send me one. Appalled, they were.'

'Kenny's fine and you know full well I always bring your card and present. 'Ere you go.' Sharon handed Vera a carrier bag.

Vera unwrapped the first present. 'Oh, another bottle of Rive Gauche.'

'I thought that was your favourite perfume?'

'Well, it's all right. But I got three unopened bottles upstairs, including the ones you bought me at Christmas and me last birthday.'

Donny gently nudged his mother. 'Oh well, at least you're well stocked up on it, Nan.'

Vera opened her second present. A satin-looking puffy-sleeved blouse. She instantly turned her nose up. 'You got the receipt? Where'd you get it from?'

'Marks and Sparks. Receipt's in the pocket,' Sharon replied, rolling her eyes. Like Kenny, she could do no right where Vera was concerned. Back when she and Kenny had first got married, Sharon referred to Vera as 'Mum' – it was a mark of respect where she came from. But Vera had told her, 'No disrespect, Sharon, but could you please refer to me as Vera in future? I never had two children. One was enough and look how he turned out!'

Struggling to stifle a fit of giggles, Donny coughed, then said, 'That one's from me and Sherry, Nan.'

Vera ripped the present open. 'Ahh, Black Magic. My favourites. You always get it right you do, Donny. Where is Sherry, by the way? I thought you would've let her take the afternoon off school to visit her gran on her birthday, Sharon. Not like I have any other grandchildren.'

Sharon trotted out the story about Sherry having chickenpox.

'Ahh, me poor girl. Give her a kiss from her nan, Donny. Oh and give her this.' Vera delved into her shopping bag and handed Donny two Jamboree bags. She then took two ten-pence pieces out of her purse. 'Treat yourself to some sweets too.'

'Cheers, Nan.' Donny couldn't look at his mum; he knew if he did he would burst out laughing.

Vera pinched her grandson's cheek. 'So handsome now, you are. Then again, you've always been a looker. Thank gawd you never inherited your father's ginger nut and ugly mug. Bet you got all the girls after you. You got a girlfriend yet, have ya?'

Apart from fingering one girl at a party and titting two up behind the bike sheds at school, Donny's sex life hadn't quite taken off yet. Debbie Ellis had given him a wank once inside a garage, but she was nineteen and minging. She also looked like a bloke. 'I did like this girl at school, Melanie Drake, but then we moved away.'

'Moved! Moved where?' Vera pursed her lips.

Sharon gave Donny a sharp kick on his ankle, before smiling at her nightmare of a mother-in-law.

'Essex, Vera. Me mum and dad are rattling about in that big ole property on their own. It's a lovely area, Ongar. Ya know, lots of countryside. Better schools for the kids an' all.'

'So, you've run out of readies, have ya? Told you not to marry him, didn't I? He was always gonna leave you and any kids you had destitute. Like father like son.'

'I can assure you Kenny has not left us destitute. Open your card now,' ordered Sharon.

Vera's eyes lit up as she did so and the two twenty-pound notes, plus a tenner, fell out of the card and onto her lap. 'Ooh, this'll come in handy. Gonna get meself some bits and bobs for indoors and I'll save whatever's left and treat meself to a decent winter coat this year.'

Sharon pinched her son on the knee. There would be no bits and bobs bought for indoors. Neither would Vera be buying any winter coat. The whole fifty quid would be frittered away on the bingo, slot machines, horse racing and football pools in less than a fortnight, unless she had a decent windfall in return.

'I know it's not your birthday yet, boy. But I'll give you your present now, in case I don't see yer beforehand.' Vera dashed out the room, returned with a gift and handed it to her grandson. 'Open it now. It's not a toy. I know you're too old for toys now.'

Donny tore off the wrapping paper and was dismayed to hold up a West Ham scarf. He looked at his nan in bemusement. 'I don't support West Ham. I support Spurs.'

'Yer can't support bloody Spurs. Your father's West Ham. So am I. We're East Enders, Donny, not North bleedin' Londoners. I thought all boys took after their father in supporting their football teams?'

'But you hate me dad. You always told me never to be like him in any way. That's why I chose to support Spurs.'

Vera pursed her lips. 'Your father might be a terrible son, a cop killer and whatever else he is, lad. But you still could've supported his football team.'

Unable to suppress her laughter anymore, Sharon spat the last of her tea back inside the cup.

Kenny was walking around the yard, enjoying the brisk air and stretching his legs when another lag tapped him on the shoulder. 'I hear you're sharing a cell with Freddie Tamplin, Ken?'

'Yeah. Unfortunately.'

'Be careful. He's a proper wrong un. I was banged up with him a few years ago back in the Ville. He was in there for robbing old people. Ya know, pensioners. He got a few digs when some of the lads heard what he'd done.'

Kenny's jaw twitched. He had no time for anybody who robbed or conned the elderly. Pure scum in his eyes. 'Cheers for the heads-up, Dazza.'

As Kenny continued with his stroll, he was already planning Tamplin's comeuppance.

'You going to the hospital later, Mum?'

'No. Not today. Nan and Granddad were staying up there all afternoon. I'll go again in the morning.'

'Weren't it funny round Nan's?' They were now in the car, on the journey back home.

'Hysterical.'

'I ain't wearing that poxy West Ham scarf.'

'When you start your new school, you can give it to a classmate. Help you make new friends.'

'Erm, I wanted to talk to you about that. When me and Granddad were playing pool last night, he suggested I start work up the nursery. He said it's pointless me starting a new school at fifteen, and I really don't want to. I wanna bring home a wage to help out. Please say yes.'

'But what about your exams? No point going to school all these years and not taking any exams, is there?'

'Dad never took no exams. He left school well young and went out to work. I got a job to go to. Granddad'll see me OK, wages wise. I ain't even that clever at school. But I will be at work. I know I will.'

Sharon sighed. 'I'll have to speak to your father. See what he says.'

Donny grinned. His dad would be all for him starting work. He knew that for a fact.

Since their little altercation, Tamplin had kept his trap shut, stopped the singing and been as quiet as a mouse. But for once, Kenny fancied a little chat. 'So, what you in 'ere for, Tamplin?'

Tamplin was wary of Kenny, had done a bit of digging and found out off a couple of Travellers who were also in the Scrubs that Bond had blown a gavver to smithereens. 'Erm, robberies.'

'What kind of robberies?'

'Just normal robberies, ya know.'

'No. I don't know. Bank robberies? Post offices? What did you rob? And who?'

As Kenny's piercing blue eyes bore into him, Tamplin felt edgy. 'Grunting' they called it in his world. He would prey on the elderly, become their friend, do odd jobs for them. The more senile they were and the less close family they had the better. Then, he would get them to sign their property over to him. If they refused, he would quote ridiculous prices, pretend their whole roof needed replacing, stuff like that, then rob them blind anyway.

'Well?' prompted Kenny.

Freddie Tamplin was twenty-nine, skinny and had always lived off the reputation of his eldest brother, Bobby. He nervously ran his hand through his thick blond hair. All his other siblings had dark hair. He was the black sheep of the family in more ways than one. Even Bobby had washed his hands with him after this latest turnout, so no way a gorger like Kenny Bond would understand

31

his way of life. 'Jewellers, mainly. Always go for the gold,' lied Freddie. 'Can sell gold all day long where I come from.'

Kenny smirked at the skinny, lying piece of shit. He'd already had a word with Scrapper Hughes. Scrapper was a scouser, a bank robber with morals like himself. Scrapper was the man to go to if you needed a decent tool or a bit of info.

'We gonna be pals now, are we?' grinned Tamplin, showing off his uneven set of teeth with one missing left-side of the front two. 'Only it gets a bit lonely sharing a cell with a mush and we don't rabbit at all.'

'Yeah. I suppose. But no more bunnying tonight. I'm shattered, gonna crash.'

The following morning, Kenny was awake with the larks. He already had the tool in his possession. Scrapper had slipped it to him yesterday evening in the queue for the phone. A razor blade, moulded into the head of a toothbrush.

'Morning, Ken. Sleep well, mush?' asked Freddie Tamplin.

Having lain awake the past hour thinking how terrified those pensioners must have been when they realized they'd been conned by Tamplin, Kenny could already feel the adrenaline running through his veins. Any scumbag ever conned his mum or Aunt Nelly, he'd kill them with his bare hands – and they were youngsters compared to the poor old sods Tamplin had targeted. 'Yeah. I was soundo the moment me head hit the pillow.'

When Tamplin began talking gibberish in that annoying bastard accent of his, Kenny wanted to smash his lights out there and then, just to shut him up. He wasn't that daft though, knew he had to lull him into a false sense of security. 'Don't talk, eh. Sing instead. Ya got a good singing voice.'

Tamplin grinned, then belted out Johnny Cash's 'Ring of Fire'.

Kenny grinned back at the no-good, pensioner-torturing bastard. Tamplin would be walking into more than a ring of fire when he got in that shower this morning.

Kenny was respected in the Scrubs. He was also feared, even though he was no bully. A fair man, who would stand up for some of the less fortunate if they were being targeted, especially if they weren't the full ticket.

Killing a copper gave Kenny the kudos to sail through prison life. The inmates wanted to be his friend rather than his enemy. So he knew nobody on his wing would grass on him. Grasses were worse than sewer rats.

'You keep watch,' Kenny whispered to his pal Stevie Brown. 'Just shout "bundle" when Big Dave clumps someone and starts the ruckus. That's when I'll strike. It'll be over in seconds, and I'll be out the showers along with everyone else.'

'Gotcha, Ken. Good luck,' replied Stevie. The screws lurked outside the showers, would only ever step inside if a fight broke out. They were called every nonce name under the sun if they stepped inside otherwise.

Tamplin caught up with Kenny. 'Now we're muckers, all right to sit with you and your mushes at breakfast?'

'Yeah,' Kenny replied, aware of Perky's stare fixed on him as they sauntered past the pillock.

Tamplin was undressed and inside the shower within a minute. Kenny quickly undressed too and barged a geezer out the way to nab the shower next to Tamplin. He couldn't risk blood spurting over his clothes.

The water was never hot, lukewarm if you were lucky. Kenny had barely begun soaping himself down when he heard Stevie bellow, 'Bundle!'

All the inmates, bar the odd pussy, loved a ruck. Kenny's tool was hidden inside a sock. He grabbed it before even putting a towel around his waist and, as the showers started to empty, he grabbed hold of Tamplin and sent him sprawling.

Tamplin was shocked, his eyes like organ stops. 'What the fuck, Ken. What ya doing, mate?'

Without further ado, Kenny plunged the razor blade deep into Tamplin's right eye. As he screamed, Kenny put his left hand over Tamplin's mouth. 'I ain't your mate and never will be,' he hissed. 'Call this payback for all those pensioners you've ripped off. Grass, or rob any more old people, and believe me I will hunt you down, take your other eye out and chop your fucking hands off. Comprende?'

Within seconds, Kenny had stuffed one of Tamplin's own socks into his gob to drown his screams, handed the tool to young Glenn to dispose of, cleaned the gunk and blood off himself and strolled outside the shower with the four men who'd hung around for the deed to be done.

The mayhem that greeted Kenny's eyes was a joy to behold. Big Dave had somehow managed to start a riot. The screws were rolling around on the floor trying to restrain those fighting.

Stevie Brown walked over to his pal. 'You'll deffo get away with this one.'

Kenny winked. 'Too right I fucking will.'

CHAPTER THREE

The summer of 1975 turned out to be the most joyous of Donny Bond's young life. He loved working at his grandparents' nursery up at Stapleford Abbotts and having dosh in his pocket. On a Sunday, he and his nan would pitch up in a lay-by along the A127 and sell bunches of overpriced flowers to passing motorists. A brilliant little earner that was.

His mum and Sherry worked at the nursery too, but not full-time like he did. Sherry refused to return to school until her hair grew back, so Granddad Charlie organized a private tutor to teach her at home. Sherry's scars weren't too bad, but she was very conscious of her burns and hated wearing anything sleeveless.

Chipping Ongar was where they all lived, in a four-bedroom gaff down a quiet little lane. It was spacious, had a couple of acres around it. Donny loved having a man around the house again. While the women were cooking, cleaning, or watching some crap on TV, he and his granddad would lift weights in the gym or play darts, snooker, pool or table tennis in the enormous games room.

Unlike other grandparents, the Saunders didn't look or

act old. They were trendy, cool and such fun to be around. Granddad wore Levi jeans, Adidas tracksuits and trainers. Nan was very pretty, had her dyed-blonde hair cut in a modern feathered style. She dressed hip, wore halter-neck tops, flared jeans and high wedge sandals like the girls in the audience of *Top of the Pops*. Donny didn't know any other nan who could drive, let alone drive a sports car and a big van.

Donny's biggest dread about moving to Essex had been that he'd have no mates to hang out with. As luck would have it, it turned out he hadn't needed any. Granddad Charlie had a mate, Wally Wicks, who had a grandson Sam. They lived nearby, so Donny and Sam started to knock around together. Sam was seventeen and a bit of a handful. The type to get you into trouble if you weren't careful. But that didn't matter anymore, not since Donny had met Tansey Turner.

Love had been the last thing Donny had expected to find shortly after moving to Essex. Knocking about with the lads was much more fun. Or so he'd thought.

Donny had only just turned fifteen when he'd first spotted her. She was riding past the nursery on a big grey horse. She had such a pretty face; Donny could not take his eyes off her. She clocked him too, he sensed that. Then she started trotting her horse past the nursery more often.

It only took him a couple of days to pluck up the courage to talk to her. She was even more gorgeous up close. Slim, long chestnut hair, blue eyes, perfect cheek-bones, big lips and a pert pair of knockers. Her horse was called Trigger and while stroking its nose and asking if it wanted some water, Donny made the mistake of telling his first lie. He'd asked her how old she was and when she'd replied 'nearly seventeen', he'd blurted out he was the same age.

His second lie came on their first actual date, at the pictures in Romford. He'd nearly died when she'd told him her father was a copper, so when she'd asked immediately afterwards what his did, he didn't have time to think properly. 'Me dad's erm, away a lot. He's in the army.'

From that first date, true love sprang like a shoot blossoming in the garden. They were so compatible. Tansey had never had a proper relationship before either, so it was a first for the both of them. Donny looked and acted far older than his age and, now he was working, was able to treat Tansey like a princess. She lived in Havering-atte-Bower, which wasn't that far from the nursery. They'd spend hours down at the stables, planning their future and making love on the hay.

Tansey was really funny too. She wouldn't allow him to touch her in front of Trigger, reckoned it was morally wrong and her horse would be jealous. And when he discarded his johnnies, Tansey would shriek, 'Put that straight outside in the bin – Trigger might choke on it!' They were lover, boyfriend/girlfriend and best mates all rolled into one. The perfect combination.

Deep down though, Donny could never shake the worry off. The worry of her dad finding out who his dad was. Little did he know his happy bubble would burst sooner rather than later.

'Tansey! Tans. Get your arse in 'ere. I've got a bone to pick with you, girl,' bellowed Terry Turner. Terry rubbed his thumb and forefinger over his moustache, a habit of his when peeved.

'Don't go all heavy on her. She's not a kid anymore,' warned Penny, Terry's wife. He was ever so protective over their two daughters, he would've kept them in ankle socks and hair in bunches until they were twenty-one if he could.

Thirteen-year-old Charlee followed her elder sister down the stairs. She knew by her father's tone that Tansey was in some kind of trouble and she bet she knew what it was.

'What's the matter?' asked Tansey innocently.

'I want to know who this lad is you're knocking around with.'

'What lad?'

'Don't start with that old flannel, Tans. The lad who you've been spotted with numerous times and was on the back of your fucking horse with you yesterday. You don't let anyone on that horse, not even your sister. So who is he? Gotta be special to you, if he's allowed to ride Trigger.'

'Oh him. That's Donny. He's not allowed to ride Trigger. I was just giving him a ride to where he works. He's new to the area, doesn't know many people. We're just friends,' lied Tansey, her cheeks beetroot red.

Penny squeezed her husband's arm. 'There you go. I said it would just be a friend. Interrogation over. You're not at work now, love.'

'Hang on a minute. We know all of the girls' friends, so why haven't we been introduced to Donny yet? There must be a reason.'

''Cause he's her boyfriend,' giggled Charlee. She couldn't help but feel a bit jealous. Donny Bond was drop-dead gorgeous.

Tansey glared at her trappy sister. 'He is not my boyfriend!'

'Why don't you just bring him round, love. It'll put your dad's mind at rest if he meets him,' advised Penny.

Tansey shrugged. 'All right. I'll ask him. But if he doesn't want to come, I can't force him, can I?'

Terry Turner smirked. 'If he refuses to come, there must be a reason he's hiding from us, so you won't be allowed to see him again.'

'How's it going with the girlfriend?' grinned Kenny Bond. He liked the fact his son had bagged himself his first proper bird. One of his pals in the Scrubs had a son who'd turned out to be gay. Kenny would go ballistic if that were to happen to him. He wouldn't be able to deal with it.

Sharon nudged Donny. 'Tell him. Go on.' She'd noticed Donny had been quiet on the journey, had questioned him and found out why.

'I've got meself into a bit of a pickle, Dad, and I dunno what do about it,' admitted Donny.

'You ain't got her up the spout, surely?'

'No,' Donny tutted. 'Nothing like that. It turns out Tansey's dad is Old Bill. He knows we've been seeing one another and he's demanded to meet me. Trouble is, I've lied. I panicked when Tans first told me and blurted out you were in the army.'

Sharon had expected her husband to be angry, so was rather taken aback when Kenny burst out laughing. 'I know he's Old Bill. Get yer arse round there and tell him your father's SAS,' chuckled Kenny. 'You getting your nuts in? If so, make sure you put a rubber on. You can't be getting her in the family way.'

Seeing Donny blush, Sharon hissed, 'Kenny! Stop it! You're embarrassing the boy! How did you know? About the dad?'

'Got eyes and ears everywhere, me. Put it this way, Shal, you'd never get away with having an affair,' laughed Kenny.

'I wanna marry Tansey one day, Dad.'

'You're fifteen years old, boy. Don't talk such bollocks.'

'But you and Mum weren't much older than me and Tansey when you two met. You're still together,' argued Donny.

'Yeah, but Granddad Charlie weren't Old Bill. No copper is gonna allow his daughter to be with my son, Donny. As soon as he finds out, he'll cull it. Which is why I say just have fun and enjoy it while it lasts.'

'But you don't get it. I love Tansey. I will always love her.'

Aware his son's eyes had welled up, Kenny glared at him. 'Stop acting like a pansy. Man up, for Christ's sake.'

Sharon sent her teary-looking son to the snack bar. As soon as he'd gone, she urged Kenny to take it easy on Donny before changing the subject: 'Any more news on that gypsy bloke you had a to-do with?'

Kenny grinned. 'Yeah. He lost an eye and got moved to Standford Hill on the Isle of Sheppey. That'll teach him to rip off old people. As for Donny, ya need to toughen him up a bit, Shal. No son of mine is gonna be acting like a pansy. Not on your nelly!'

Terry Turner looked and acted like a typical copper. He had an overpowering personality, a loud voice, chain-smoked, and a moustache he kept fiddling about with. Tansey's mum seemed nice, but it was the old man firing all the questions his way.

'Tansey says you're new to the area. Where'd you live before, lad?' asked Terry.

'London. We moved here end of April,' Donny replied. With his father's warning still on his mind, he was crapping himself. No way could he lose Tansey, no matter what his old man said.

'Big place London. Whereabouts?'

'South London.'

'What made you move 'ere then?'

'Let the boy drink his lemonade and eat his biscuits, Tel,' advised Penny.

'I'm only chatting to the lad. You're all right, eh Donny?'

Donny gulped at his lemonade. He couldn't wait to leave. The old man had evil green eyes that seemed to bore straight through him.

'You work in Stapleford Abbotts, Tansey tells me.'

'Yeah. In the garden nursery near where Tansey keeps Trigger. My granddad owns it.'

Terry Turner frowned. He'd heard that nursery was owned by some old-school villain. He'd never seen the bloke. On the few occasions he and Penny had popped in there, there was a woman working. Quite attractive for her age, but definitely mutton done up as lamb. 'Your Nan work there, does she?'

'Yes. And my mum and little sister.'

'Enough questions now, Terry. You'll scare the poor lad off.' Penny smiled at Donny. He was a lovely looking lad. No wonder her Tansey had taken a shine to him.

Tansey stood up. 'You've met Donny like you asked to. Can we go out now, please? I need to muck out Trigger's stable.'

'Hold your horses,' said Terry. 'Why you so keen to leave? The lad's not been 'ere ten minutes.'

'What does your dad do, love?' Penny asked Donny.

'He's in the army.'

'Where's he based?' asked Terry.

''Erm, I don't know. He's in the Special Forces and me mum doesn't tell us anything.'

'What's his ranking then?'

Donny shrugged. 'Dad never talks about his job when he comes home on leave. Well, not in front of me and my sister anyway.'

Seeing Donny looking flustered, Tansey stood up. 'Right, you've met him. Come on, Donny. We're going.'

When the front door slammed, Terry rubbed his finger over his moustache. He glanced at Penny. 'Special Forces, my arse.'

'I thought he was a lovely, well-mannered boy,' piped up Penny.

'I'll do some digging; find out what the lad's father really does. We don't want our Tansey knocking around with any Tom, Dick or Harry, do we? She's smitten with him. Written all over her bleedin' face.'

CHAPTER FOUR

'Bent cops are the lowest of the low. Reason being,
they'd like to be one of us. But they ain't got the
brains or the balls.'

*I was spot on with my prediction. Soon after Donny met
Tansey's family, the shit hit the fan and their relationship got
culled. The Turners then swiftly moved away from the area.*

*Donny didn't take the break-up well. I couldn't help
but get annoyed with him, especially when he burst into
tears on a visit. Talk about embarrass me.*

*The summer of 1976 was a scorcher, not that I did
much sunbathing. There were hosepipe bans and water
shortages across the country. It was stifling inside the
prison, especially in me cell. I coped with it by daydreaming
about Shal, the kids, our future.*

*That autumn, I got hit by a double whammy. After
playing the field for a while, my thick son took up with
another bird, Lori Boswell. She was eighteen months older
than him, and I'd warned Donny until I was blue in the
face to always take precautions. Did he listen? Did he
fuck. He got Lori up the duff, not with one kid, but twins!*

As if that wasn't bad enough, the silly little sod then decided to hold up a security van with his pal. They got chased for a couple of miles before Donny's mate lost control of the car, crashing it and getting them both caught.

Five years Donny got, was sent to Feltham. While he was in there, Lori gave birth to my grandsons, Beau and Brett Bond.

The last few years of my sentence dragged, but finally I got the news I'd been gagging to hear. My parole had been granted. At long last I would be reunited with my family.

Little did I know, at that point, what the future had in store for me . . .

Summer 1979

'Kenny,' Sharon ran towards her husband, beaming from ear to ear.

Lifting his wife up, Kenny swung her around. 'Onwards and upwards for us now, treacle. The past is over and our future's about to begin.'

Tears of joy ran down Sharon's face. This day had been a long time coming and it was hard to digest it had finally arrived. 'I can't believe we'll be waking up together every morning. I never want to spend another night apart.'

'You won't have to, I promise.' Kenny kissed Sharon passionately and immediately became erect. 'I told you not to bring the kids and to bring some dosh with ya as I thought we'd stop at a hotel, grab an hour or two alone before going back to your parents.'

'We can't, Kenny. Everyone's at home waiting for you.'

'Whaddya mean, everyone? I told you I didn't want a big fuss.'

'Just all the family. Your mum and aunt will be there by the time we get home too. Donny's gone to pick them up.' Sharon's dad had given Donny a crash course in driving lessons and he'd passed his test first time. Her dad had treated him to his first set of wheels too. A mustard-coloured Hillman Imp.

Kenny rolled his eyes. 'Glad you invited me muvver. Happy bleedin' days.'

'I couldn't invite Aunt Nelly and not invite her,' chuckled Sharon.

'Let's get going then. Best you pull over somewhere quiet on the way though, Shal. Me cock feels like it's about to explode. Seeing as I've gotta suffer Mum, the least you can do is gimme a nosh first.'

'Only if we can find somewhere really quiet,' laughed Sharon.

'Course we can!' Kenny winked.

Donny drove up the East End deep in thought. When he'd been released early just over six months ago, he couldn't believe how much everything had changed. Nobody wore flares anymore, or shirts with big collars. He'd had to invest in a whole new wardrobe. His old clothes probably wouldn't have fitted him anyway. He was five foot eleven now, the same height as his dad. God, how things had changed since his dad got put away.

Skinheads and mods were the latest craze, and there was even a woman in charge of the country. Margaret Thatcher had been the Prime Minister since May. Music had also altered. Squeeze and The Jam were among the bands Donny liked these days.

Because he had the twins, moving in with Lori seemed the right thing to do. His dad had urged him to man up to his responsibilities, so he had. There weren't fireworks between himself and Lori, not like there'd been with Tansey, but there was a cooked dinner on the table for him every evening, he adored his boys, and sex was on tap whenever he fancied it.

All in all, life was good, apart from two things. Donny had always lived in decent-sized gaffs and he hated the house the council had given Lori. It was a two-bedroom terraced in Harold Hill, and everything about it was poky. Even the garden was the size of a postage stamp, which was why Donny was currently saving for a mortgage.

The other issue he had was Lori kept banging on about getting married. He'd recently turned nineteen and didn't feel ready for such a massive commitment, so he'd compromised by proposing to Lori and buying her an engagement ring instead. He was adamant, though, that they needed to move to a new home before they actually wed. Thankfully, she'd agreed. The twins were now two-year-old bundles of energy and needed a bigger garden.

Donny pulled up outside his nan's house.

'Oh, it's you,' said Vera. 'I thought your dad was picking me up.'

'Don't be daft. He ain't even got a car. Mum's gone to pick Dad up. I told you on the phone that I was picking you up first, then Aunt Nelly.'

'But you haven't long passed your test. I'm not a good passenger at the best of times and you're a novice.'

'I ain't had no accidents, Nan, and I drive vans up the nursery.'

Vera sighed. 'Don't say that! You'll jinx us. I'll just have

46

to sit in the back, shut me bleedin' eyes and pray to God, I suppose.'

Having been relieved by his wife in a quiet lay-by, Kenny arrived at Shal's parents with a big smile on his face. There was a huge banner above the door that read WELCOME HOME KENNY.

Before Sharon had a chance to put the handbrake on, the front door opened and out dashed Sherry. She was all grown up now at sixteen, and worked at the nursery full-time.

Kenny hugged his daughter tight to his chest. 'Missed you so much, darlin'.'

'Donny gone to pick up Lori and the boys?' Sharon asked her mum.

'No. He's not back with Nelly and Vera yet. I hope he's OK. He's been gone ages.'

'Knowing Donny, he's probably got lost,' laughed Kenny. 'Come on. Let's get inside. I could murder a cold beer.'

'I bet you could, ya greedy bastard,' piped up an unmistakable croaky voice.

Kenny swung around, beaming from ear to ear. Alan Davey was his best mate. They'd met at school after Kenny had moved in with his grandparents. 'Blimey! You ain't changed a bit. Well, apart from all those wrinkles on your mooey,' joked Kenny, 'and someone seems to have half-inched your hair!'

Alan laughed and gave Kenny a bear-hug. They'd been ribbing one another since they were teenagers. 'Welcome home, ya ginger bastard. It's been a long time coming.'

Charlie had paid for all the booze and grub. There was every type of seafood and a lovely buffet laid out on a long table that had everything from cheese and pineapple to sausages on sticks, pork pies, big lumps of cold beef and ham, whole chickens, crusty loaves, salad, pickles – the works.

'How I've missed me jellied eels,' Kenny said, dipping a piece of bread into the jelly that was smothered in pepper and vinegar.

'Thank God for that! Donny's just pulled up,' Sharon hollered. She'd worried about her son, had been glued to the window for the past ten minutes. The car looked OK and Vera and Nelly were with him.

Dressed in a peach, floral dress that was as young as it was short for her, Vera marched inside the house, beehive as big as ever, holding her forehead. 'Get me a brandy. A large one. What a journey! Never again!'

'Whatever's wrong?' asked Sharon.

'Take no bleeding notice of her,' Nelly sighed.

'We had a puncture and it took me ages to change it as I couldn't get the wheel nuts off,' explained Donny.

Charlie handed Vera a drink, which she promptly necked in one. 'But it weren't just that, was it? You nearly hit a van, thought I'd broken my bastard neck as me head flew into the back of the seat. Good job I sat in the back. I would've gone straight through the windscreen otherwise.'

'The van pulled out on us, Nan. I had to brake,' Donny argued.

'Not like that you didn't. As for that racket you forced us to listen to all the way here, it's given me a migraine. That's not music, it's a load of old pony!'

Kenny burst out laughing. 'Hello, Mum. It's good to see you. You haven't changed a bit, cherub.'

'Look! There's Gramps. You can see lots of him now as he hasn't got to work away anymore,' Lori told her beloved

48

sons. 'Go on. Don't be shy.' Kenny's last home visit had been for a week and he'd seen the twins virtually every day.

Kenny leapt out of his garden chair as he clocked who was ambling towards him. ''Ere they are. Me little bruisers.' He grinned, picking Beau and Brett up in his arms.

'Gramps,' mumbled Beau, poking his finger into Kenny's cheek.

Laughing, Kenny pretended to nibble on Beau's finger. Handsome boys, they were, with their straight blond hair and big brown eyes. Brett had a little mole behind his earlobe, which was the only way Kenny could tell who was who at first. He'd soon realized that Beau was the more brazen out the two, could easily separate them now.

'Hello, Kenny. Welcome home. The boys coloured in a card for you. I've left it in the kitchen.'

'Ahh, lovely. Cheers, Lori. How you doing, darling? That son of mine taking good care of you?' Kenny had only met Lori a few times, but liked what he'd seen. Medium height, slim, with long blonde hair, she wore little make-up, yet was pretty in a natural way. She dressed the boys identically and they always looked clean and smart. Today they were wearing pale blue shorts, crisp short-sleeved white shirts and white plimsolls.

Beaming like a Cheshire cat, Lori proudly showed Kenny her engagement ring.

'He told me he'd finally taken steps to make an honest woman out of yer. About bleedin' time too. On a serious note, I think you'll make a cracking couple. You're both good parents and these two'll keep you busy,' Kenny said, as he put his wriggling grandsons down.

Brett immediately tried to run, tripped and fell flat on

his face. When he burst into tears, Kenny lifted him up. 'Where's it hurt?'

Brett pointed to his left knee. There was a slight graze. 'Nothing wrong with it. You're a big boy now and big boys don't cry. Only girls do.'

Lori laughed as her son immediately stopped crying. 'I know what to say in future myself now. I knew dressing them in white was a big mistake. I'll buy navy shirts next time.'

'Come out the front, I got something to show you,' Alan urged Kenny.

Sitting with Aunt Nelly, Kenny excused himself and followed his pal.

Alan pointed to the white Mercedes-Benz 300D he'd arrived in. 'You like it?'

The car was two years old, an R reg. 'What's not to like, it's a beauty,' gushed Kenny. He'd always loved a nice set of wheels and was amazed by how much motors had changed since he'd got banged up. No more freezing your nuts off in winter like the old days.

'Glad you like it. Only, it's yours.' Alan grinned, chucking his pal the keys.

'You're kidding me! How much do I owe ya? Take it out the dosh you're looking after for me.'

'Never! It's my coming-out gift. I know if the boot was on the other foot you'd do the same.'

'Ahh, mate. That's so nice of you. Come 'ere,' Kenny hugged his pal and smacked him on the back. Even though he wasn't short of dosh, it was courtesy in his world to give a man who'd done a long stretch a gift, usually cash. Alan had gone straight now – well, straight-ish – so he'd feel insulted if Kenny knocked the car back. To refuse a coming-out

50

gift was seen as a rebuff, usually meaning you didn't like or trust the bastard offering it. Kenny trusted Alan like a brother. 'How you getting back to Blackheath then, Al?'

Alan pointed to a red Ford Capri. 'Julia brought her car an' all. Keep this between us, Ken, but she's pregnant again. Only ten weeks, mind, which is why we're not shouting it from the rooftops. Our youngest is fifteen. It wasn't planned. But now I've got me head around it, I can't wait.'

Kenny slapped his pal on the back. 'Blinding! So chuffed for you both. Me and Shal will hopefully be joining you soon. I want another nipper and she agreed to it while I was in the can. I got plenty of making up to do on the bonking front, so watch this space.'

Alan laughed. 'You remember before we met Julia and Sharon, all them birds that used to fancy us and hang around outside the boxing gym? How many did we end up shagging round the back?'

'Dunno. I lost count. We were only about fourteen or fifteen. A lifetime ago.'

'I remember you losing your virginity to Randy Mandy at thirteen, Ken.'

Kenny pulled a face. 'Please don't remind me of that one. What a minger! Face like a smacked arse, fanny like a bucket.'

'Kenny. What you doing?' asked Sharon. 'You better come inside. Your mum's not happy. Reckons the seafood's off and she's been poisoned.'

'Bit of luck it is and she has,' smirked Kenny. And they made their way back indoors, happy as Larry.

With the sun having gone down, Donny picked up his sleeping son, took him inside and sat next to Lori on the sofa, lying Brett across both of their laps. 'Turn that down a bit, Sherry. The boys are tired,' ordered Donny. His sister had invited a couple of her mates and all three were singing at the top of their voices while dancing to Blondie's 'Sunday Girl' in the kitchen.

Sherry put her head around the door and flicked her long hair in that annoying way she had when dancing. 'No. It's a party for Dad. Not you.'

Across the room, Vera was having problems of her own. She was eating a piece of her son's 'Welcome Home' cake, or trying to anyway. One of the twins, she didn't know which one, had suddenly become obsessed with her, kept pointing at her, trying to say something and wouldn't leave her alone. 'Go back to your mum and dad now. Look, they're over there,' she pointed. 'There's a good boy.'

'Aww, bless him. You've never been a kiddie person, have you, Vee? Look at his little face. He likes you and wants to sit on your lap and share your cake. I'd give him some of mine, if I hadn't already eaten it.'

Knowing Nelly was having a knock at her for not raising Kenny herself, Vera treated her to a look of disdain, while mumbling, 'No surprise you've already scoffed yours. You always ate like a gannet.'

'Whaddya say?' Squeeze's 'Up the Junction' was so loud, Nelly couldn't hear.

'I said, I will give him some cake.' Vera handed Nelly her plate. Unlike her sister, she was eating hers with a fork instead of her hands. She would hate to be Nell's size, valued her figure too much. 'Come on then, boy.'

Beau grinned as he was lifted onto the woman with the weird hair's lap. He'd met her before, was sure he had.

'You feed him then, Nell, and don't get it over me frock.'

Before Nelly had a chance to do anything, Beau grabbed

the cake with his right hand and shoved it in the weird woman's face.

'Me hair! He's got it in me bastard hair. Get him off me, the little bugger. I can't see sod all. It's in me eyes. I'm blinded.'

Kenny looked at Donny. Both ran from the room in fits of laughter. Nelly couldn't hold it in either. 'I'll get you a tissue,' she said, before darting into the kitchen, holding her sides. Maggie and Charlie were next to follow suit.

Lori was horrified. She'd only met Donny's gran once before. 'I'm so sorry, Vera.' She grabbed her son by the arm and slapped him gently on the backside. 'You naughty boy,' she scolded, before wiping his hands clean of chocolate cake.

Trying to stifle her own hysteria, Sharon handed Vera a wet flannel. 'There's not too much in your hair. I'll try and get it off for you.'

'No. Don't you dare touch it! I only had it bastard well set today. Horrid child. Don't you ever bring him round mine. Must take after Kenny.'

Having ordered his daughter to turn the music off, Kenny poked his head around the kitchen door. 'Did you call me, Mother?'

'No. I didn't. Been laughing at me misfortune though, ain't ya? I heard you.'

'Well, it was funny. You look like a badger!'

'Stop it, Kenny,' scolded Sharon. 'Go and look in the bathroom mirror, Vera. You'll get that out your barnet easily enough.'

Vera dashed to the bathroom to inspect the damage.

Everybody apart from Lori and the boys was now in the kitchen. 'Get in the front room now, Kenny, and you, Donny. As for you, Sherry, stop acting silly and get up off the floor. Your dad said you could have a couple of drinks. How many you had?'

'Two,' Sherry lied.

'Funniest thing I've seen in years,' Nelly chuckled. 'Best we be getting off soon. You gonna drop us home, Donny?'

'If Nan'll let me.' Since the twins had been born, Donny wasn't a big drinker. He'd only had a couple of beers and a glass of bubbles to toast his dad. 'I'll have to drop Lori home first though, the boys are tired.'

Vera came into the kitchen, lips pursed. The damage to her beehive wasn't as bad as feared, but she wasn't about to tell Kenny that. She'd left the bits of cake in it, but was sure with a careful bit of backcombing, she'd get them out quite easily at home.

'Your hair all right?' Sharon enquired.

'No. Gonna have to shell out to get it done again tomorrow. It ain't cheap either.'

Sharon grabbed her purse and handed Vera a tenner. 'Will that cover it?'

'I suppose it'll have to.'

'Thanks for coming, Mum. It's been a pleasure, as always. Donny's gonna drop you home now,' Kenny said, his tone laden with sarcasm.

'Oh, no he isn't! Not after that journey 'ere. I'd rather walk.'

'We'll drop your mum and aunt off,' Alan offered.

'But you're half-cut,' Vera replied. 'You've been guzzling Scotch like it's been going out of style.'

'Julia's driving. She's not been drinking.'

'But she's a woman. Can she drive?'

When her grandkids and the men all chuckled, Maggie became quite indignant. She'd never liked Vera. The miserable cow had very nearly ruined her daughter's wedding.

'Well, I drive and Sharon can drive. Why don't you just get in the car and see if Julia can drive? If not, walk.'

Giving Maggie daggers, Vera turned to Julia and smiled. 'I was only pulling your leg. Thank you, dear. A lift home would be lovely. Very kind of you to offer.'

Kenny lay in bed, content, his arms wrapped around his wonderful wife. 'Sorry for coming so quickly. I'll be all right in a few days.'

'Christ, Ken. You haven't got to apologize. You've been banged up for years, whaddya bleedin' well expect? Anyway, we're hardly spring chickens anymore. I'm just happy to have you home.' Sharon stroked his handsome face. With his rugged, manly looks, Kenny wasn't your conventional Adonis, but his piercing blue eyes could hypnotize anyone. They were the first thing Sharon had noticed about him when they'd met.

Kenny chuckled. 'Jesus wept, Shal. We're only in our thirties. You're making us sound like *George and Mildred*. Alan had a chat with me on the quiet earlier. Julia's pregnant again. Early days like, but he's well excited. You still up for having another nipper?'

'Oh, I don't know, Ken. There'd be such a gap between the other two. Plus, we've got our grandsons now. I'd feel a bit silly if our kid was younger than our grandkids, wouldn't you?'

Kenny propped himself on his elbow. 'Nah. Bollocks to what anyone else thinks. It's nobody else's business. I thought you wanted another one?'

'Not really. I played along with the idea while you were in prison as I wanted you to have things to look forward to, to help you through the rest of your sentence. I like working up the nursery. I don't really fancy being pregnant

55

again at my age. We've got one of each. Why don't we just concentrate on the grandkids, spend more time with them?'

Feeling a bit deflated, Kenny tried not to show it. He'd spent so many years cooped up in a cell, still felt young at heart. 'Whatever you want is fine by me.'

Sharon ran her hands through Kenny's hair. She couldn't tell him the truth. She hadn't told a soul, not even her own mother.

CHAPTER FIVE

Sharon woke up early hours, her nightie soaked in sweat. This was a regular occurrence since sharing a bed with Kenny again. He radiated heat and she couldn't just chuck the quilt off like she had when sleeping alone.

Kenny rolled onto his side, one eye open. 'What's the time?'

'Just gone five. You go back to sleep. I'm gonna get up, make a cuppa.'

Aware that his wife was naked, Kenny felt his penis stiffen. 'Not so fast,' he grinned, grabbing Sharon's hand.

'Not this morning, Ken. I got a headache,' lied Sharon.

Feeling hurt, Kenny sat up. 'You had a headache last night. What's up? Don't you fancy me anymore?'

'Of course I do, ya daft sod.'

'Well, you got a funny way of showing it. You don't even get wet down below anymore, let alone come.'

Sharon got back into bed and fondled Kenny's penis. 'I'm just a bit out of practice, that's all. I've spent a long time alone.'

'Which is why we've got a lot of making up to do.'

Feeling guilty, Sharon took his penis in her mouth.

*

'What can I get you, gentlemen?' asked the young waitress.

'Full English for me with two slices of crusty bread and a mug of tea,' Kenny replied.

'Same for me, but no black pudding,' smiled Donny at the pretty young waitress. He'd never cheated on Lori, but still appreciated a good-looking bird.

Kenny picked up the *Daily Mirror*. Sebastian Coe was front page for setting a new record for running a mile. 'How the hell can anyone run a mile in under four minutes?'

'Lots of training and long legs, I suppose. So, what's this boat like then? Is it like, big?'

'It's big enough. You'll see it soon enough.' Kenny chucked the paper back on the table and leaned forward. 'If I ask you something, son, you mustn't say sod all to your mum.'

'All right.'

'Was there any geezers sniffing round your mother while I was away? She have any male mates, like? Ya know, up the nursery or anywhere?'

'No. Why you asking that?'

'What about going out of a night and stuff with pals?'

'Mum never goes out. Only shopping with Nan and Sherry, or lunch with the family. Surely you ain't insinuating what I think you are? Mum loves you, Dad. She would never look at another geezer.'

'Nah, I know that. But I dunno, she seems to have changed. Perhaps it's 'cause she spent all those years without me?'

'Of course it is. Nobody was happier than Mum when you got your parole granted.'

'Forget we had this conversation, yeah – it's just me being paranoid.'

'What conversation?'

Kenny grinned. 'That's my boy.'

Thanks to his wonderful nan raising him, and the sound advice from his grandfather, Kenny Bond wasn't your average man. Five foot eleven with copper-coloured wavy hair and a biggish nose that suited his craggy face, he was handsome in a rough kind of way. His intensely blue eyes were his best feature, but it was his East End banter, mannerisms and gift of the gab that seemed to draw people to him. Women loved him and men respected him. Well, apart from the Old Bill, of course, which is why Kenny knew he now had to keep his nose clean. The filth would be watching him like a hawk, waiting for him to make a wrong move so they could bang him up again, which is why he'd come up with a legal business plan.

'Cor, look at the size of that, Dad.' Donny pointed to the biggest boat out of the lot. 'Is that the one?'

Kenny chuckled. 'Nah. Bit out of our league that one, boy. That's it. Look over there,' pointed Kenny. '*The Duchess.*'

Donny stared at the boat. It was the tattiest one of them all. 'Really?'

'Bit of tender loving care and she'll look beautiful.'

A short stocky bloke approached, accompanied by a young skinny lad. 'You must be Kenny?' the short one said.

'That's right and this is me boy, Donny.'

'I'm George's mate, Reg, and this 'ere's the skipper, Bobby. Jump aboard, lads.'

Half an hour later, Kenny handed over the wonga and was the proud owner of a boat he planned to hold parties on down the Thames. Donny was his new business partner.

They'd split the profits straight down the middle. Fifty-fifty.

'Brett, Beau, stop that now. You mustn't do things like that. It's naughty and cruel. Now go and wash your hands, the pair of ya.' The boys had been chopping up live worms and it wasn't the first time Lori had caught them doing that. She knew boys would be boys, but was determined to teach them right from wrong.

Hearing the front door open and close, the twins shrieked 'Daddy!' in unison.

'Wash your hands before you touch your father, please. You'll infect him with your germs.'

'What they been up to now?'

'Chopping up bloody worms again. How'd it go with your dad?'

'Good,' grinned Donny. 'Boat needs a lot of doing up, but we're hoping to have it up and running within a month. Exciting times, eh? I'm still gonna do the flowers on a Sunday with me nan, 'cause that's too much of a good little earner to give up. Once the money starts rolling in from the boat, I'll take out a mortgage and we can get out of this shithole.'

'So how many nights a week will you be working when the boat is up and running?'

Donny was about to reply when the boys threw themselves at him. He picked one up in each arm. 'I dunno. Mainly be weekends, I suppose.'

'Bound to be full of drunken women chucking themselves at you.' Lori saw the way girls looked at Donny whenever they were out together and she couldn't help but feel a bit jealous about this new business of his.

'I'll be working with me father. Whaddya think we're gonna be doing? Orgy cruises down the Thames?'

'No. But you're bound to get lots of female attention, especially when they know you're part owner of the boat.'

'As if I'm gonna be interested! I wouldn't be engaged to you with two kids if I was on the lookout for a bit of skirt, would I?'

'I suppose not. Perhaps once the money starts rolling in we can finally book the wedding?'

'Yeah. We will. But moving's gotta be our priority. I can't tell you how much I hate this fucking rabbit hutch of a house.' Donny glanced at his watch. 'Right, I'm gonna jump in the bath. It's Divvy Dave's fortieth and I can't not turn up at his birthday drink-up.'

'Oh, I forgot you were going out,' sighed Lori. 'Do you really have to go? The boys have been right little bastards today and I was hoping we could have an early night once I put them to bed.' Lori could not get enough of Donny since his release from prison, and vice versa. They made love virtually every night.

'We can. I won't be back late, babe. I'll spend a couple of hours at the boozer, then make me excuses.'

Lori smiled. 'Love you.'

'Love you too.'

'How'd it go?' Sharon dried her hands with the tea towel and put away the last of the plates.

'Yep. All good, we're celebrating this evening. Go get your glad rags on,' replied Kenny.

'But I got us skate for dinner.'

'That'll keep until tomorrow.'

'Where we going then?'

'It's a surprise. Go on, chop chop. Otherwise we'll be late.'

*

61

Stapleford Abbotts was a rural part of Essex that had very few shops, lots of greenery, but did have three pubs. Two were called The Oak and were differentiated by the locals as the Bottom Oak and Top Oak.

Tansey Turner hadn't returned to the area since she'd moved away and as she passed familiar places, including Trigger's old stables, she couldn't help but think of Donny Bond. They say you never forget your first love and she hadn't, even though she was now happily married with a son.

Visions of their love-making in Trigger's stable flashed through Tansey's mind. Sex with Matt was fine, but it couldn't compete with the lust and togetherness she'd experienced with Donny. Sometimes they'd lie in that stable for hours and hours; even after sex, they couldn't stop kissing and cuddling.

'You're quiet, Tans. You OK, mate?' asked Vicki Wainwright, the bride-to-be.

'Yes, fine,' smiled Tansey, looking out the window again. Her father had been in his element telling her Donny had got nicked for armed robbery and what a lucky escape she'd had. She wondered if he was still in prison. Hopefully he wasn't, but wherever he was, she hoped he was healthy and happy.

Dressed in a black Fred Perry polo shirt, light Wrangler jeans and tan desert boots, Donny walked into The Oak. It was busier than usual, rammed with women.

The DJ was playing Elvis Costello's 'Oliver's Army'.

Spotting Dave and the others in their usual spot in the corner, Donny walked over and slapped Dave on the back. 'All right, you old git? Whaddya want to drink?'

'I'm OK at the moment. I got three in the pump. Some crumpet in 'ere tonight, ain't there, Don?'

Donny smiled. Dave was six foot five, skinny with carrot-coloured hair. He'd only had one proper girlfriend in his lifetime and she'd resembled Olive off *On the Buses*. Now and again he'd pull some plastered old scrubber, but other than that he got his thrills down at the massage parlour in Goodmayes. Dave was a regular, probably spent most of his wages there.

'Cor, she's well fit that bird. Look, Don. She's got them black shiny leggings on and leather jacket. She reminds me of Olivia Newton John in *Grease*, but with a different barnet.'

Donny turned around. He'd been banged up when *Grease* had become a phenomenon, so had never seen the film. The girl in question had her back to him, was dancing with friends to Janet Kay's 'Silly Games. 'She looks fit enough from the back, mate, so your type of bird,' Donny laughed, turning to the bar.

Divvy Dave nudged Donny. 'Look, you can see her face now. I wouldn't mind her lips around me cory later.'

Donny turned around and was totally dumbstruck. The bird Dave was referring to was his one and only true love: Tansey.

''Ere, there's some bloke keeps looking at you and I'm sure it's your ex who used to come up the stables,' Vicki informed her friend.

Tansey felt the colour drain from her face. 'Donny?'

'Yeah. Turn around. He's standing up the bar towards the back, left-hand side. I saw him looking over earlier and was sure I knew him from somewhere. I've just cottoned on where from. I bet he don't recognize me though. I was into glam rock back then,' chuckled Vicki.

Legs feeling like blancmange, Tansey turned around.

Their eyes locked and both of them felt as if they'd been struck by a thunderbolt.

'I can't believe you've bought me back here, Kenny. You sure know how to make a woman feel special,' smiled Sharon. She hadn't returned to South London since the evening the petrol bomb had been slung through her window and it had felt like a trip down memory lane. The Italian restaurant was at the Elephant and Castle, and that's where Kenny had proposed to her. They were even sitting on the very same table with a red rose in a vase, exactly how it had been that night, although the decor had changed somewhat.

Kenny held his wife's hands and stared into her big brown eyes. 'For better or for worse, eh babe? And we've certainly had our fair share of the latter. Your visits and letters kept me going while inside. I could never have coped without yer. You're my rock, and now we got only good times to look forward to.'

'Let's hope so, Kenny. As long as you keep to your promise. Only I couldn't do all those prison visits again.' They both knew she'd stick by him no matter but he wouldn't do it to her.

'I wouldn't expect you to, love. That's why I bought the boat. All above board, excuse the pun.'

'That won't be enough cash for you, even if you weren't sharing the profits with Donny. Remember, I know you better than anyone; you live life in the fast lane. You always have.'

'Not anymore, Shal. Prison changes yer, makes you realize what's important in life. It's all about family for me now. Spending quality time with you, the kids and our grandkids. Anyway, I still got plenty of money stashed away. We ain't short on cash, girl. We got enough to buy our own home. In fact, I'm gonna build you one, my queen. You shall have your very own dream home.'

'Oh, don't be daft. I'm not materialistic like that. All I want is you, our kids and grandkids to be happy and healthy, and my parents, your aunt and mum. That's all I've ever wanted. That and a few bob in the bank suits me fine.'

'You got more chance of hell freezing over than my muvver ever being happy,' chuckled Kenny.

'Be happy with what we've got, Kenny.'

'My darling, if I've got you by my side nothing else in the world matters.'

Kenny looked into her eyes and for that moment, he believed every word.

Having been a big fan of the film *Grease*, Tansey actually felt as if she were starring in it as Donny walked towards her and said her name. Not only was she dressed up as Sandy, it reminded her of the moment Sandy bumped into Danny Zuko again after their summer fling.

'Donny! How are you?' Tansey could actually feel her legs trembling. His hair was shorter, cropped, which suited him. But it was those big brown eyes. She'd almost forgotten how absorbing and gorgeous they were.

'Can't hear yourself think in 'ere. Shall we talk outside?' Donny suggested. She looked stunning, his stomach was in knots.

Tansey nodded. Then like a lamb being led to the slaughter, she followed Donny.

It was a lovely July evening, so Donny suggested they take a stroll. They got the niceties out the way. Each was shocked to find out the other was a parent now.

'So what's he do, your old man?' Donny enquired. He couldn't help but feel jealous, even though he was engaged to Lori.

'Matt's a policeman, like my dad. In fact, it was through my dad I met Matt.'

I bet it was, Donny thought bitterly. 'So, he treats you well, like?'

'Yes. Matt's a good man and a good father. He's been promoted recently to a DS. What about your fiancée? Where did you meet?'

'In a pub. To be honest, I was gutted when you left the area and I went off the rails a bit. Was boozing heavily. I met Lori around that time and she fell pregnant with the twins. They certainly weren't planned – I was only sixteen, and she was supposed to be on the pill – but obviously I wouldn't be without them now. As you can imagine, I freaked out when she told me she was having twins. That's when I did something really dumb: an armed robbery. I only did it 'cause I knew I had to put a roof over me kids' heads. But it all went tits up and I ended up in Feltham. I've not long been out.'

Tansey squeezed Donny's arm. She admired his honesty. 'I know. My dad had great pleasure in telling me at the time. I was so upset for you, even though I'd met Matt by then. I never forgot about you, Donny.'

Donny cupped her face in his hands. 'I thought about you every day while banged up. What we had was so special. What I've got now don't even come close.'

Tansey looked into those soulful eyes she had never been able to resist. For a moment she tried but, seconds later, they were kissing.

Kenny returned from the Gents to find his wife in conversation with the geezer he'd clocked craning his neck and looking over at their table earlier.

'Kenny, this is Duncan, an old classmate of mine from senior school,' Sharon explained, her tone a tad edgy.

When the bloke held out his right hand, Kenny accepted the handshake. 'You got a right cracker there, mate, you lucky sod. Shal was my first love, weren't you, darlin'?'

Glaring at the blond-haired prick with hatred, Kenny then turned to the wife who'd always assured him that he was her first boyfriend. 'That right, is it, darlin'?' he asked sarcastically.

Sharon laughed nervously. Duncan had told her he'd been out with pals earlier celebrating his divorce papers coming through and it was clear he'd had a few too many shandies. 'We were only youngsters. It was all innocent,' Sharon insisted, hoping Duncan would take heed of the warning look she gave him.

'We weren't that young, darlin'. We were fourteen. You still got that beautiful smile of yours,' Duncan gushed.

Kenny's jaw began twitching as Duncan squeezed his wife's shoulders.

'Kenny, no,' shrieked Sharon, as her husband grabbed Duncan around the throat, smashed the back of his head against the wall, then kneed him in the nuts, leaving the man in a crumpled heap on the floor. Everyone was looking. It was embarrassing.

'You ever lay another hand on my wife, I'll chop your bastard hands off. She ain't your darlin' either, she's mine, yer cheeky cunt.' Kenny took a wad of notes out of his pocket and chucked a few on the table. 'Get your fucking coat, Shal. We're going.'

*

Hearing a car engine, Lori was relieved Donny was home.

Donny let himself in. 'Sorry I'm late.'

Lori glared at him. 'And so you bloody should be. Beau's been really ill. He hasn't stopped vomiting and needs to go to casualty. I would have rung my stepdad, but he and Mum are down the caravan. Where the bloody hell you been? It's nearly one!'

Donny felt a twinge of guilt. 'The guvnor had a lock-in for Dave and he begged me not to leave early,' he explained. Part of that was true; there had been a lock-in. But Dave hadn't begged him to stay. Tansey had left the pub around eleven thirty and he'd needed to collect his thoughts and have a couple of stiff brandies before driving home. It had literally blown his world apart, seeing her again. As for kissing her, her lips felt like pure silk against his, just as they had back in the day. 'Do you wanna go hospital now?'

Lori hated Donny being out late; it brought out a jealous streak in her. So she'd laid it on thick about Beau. 'He's asleep now. Hopefully, and no poxy thanks to you, he'll be all right in the morning.'

Sharon was fuming. 'I truly can't believe you made a show of us like that. Say the police had been called? You know if you break your parole conditions, you're straight back inside.'

'That's why I never clumped the mug. The thought of you and him together turns my stomach. What the hell were you thinking, Shal? And you bastard well lied to me.'

'Slow down, for Christ's sake. You're gonna kill us in a minute,' Sharon pleaded, as Kenny overtook another car at high speed, very nearly colliding with it.

'A liar is worse than a thief. That's what my granddad always drummed into me, God rest his soul.'

'Oh, stop being so overly dramatic. Your grandfather was a thief. That's why he said that. I have never lied to you, Kenny. When we met, I told you I'd never had a serious boyfriend. Duncan wasn't serious, was he? I was thirteen! We didn't even meet up out of school.'

'Fourteen. He said fourteen.'

'Thirteen, fourteen. Does it bloody matter? Stop acting like a child and grow up. You know full well I was a virgin when we met. You bloody weren't though, was you? You poked your John Thomas up anything you could before we got together.'

'It's different for blokes.'

'You're such a male chauvinist at times. I'm glad Donny has grown up with my values and not yours. He's a proper little family man. He doesn't run around shoving his dick up every old slapper.'

'He did when he got his heart broken that time. He told me. How could you go out with a bell-end like that, eh? And what I did before I met you is neither 'ere nor there. I have never cheated on you.'

'Well, I'm not surprised. You've been banged up for most of our married life. I'm not talking about this any more, so stop being so bleedin' immature and concentrate on getting us home in one piece.'

'OK. Can I please just ask one more question though?'

'What?' snapped Sharon.

'How long did you go out with Dunky for?'

Sharon punched Kenny on the leg. 'You're such a tosser.'

Kenny was the first to burst out laughing. Sharon then saw the funny side. A typical Bond evening out. Just like the good old days.

CHAPTER SIX

'Men are like dogs. If they ain't properly trained,
they'll shit all over their own carpet.'

To say I was enraged when Donny finally confided in me
as to what was going on is putting it mildly. He's lucky
I never shoved him off the boat and into the Thames.

Family meant everything to me and I was upset my boy
didn't share mine or me granddad's values. Not only was
the idiot knocking off that bloody Tansey again, he
was insistent it was true love and he was going to leave
Lori and the twins for her.

I said and did everything in my power to make Donny
see sense; including telling him his mother would disown
him. But it went in one ear and out the other. He was
like a lovesick puppy, the drip.

In the end I lost my temper. 'You end this nonsense
with Tansey immediately. Because believe me, if you don't,
you're gonna start a fucking war and I'm bound to get
caught up in it too.'

Unfortunately, my warning fell on deaf ears . . .

*

Matt Jackson felt as though he had the weight of the world on his shoulders. Not only was he currently investigating the brutal murder of a four-year-old boy, his marriage was falling apart before his very eyes.

Matt sighed. Before that hen night, Tansey had never been interested in going out with the girls. Now she was out every Friday, supposedly drinking with her mates in the Cross Keys in Dagenham.

Something was definitely amiss; Matt was sure of that. He could see it in her eyes when they made love and he could sense it in her all-round behaviour. It was as though she was at home in person, but her mind was elsewhere.

Having come to the conclusion that Tansey must be having an affair, Matt had spoken to her father about it. Terry had all but laughed in his face. 'Don't be daft. My Tans would never cheat on you. You've got a lot to learn about women, son. My Penny's mood can change on the turn of a sixpence, especially around her time of the month. I just sod off down the pub, me,' he'd chuckled.

Still suspicious, Matt decided he had to find out the truth for his own sanity. So tonight, a good friend and colleague of his, PC Jayne Clark, would be following Tansey to find out where she was really going and who the hell with.

'Right, I'm off out then. I won't be too late home,' Donny told Lori.

Lori eyed her fiancé with uncertainty. Friday was the only day he ever seemed cheerful of late and she was sure that was because he was seeing *her* – his bit on the side. 'You should be staying in tonight, seeing as you'll be out working on the boat tomorrow night. It's not fair on me and the boys,' hissed Lori.

'Friday night is the only night I have out with my mates, Lori. Tomorrow is work. Entirely different. I work damn hard to put a roof over our heads and food on the table. Please don't begrudge me a few beers with me pals.'

'That's if you're actually going out with your pals.'

'Oh, don't start all that again. You should see a doctor about your paranoia. See ya later.'

Having been told what direction Tansey went off in, PC Jayne Clark parked her Ford Cortina at the top of the road. She'd met Matt at Hendon, they'd done their training together and she thought the world of him. She was the only colleague he'd confided in about Tansey and it pained her to see him in such turmoil.

Jayne tilted her interior mirror so she'd have a view of Tansey when she left the house. She didn't have to wait long. Dead on 6.15 p.m., just as Matt had predicted, she saw Tansey walking towards her car. She'd never met Matt's wife, had cried off going to his wedding, pleading illness. The thought of watching the only man she'd ever wanted to marry walking down the aisle with someone else was more than she could stand. But she'd seen their wedding photos. She had one in her handbag now.

As Tansey walked past her car, Jayne waited thirty seconds before stepping out of the driver's side.

Donny was parked up outside Hornchurch Station. He literally lived for Fridays of late. Every other day of the week was as dull as dishwater to him. Tomorrow would be good though. The boat had its first booking, a fortieth birthday bash. The start of a new era, where he could hopefully save a load of dosh for his and Tansey's future. He knew it was fate they'd met up again, could feel it in his bones.

Donny thought of Lori. He couldn't even get a hard-on the last time he'd been forced to give her one. She'd gone ballistic that night, had told him if she caught him out, he would never see their sons again. That had preyed on his mind, along with his dad's stark warning.

At 6.55 p.m., Donny saw the love of his life walk out the station. He leapt out of his motor, held her in his arms and kissed her. 'I've missed you so much this week. It's doing my nut in.'

Tansey smiled. 'I've felt the same. Come on, drive to the nursery, quickly. I need to feel you inside me again.'

What neither realized as they pulled away sharpish, was that Jayne Clark was a keen photographer in her spare time and now had all the evidence she needed.

The following day Matt was at the Thatched House at noon, as planned. It was his first day off for over a fortnight and Jayne had pulled a sickie to meet up with him. 'Well?' Matt asked. He'd barely slept a wink last night. Not only was it too bloody hot to sleep, his mind had been torturing him with thoughts of what Tansey was up to.

Having been the first to arrive, Jayne pushed the large brandy she'd bought towards Matt. 'Drink up, you're gonna need it.'

Matt's face drained of colour. He downed his drink in one.

'I'm so sorry, Matt. I truly am,' Jayne sympathized as she handed him the four photos. One was of Tansey and Donny embracing, two of them kissing and the other, Donny's number plate. 'I've already found out who he is. His name is Donny Bond and I have an address for him in Harold Hill.'

Matt felt physically sick as he studied the images. How

73

could Tansey do this to him and Jamie? He smashed his fist against the table. 'I'm gonna fucking kill him, then I shall kill that slag I made the mistake of marrying.'

Penny Turner opened the front door and was amazed when her usually well-mannered son-in-law barged past her with a woman she'd never seen before, bellowing, 'Where the fuck is Terry?'

'Still in bed. He's on nights. Whatever's wrong?'

'Your daughter. That's what's fucking wrong.'

'Terry! Terry! You need to get up. It's urgent,' yelled Penny.

Feeling awkward, Jayne held out her right hand. 'I'm Jayne, Matt's work colleague and friend. We did our training together too.'

Not knowing what the hell was going on, Penny mumbled. 'Oh, right,' then shook the woman's hand.

Terry appeared, bleary-eyed, in a navy-blue dressing gown.

'I told you your darling daughter was at it, didn't I?' Matt bellowed, handing Terry the photos.

Terry's complexion turned white. 'I'll bloody kill her. That's Donny Bond,' he fumed, handing the evidence to Penny.

'Please God no,' gasped the horrified Penny.

'I want her out the house, Tel,' raged Matt. 'She ain't taking my boy with her either. I'm paying that no-good arsehole a visit an' all. I've got his address.'

Terry ran his fingers across his moustache. 'Let me get dressed, son, and I'll come with you.'

As Terry drove them to Harold Hill, Matt was quiet but, understandably, very hurt and angry. Matt was a good copper and a decent bloke. Terry's heart went out to him. 'If you chuck Tansey out, son, you'll only be pushing her further into Donny's arms. I know how mad you are – I would be too – but don't you think your marriage might be worth saving?'

Matt glared at Terry as though he were barmy. 'No. I don't. I never want to see the slag again, let alone share a bed with her. What, after he's been up her? You're having a laugh.'

Usually Terry would deck any man who referred to his daughter as a 'slag', but he decided to swallow his pride for once, seeing as it was warranted. 'Not even for Jamie's sake? If Tans moves out, she'll take Jamie with her, pal, and you know what the courts are like. They always give custody to the mother.'

Matt looked at Terry with a dangerous glint in his eyes. 'Over my dead body. She ain't taking my son anywhere.'

'Your call, but you're taking a gamble.' No way did Terry want his daughter ending up with Donny Bond and his grandson having contact with his other grandfather – the cop killer. 'He's done bird, this Donny, ya know. Armed robbery. He ain't been out of Feltham long. As for his father, he's not long out. Shot a cop over a dozen times, the wrong un.'

Matt looked aghast. 'You're kidding me!'

'Nope. Afraid not. Do you really want Jamie being raised around a family like that?'

'How d'ya know all this?'

'Donny was Tansey's first boyfriend. That's why I moved the family away from Havering-atte-Bower – to get her away from him.'

Matt's mouth was wide open. Not once had Tansey mentioned an ex-boyfriend. When they'd made love for the first time, she'd sworn he was her first. He'd thought it funny at the time that there was no blood on the pure white sheets. Not only was the slag he'd married a cheat, she was also a liar. What the hell had he married? It seemed he really didn't know Tansey at all.

'Beau, stop that now! You're hurting Brett.' Beau was twisting his brother's ear and trying to use it to lead him round the garden.

When Beau ignored her and Brett started to cry, Lori rushed into the garden, grabbed her naughtiest son by the arm and gave him a wallop on his bottom. Both the twins were little sods, but Beau had more of the devil in him. 'Now behave your bloody self, otherwise I will send you to your room. Brothers don't fight, especially twins. How many times have I got to tell you that?'

'Didn't hurt,' smirked Beau.

Lori berated Beau then took the washing outside. She was just about to peg up Donny's pants, which she scrutinized on a regular basis, especially after his Friday nights out, when the doorbell rang.

'Play nicely now,' Lori ordered her sons, before dashing to see who it was. She was surprised to see two strange men on her doorstep. One older and stocky, the other tall and quite handsome. They certainly didn't look like Jehovah's Witnesses. 'Hello. How can I help you?'

'Donny in?' hissed Matt.

'Erm, no. He's working today.'

'Where?' asked the older bloke.

'On his boat. You won't be able to get hold of him. Who shall I say wanted to speak to him?' Lori was worried. Neither man looked happy, especially the younger one.

The older guy turned away, taking his mate by the arm and telling him, 'Come on. We'll pop back and see Donny another time.'

All of a sudden, the twins appeared at the door. 'Mum, hurt arm,' cried Brett.

At the sight of her boys, the younger man's anger turned to fury. He swiped away the other man's hand, telling him, 'If I'm going to lose my son, I'll see to it he loses his kids too.' Then he reached into his pocket, took out some photos and handed them to Lori. 'I'm Tansey's old man. I think we need to have a chat, love.'

Lori stared at the photos in complete horror. When she'd first met Donny all he had gone on about was bloody Tansey, but she'd had no idea they'd met up since. Until now. Donny had the outfit on he'd gone out in last night. Unable to stop herself, Lori burst into tears. 'You'd better come in,' she wept.

'OK, I'll be back tomorrow at ten a.m. You sure you're gonna be all right?' Matt asked Lori. She'd invited him to come back tomorrow to confront Donny, wanting to see the cheating bastard cringe when he was confronted by his tart's old man. She was going to act dumb up until then.

'Make sure you give him a good clump an' all,' Lori said, fighting back the tears.

'Oh, he'll get a good hiding all right,' spat Terry.

'See you tomorrow then,' Matt said.

'Yeah, bye.' Lori shut the front door and crumpled to her haunches. She'd always dreaded this moment and now it had arrived. She would fight tooth and nail to keep Donny, mind. No way was she chucking him out so he could run straight into that slapper's arms. Not only was her fiancé the love of her life, he was also her meal ticket and the father of her children. Without him, she'd never be able to cope with the twins.

Tears streaming down her face, Lori lifted the lid of the record playing and put on *her* song. The Alessi Brothers' 'Oh Lori' was a love song Donny had asked his mum to buy her for her birthday while he was incarcerated. It had beautiful words about being made for each other, wanting to be together.

The twins suddenly appeared. 'What a matter, Mum?' asked Brett.

Tears turning to anger, Lori snatched at the record, chucked it on the floor and repeatedly stamped on it until it smashed to pieces. Those lyrics had once meant the world to her, but not anymore. She never wanted to hear the poxy song again.

It was a baking hot day. Tansey was in the garden playing with Jamie. Matt had bought him a small blow-up paddling pool and he was happily sailing his boat and splashing about in a couple of inches of water.

As soon as Matt appeared with her father, Tansey could tell something was wrong. Both had faces like thunder. Her heart sank. Surely they hadn't found out her sordid secret? 'What's up? Is Mum OK?'

'Dry Jamie off and put him in his playpen,' Matt seethed. 'Then start packing your bags, you slut. I want you outta my house within the hour. Oh, and you won't be taking Jamie with you. He stays with me.'

The enormity of what she had done suddenly smacked Tansey in the face like a stocking full of hot shit. She had never seen her mild-mannered husband look so angry. As for calling her a slut, why wasn't her dad sticking up for her? 'Whatever are you talking about?' Her whole body was shaking with fear.

Terry walked over to the paddling pool and lifted his grandson out. He glared at his daughter. 'You've disappointed both me and your mother. Even your sister is appalled by your recklessness. I'll sort Jamie out while you two talk. I hope Donny was worth it, treacle, 'cause Matt now hates your guts and I don't blame him. A convicted armed robber who just happens to be the son of a cop killer. You've really excelled yourself this time. I hope you're ashamed of yourself 'cause you've shamed your wonderful husband and the rest of your family. You're nothing but a common tramp.'

Tansey burst into tears. The words were like a knife to her heart. 'But I haven't done anything wrong. Donny and I are just friends.'

Matt took the photos out of his pocket, stormed over to Tansey and nigh on rammed them in her face. 'Really! Explain these then—'

'Matt, enough, mate. Not in front of Jamie,' warned Terry.

'I'm so sorry. I truly am,' sobbed Tansey.

'It's too late for sorrys. Now go pack your bags. Oh and first thing on Monday I'll be filing for divorce – and custody of Jamie.'

Donny Bond was full of the joys of spring as his father drove him home. Not only had the fortieth party been a great success, it was amazing to be part owner of a Thames pleasure boat.

'You all right, boy? Good little earner, eh? We need to book more of these open-bar parties. The bill tots up proper nicely as there are so many greedy bastards out there, especially when the host is paying,' chuckled Kenny Bond.

His dad had been much more relaxed around him since he'd stopped talking about leaving Lori and the twins for Tansey. In fact, he no longer mentioned Tansey in front of his father. Best to let his old man believe his sharp words and stark warning had made him see sense. Until Tans finally made the decision to leave Matt, it wasn't worth the grief of bringing it up. Donny laughed and counted the huge wad of money in his hand again. Even though they'd had to pay the captain, his mate, the bar staff and DJ, he'd still earned far more money than he'd ever been paid for a week's work before, let alone a day's.

'Don't spend it all at once, eh?' winked Kenny as he pulled up outside his son's house.

'No way. I'm saving every penny for a better future. I will treat the twins, though.'

Kenny ruffled his son's hair. 'Good lad.'

'Night, Dad. Thanks for everything.'

'You're welcome.'

Wide awake, Lori shut her eyes as she heard Donny open the front door, then come up the stairs.

'You awake? Tonight went so well.' Donny was buzzing and desperate to tell his good news.

Lori said nothing. She just thought of the bread knife downstairs and visualized stabbing Tansey straight through the heart with it.

Unable to sleep, Lori was up early the following morning. She didn't want her sons to witness the chaos that was about to happen, so had rung her mum the previous evening and asked her to look after Beau and Brett for a few hours. She hadn't confided in her mum what had occurred, because she knew her mother would go ballistic and demand she kick Donny's arse out. Lori's real dad had had an affair and her mum was a tough cookie. She'd cut all ties with him immediately and told him where to go. Her mum referred to him now as 'the tosspot'.

Lori sighed as she put the kettle on. Unlike her mother, she was a weak woman. Perhaps she took after her father? But if so, there was nothing she could do about it. The only thing she could do was hope and pray that Donny would stay with her and the kids. He loved the twins, and she could never see him walking away from them. But, if he did, she would make damn sure he never saw them again.

Lori looked at the clock on the kitchen wall: 9.30. Roll on 10 a.m., she thought. The waiting was all but killing her.

Knowing he wouldn't be home until late last night, Donny Bond had arranged for Divvy Dave to help his nan today, flogging flowers down the A127. This would be his first Sunday-morning lie-in since last winter, and he'd been determined to make the most of it. But Lori had other ideas.

'Donny, you've got visitors,' she shouted up the stairs. How she'd kept a lid on it when he'd climbed into bed, slung an arm around her and told her how wonderful last night on the boat had been, she would never know.

Matt winked at Lori. 'You OK?' he whispered.

'So-so. Just make sure you hit him fucking hard and don't do it out the front. The neighbours are nosy.'

Terry pushed Matt inside the house and the pair of them glared at Donny as he came down the stairs.

Donny's eyes widened in alarm as he clocked who his visitors were. He obviously recognized Tansey's dad, and it didn't take much to work out that the younger man

81

was her husband. 'Go out in the garden, Lori. Me and the lads need to talk a bit of business.'

'Business! I'll give you fucking business, you lowlife piece of shit,' bellowed Terry, literally grabbing hold of Donny by the scruff of his neck and dragging him down the rest of the stairs.

Donny lost his footing, his dressing gown flew open, and Lori thoroughly enjoyed the sight of him getting a good kicking. Matt was a keen rugby player and Donny didn't stand a chance against him and Terry.

'You can have that slut of a wife of mine now.' Matt dragged Donny to his feet and gave him a right-hander with such force that Donny flew backwards and landed on the stairs. 'But you won't be raising my son. Jamie stays with me. As for Tansey, I wouldn't touch her with a bargepole now you've been up her.'

Aware that Lori was watching, and desperate to stop the beating, Donny croaked, 'Me and Tans go back years. We're old pals, that's all.'

'You're a scumbag, Bond. From scumbag stock. You stay away from my daughter, do you hear me?' spat Terry, aiming a kick at Donny's bollocks. It was a shame he had pants on.

Matt shoved the photos in Donny's face. 'Really, ya lying prick!' He then handed the photos to Lori. 'You keep these, sweetheart. I had a couple of sets printed. Use these to get the money you deserve for your kids.'

'Thank you,' Lori mumbled, even though she had no intention of letting Donny leave her.

Terry Turner stamped on Donny's stomach one last time. As much as he loathed his daughter right now, no way did he want her ending up with vermin. He wasn't worried about himself or Matt getting into trouble at work. There

82

was no chance of Donny involving the Old Bill, not with a father like Kenny.

Donny clutched his stomach. Terry had winded him big time.

'Come on, Matt. Let's go, son.'

Matt turned to Lori. 'You look after yourself, sweetheart.' He gestured towards Donny. 'You certainly deserve better than him.'

Lori saw Matt and Terry out before slinging the photos at Donny. 'How could you do this to me? I knew you were at it and you made me feel like I was mental. What type of man does that to the mother of his children? You've broken my heart.'

'I'm really sorry. I didn't mean to hurt you. But I can't help the way I feel. I love Tansey and she loves me.'

That wasn't what Lori had wanted to hear. She'd expected Donny to grovel, beg her forgiveness, not tell her he was in love with someone else. Unable to stop herself, Lori went apeshit and began slapping Donny around the face.

Donny managed to restrain her by grabbing her wrists. 'I'll pack some stuff, yeah, and get out your hair. I'll stay with me nan and granddad for a bit.' His mum, dad and sister were still all living with his grandparents, as his dad was currently having their dream home built from scratch.

Lori chased Donny up the stairs. 'You can't just walk out. What about the twins? They'll be devastated.'

'I'll still see 'em regularly. They'll be OK. They've got each other and you.'

Lori burst into tears. 'Please don't walk out today, Donny. We're engaged to be married, for Christ's sake! We need to talk about what's happened. Please?'

Donny shrugged. 'All right,' he agreed reluctantly. 'I'll stay today.'

CHAPTER SEVEN

Donny felt as if he'd been hit by a bus as he tried to swing his legs over the edge of the bed. His spine was killing him, and his ribs.

'You OK? Shall I get you a cup of tea and some painkillers?' asked Lori. She seemed to have decided that, however much she hated him right now, being nasty wasn't going to get her anywhere. She would put on an act for ever if she had to, to stop him jumping ship with Tansey.

Donny studied his appearance in the wardrobe mirror. He had a right shiner and a fat lip. 'Nah. It's OK. I gotta go to work. You get back to sleep.'

Lori sat bolt upright. 'Don't be so stupid. You can't go to work like that. You can't even walk properly. You're hobbling. I'll ring the nursery for you, say you're not well. Besides, we need to talk, properly talk.' When he shook his head, she added, 'I'll call Mum, tell her to drop the boys off early.' It was obvious she wanted to remind Donny exactly what he'd be losing. Even if he didn't love her anymore, she knew he loved Beau and Brett and couldn't walk away from them.

'I have to go to work. We're short-staffed today as it is

84

and I can't trust Divvy Dave,' lied Donny. 'I'll be fine. I'm stiff, that's all. A couple of painkillers, I'll be right as rain.'

'You are coming home this evening, aren't you?'

He could hear the anxiety in her voice; she was terrified he was going to see Tansey.

'Yeah. Course.'

Lori breathed a sigh of relief. 'I'll cook us the roast we never got to have yesterday.'

'Sounds good,' Donny said as he gingerly finished getting dressed. He felt too rough to have a wash. 'See ya later then.'

'Bye. Don't overdo it,' Lori replied, forcing a jovial tone.

'Don't tell anyone what happened yesterday, will ya? I'm gonna tell my family I got into a fight at the boozer.'

'OK. I'll say the same.'

As Donny left the room, Lori put her head under the quilt and began crying like a baby.

'Donny, there's a young lady on the phone, says it's important,' shouted Maggie Saunders.

Heart in his mouth, Donny snatched at the phone. Tansey was crying. 'I can't stay here with my parents, Donny. They've been so horrible to me. Both have sided with Matt. What happened when my dad and Matt come round yours? Did they hurt you?'

'A bit. Could've been worse. Ya can't blame 'em, can ya?'

'I suppose not. Oh well, at least we can be together now, and that's what we both wanted. All my belongings are still at Matt's. He took my door key off me but I know my mum has a spare. Where will we live? I honestly can't stay here another night. I'm missing Jamie terribly. Matt can't keep him. Jamie needs his mum.'

'Is your dad there now?'

'No. He's at work. My mum's here though.'

'Give us the address and I'll come and get you. Then we'll try and pick up your clobber and Jamie. We can stay at my nan and granddad's until I sort us out a place to live.'

'OK. That's great. I'll ring home. I know Matt was on days this week, so hopefully he's at work too. I reckon his mum or sister will be looking after Jamie. I'll grab the spare key and get my bits together now. See you soon, Donny.'

Donny arrived at Tansey's parents' gaff thirty-five minutes later and was surprised to see her having some kind of barney with her mum out the front. He jumped out of his work van. He'd been in terrible pain until Tansey rang him, then the adrenaline kicked in. 'You all right, Tans?'

Penny Turner looked Donny up and down as though he was something nasty she'd trodden in. 'No. She's not all right. She's a stupid little tart who has thrown her perfectly good marriage away on a cocky toerag like you. I'll say this once more, Tansey: if you drive off now with *him*, I will never forgive you and neither will your father. We will disown you.' Penny was pleased to see Donny's left eye was swollen. He had a shiner there and she hoped it bloody well hurt.

'Put my bags in the van, please, Donny,' said Tansey.

Penny shook her head in total despair. 'Your father will go mental when I tell him this. Don't come running back here with your tail between your legs when it all goes wrong with Romeo.'

Tansey got into the passenger seat and as Donny drove away the last thing she heard was her mother screaming, 'You're dead to us, young lady. Dead!'

*

Even though she'd taken the precaution of ringing her landline to see if Matt was home, Tansey was relieved to find the house empty.

'I've cleared out the back of my van, so we'll just grab as much as your stuff as quickly as we can.' Donny really didn't fancy Matt turning up and him having another run-in with him.

'You load up all my clothes and shoes, Donny, and I'll put all my other odds and sods together and Jamie's things.'

Forty-five minutes later, the back of the van was crammed full. 'You're gonna have to leave anything else now, Tans.'

Tansey took one last look at the house she'd once been so proud of. It belonged to Matt now, not her, so she posted the spare key through the letterbox.

Their next stop was Matt's mum's place in East Ham. Tansey gave Donny directions, then told him, 'Park away from the house and wait in the van.' She could hardly allow Matt's mum and Donny to meet.

The old dear next door was scrubbing her step. 'She ain't in, lovey. Went out about an hour ago. Probably at the daytime bingo.'

'She didn't have her grandson with her then?'

'Nope.'

'Thanks.'

Tansey got back in the van. 'Head to West Ham and I'll give you directions when we get near there.'

Donny was dreading picking his clobber up later. Lori was bound to go hysterical. She'd even tried to have sex with him last night, that's how desperate the poor cow was. He hoped in time their relationship could be amicable because of the twins, but he very much doubted Lori would ever forgive him. She loved him too much to

87

forgive or forget. He couldn't see her moving on with another bloke either, although that quite pleased him. He wouldn't mind her dating, but wouldn't like another geezer raising his boys. That'd do his head in.

Lyndsey Jackson lived with her bus driver partner Brian and their two children Jessica and Jacob.

They lived in a ground-floor council flat but were lucky to have patio doors that opened onto a big green where the kids loved to play, especially on hot days such as today.

Lots of the neighbours would sit on the green too, so it was as safe as houses for the kids. One of the neighbours had bought a big paddling pool a while back. Jessica and Jacob were currently splashing about in that while little Jamie was sleeping in his pushchair nearby. She'd made sure she'd put plenty of high-factor sun cream on all three of them.

'Look! Jamie's outside with Jessica and Jacob. Turn around, then stop while I grab him. I'll have to leave the pushchair there – we can get him a new one tomorrow.'

'You can't just snatch him without saying something, Tans. The poor woman will think he's been abducted, and Matt'll send out a search party.'

'I'll tell the kids to tell their mum. Wait here and get ready to put your foot down.'

'Auntie Tansey,' squealed six-year-old Jessica. 'We been babysitting Jamie and he's been a good boy.'

'I know, darling, but he's coming home with me now. Do me a favour, run and tell your mum I've picked him up, yeah.' Tansey unstrapped her son and literally ran back to the van with him in her arms.

'Oi! Whaddya think you're doing?' Tansey heard some bloke shout.

'Drive, Donny. Quickly!'

Donny did exactly as he was told.

Relieved to see the only car on the drive was his mother's, Donny squeezed Tansey's hand. Jamie was asleep on her lap. 'Best I speak to my mum alone and explain what's happened. You wait 'ere. I won't be long.'

Dreading the conversation he was about to have, Donny let himself in the house. His mother was lying in the back garden reading a book.

'You not at work, love?' Sharon put her book down and did a double-take. She took off her sunglasses to make sure the dark lenses weren't deceiving her. 'What you done to your face, Donny? You been in a fight?'

'It's a long story, so I'm gonna cut it short. Please don't hate me though. I can't help the way I feel.'

Startled, Sharon scrambled to her feet. 'Whatever's wrong?'

'I've been seeing Tansey again and it's all come on top. I love her and we wanna be together. Her husband found out and chucked her out. He's the one that did this.' Donny pointed to his black eye. 'I know it's a mess, but she's outside in the van with her son. Can she stay 'ere, Mum? Me an' all?'

Sharon looked at her son in amazement. 'Hold your horses. What about Lori and your sons?'

'I'm not happy with Lori. I never have been.'

'But you asked the girl to marry ya, so you couldn't have been that bastard well unhappy! You can't just walk away and leave the twins. They're your flesh and blood. They depend on you.'

'I'll still be a good dad to 'em and see 'em loads.'

Not quite believing what she was hearing, a disgusted

Sharon marched towards her son and clouted him as hard as she could around the face. 'You can't raise another man's son and leave Beau and Brett. Does Lori know you've cheated on her?'

'Well, yeah, but—'

'No buts. You get your arse back home and make things right with that poor girl. You were raised with morals, Donny. Family means everything. Not somebody else's family – your fucking own.'

'Say your granddad turns us away too? What will we do then?' Tansey asked worriedly. Donny had already said that, worst come to the worst, they could stop in a hotel for a few nights until he found them somewhere to live, but she really didn't fancy leaving all her belongings in the back of a van. She had packed in such a hurry; she had no idea where any of Jamie's bits were offhand.

Donny swung into the nursery. He knew his grandfather was there because he'd rung from a phone box to make sure. 'It's my granddad's house, not my parents', Tans. I know he won't turn us away. Stay 'ere while I talk to him.'

'Dear, oh dear, oh dear,' chuckled Charlie Saunders. 'Your nan said you'd got yourself into a spot of bother. You need to put a lump of steak on that eye.'

Donny explained what had happened with Tansey, his mum, Matt and Terry. 'We ain't got nowhere to go, Granddad, and all Tansey's worldly goods are in the back of the work van.'

Unbeknown to Maggie, Charlie had been a ladies' man back in the day. Not anymore, but he had messed around early on in their marriage. And he was no fan of Lori's. Aside from purposely trapping his grandson by getting pregnant, she was as dull as ditchwater. Pretty and a decent enough mother, but zero personality. He could understand why Donny's head had been turned.

'Listen, boy, I'm on your side. But Tansey comes from and is married to bad stock, and I don't want or need no agg round mine. Neither will your father. You can kip in the caravan up 'ere until you sort somewhere.'

'Granddad, please let us stay in my old room? Just for a couple of nights, until I sort something. That caravan's minging. It stinks to high heaven. I can't expect Tans or Jamie to sleep there.'

'Go to a hotel then, boy. I'll give you some wonga.'

'But we need to unpack some stuff from the van. Two nights, that's all I'm asking. Tansey's husband and father have already clumped me, they ain't gonna do sod all else. I swear they won't. I'll be out your hair within forty-eight hours.'

Charlie sighed deeply. He idolized his only grandson; much preferred him to his son-in-law. 'Two nights. But I'm telling yer now, Donny, if the filth turn up at mine, I won't be a happy man. Understand me?'

'Yes, Granddad. They won't, though. I swear on my life they won't.'

After unloading the van, Donny decided to get the inevitable over with. It had to be sooner rather than later.

'Good luck and don't forget to get some food on the way back,' Tansey reminded him. She had some Farley's rusks that she'd picked up from Matt's, so they'd have to do for now. Jamie was obviously hungry as he'd been grizzly ever since she'd picked him up earlier.

Donny got in the van and cranked the radio up. Cliff Richard's 'We Don't Talk Any More' was playing. Lori probably wouldn't be talking to him ever again after he'd picked up his stuff.

The journey to Harold Hill only took about half an hour from his granddad's house. He put his key in the door.

Lori dashed into the hallway. 'This is a nice surprise. You knocked off work early?' she smiled.

Donny took a deep breath. 'I've come to collect me stuff, Lori. I am so sorry, but it's not gonna work for me staying 'ere, and you deserve better than that.'

Lori's face crumpled. She threw herself on the hallway carpet and clung to Donny's ankles. 'Please don't leave me and the boys. We need you.'

The boys ran in from the garden. 'What matter, Mum?' asked Beau.

'Daddy's leaving us for another woman and her son,' shrieked Lori.

Not understanding what was going on, Brett and Beau stared at one another, bemused.

'I got some bits and bobs so Jamie don't starve. But let's go out. Get a proper meal down us.' Donny sighed, handing a carrier bag to Tansey.

'How'd it go?'

'As awful as expected. The boys didn't get it, but were still upset, and Lori was in bits. She then went into lunatic mode. Ripped some of my clothes up and chucked shoes and trainers at my head. One hit Beau smack in the face, so I told her to get a grip. I dunno when I'll see the twins again. She reckons she ain't letting me see 'em. I didn't tell her we were together. She asked if I was with you and I told her you were at your parents and I'd be staying with mine.'

'She can't stop you seeing your sons, Donny. She'll come round in time. You'll see.'

Donny shook his head. 'Doubt that very much. You don't know her like I do.'

Kenny shook his head in despair when Sharon explained the day's happenings. 'I thought he'd ended things with Tansey. I warned the silly bastard this would happen.'

'You knew! Why didn't you bloody well tell me?'

''Cause I didn't wanna upset or worry yer. I knew you'd be furious. Lori ain't a bad girl. She don't deserve this. Neither do the twins. Poor little mites. I could swing for Donny, I really could.'

'In fairness to Donny, Lori did trap him at sixteen years old, Kenny. She was meant to be taking the pill. He was no more than a child.' After her initial furious reaction, when Donny had returned asking her to store some of his belongings, he'd sat her down and explained things in more detail. It was clear her son's head was all over the place; she didn't want Kenny making things worse with his bull-in-a-china-shop approach.

Surprised his wife wasn't losing her rag, Kenny ran his hands through his hair. 'Get in the motor. Me and you are gonna pay Lori a visit, make sure she's all right and see if she needs anything. I can't not see Beau and Brett regularly, so we gotta make it look like we're on her side, Shal. Where's Donny now?'

'Gone out to get something to eat. Listen, I already suggested we pay Lori a visit and Donny was adamant we shouldn't get involved. "I'm a man now, not a boy, and I'm quite capable of sorting out my own problems" were his exact words.'

'Well, best he starts acting like a fucking man then, for the twins' sake.'

After a stressful day at work that had involved losing a car full of armed robbers and dealing with a particular nasty domestic violence incident, Matt Jackson arrived at his sister's later than expected to pick up his beloved son. The only thing that was keeping him sane right now was Jamie. His sister opened the door, red-eyed. 'Whatever's the matter?' asked Matt.

'It's Jamie. Tansey turned up here in a van earlier and took him. I'm so sorry. He was only getting a bit of air outside with Jessica and Jacob. He wouldn't settle indoors, kept crying.'

Matt smashed his fist against his sister's hallway so hard; he very nearly broke his wrist. 'You dumb prat. I told you not to take your eyes off that boy, didn't I?'

'Matt, I'm sorry. I really am.'

Matt didn't reply as he leapt in his motor. He would hunt down that lying, cheating bitch he'd married and get his son back before it got dark.

Terry Turner was raging. He'd just arrived home from a hard day's graft to be told his eldest daughter had sodded off to move in with Donny and that notright villainous family of his. 'That's her fucking lot, Pen. Never will she darken this doorstep again. What an embarrassment for me at work, eh? I will never live this down. I'll be the laughing stock of the station. I will never forgive her for this, Pen. Not ever!'

Just when Terry was thinking his day could not get any bloody worse, the doorbell rang. Penny answered it and an enraged Matt stormed into his front room. 'Tansey turned up at my sister's and snatched Jamie. Where is she? I want my son back.'

'She ain't 'ere. She's with him,' explained Terry.

'You what! No way is my boy living with that scumbag family, Tel. You either back me, or I go collect him alone.' Matt was livid.

'I've got your back,' replied Terry.

As both men stormed out of the house, Penny chased after them shouting, 'Please be careful. They might have guns up there and all sorts.'

Matt turned, his eyes gleaming with anger. 'Don't worry about that, Pen. I've got one of me own.'

Tansey wrapped her bare legs and arms around Donny and sighed deeply. Nothing about today had felt normal, until they'd made love. All the doubt and heartbreak had immediately vanished. This would be the first whole night they'd ever spent together and they fitted like a glove in more ways than one. Soulmates, for sure. 'I love you, Donny,' Tansey whispered.

She was leaning in for a kiss when Bonnie and Clyde, the two Rottweilers who roamed around his grandparents' property, guarding it, began to bark madly. Donny leapt out of bed at the same time Jamie started bawling. He quickly got dressed and ran down the stairs, with Tansey following. His dad and granddad were already outside the house. Kenny was armed with a baseball bat, Charlie with a cricket bat and torch.

'Come any closer, I'll make sure the dogs fucking eat you alive. One word from me and they will, trust me,' bellowed Charlie.

'I just want my son back, then I'll leave quietly,' Matt shouted back.

'And I want my grandson back. No way is he living with your mob,' shouted her father.

Feeling brave because there were electric gates surrounding the property and he had back-up with his dad and granddad this time, Donny yelled, 'Jamie's going nowhere. He's staying with his mother, so do one.'

Charlie glared at his grandson. 'Shut the fuck up, you. I've now got two Old Bill at my gate thanks to you, ya soppy prick.'

'They're not taking Jamie away from me, Donny. They've no right to,' shrieked Tansey.

'You stay 'ere with Jamie while I sort it. Don't panic. They ain't getting their hands on Jamie,' Donny reassured her.

'Who is it? What's going on?' Sharon Bond appeared, grabbing Kenny's arm.

'Get back inside the house, you,' Charlie ordered, glaring at his grandson once more. 'You've caused this shit,' he added, before marching down his driveway, cricket bat in hand.

'Charlie. No,' warned Maggie.

'Well done, Donny,' said Sherry, clapping her hands slowly. She wouldn't have minded if her brother didn't slate her taste in lads so much. How dare he, when he had brought trouble to their family home.

'Get back inside, girls,' Kenny ordered as he followed Charlie down the driveway, baseball bat in hand. The dogs were still going absolutely mental, frothing at the mouth by the sound of it.

'Please don't do anything stupid,' Sharon pleaded.

Terry Turner locked eyes with Kenny, staring down the cop killer. 'My son-in-law wants his son back. I've disowned my daughter for the anguish she's caused Matt and her mother. Just give us the lad and we'll be out of your hair.'

'The boy stays with his mother,' snapped Kenny. He knew this bastard was as bent as a nine-bob note. He'd heard it through the grapevine in prison, and if there was anything in life Kenny loathed, it was a bent cop. In his eyes, you were either one side of the fence or the other. End of.

With a howl of rage, Matt pulled a gun out of his jacket pocket. Tansey screamed; she'd left Jamie inside with Sharon, wanted to see what was happening for herself. She had never known Matt to carry a gun. He must have stolen it from work, and from the look on his face she had no doubt he would use it.

'Don't be so fucking stupid,' Terry bellowed, trying to knock the gun out of Matt's hand. But it was too late. A shot had been fired and Charlie Saunders was now lying on his driveway, screaming, 'Me foot. You've shot me fucking foot off!'

Giving Donny a good dig on Sunday morning was something Terry knew he and Matt could get away with. However, this was different gravy. 'Get in the fucking car now,' Terry ordered, grabbing the gun out of Matt's hand.

The sight of blood pouring out of his father-in-law's foot was like a red rag to a bull for Kenny. He climbed over the gate, baseball bat in hand, and went for Matt.

Knowing that he and Matt could lose their careers if word of the shooting got out, Terry Turner allowed Kenny to wallop Matt a couple of times before pushing Matt inside the car. 'Listen, I'm sorry about this, but I seriously didn't know my son-in-law had a gun on him. Keep schtum on this, Kenny, and I'll make sure we leave you all alone in future. I know Tansey loves your Donny – the two of them can bring up the boy. We won't be in touch no more, I promise.'

Kenny Bond grabbed Terry by the neck. 'You or him ever come near my family again, you'll end up in a worse state than DS Harry Harrison did. Only I won't be doing bird again. A pal of mine has a farm. I'll feed you to his pigs. You'll be gone. Finito.' Kenny clicked his fingers, his jaw twitching furiously.

Kenny Bond had the most evil eyes Terry had ever seen in the flesh. 'Yeah, I get it. Please though, for Matt's sake, don't grass on him. He's lost his wife and son and he's hurting badly. We'll give you no more trouble, I swear on the bible we won't.'

'Glad to hear it. Now fuck off as I need to think up a story and get my father-in-law to a hospital. Go back on your word, Terry, and I swear I will do what I said.'

'My word is my bond,' Terry replied as he got in his motor and tried to put the key in the ignition. His hands were trembling that much, he couldn't find the bloody ignition.

Terry felt a sigh of relief as he put his foot on the accelerator and raced away. 'Whatever was you thinking? You've just blown Charlie Saunders' fucking foot off. You're gonna have to forget about Jamie after this little episode, Matt. Think yourself lucky Kenny has agreed not to grass. You'd deffo get the bullet otherwise.'

'Don't give a shit anymore – and if you think I'm giving up on Jamie, you got another think coming. I'm still applying for custody.'

'You can't do that. Not after I swore to Kenny. Fucking lunatic the man is. You're gonna have to move on with your life, meet another young lady and start a new family. I know it's tough, but that's what needs to be done, son. For all our sakes. Once a cop killer always a cop killer. Trust me on that one.'

CHAPTER EIGHT

'Always trust your gut instinct and I promise yer,
ya won't go far wrong in life.'

*Charlie had to have two operations to repair the damage
the bullet had caused. The first went OK, but after the
second, gangrene set in, and my father-in-law had to
have his leg amputated from the knee down.*

*Obviously, the family were beside themselves. Maggie
and Sharon cried a bucketful of tears and Donny blamed
himself. Only Sherry didn't seem that arsed, and neither
was I. Reason being, I remembered only too well what a
flash, womanizing tosspot Charlie Saunders had been back
in the days when he'd been on the blag and seen himself
as the kingpin of South London.*

*Prison had taught me loads, including faith – to a certain
degree. I believed karma had finally caught up with Charlie.*

*I took the advice of my missus and kept out of Donny's
ugly feud with his ex. Lori went proper on the turn anyway.
Donny had to take her to court in the end to get access
to his sons. I'd sided with my boy by that point. It was
clear he and Tansey were in love, so I gave him a deposit*

for a mortgage. He bought a nice little two-bedroom gaff in Havering-atte-Bower with a decent-sized bit of land attached.

As the seventies moved into the eighties, life was pretty good. Apart from my concerns over my grandsons.

Beau and Brett were a chip off the old block. But they had turned into right little fuckers, proper naughty boys. They were skinny as rakes, and I was sure something was amiss with them at home. I questioned Donny and he reassured me all was fine and Lori was looking after them properly.

I should have known better than to trust or believe my weakling of a son. If only I had gone with me gut instinct, things would have turned out so differently . . .

Autumn 1982

Lori Boswell lit up a joint, took a deep drag, then handed it to her new man. She had fancied the pants off Gary Acorn for ages. Tall with mousy brown hair and a moustache, he was the only looker in the crowd who regularly hung out around her place.

Gary had been dating Sandra Smith up until recently and Lori had been elated when they'd split up. Gary had big brown eyes like Donny, doleful and sexy. They'd finally got it together last weekend and Gary had stayed at hers every night since. It felt good to be having regular sex again and to wake up with a man. This was Lori's first proper relationship since Donny. She didn't include the drunken, drug-fuelled one-night-stands, as they'd meant nothing. She couldn't even remember much about them.

Downstairs in the kitchen, Beau and Brett were making

themselves some breakfast. They'd had to learn how to do so and to dress themselves as their mother was no early bird. She said she felt too tired to get out of bed of a morning, and that was their dad's fault as he'd left her to bring them up alone.

'Mum, Mum. There ain't no milk for our cornflakes,' yelled Beau.

'You'll have to eat 'em dry. I'll get some milk later,' Lori shouted back.

Brett pulled a face. 'I can't eat 'em dry.'

Beau climbed onto the small steps they used to reach things. He turned on the tap and put water on both bowls of cornflakes. 'That'll have to do. We'll be hungry otherwise.'

Both boys munched away hungrily. They hadn't had a proper dinner last night, only egg and beans. 'Do you like Mum's boyfriend?' asked Brett.

Beau shrugged. 'He don't really talk to us much, does he? I prefer him to his brother, though.'

Brett pulled a face. 'Yeah. Me too. He's creepy.'

Having turned five in the summer, Beau and Brett had started school in early September. Both were quite bright compared to some of the other kids, but were the bane of the teachers' lives and their out-of-control antics were the main topic of discussion in the staffroom.

Miss Clark, their form teacher, was frequently driven to despair by the twins' naughty, uncouth, unruly behaviour and today she wasn't in the mood for any nonsense, as yesterday evening she'd had to have her beloved eighteen-year-old cat Boris put to sleep. 'Settle down now, children, please,' ordered Miss Clark, as she picked up the chalk to write on the blackboard.

'Fuck off,' said a voice.

Some of the children giggled, some didn't dare but looked as if they wanted to. Miss Clark spun around. 'Who said that awful word? Put your hand up at once.'

Miss Clark clocked the culprit or culprits immediately. The awful Bond twins were chuckling away, resembling two laughing gnomes. 'Which one of you two said that terrible word? I demand you own up immediately.'

Glancing at one another, the twins replied 'Fuck off!' in unison.

Absolutely furious, Miss Clark marched over to the twins' desks, grabbed both boys roughly by their arms and dragged them to the front of the classroom. 'I am sick to death of your foul behaviour. I will not tolerate it in my classroom any longer,' she shouted, picking up a ruler and clumping Beau on the bottom with it.

Having always been told by his dad and gramps that if anyone hit him, he was to clump 'em back twice as hard, Beau began kicking and punching Miss Clark with all his might.

The other children sat in amazement, mouths open, as Brett also joined in with the assault on their teacher.

Miss Clark managed to get away from the deranged twins and ran straight to the headmaster's office. No way was she teaching the Bond boys any more. She would rather quit her job.

Lori's phone had been cut off, so it was Donny who the school contacted. The twins were sitting on chairs outside the headmaster's office. Donny had been told over the phone what they'd done. 'Why did you attack your teacher?'

''Cause she hit me with a ruler and was gonna do the same to Brett,' explained Beau.

'You told us if anyone hits us, we gotta hit 'em back twice as hard,' Brett reminded his father.

'I didn't mean your bloody teacher, ya pair of doughnuts.'

'She's a cow,' grinned Beau.

'And a bitch,' Brett added.

'I'll deal with you pair in a minute,' Donny hissed, before tapping on the headmaster's door.

'Come in,' barked a stern voice.

Donny entered the room. The headmaster glared at him, as did the teacher, who had clearly been crying. 'I'm Donny. The twins' dad.'

'You're not doing a very good job of raising them,' the headmaster bellowed. 'Those boys are totally out of control. Look at poor Miss Clark's legs. She's even been bitten. I will not tolerate such vicious behaviour at my school, Mr Bond. The twins are expelled with immediate effect.'

Donny glanced at the woman's legs. 'I'm extremely sorry for my sons' behaviour, Miss Clark. They don't live with me. They live with their mother.'

'Well, I suggest you take them in hand, Mr Bond. You can leave now and please escort your sons off my premises,' the glowering headmaster brusquely dismissed him.

'All right. Take a chill pill. They're only five!'

When Donny shut the headmaster's door, he grabbed Beau and Brett by their ears and literally marched them down the corridor.

Having scored earlier, Lori and Gary were lying on Lori's dirty quilt cover, completely smashed out of their faces.

The doorbell rang. 'Don't answer it,' slurred Gary.

Lori had no intention of answering it, but it was rare

103

that she got any callers before noon, so she staggered over to the window to have a peep through the filthy curtain. 'It's my ex. That's his car. I wonder what he wants? He only ever comes here on Sundays to pick the boys up and drop 'em off, and he never knocks, just bibs outside.'

'Want me to go down and sort him out?' Before the drugs had taken hold of him, Gary had been a doorman in a nightclub.

'Nah.'

'Fuck him then. Come back over 'ere.'

Lori stayed put. 'He's got the twins with him,' she said, as Donny walked back towards his car with their sons. 'I wonder if one or both of 'em have been ill at school? Oh well, I don't fancy clearing up spew. Let Donny do his fatherly duties for once and nurse 'em while they're ill.'

With his day now totally ballsed up, Donny decided to skip work altogether and treat his sons to a decent meal. They were quite tall for their age but needed some meat on their bones.

Donny looked at his boys' excited little faces in the interior mirror when he told them he was taking them to a carvery for a nice roast dinner. He knew by the state of Lori's curtains and her appearance these days, as well as the threadbare, unwashed clothes and trainers that the boys would be wearing whenever he picked them up, that life was crap for them at home. They rarely looked clean either. As soon as he picked them up, he would take them swimming then have them change into the designer gear that he kept for them, having learned that if he sent them home wearing decent gear, Lori would flog it. His parents would go apeshit if they knew of the boys' plight. But the twins were good, knew when to keep their traps shut, even at their young age. He'd had to lie, drummed it into them enough never to tell Nan or Gramps about anything that went on at home. Told them if they did, their mum would stop their visits and he'd be banned from seeing them.

Listening to them chat so excitedly about what they were going to eat, Donny felt the usual surge of guilt flood through his veins. Instead of turning a blind eye, he knew he should be insisting they came to live with him instead of that mess of a mother of theirs. Trouble was, they were hard to handle, and he knew Tansey could never put up with them. Plus, he had Jamie and now little Harry to consider. The twins would terrorize them without a doubt.

Tansey had given birth to their son Harry in autumn 1980. He was two now and such a little character. Both Donny and Tansey doted on him. He never failed to make them laugh.

Tansey's son Jamie was now four. His real dad Matt Jackson had kept to his word, as had Tansey's old man. Neither had ever tried to make contact with his family again. Matt and Tansey were divorced now. As for Jamie, he was a quiet kid, ever so well behaved. Unlike the twins, you could take Jamie anywhere and not be shown up.

Both Beau and Brett had a man-size plateful of grub and as Donny clocked them scoffing it like two starving foxes, he started to worry even more. He waited until they'd finished eating before questioning them. 'Did your mum not make you any breakfast this morning, boys?'

'Mum's got a boyfriend now and they was in bed when we got ready for school. We had cornflakes, didn't we, Brett?'

'Yeah. But no milk. We had to have water. Tasted nasty.'

Donny felt the guilt flood through his veins once again.

His father was a proper man, would have done something about this already. 'Tell me more about Mummy's boyfriend.'

He took a piece of beef from his own plate and divided it between them. Beau stuffed it in his mouth and swallowed it whole before answering. 'Him and Mum smoke funny fags and then they sleep for ages afterwards.'

'Gary has a brother, Eric, who comes round some nights too. Me and Beau don't like him. He's creepy and keeps asking to play games with us.'

Alarm bells rang loudly in Donny's head. He knew Lori's mum loathed him, but he needed to speak to her to find out what the hell was going on. Perhaps the boys could move in with her and she could raise them?

'Can we have afters too, Dad?' asked Brett. 'We ain't had much to eat this week.'

'We only had egg and beans last night,' Beau added.

'And the night before we had spam and spaghetti.'

Donny was appalled. Not many men gave as much as he did every week to an ex to support their kids. A oner was more than enough to feed and clothe two five-year-olds. Lori was on all kinds of benefits too, even got her rent paid. Where was all this money going? It had to be on drink and drugs.

Something had to change for his sons' sake, and he had to man up and make sure it bloody well did.

Tansey had never met the twins, but always asked after them. When Donny told her later that evening that there'd been an incident at their school and he would have to sort them out another, he played down what had actually happened. He was too embarrassed to admit Beau and Brett had attacked their form teacher. Tansey would be horrified.

'That money I'm giving Lori – hardly a penny is being spent on those boys. Their clothes are threadbare. Brett had a great big hole in the bottom of his trainers last weekend and Beau's are clearly too small for him. Now Lori has moved in some geezer called Gary, and his weirdo brother turns up most nights and keeps asking to play games with me sons. That ain't fucking right, is it? I'm having 'em Saturday and Sunday next weekend 'cause we're gonna do a firework display for 'em at me dad's. I'll kip there on Saturday night and be back Sunday evening. I was thinking of paying Lori's mum a visit. I know she bastard well hates me, but surely she must know what's going on. Her and Lori were ever so close. I was hoping when I tell her how bad the situation is, she might allow the boys to live at hers. They're the only grandkids she has. What d'ya reckon?'

'Yes. I think you should pay the other nan a visit. I also think you should stop giving Lori cash. Why don't you spend fifty quid on all the food you know the boys like, and buy them fifty quid's worth of new clothes and things every week? That way, they will eat and be dressed well and Lori can't spend the cash on herself.'

'Genius!' Donny smiled.

On Friday afternoon, Lori Boswell was becoming more and more anxious. Divvy Dave always dropped her dosh off by 1 p.m. at the latest and now it was nearly 2 p.m.

Gary Acorn had his head in his shaking hands. 'I'm fucking desperate 'ere. Where is this prick?'

Just as desperate for a fix as her lover, Lori came up with an idea. 'You stay 'ere and I'm gonna run round the phone box and call the nursery.' There had been a time when Lori could have asked one of her neighbours if she could use the phone, but they all hated her now. All they ever did was complain about the loud music she and her pals blasted out of a night. Usually Pink Floyd.

'Go on then. Go now and hurry up. I feel like shit.'

There was a phone box on Hilldene Avenue and thankfully for once it was working. Lori dialled the number of the nursery then put ten pence in the slot. Sharon answered.

'Hi, Shal, it's Lori. Dave has usually dropped my money off by now, but there's been no sign of him. Is he there? Only I have no food in the cupboards for the twins.'

Sharon Bond pursed her lips. Donny had already clued her up on what to say if Lori were to ring. 'Dave's off sick today,' she lied. 'But Donny's here. Do you want to speak to him?'

'Yes. Yes, please.' Lori noticed her hands trembling as she placed another ten-pence piece over the slot.

Donny grabbed the phone off his mother. 'Listen, I'll sort you out in the morning when I pick the boys up.'

'No! You can't do that. I need the money today! Now! There's no food in the house for your sons.'

Donny had given the boys money the other day and told them to go to the chippy on their way home from school every day until he sorted the food situation at the weekend. 'No can do, I'm afraid. Too busy working up 'ere. See you at ten in the morning.'

'You lousy useless no-good bastard. I fucking hate your guts,' screamed Lori.

Donny smirked as he cut her off. No way was she starving his sons any more. Over his dead body.

The following morning, Donny arrived promptly outside Lori's and bibbed his hooter. The boys ran out dressed like two little orphans as per usual, and Lori followed them. 'Get in the car, boys,' Donny ordered, before opening the boot.

'What's that?' asked Lori, as he began lifting carrier bags out.

'It's food, Lori, for our sons to eat. That bag there needs to go into the freezer.'

'Oh, that's nice of you to bring me extra.'

Donny carried all the bags to the doorstep, then got back inside his car.

Lori held her hand out. 'Where's me money?'

'There is no money. From now on I will be bringing food and clothes round for the boys every weekend. 'Cause that oner I've been giving you isn't being spent on our sons, is it?'

'You can't do this! I do spend it on the boys. I'll take you to fucking court if you break our agreement.'

'Nah. You won't. 'Cause if you do, I'll tell the court what a dreadful mother you really are. The boys will then be taken away from you in a flash. Trust me on that one.'

'Cunt,' screamed Lori, kicking the side of Donny's car.

Donny smirked, put his foot down and sped away.

By the time Donny drove up to the house his dad had built from scratch, the twins had been swimming, had a lovely hot shower and were looking a million dollars in their designer clobber. The latest craze was casual, so he'd purchased his lads the best trainers and tracksuits. He'd also taken Beau and Brett into Romford town centre to buy them some new school shoes and clothes. He bought half-decent clobber, actually spent far more than the fifty quid he'd told Lori he was spending, but not designer makes. Hopefully that way the skank wouldn't try and flog it for drug money.

Lori's mum hadn't been at home when he'd called in at her gaff in Collier Row on his way to pick the boys up. He would swing by again tomorrow, with the twins in tow, see what she had to say for herself.

Kenny loved the home he'd had built for him and Sharon. It was situated on a private lane that ran off the A127, not too far from the Upminster turn-off. Kenny's pal was a property developer as well as an ex-villain, and it had been his idea to only sell to proper people. A select community, so to speak. He now lived there too.

There were eight houses in total and one bungalow that'd been built especially for Kenny's mother- and father-in-law. Even though Charlie had a false leg fitted, he hadn't been able to manage the stairs at his old gaff in Ongar, so had sold up.

'How's me two main men doing?' Kenny grinned at his grandsons when he opened the door to them. 'Looking forward to your first sleepover and firework night down Dark Lane?' Kenny had come up with the name for the lane, much to the amusement of his pal. It was very apt as it was full of dark characters.

'Yes, Gramps. And the burgers and hotdogs,' beamed Beau.

'And the taters,' added Brett.

Donny hadn't stayed over a single night since getting with Tansey. Kenny had decided to make the most of the opportunity by plying his son with alcohol this evening to get him to open up a bit. Every time he asked the twins about their mother, they would glance at one another, then clam up.

Those twins were his flesh and blood, and he idolized them. If they were being wronged in any way, shape or

110

form, there'd be hell to pay. Kenny would make damn sure of it.

Guy Fawkes Night had been the previous evening, but that didn't stop all the neighbours from Dark Lane turning up for Kenny's party. The twins had a ball. There was one little incident when Donny caught them picking on one of the neighbour's grandkids. Donny ordered his sons to shake hands with the other lad. Rather reluctantly, both did.

When the neighbours started to depart, Donny told his dad he was going to put the twins to bed and have an early night himself.

'Don't you go to bed yet, son. As soon as these last few stragglers leave, I've got a vintage bottle of Scotch for me and you to crack open,' Kenny winked.

'Sod that, Dad. I don't want a hangover in the morning. I've got stuff to do.'

'Don't be boring. Your nan won't be serving up the roast too early. She's been on the gin tonight,' chuckled Kenny. 'Come on, apart from working on the boat, when do we ever get together since you got with Tansey? You're my boy. I love ya. Is it wrong for a father to want to crack open an expensive bottle of plonk he's had for donkey's years with his only son?'

Donny rolled his eyes. 'All right then. You've twisted me arm.'

Kenny grinned. 'Good lad.'

The twins were tired, but still buzzing, Beau especially. 'Can Gramps do us another fire so we can burn another Guy, Dad?'

'No. We'll do it again next year, though. I promise.'

111

'Aww. But I wanna see him burn again. Don't you, Brett?'

Brett's eyes were virtually shut the moment Donny tucked him in.

Donny kissed Brett on the head and then urged Beau to go to sleep too.

Beau smiled. 'OK, Dad. Today been the best day ever. Promise I will sleep.'

Donny felt so sad as he ruffled Beau's blond hair. The twins were handsome little mites, stood out against other kids even in their rotten clothes. Apart from their hair colour, they'd obviously inherited sod all else from that awful mother of theirs. Both had his smile and big brown eyes. 'Na-night, boy. Love you.'

'Love you too, Dad.'

Donny turned the light off and had tears in his eyes as he left the room. That was the first time either of the twins had ever told him they loved him.

Kenny Bond poured his son another Scotch. His pisshead of a daughter had been the last to go to bed.

'Me granddad's never gonna forgive me, is he? For getting his foot blown off,' Donny slurred. His relationship with his grandfather had never been quite the same since the shooting and Donny missed the connection they'd once shared, the times they'd worked out in the gym, or played pool and darts in the games room, while laughing and joking about all sorts of things.

'Listen, I've said it time and time again, what happened that night wasn't your fault. As for Charlie, he's turned into a bitter old bastard. That ain't your fault either. He was always cantankerous and led your nan a dog's life in many ways. I remember him back in the old days, if you get my drift.'

'What do you mean?'

Kenny topped up his own glass, then Donny's. 'We'll chat about that another time. Right now, I'm more concerned with the twins. What's going on there? And please don't lie to me. I know they've got problems at home. Beau told me earlier,' lied Kenny.

It was at that point Donny broke down. Tears in his eyes, he told his father everything, but failed to mention Lori's new bloke, or his brother.

That would prove to be one of the biggest mistakes of his life.

CHAPTER NINE

Donny woke the following morning with a splitting head-ache. He could still taste the Scotch and vowed there and then never to drink it again.

The boys were already up. He could hear them playing in the garden.

Kenny opened the bedroom door. 'Morning. I thought me and you would take a drive round Lori's mum's this morning with the twins. Where's their shitty old clothes?'

'In the boot of me car.'

'We'll stop down the road and dress 'em. I don't want to worry your mum. We'll do the same on the way back; put their tracksuits back on 'em.'

'I feel proper ropey, Dad. Got a terrible headache.'

'I'll bring you up some tablets and a pint of water. That'll sort you out. Jump in the shower. Come on, get yer skates on. No way are those boys living with that wrong un any more.'

Very gingerly, Donny swung his legs over the edge of the bed, wishing he'd kept his big mouth shut.

*

Sandy Boswell lived in a three-bedroom semi-detached house in Collier Row. Her partner, Steve, was a driver for a local minicab firm and was out grafting at present.

Not expecting visitors, Sandy opened the front door and was horrified to see that no-good-bastard on her doorstep with an older man and her grandsons.

As Sandy went to slam the door, Kenny put his foot in the way to stop her from doing so. 'No so fast. Not until you've heard what my son has to say.'

Aware now that this was the infamous cop-killing Kenny Bond, Sandy chose her words carefully. 'I have nothing to say to your son, I'm afraid. He ruined my Lori's life. She's never been the same since the day he left her in the lurch.'

'Hello, Nan,' said Brett.

Beau smirked. 'Hello, Nan.'

Sandy looked daggers at the twins without replying.

'It's Lori that Donny wants to talk to you about. He has grave concerns over the twins' welfare,' Kenny explained. 'Can we do this inside?'

'No,' Sandy replied. She gestured towards her grandsons. 'They've already wrecked my home numerous times. They ain't bleedin' well doing it again.'

'Have you visited Lori lately?' enquired Donny.

'No. Last couple of times I went round there, she shouted out the window she was ill and refused to answer the door. I know she drinks all day long and smokes those funny fags. I offered to get her professional help. Me and Steve were willing to pay for it, but she told me to mind me own bleedin' business. She's a shadow of the daughter I once knew, all thanks to you,' Sandy spat.

Donny explained that he'd religiously given Lori a oner a week to feed and clothe the boys. He told Sandy the kind of meals the twins were being fed at home and how they had to dress themselves and sort their own breakfasts out. 'There's rarely any milk in the house. The poor little mites are having to put water on their cereal. As for the state of their clothes – look at 'em.'

'I'll go round there tomorrow, find out what's going on,' Sandy sighed.

'If Lori don't get herself clean, then I'll have no choice but to involve Social Services. She'll lose the twins for good if that happens. I've started buying food for the boys now and clothes rather than giving her money. I've had to,' explained Donny.

'At least that way she can't spend the money on drink and drugs. You've done her a favour, for once!'

'I was wondering, Sandy, could you have the boys stay with you until Lori gets herself sorted? I'll give you a hundred and twenty quid a week for their keep.'

Sandy glanced at next-door's house, then ushered her visitors inside the hallway. She shut the front door. 'Not on your nelly! You know what he did last time he came round 'ere?' Sandy said, pointing at Beau. 'Strangled the cat that belonged to the poor old dear next door. Caught the little bastard red-handed, I did.'

Kenny was disgusted. He grabbed Beau by his throat and dirty sweatshirt and lifted him off his feet. 'If I ever hear about you torturing a poor defenceless animal again, I will strangle you.'

Eyes bulging as his feet touched the floor, Beau croaked. 'But it bit me, the cat.'

'I don't give a shit what it did,' hissed Kenny. 'You never hurt another animal. Understand?'

Donny felt sick. There must be something wrong with his sons, there had to be. 'I'm so very sorry you had to witness that, Sandy.'

'Witness it! Steve had to bury the poor thing in the dark down the bottom of our garden. Loved her Barney, did Flora. She's eighty-one and has been a broken woman since he never came home. You could offer me a grand a week and I wouldn't take them on. You're their father, you look after 'em. Now, if you don't mind, I've got a roast to prepare.'

Donny scribbled down the phone number on a piece of paper and held it out to her. 'Ring me once you see her?'

Sandy snatched it off him. 'OK. But don't ever show your face around here again. If it wasn't for you, my daughter would still be the fun-loving, beautiful girl she once was.'

When Donny bowed his head, Kenny decided to speak up on his behalf. 'No disrespect, but my boy was only sixteen when your daughter pretended she was on the pill, then got herself knocked up purposely. The words pot, kettle and black spring to mind, treacle.'

The following morning, Sandy drove round to Lori's. The nets were filthy, looked yellow, stained with nicotine, Sandy imagined. She banged on the door.

Beau answered. 'All right, Nan?'

'Why aren't you at school?'

Brett appeared by his brother's side. 'We been chucked outta school.'

Sandy rolled her eyes. 'Where's Mum?'

'In bed with Gary,' Brett replied.

Sandy marched up the stairs and rapped on her daughter's bedroom door.

'Who is it?' shouted Lori.

'Your mother.'

'Oh, shit,' Lori whispered. 'You stay 'ere. I'll get rid of her,' she told Gary.

'Be quick then. I gotta sign on soon.'

Wrapping her dressing gown around her, Lori walked out of her bedroom and swiftly shut the door. 'What's up?'

'Look at the bloody state of you. You look dreadful.' Sandy had never seen her daughter look so rough. Her once lovely shiny blonde hair was matted and greasy. Her once radiant complexion, spotty. Her dressing gown was filthy, and she looked as though she could do with a bloody good scrub. 'Have you looked in the mirror lately? Only I'm surprised it didn't crack, if you have. What's going on, Lori?'

'Nothing. Fancy a cup of tea?' At least if she took her mother in the kitchen and shut the door, Gary could sneak out to sign on.

The state of the kitchen was appalling. The worktops were rotten, as was the sink, and there were dirty plates, glasses, cups and saucepans everywhere. As for the hob, that was disgusting. Sandy had tears in her eyes as she took in the full horror of it all. The front room looked as though a bomb had hit it. 'How can you live like this? Your home is like a pigsty. No wonder your sons have been expelled from school if this is the way they are forced to live. What type of mother are you? And who is this new bloke you've shacked up with?'

'It weren't Mum's fault,' explained Beau. 'We hit our teacher, Miss Clark, 'cause she hit me and was gonna hit Brett with the ruler too.'

'Out in the garden, you two,' bellowed Lori. She needed her daily fix, so the quicker she got rid of her interfering mother, the better.

'What are you taking, Lori?' Sandy asked, once the boys were out of earshot.

'I just like a puff and a booze,' lied Lori. 'Not that it's any of your bloody business.'

'I had Donny and his father turn up at mine yesterday. They're worried about the twins' welfare.'

'I know. The twins told me. They had no fucking right turning up at yours,' snarled Lori. 'As for that bastard, Donny. He's stopped my money.'

'He told me he was bringing you clothes and food for the boys.'

'Well, yeah. But I have bills to pay. How am I meant to pay those now?'

'Perhaps if you stopped wasting money on drugs and alcohol, you'd have money for your bills? This can't go on, Lori. For the sake of your sons, this has to stop now. Those boys will go totally off the rails otherwise and you'll lose them. And you still haven't answered my question. Who is this new bloke you're shacked up with?'

'His name's Gary and he's the best thing that's happened to me in ages. As for the twins, they're little shits. They drive me insane. You try looking after 'em if you don't believe me.'

'But they're your sons, Lori. Your responsibility. Look at this shithole. What kind of example are you setting them? No wonder they have issues. Do you want to lose them? Only Donny says, unless you sort yourself out, he'll have no option but to go to Social Services for help.'

'Fuck Donny!' spat Lori. 'It's all his fault I'm in this position in the first place, as you well know.'

'You're stuck in a rut. Only you can get yourself out of it. The offer's still there if you want to go into rehab, sort your life out. Donny can look after the boys.'

'Oh, fuck off, Mum. Just leave me alone, will ya?' screeched Lori. 'Ever since you got with Steve, you've been less an' less bothered about me. Why the sudden interest?'

Sandy was hurt. That wasn't the case at all. 'How can you even say that? I have never put Steve ahead of you. I just want to help you, Lori. Somebody has to. I don't want to get a knock on the door from the police one day and hear something terrible has happened to you. I'm worried. You look like you're at death's door.'

'You live your life and I'll live mine. You can see yourself out and don't come back anytime soon.'

With tears in her eyes, Sandy picked up her handbag; Lori was a lost cause, way beyond help. It broke her heart to see the state of her daughter and her once lovely home. Well you can lead a horse to water, but you can't make it drink, she thought bitterly.

Donny put the phone down. Sandy had given him another barrage of abuse, blaming him for everything that had gone wrong in Lori's life since he'd left her. But it was her parting sentence that had really hit home: 'The state of that place – it's a disgrace. Lori isn't fit to be a mother anymore and the only person who can step in to give those twins a better life is you.'

'What's up?' asked Sharon. Her son's face was deathly white.

'Nothing. Just Lori kicking off about money as usual.'

Having sneaked out while her mother was there, Lori was furious when Gary finally arrived home in the evening, his eyes glazed and his notright brother in tow.

Lori didn't like Eric Acorn. Bald, short, overweight with beady eyes, it was hard to believe he and Gary were brothers.

'Where you bloody been all day?' she demanded. 'You better have bought me some gear back. I had to sell some of the boy's new clothes to get a bit earlier. I would've been ill otherwise. I ain't even got no methadone left.'

Gary handed Lori what she craved. 'Eric's been slung out his flat. I said he could kip on the sofa until he sorts himself out.'

'There's no room here for anyone else to stay.'

Gary shrugged. 'Well, in that case I'll move out tomorrow and get a place with Eric. He can't afford all the bills and stuff otherwise.' Gary had been living with Eric until he'd got with Lori.

Not wanting to lose her man, Lori relented. 'Oh, I suppose he can kip on the sofa for a while. Not permanently, though.'

'Cheers, Lori,' grinned Eric, showing off his rotting yellow teeth.

'Mum, we're hungry. Can you cook us the steak Dad bought us?' asked Beau. The boys had been elated when looking through their food parcel.

'I had to sell the steak to get some electric,' lied Lori. She'd actually swapped it for a bit of puff.

'Awww. But we're hungry,' Brett replied, lip pouting.

'Blame your father, not me. He's not giving me any money to pay the bills anymore,' snapped Lori. 'There's plenty of other food you can eat.'

Eric smiled at the twins. 'Come on, I'll cook you something. Follow me and you can choose whatever you want.'

Donny picked the twins up on the Sunday morning. He'd struggled to find a new normal school for them, but had finally received a phone call on Friday afternoon saying there was a place for them at a school in Rainham that dealt with kids who had behavioural problems. Problem was, they wouldn't be able to start there until after the Christmas holidays.

Donny was peeved when his sons got in his car wearing tatty old clothes. 'Where's your new clothes?' he enquired.

'Some is dirty and some gone missing,' Beau explained.

'Whaddya mean, gone missing?'

'Can't find our new trainers,' Brett replied.

Donny's lip curled. If that wrong un had sold her own sons' trainers after being warned of the consequences, he'd give her what for. 'You been eating well this week? Has mum cooked all the nice food I brought? I've got another load of grub for ya. It's at Nan and Granddad's. We'll bring it with us when I drop you off later.'

'Mum sold the steak 'cause we had no electric. But Eric cooked us burgers and hotdogs,' Beau replied.

'Gary and Eric ate most of the food. None left now. We had to have egg and beans last night,' Brett added.

To say Donny was furious was putting it mildly. 'Eric's Gary's brother, isn't he?'

'Yeah,' replied Beau. 'Eric lives with us now. He sleeps on the sofa. Me and Brett don't like him, but he does cook us food.'

Raging, Donny did a U-turn and headed back to Lori's.

Having not gone to bed until 4 a.m., Lori and Gary were both fast asleep. The sound of someone hammering at the front door had them wide awake in no time.

Gary leapt out of bed. 'Shit. Gotta be the Old Bill. Where's the smack?'

'Open this fucking door, Lori, before I boot it down,' bellowed Donny.

'You stay up 'ere, Gal. I'll deal with him.'

A born coward, Eric leapt off the sofa and decided to hide in the back garden.

Lori opened the front door and was furious as Donny marched inside *her* house. 'Get out! You don't live here anymore.'

Donny couldn't believe his eyes as they took in the squalor. His once lovely furniture and carpet were filthy and full of burn-holes. The wallpaper was ripped off one wall and had been replaced with graffiti.

The room reeked of stale smoke. There were overflowing ashtrays, empty bottles of cider and screwed-up cans. There were even plates with what looked like rotting food on them, and bits of tin foil stuck to the carpet. It was atrocious. 'Jesus fucking wept! You disgust me. As for flogging the boys' clothes and food – you couldn't sink any lower if yer tried.'

'Get out!' shrieked Lori.

'You're the worst fucking mother ever.'

'And you're the worst father, for walking out and leaving 'em for your bit on the side, so don't come throwing your weight around 'ere, Donny Bond.'

Gary Acorn put his jeans on and ran down the stairs. 'The lady asked you to leave, mate.'

Guessing that this must be Gary, Donny sized him up. He was tall, lean, but looked a mess, like a druggie. 'She ain't no lady and I ain't your mate. Where's the other geezer who lives 'ere?'

Feeling braver because Gary was now present, Eric came in from the garden. 'Hi. I'm Eric.'

Donny pointed at the ugly, dumpy bastard, then pointed at Gary. 'That food I bring round 'ere is for my sons to eat. You buy your own fucking grub to scoff. 'Cause if I find out you've eaten as much of a morsel of

123

their food again, you won't just have me to deal with, you'll have my old man round 'ere too. Lori'll tell you all about him – and believe me, he ain't a man to be messed with.'

Sharon Bond seasoned the leg of lamb, then shoved it in the oven. Sundays were her favourite day of the week, as it was all about family. Donny and her grandsons would arrive before noon and stay until early evening. Sherry would be in and out all day with pals, but always enjoyed her mum's roast even if it had to be warmed up for her. A seafood tea with her parents was a ritual, and today they had four extra guests. Alan, Julia, and Kenny's mum and aunt.

'I'll be off now,' Kenny said. It was the anniversary of his grandfather's death, so he was picking his aunt and mum up, then going to the cemetery first.

Sharon walked over to her strapping husband. He looked so handsome in the expensive sheepskin coat she'd bought him last Christmas. He'd been out of sorts these past couple of days, spent a lot of time in his office, alone. 'I know how much your granddad meant to you, Ken, but you sure nothing else is troubling you?'

Kenny kissed his wife on the forehead. 'Nah. I'm fine. Just a bit down 'cause of me granddad,' he lied. It was pointless worrying Sharon at present, but the twins' home-life had been playing heavily on his mind and he'd come to a decision. If Donny wasn't man enough to stand up to Tansey and take the twins on, then he would. He'd go and see a brief, apply for him and Shal to get custody. Beau and Brett would be far better off here than with that wrong un who'd given birth to them.

*

124

Kenny took the flowers out of the boot, then urged his mum and aunt to hold on to an arm each. It was horrible weather, strong winds and heavy rain, and his mother had a ridiculous pair of high heels on.

'Bloody Nora! That's the second time me brolly's gone inside out. I'll pay my respects in the car, Kenny. Give me your keys,' said Vera.

Kenny handed his mother the keys willingly. She wasn't the most compassionate of women, even at a graveside.

Both his grandparents were buried in the same plot in Bow Cemetery and as Kenny continued to walk, Nelly was unusually quiet. 'You all right, Auntie? Tough day, I know.'

'Yeah, boy. I'm OK.' Nelly was anything but all right, but not for the reason Kenny surmised. She couldn't tell him the news today though. She'd wait until she saw him alone next. He was bound to blow his top – and he had every bloody right to.

'You don't mind if I don't come to dinner, do you?' Vera asked the moment Kenny stepped back inside the car. 'I've got a stinking headache.'

'Erm, no. If you don't feel well, you don't feel well, Mum. You ain't been on that Cinzano Bianco again, have yer?'

'Don't be daft. Just one of me migraines. It'll soon pass once I have a kip,' fibbed Vera.

Kenny dropped his mother off, then was surprised when his aunt asked him to drop her back home too. 'It's silly, you having to drop me home later if your mum isn't coming, boy. You've got your friends round too. You have a good drink and toast your granddad. I need to catch up with me housework anyway.'

Kenny waited until he pulled up outside Aunt Nelly's

before confronting her. 'I know you better than you know yourself. Spill the beans. Have you and Mum fallen out? Only, you could cut the atmosphere with a knife earlier.'

Nelly sighed deeply. She was dreading telling her nephew but owed it to him. Kenny was more like a son to her. 'Don't say this has come from me, especially to your mother. Pete's out of prison and she's back with him. They've been seen out gallivanting. That's why she didn't want to come over yours for dinner today. Migraine, my arse. They were down the Rose and Crown last Sunday. One of my customers saw 'em. Like a pair of lovestruck teenagers. She was all over him like a rash, by all accounts. The silly old cow.'

Kenny's jaw twitched frantically. As memories of the beatings he'd taken as a child flooded back, he smashed his fist against the steering wheel. He'd heard the no-good bastard had been released, but hadn't thought in a million years his mother would take him back. 'Thanks for telling me, Auntie. Does Mum know you know?'

'No. But it was a struggle to act normal in front of her earlier. I despair of her at times. I truly do.'

Kenny gently touched his aunt's arm. 'Me too. Keep schtum. I'll deal with this my way.'

Nelly rubbed her nephew's cheek. 'I thought you might. You're a good man, Kenny. Your granddad would be very proud of you.' Nelly had a slight struggle getting her large frame out of the car, then poked her head back inside. 'Oh, and the Crown is his local. He's in there most lunchtimes and evenings.'

Due to a bad accident along the A13, by the time Kenny got home, Alan and Julia had already arrived. He'd also had time to calm down while planning his revenge.

'Ricky!' Kenny grinned as Alan and Julia's son ambled towards him, arms wide open and a big grin on his handsome face. Unfortunately for Alan and Julia, Ricky had been born with Down's syndrome. But he was a little belter, always happy, and Kenny had been honoured when his pal had asked himself and Shal to be Ricky's godparents. 'If anything ever happened to me and Julia, I couldn't think of anyone better to take care of my special boy.' Alan's words had brought tears to Kenny's eyes that day. He adored his pal and loved Ricky to bits.

'Where's your mum and aunt?' enquired Sharon.

Kenny lifted his chuckling godson in the air. 'Mum had a migraine and Aunt Nell weren't herself either. A least I can have a booze now. Every cloud an' all that lark.'

Brett and Beau ran into the kitchen. 'Gramps,' they shouted in unison.

After making a fuss of his grandsons and chatting to Julia, Kenny gestured for Alan to follow him into his office. The room wasn't overly furnished but had everything Kenny needed in it. A phone, a leather swivel chair, a desk, a sofa, TV and most importantly, a drink's cabinet. Kenny poured two large brandies and handed one to Alan.

'You OK, mate? I know today's a tough one for you.'

Kenny explained Pete was out of prison and was seeing his mother again. Alan was the only one who truly knew the awful childhood he'd had and the mental scars that bastard had left him with.

'What you gonna do? He ain't worth doing time over, Ken.'

Kenny's jaw twitched. 'Oh, I know that. I ain't completely doolally. No way is he having it away with my muvver again though. He made her life a misery last time. He'll shag anything with a pulse, him. Don't say nothing to Shal or Julia. Between us, this is. I want today to be about friendship, family and me granddad, so let's change the subject.' Kenny opened the safe, took out two envelopes and handed them both to Alan. 'Hide 'em in your motor, mate. The smaller envelope is obviously yours.'

'I'll do it now. Going all right, this little arrangement, eh?' grinned Alan.

'Sure is.' Neither Sharon nor Julia knew about their latest venture. A pal of Kenny's specialized in flogging cut-and-shuts abroad. Top-of-the-range vehicles that consisted of two or more cars welded together to create a new motor. A pal of Alan's was doing all the welding, mechanical stuff and bodywork. He and Al were just the middlemen, but they were still earning a decent bit of wedge from it.

Kenny lit up a cigar. He had to take the odd chance here and there, not just to relieve the boredom of going straight, but to keep the money rolling in. The boat business was seasonal. There were very few bookings with winter rapidly approaching. It would be March or April before *The Duchess* started paying dividends again. He and Donny had raked in a nice few bob during the summer though. He bought all the booze cheap off a pal. 'What you laughing at?' Alan asked as he re-entered the office.

'Was thinking about those tourists' events. I can't wait to start 'em up again. You gotta come on some more, Al.' It had been Kenny's idea to add tourist events in the daytime – and what a blast they'd been. A boat full of mainly Japanese, Chinese and Americans, lapping up any old crap he cared to spout over the mike.

Alan was laughing so hard it was all he could do to light the cigar Kenny handed him. 'Remember when you told 'em you originated from a tribe called "The

128

Cockerknees", then pointed out Westminster Palace and said your great-great-great nan and granddad were so poor, they'd sit outside the palace begging for scraps of food, and were made to sing and dance for it. All I could hear was yap, yap, yap from the Chinese and the Yanks were horrified. Love the royals, that mob do.'

Kenny chuckled. 'My favourite was when I told 'em I knew who Jack the Ripper was, as I was related to him. Their north and souths were agog at that! I got proper told off by Donny afterwards. Reckoned the tourist board would take a trip undercover and put the block on us doing any more.'

Alan chuckled. 'Yeah, Donny was proper irate. He certainly ain't got your sense of humour, pal.'

'Nope. Unfortunately, he ain't got my brains either.'

Sharon knocking on the door ended the humorous reminiscing. 'Dinner's ready, you two.'

While Sharon was getting the tea ready, Kenny gestured Donny to follow him into the gym. He hadn't had a chance to speak alone with his son since he'd spilled his guts the other night and Donny had been avoiding his phone calls. 'Why haven't you got back to me? I rung you at me nursery and left a message with Tansey for you to call me back.'

'Sorry. Yesterday was manic at work. We had a load of Christmas stuff delivered.'

'How'd it go with Lori's mum?'

'Yeah, good,' lied Donny. 'She gave Lori what for, then I stormed round there and did the same. Lori's promised to change her ways, put the boys first from now on.'

Kenny eyed his son suspiciously. A leopard don't change its spots, not that quickly anyway.

Sharon poked her head around the door. 'There you

are! I've made the twins their winkle and prawn sand-wiches, but I can't find 'em anywhere. They've nicked the matches I light the gas with an' all.'

Both Donny and Kenny sprang into action, searching the house and repeatedly calling Beau and Brett's names. There was no reply.

Giggling behind the garden shed because they could hear their names being called, Beau ripped off a piece of the foil that he'd stolen from his nan's kitchen. He rolled it up like Gary did, then ripped off a bigger piece.

'Serves Gramps right he thinks we're lost. He likes Ricky more than us,' a jealous Beau informed his brother.

'Don't say that. Gramps loves us too.'

'I think we should play with Ricky later, then trip him up as we come back downstairs, so he falls and hurts himself.'

'We can't do that, Granddad will go mental.' Brett was always the softer of the two.

'We're brothers.' In other words, they were going to do it regardless. 'Pass me the pepper.'

After a desperate search, it was Kenny who decided to look behind the shed. 'Donny, Donny,' Kenny bellowed. He could barely believe his eyes. His grandsons had made straws out of foil and looked like they were about to chase the dragon. Kenny snatched the foil with the powder on it out of Beau's hand. He sniffed it and was relieved that it made him sneeze and was only pepper.

Donny's face turned a deathly white. 'What the hell you doing, boys?'

'Copying Gary,' Beau explained.

Realizing they were in big trouble, Brett handed his

father the pepper pot minus the lid. 'We're sorry. Ain't we, Beau?'

For the second time that day, Kenny's jaw twitched furiously. 'Get inside now, boys. Nan's made your sandwiches. Go eat 'em.'

When his grandsons scarpered, Kenny prodded his son hard in the chest. 'Your ex's geezer is a fucking smackhead. You take them boys away from her today. She's vermin and so is he. She must be on the gear too. Bollocks to Tansey. It's time for you to man the fuck up.'

Still livid, Kenny waited until Alan left, then insisted on accompanying his son to confront Lori. On the journey, he urged his son to barge inside the house, pick up whatever was worth collecting of his sons' belongings, then take them home with him.

'I can't just turn up at home with the boys without speaking to Tansey first, Dad. I'll talk to her tonight. I promise I will.'

'Well, the boys will stay with me tonight then. Say they get their hands on the real stuff and try smoking that next, eh?'

In the back of the car, Beau nudged Brett. Both would much prefer to live with their father. He bought them loads of presents and fed them good food.

Beau thought of Ricky and smirked. Because he and Brett were already in the doghouse, he hadn't had a chance to trip Ricky up and watch him fall down the stairs. He would in the future though. Something to look forward to.

'Let me deal with this, Dad. They're my sons,' Donny said when he pulled up outside Lori's.

'And they're my grandsons. You couldn't be trusted

organizing a piss up in a brewery lately,' Kenny hissed, opening the passenger door.

Lori was horrified to see Kenny standing on her doorstep next to Donny, but not overly surprised. Her mother's visit, followed by Donny turning up and threatening her, had given her a bit of a wake-up call. Afraid of Social Services or Kenny turning up, she'd taken only enough heroin to stop her clucking today, cleaned the house as best as she could and had spruced herself up a bit and put some make-up on.

Donny ordered his sons to play in the postage stamp of a garden before telling Lori what his dad had caught them doing, then calling her every name under the sun. 'You disgust me. You're not fit to be their fucking mother,' he cursed.

'I swear on my life, I don't take smack,' lied Lori. As much as her sons did her head in, she had no intention of parting with them. They were the only hold she still had over Donny. Plus, the thought of that relationship-wrecking whore Tansey raising her sons with her ex, playing happy families, didn't bear thinking of.

Kenny was shocked by Lori's appearance. She was all skin and bone, her eyes were sunken and her former youth and vitality seemed to have deserted her. 'You can't kid a kidder. You should be ashamed of yourself. Where's Gary?' Kenny spat, barging past Lori. 'No way are my grandsons living with junkies. They'll be staying with me tonight, then moving in with Donny,' he bellowed, as he began searching the shithole Lori called home.

Lori sank to her knees and clutched Donny around the ankles. 'Please don't take the boys away from me. They're all I've got. On their lives, all I've ever done is have a puff and a drink. It was Gary who was doing heroin. I didn't know, I swear I didn't. As soon as I found out, I slung him out – and Eric. Please Donny, please,' she pleaded.

Donny felt a pang of guilt as he looked down at his bedraggled ex. He knew in his heart that he was the cause of her downfall. It also suited him for her to sort herself out, as he also knew that Tansey would not welcome the twins with open arms – if at all.

When his father flew back down the stairs, Donny grabbed his arm and led him out the front. He explained the situation. 'Please, Dad, we can't just take the boys away from her. It isn't right. We need to do this properly, go through the proper channels. No way will a court give you custody, not with your record. I will keep a close eye on Lori from now on and, cross my heart, if she doesn't sort herself out, the twins'll be living with me. As you said, bollocks to Tansey.'

Shaking his head in despair, Kenny stomped back to the car before he truly lost it. There was blokes' clothes and shoes in the wardrobe, so no way had Gary gone far. His son was so naive. If he didn't trust Sharon so much, he might have suspected their old milkman was Donny's real father. The lad certainly didn't behave like a Bond. 'Let the blood be on your hands if this goes wrong, boy,' Kenny yelled, slamming the car door.

Thanking Donny profusely, Lori sank to her knees once again as she heard his car drive away. It was a good job she'd told Gary and Eric to make themselves scarce today. Now all she had to do was think of another way to bribe her sons.

Donny broached the subject of his sons' plight with Tansey that evening. He knew deep down his dad was right.

Without professional help, Lori seemed far too up the wrong path to sort herself out.

Tansey looked at Donny in bewilderment. 'No disrespect to the twins – obviously I wish them well and want them to be happy – but I'm not raising another woman's sons. Jamie and Harry are enough for me, thanks very much.'

Donny said no more. That was the response he'd fully expected and, in his home, Tansey wore the trousers.

While he wasn't happy about it, Donny thought he'd made the right decision. Little did he know, his boys were in more danger than he realized . . .

CHAPTER TEN

Unlike his brother, Eric Acorn wasn't a user of heroin. He preferred taking speed or smoking weed, hence his rotting teeth.

At school, Eric had no friends whatsoever. He'd been beaten up regularly. Once Gary was old enough to defend him, the beatings stopped, but Eric's schooldays had scarred him for life.

When Eric wasn't out of his nut on drugs, he'd turn to his other passion, food. He had a real sweet tooth, could eat a whole packet of biscuits in one go. As for chocolate, Eric would live on that if he could.

But Eric's biggest passion of all was little boys. He had no interest in women or men, had never slept with either. Gary didn't know his brother's sordid secret; he would probably have disowned him.

As Eric watched the twins play in the garden, he couldn't help but smile. They truly were handsome. Too bloody handsome, in fact.

As Christmas approached, Donny started to worry less about the twins. Both had put on weight. None of the clothes he'd bought them recently had gone missing, and they insisted their mum was looking after them better.

Always one to turn a blind eye rather than face reality, Donny was blissfully unaware that Lori had frightened the living daylights out of his sons. She'd told Beau and Brett if they ever mentioned that Gary and Eric were still living there, they would be taken away by Social Services, put in a children's home and never allowed to visit her, their dad or granddad ever again.

'I thought it might be nice if we book a restaurant and eat out this Christmas, Donny?' suggested Tansey. The festive season was awkward. Not only was Tansey not welcome around Donny's family anymore – because his mum, nan and granddad blamed her for Charlie losing a leg – she was no longer welcome around her own family. And she missed them, especially her mum.

'Yeah, let's do that. We'll go over Romford Dogs on Boxing Day an' all. The boys'll love that.' Donny found the festive season tough too. It was a messed up situation, but what family wasn't? Tansey didn't want Harry visiting his family because, apart from his dad, none of them spoke to her; therefore his youngest son had very little contact with them, which upset him. ''Ere, I meant to tell you, my dad says they've got planning permission to build another couple of houses down Dark Lane. He reckons we should move there, said it will definitely help build bridges. He even said he'll help us out with the mortgage, if need be. If you still want us to try for a daughter, we're gonna need a bigger place, ain't we?'

Tansey glared at Donny. 'But what about Jamie? Your family loathe me, so they aren't going to give him the time of day, are they? In case you'd forgotten, it was his father who shot your granddad.'

Donny rolled his eyes. Sarcasm wasn't one of Tansey's finest attributes.

Every time he cashed his giro, Eric Acorn would head to the local shop and treat the twins to a big bag of penny sweets each. Flying saucers, blackjacks, fruit salad, strawberry laces, cola bottles, no expense spared.

Eric smiled as he headed towards what he now called home. He was a big man, over eighteen stone, so Lori's sofa wasn't the most comfortable bed. On the other hand, being around the twins made up for it. He'd been ever so pleased when they'd got themselves expelled from school, as it meant he could spend more time with them. He was dreading them starting their new school, mind. Watching them all day long gave him a thrill.

Eric was yet to act on his urge for young boys. The reason being, he'd never had a chance to before. He had one friend, Jonathan, who shared his cravings. He would often pop round Jonathan's to watch one of his special videos that he ordered from Holland, which he'd then fantasize over for days on end. But Eric had never had any other like-minded friends, let alone ones who had access to young boys.

'Hello, Lori, Gary not in?' Eric didn't particularly like Lori. She wasn't a good mother and those gorgeous little boys deserved better. She wasn't a good influence on his younger brother either. But at least she had given them a roof over their head.

'Gary's gone to see a man about a dog. You treating me, Gal, and the boys to something from the chippy then? It's your giro day.'

'Of course. Don't I always treat us? And the boys.' Eric smiled, waving the two big sweetie bags in the air.

'They've been little shits today, climbing over all the

137

neighbour's gardens. That witch Janice knocked and gave me a right mouthful 'cause they set her dogs off. As if it's my bloody fault.'

'Where are they now?'

'Out the front somewhere.'

Eric bolted out the front door and called the boys' names. Even though lots of people couldn't tell the difference between them, he could. Brett was his favourite. Beau definitely had the nastier nature out the two. He'd studied them for hours, knew all their traits.

Knowing full well they'd be getting a big bag of sweets as it was Fat Eric's giro day, the boys appeared out of nowhere. Beau went to snatch a bag as usual.

'No. What do we say first to Uncle Eric?'

'Ta.'

'Thanks, Uncle Eric,' Brett said, as he was handed his bag.

Eric smiled happily as the boys excitedly delved inside their goodie bags. He wasn't brave enough to act on his fantasies. His brother would never forgive him and he'd be made homeless.

However, a man such as him could still dream . . .

Sharon twiddled her fingers anxiously, waiting for her name to be called. She'd finally spoken to her mum about her problem and her mum had insisted she get herself checked out in case there was something seriously wrong. Her own GP was a man, so Sharon had paid to see a private female gynaecologist. No way could she talk to a man about it.

'Sharon Bond. Dr Morgan is ready to see you now. Second door on the left.' The receptionist pointed towards a corridor.

A tall lady with long, wavy red hair, Dr Alison Morgan greeted Sharon warmly, then urged her to take a seat. She smiled. 'How can I help you today, Sharon?'

Up until she'd got with Kenny, Sharon was quite prudish and, apart from larking around with some of her friends on the subject, had little knowledge about sex. Her mother had only ever told her not to have sex before marriage as no decent man would marry an easy girl. Other than that, the subject was taboo at home and there had been no sex education lessons when she was at school.

Sharon gabbled as she explained her issues to Dr Morgan. 'I'm sure my husband thinks I don't love him anymore. But I do. I adore him. I told my mum recently and she's worried I might have womb cancer. She said it can't be the change 'cause I'm far too young for that.'

When Sharon's eyes welled up, Dr Morgan squeezed her hand. 'If I had a pound for every woman that came to me with similar issues to yours, I'd be extremely rich.'

Feeling less like a freak of nature, Sharon forced a smile. 'Really?'

Dr Morgan picked up a pen and began making notes. 'When did you last menstruate, Sharon?'

'What?'

'Your last period. When was it?'

'Years ago. I think it was around the time my son got himself into a bit of bother. It was nothing serious, like. Teenagers will be teenagers, won't they? He's a hard-working father of three now, my Donny.'

Dr Morgan smiled. 'I have all that to look forward to. My son Sebastian is only eight. Do you suffer from anxiety at all, Sharon? Any hot sweats?'

'Yes. Both. Especially of a night. My husband . . . erm, worked away for years, on oil rigs, but since he's moved back home I sweat like a pig. Kenny seems to generate heat and when he was away, I could just throw the quilt off. I know Kenny loves me, but because he still has a high sex drive and I don't anymore, I can't help but worry that he'll stray. I know deep down he wouldn't, 'cause he's a family man, but we have argued over the subject. Not recently, this was all a while back. I can't tell him it hurts me when we have sex now. It's embarrassing. If only it didn't hurt, I would just lie back and think of England, so to speak. I wanna feel normal again, Doctor. Like a woman should with her husband.'

Having been raised in Hampstead, Dr Morgan was fascinated by the attractive woman in front of her, the common accent combined with her way with words. She would have put money on Sharon's husband never having seen an oil rig in his life. Most likely he'd been in prison. Since starting her clinic in Brentwood, Essex, Alison had come across many Sharons. Villain's wives. Some even told her their life stories.

'I'm sure you will feel like that woman again, Sharon. All your symptoms suggest to me that you have gone through an early menopause. The change, as you call it. But let's examine you anyway, to put your mind at rest regarding womb cancer. Pop behind the curtains, undress and put the gown on. I will perform a smear test.'

Blushing furiously, Sharon did as asked. Nobody had ever looked closely at her fanny other than Kenny. She was mortified.

Eric Acorn wasn't a big drinker. Neither did he like pubs. He felt awkward and sweaty, and was sure everybody was looking at him and laughing at his size, like they had at school.

Gary and Lori rarely ventured to pubs either. It was so much cheaper to drink at home, and they preferred to spend all their extra cash on the brown. Heroin took them to another level. However, Gary'd had a result this week. He'd gone out on the thieve with a pal of his, stolen a couple of generators and got a good price for them off Gypsy Dave.

'Seeing as you don't fancy the pub, can you babysit the twins tonight?' asked Gary.

Eric's eyes lit up. Even if he could only watch TV and have a cuddle with Brett, that would be the best Christmas present he could wish for. He didn't want to sound too excited though, that might give his true feelings away. 'Erm, what pub you going to? Only I didn't actually say I didn't fancy coming. I just said I'd already made plans to pop round my mate Jonathan's.'

'The Pompadours. I told you earlier what boozer we were going to. Well, can you look after the twins or not?'

'Erm, OK. What I'll do is visit Jonathan now instead. We need to exchange presents.'

'Cool.'

Eric trotted off excitedly. Jonathan had a new video that had arrived from Holland yesterday. One that Eric couldn't wait to see.

Donny Bond relaxed in the armchair, cold beer in hand. It had been manic at the nursery recently. They'd sold more Christmas trees than ever this year, and he was glad to have a break from work. He picked up the remote and put the stereo on. Wham's 'Young Guns' was playing. Tansey definitely had the hots for Andrew Ridgeley, but her little crush didn't bother him. She would never cheat on him and vice versa. Fact.

Feeling chilled, Donny put his hands behind his head. He'd left most of the kids presents to Tansey, but it had been his idea what to buy the twins. Donny couldn't wait to see Beau and Brett's faces tomorrow when they saw the Raleigh Budgies he'd bought them. They'd been on about wanting a bike for ages now and he knew they'd love his choice. Proper little geezer's bikes they were, suited his pair of rascals to a tee.

'Both boys bathed and finally asleep,' Tansey said. 'What you so happy about? I heard you singing away.'

'Life. You. And I got you a nice surprise for you. A special present. But if I tell you any more, I'll have to kill ya,' grinned Donny.

Tansey sat next to Donny, draped her arms around his neck and kissed him passionately. Whatever his surprise present was, it wouldn't beat hers.

Eric Acorn felt tipsy but very happy as he sat on the sofa with his two favourite boys. 'Do you want to watch TV? Or shall we play some more games?'

'Snakes and Ladders,' Brett replied.

'Go and get the board then and I'll get the chocolate and crisps I bought you,' smiled Eric. Today had been a good day. As for Jonathan's new video, it had been one of the best Eric had ever seen. He couldn't stop thinking about it. The blond boy had reminded him of the twins. Around the same age.

Eric cracked open the bottle of Scotch his friend had kindly given him for Christmas and as he watched Beau bend over the Snakes and Ladders' board, he felt his penis unexpectedly spring into life.

Sighing, Eric put a pillow over his crotch. Perhaps watching that boy being raped today hadn't been a good idea after all. He should have watched the film *after* his babysitting duties, not beforehand.

Kenny was amazed when, out of the blue, Sharon started whispering filth in his ear and suggested an early night. When they'd first met, Sharon was very shy sexually. He'd liked that. He'd slept with enough slags to know a decent girl when he met one.

Even when they'd first got married, Sharon was a bit of a prude. Then he'd brought her out of her shell. They'd connected in a way in the bedroom that only two people truly in love, who trusted one another implicitly, could.

'Oh, Shal,' Kenny groaned, as his wife unzipped his trousers and shoved her mouth lovingly around his prized piece. He missed her dressing up, her wearing the fancy lacy knickers, stilettos with sod all else and talking dirty to him. He'd known she'd knocked back a fair bit of booze this evening, but nevertheless, this made him happy. The best Christmas present he could wish for, in fact.

Kenny gave another loud groan. 'Get your drawers off, babe. I'm gonna fuck you hard and proper. Like the old days.'

'OK. But I need a wee first.'

Once inside the bathroom, Sharon grabbed the tube of lubricant Dr Morgan had advised her to buy earlier. Sharon had felt ever so embarrassed paying for it in Boots in case the cashier knew what it was for.

Sharon said a silent prayer as she rubbed it around her intimate parts. Dr Morgan said it should help with the pain, but Sharon was hoping for more than that. She was hoping it would relight her desires.

*

Half a dozen Scotches and three joints later, Eric was struggling to control his urges. Beau was curled up in the corner of the sofa, but Brett had fallen asleep next to him and his head had now flopped onto his genitals. That alone was making him extremely excitable.

While reliving the video he'd watched earlier, Eric stroked Brett's hair, then glanced at Beau to make sure he was still soundo. He was. Eric quietly stood and lifted his favourite boy in the whole wide world up. He then crept up the stairs with him and did the unthinkable. That thing he'd always dreamed of.

CHAPTER ELEVEN

'What a matter, Brett? Why you crying?' asked Beau at 6 a.m. the following morning.

Brett was in excruciating pain, but was far too scared to say how it had occurred. The reason being, Eric had told him that nobody would believe him and, if he told anybody, the police would come and arrest him and he'd be taken away from Beau and put in a children's home. 'I didn't mean to hurt you. I love you. I promise you this will never happen again,' he'd told him. 'But it has to be our little secret. Is that OK? And if you are in a bit of pain tomorrow, say you have a tummy ache.' Those were Fat Eric's parting words before leaving Brett alone to sob himself to sleep.

'I don't feel well,' he told Beau.

'Where don't you feel well?'

'Me tummy. It hurts.'

'Dad'll give you some medicine. Get up. He'll be 'ere soon. I wonder what he's bought us?'

Brett burst into tears. For once he didn't care what their father had bought them.

*

Eric Acorn woke up on the sofa, sweating like a rapist, which he now was. He put his hands over his face. Why had he watched that film, then got himself so stoned? He knew cannabis had a tendency to make him overly horny.

Hearing light footsteps coming down the stairs, a white-faced Eric sat bolt upright. 'Merry Christmas. Where's your brother?'

'In bed. Don't feel well. But he gotta get up soon 'cause our dad's picking us up at nine and I wanna see what he bought us.' Beau stared at the leaning, crappy fake Christmas tree his mother had put up. There were more presents than usual underneath, but Beau knew they would be a load of old crap. They always were.

Seeing what Beau was looking at, Eric forced a smile. He felt bad, scared, terrified, in fact. Lori and Gary had come home smashed last night and were still in bed. Say Brett told his mum? Or worse still, his dad? He had to get out of the house before Donny arrived. 'What's wrong with your brother? Did he say?'

Stuffing some of the chocolate in his mouth that was left over from last night, Beau replied, 'Gut ache.'

Eric breathed a sigh of relief. He'd had to cover the boy's mouth so his screams would not wake Beau. He glanced at his watch. It was nearly 8 a.m. 'I'll pop upstairs and make sure Brett is OK. Then you can open your presents from me.'

In absolute agony and shock, Brett was sobbing underneath his shabby blankets when Eric entered the room. 'Brett, it's me. Are you OK?'

'No.'

'Please don't tell anybody, Brett. You're my special boy, you know that. You won't tell, will you? I promise what happened won't ever happen again. I'll buy you anything

146

you want. Actually, I have some lovely presents downstairs for you. Why don't you come downstairs and open them with Beau?'

'Don't want 'em. Go away. I hate you!'

For the last couple of years, Donny had picked the twins up early and taken them to his parents' so he could spend a few hours with them and watch them open their presents. 'You OK, Brett? You seem quiet, boy.'

Watching Brett fidget, then stare aimlessly out of the car window, Beau decided to reply for him. 'He ain't well, Dad. He got the gut ache.'

Donny tilted the interior mirror to focus on Brett. He had tears running down his cheeks, the poor little sod. Both boys looked more dishevelled than usual this morning. They looked very dirty, so did their clothes. 'What you got all down your jumpers?'

'Chocolate and hot chocolate that Eric made us,' explained Beau. Their mum hadn't done any washing recently, so both he and Brett had the same jumpers on as they'd worn yesterday. He daren't tell his dad that though, in case they got taken away and sent to that children's home.

At the mention of Eric's name, Brett started to gag.

'I'm sure Nanny Sharon has something to make you feel better, Brett. She's got something in her magic medicine cupboard to cure everything. I'll give you a bath as soon as we get there too. I've got clean clothes in the boot for yous. Just say I got the time mixed up with your muvver if Nanny or Granddad asks though.'

When Brett burst into floods of tears, Donny began to worry. Brett wasn't usually a crier. Neither of the twins were. Perhaps he had appendicitis or something?

*

147

By the time Donny got to his parents', Brett was in that much pain, he was screaming his head off. Donny lied to his parents about getting the time mixed up with Lori, hence the state of the boys. He knew his dad didn't believe him though, could tell by his stony stare.

'Oh, darling. Whatever is wrong with you?' asked the concerned Sharon Bond. She knew the twins were little hard-nuts as a rule.

Remembering Fat Eric's warning, Brett miserably pointed to his stomach. 'It hurts 'ere.'

'He's in proper bad pain, Donny. Leave Beau with us and take Brett to Oldchurch,' ordered Kenny. 'I'd come with you, but I've gotta pick your nan and Aunt Nelly up.'

'Say there's a long wait? I got a restaurant booking at two. Tansey'll go mad if we have to cancel. We've got no dinner otherwise.'

Kenny glared at his son. 'Look at the kid. He's in agony. Fuck Tansey and fuck your dinner.'

'You go to the hospital with them, Kenny,' urged Sharon. 'My dad'll pick up your mum and Nell. There's something seriously wrong. I can tell. Call it a mother's instinct.'

'I wanna go too,' Beau said.

'No, darling. You stay with Nanny,' Sharon replied.

As Donny left the house with Brett in his arms, Sharon was surprised when Beau burst into tears. She hadn't seen him cry before. Not ever.

Donny looked on worriedly as Brett was examined. His dad had gone to find a payphone to ring Tansey and explain what was happening. As usual, Donny had taken the coward's way out. He'd known Tansey would go apeshit at him.

Dr Blake gently pressed different places on the young

boy's stomach. 'Does it hurt here, Brett? Or here? Or here?' he asked.

Unable to stand the pain anymore and desperately needing to poo, Brett as young as he was, knew he had to come clean. 'Not my tummy. My bum hurts. It hurts bad.'

Donny Bond put his hands on his head and rocked to and fro on a chair in the corridor. He'd had to leave his son alone with the doctor, could not face watching the medical assessment any longer. He'd thought he was about to throw up at one point. How could he have allowed this to happen?

Dr Blake reappeared. 'I'd like to have Brett seen by a specialist paediatrician to conduct an intimate examination, but will need your consent to do so.'

'Do what you've got to do. I'll sign whatever. Is Brett OK?'

'He's in a lot of pain, but we'll give him something to ease that.'

When Dr Blake walked away, Kenny Bond smashed his fist against the wall next to his son's thick head. He hit it so hard, he felt a knuckle or two crumble. 'How many times did I tell you those boys weren't safe with that skanky whore of a mother of theirs? You're a fucking cretin, Donny. I'm ashamed to call you my son right now.'

When Donny started to weep, Kenny whacked him hard around the head. 'No point crying after the horse has bolted, is there? Man up, grow a pair and be the dad those boys deserve. If Tansey don't want 'em living with her, tell her to fuck off. Brett, especially, needs you more than ever now.'

Dr Blake led Donny and Kenny into a room, shut the door and urged them to sit down.

'How is he?' asked Donny.

'More comfortable since we've sedated him. We'd like to keep him in overnight for observation. Brett's had a traumatic time, unfortunately. Does he live with you, Donny?'

'No. He lives with his mother. He was bawling his eyes out when I picked him up this morning. I knew something was wrong immediately, but never in a million years did I think it would be anything like this.'

'Has the specialist paediatrician examined him yet?' asked Kenny.

'Yes. Brett has severe anal tearing. We suspect a possible rape; therefore we will notify the police of our findings and they will investigate the matter further.'

Donny's eyes welled up. He was in shock, turmoil, felt like the worst dad ever. 'I can't believe this has happened,' he mumbled.

Kenny glared at his son. 'Well, it has, ain't it! Now we all have to pull together for Brett's sake and deal with it.' He turned back to Dr Blake. 'So, I take it the police will go round and question Brett's mother?'

'Yes. Most definitely. The way it works is, the police notify Social Services and it becomes a joint investigation. They work in conjunction, but the police call the shots, so to speak. They will do intelligence checks around the mother and Donny. Does Brett's mother live alone?'

'Supposedly. But she did have a bloke and another geezer living with her recently. Lori's a junkie, often has a houseful,' replied Kenny. That was all he needed, the Old Bill doing intelligence checks. Especially if they cottoned on who he was.

'Can we see Brett now?' asked Donny.

'Yes. He's still quite sleepy. We had to sedate him. I take

150

it you will be looking after your son, Mr Bond, once he is discharged?'

'Yes. Of course. Brett has a twin brother. No way will their mother ever be seeing them again, not if I have my way. I'll get out a restraining order if I have to,' Donny insisted.

'Follow me,' said Dr Blake.

Brett was in a little room on his own, his eyes shut. Donny stroked his hair and Brett flinched. 'It's OK, son. It's Daddy. You and Beau will be living with me from now on. You get some rest now and I'll be back in the morning to pick you up.'

'Where Beau?' mumbled Brett.

'At Nan and Granddad's. I'll bring him with me tomorrow when we pick you up, OK?'

Brett blinked then closed his eyes again.

'We'll keep Brett sedated to ease the pain. He's in good hands, I promise,' Dr Blake said. 'He just needs some rest.'

Kenny kissed his grandson on the forehead, then thanked Dr Blake. He and a rather reluctant Donny then left the hospital.

'Raped! What do you mean raped?' gasped Sharon Bond. She could not quite believe what she was hearing.

Charlie Saunders got up and hobbled up and down the room. He hated his false leg. It was so bloody uncomfortable. 'If there's anything I loathe in life, it's nonces. I'll hunt him down and kill the dirty fucker,' he bellowed.

Aunt Nelly's eyes welled up. 'Poor little mite. God bless him.'

Vera pursed her lips. 'I always knew that Lori wasn't fit to be a mother. Dunno what Donny ever saw in the tart.'

Kenny scowled at his mother. She was a fine one to

151

talk. Her mothering skills had been non-existent through-out his childhood and since. He was yet to catch up with that tosser she was hawking her mutton at. Twice he'd popped in the Rose and Crown and neither time had Pete been in there. He'd hunt him down soon though, after he'd sought revenge for his grandson. Brett was top of his list of priorities right now.

Maggie Saunders put her head in her hands and wept. You read about stuff like this in the newspapers, but never expected it to happen to one of your own. Poor little Brett. It was surreal. Horrific. Like a bad dream.

Beau had been upset when they'd arrived home without his brother, so Kenny had urged Donny to take the boy out on his new bike. He hadn't wanted to tell the rest of the family in front of him, obviously.

'What we going to do about dinner? I'm not a bit hungry now,' Sharon said, tears rolling down her cheeks.

'Neither am I,' Maggie added.

'Me and Nelly are hungry,' piped up Vera.

'Whoever has done this has messed with the wrong family. I'll sort this,' Charlie ranted.

Kenny gave his distraught wife a hug. 'Come on now. Starving ourselves ain't gonna solve anything. Plus, we have to act normal for the sake of Beau.' He glanced at Charlie. 'Whoever is responsible for this will pay massively, I promise ya that much. And I don't mean being shoved in the nonce wing in some cushty prison. There is more than one way to skin a cat, and trust me, I'm capable of skinning a nonce – literally.'

Absolutely livid that her and her sons' Christmas Day had been ruined, once Tansey put the boys to bed, she poured a Malibu and pineapple. It was 9 p.m. now and she hadn't heard a single word from Donny all day. To say she was furious was the understatement of the century.

Wondering how her own family were celebrating Christmas, Tansey made a decision there and then. She would contact her mum in the new year. Sod what Donny said. It was different for him. He still had all his family around him, whereas she'd literally given hers up to be with him. After today's turnout, him putting Brett in front of her and their kids, she would do what she bloody well liked in future.

Donny arrived home half an hour later with a stony expression on his face.

Tansey's expression was equally stony. 'Wonderful Christmas this turned out to be. Thanks for the regular updates as well. Do you not know how to use a phone?'

Donny held his hands aloft. 'Don't start with me, Tans, cause I really ain't in the mood. I've had the day from fucking hell, trust me.'

'Oh, and you think my day has been any better? The boys and I had burgers and chips for dinner. Why on earth didn't you pick Lori up and insist she sit at the hospital with Brett? Or is that too much to ask?'

For the first time ever, Donny looked at Tansey with distaste. She hadn't even asked what was wrong with Brett, was more bothered about her own day being ruined. 'Brett has been sexually abused. Actually, no, it's worse than that. Some fucking pervert shoved his cock up his arse and raped him. Sorry you had to eat burgers and chips. But, I'm sure you can understand now, my day has been far worse than yours. Oh, and the twins will be living with us from now on. Whether you like it or not.'

*

153

As prearranged, Kenny picked Donny up at ten on Boxing Day morning. He'd left Beau at home. He had plenty of new toys there to play with.

'How's Beau?' Donny asked, slamming the passenger door. He had the bit between his teeth this morning, even though he'd barely slept all night.

'So-so. Missing his brother. Your nan was cooking him a fry-up as I left. Have you rung the hospital? I was thinking, rather than take Beau up there with us, it'll be nice to surprise him and just turn up at home with Brett.'

'I rung Oldchurch first thing. The nurse said Brett got some sleep and seemed as comfortable as could be expected. He keeps asking for Beau. Must be a twin thing. Never been separated before, have they?'

'Nah.'

'Did you tell Tansey they're moving in?'

'Yep. She weren't overjoyed. She slept in Jamie's bed. I stood me ground though, Dad. Told her those boys are my priority now and she can like it or lump it.'

'About bloody time. I got some tools in the boot. You take the baseball bat; I'll take the monkey wrench. The druggies are bound to be spark out at this hour, so we'll catch 'em unaware. Won't take us long to find out the cunt who attacked Brett. Sod the Old Bill. We'll be dealing with this in the only way I know.'

Lori stumbled out of bed as the loud pounding on the front door continued. She looked out the window. 'You stay up 'ere, Gal. I think the twins are back and it's Donny's dad dropping 'em off.' She'd never admitted to Gary that Kenny was a murderer, was too scared it would frighten him off for good.

Squinting, Lori flung open the front door and was

stunned when Donny pushed her so hard, she lost her balance and fell backwards in the hallway. 'What you doing?' she shrieked, as Donny prodded a baseball bat hard against her chest.

'Who were the boys with on Christmas Eve?' he bellowed.

'Me.'

'No. They fucking weren't. Who were they with, Lori?'

Lori was stunned. 'Why? Where are they? Where are my boys?'

'Brett's in hospital,' bellowed Donny.

Hearing the commotion, Gary put his jeans on, ran down the stairs bare-chested and decided to play the big man. 'What the hell's going on? Oi, you leave Lori be, else you'll have me to deal with,' he shouted.

Kenny took one look at Gary and smashed him across the side of the head with the monkey wrench. Gary fell onto the stairs and Kenny leapt on top of him, hands around his throat. 'Was it you, eh? You the fucking nonce?'

Lori was petrified. 'What's happened?'

Donny lowered his face towards Lori's. She was so ugly now; he could not believe he had ever fancied her. 'Answer my question first, then I'll answer yours. Who was round 'ere with the boys on Christmas Eve?'

'Nobody. Only Gary's brother. Me and Gal went to the pub while Eric babysat the twins.'

'And where is Eric now?' hissed Donny.

'I don't know. Honest. He left a note yesterday morning, saying he was spending Christmas with a friend. Me and Gal ain't seen him since.'

Kenny whacked Gary again. 'Who does your brother knock about with?'

Gary was stunned, literally. If a smack around the right

155

side of his head with the wrench hadn't been enough to disorientate him, he'd just had another around the left. 'My brother only has one friend. I dunno where he lives though. On the Hill somewhere.'

When Kenny whacked Gary in his privates with the wrench, Lori screamed. 'What's happened to Brett? Please tell me.'

Donny looked at her with hatred. 'He's been raped, that's fucking what. The Old Bill will be paying you a visit soon, and Social Services. Now, think good and hard where Eric might be. Otherwise, I will make sure you never see those boys again.'

'I think Jonathan lives near the chippy in Hilldene Avenue,' sobbed Lori. But I don't know the actual address. Please don't stop me from seeing the boys. I know I'm not the best mum in the world, but I love 'em in my own way. They're *our* babies.'

Unable to stop himself, Donny spat in Lori's face. 'They're *my* fucking babies now. My responsibility *solely*. And believe me, while I have breath in my lungs, I will make damn sure you never see them again.' Donny stood up and picked up the baseball bat. 'Come on, Dad. Let's go.'

Kenny wasn't quite finished yet. He smashed the wrench against Gary's teeth. 'If you mention one word to your nonce of a brother, that we're onto him, believe me, you will suffer the worse death ever. Under-fucking-stand me?'

Even though he'd once been a bouncer, Gary Acorn was terrified. He'd always had suspicions his brother might be gay, but not a nonce. Donny's dad was a maniac. He had proper scary eyes, like something out of a horror movie. Blood pouring from his mouth, Gary nodded repeatedly. 'Jones,' he splattered, blood pouring down his chin. 'Jonathan's surname is Jones!'

'Where's Beau?' was the first question Brett asked when Donny arrived at the hospital.

'At Nan and Granddad's. We'll go straight there after Granddad's spoken to the doctor. How you feeling today?'

Brett shrugged.

'Are you hungry?'

'A bit.'

Donny forced a smile. 'What I'll do is get Nan to rustle you up a nice bit of lunch. You and Beau can choose whatever you want. Then after you've eaten, we'll go back to my house. That's where you'll both be living from now on. It's got a big garden. You'll love playing in that.'

'Forever?'

'Yeah.'

'Won't Mum miss us?'

Kenny's reappearance saved Donny from replying. 'We can take him home. They've given him painkillers to help him sleep and they want to see him again in a week's time. Any problems in the meantime, Dr Blake said don't hesitate in bringing him straight back up 'ere.'

When Donny went to lift his son up, Brett shrieked. 'Noooo. Don't touch me! Wanna walk.'

Beau ran out of the house and flung his arms around his brother. 'Miss you, Brett.'

Brett hugged Beau back. 'Miss you too.'

'Get inside, boys. It's cold out 'ere and you haven't got a coat on, Beau.' Nobody had told Beau what had happened. He was far too young to understand. If Brett told him and Beau started asking questions, Donny would have to try and explain as gently as he could.

Kenny grabbed his son's arm. 'I'm gonna make some phone calls, set the ball rolling to find and then dispose of the nonce. Keep the day after tomorrow free. I should have everything in place by then.'

'Dispose?'

'Yeah. And you're gonna help me get rid. My granddad taught me what it means to be a Bond. Now I'm gonna teach you too.'

Tansey had spent the day on tenterhooks. She'd fully expected a full-blown apology off Donny this morning for the way he'd spoken to her last night, but she hadn't received one. Instead he'd spoken to her quite abruptly.

Having prayed today that a miracle would occur and Donny would arrive home minus the twins, Tansey was gutted when Donny let himself in and his sons were with him. Jamie and Harry were both upstairs having an afternoon nap.

'This is Tansey who I was telling you about, boys. This is Beau, Tans, and this is Brett,' Donny said, ruffling Brett's hair.

Beau and Brett eyed Tansey with suspicion. 'Say hello then,' urged Donny.

Beau glared at Tansey. For some strange reason, he hated her on sight. 'You our new mum?'

CHAPTER TWELVE

Bernie O'Callaghan was a stout, straight-talking Irishman. His hair was bright ginger, as were the freckles he was covered in. He was a good egg though, owned a slaughterhouse out Chelmsford way, and very trustworthy.

Bernie greeted his old pal warmly. They'd been banged up together many moons ago and Bernie had a lot of respect for Kenny Bond. 'Come into my office. You can say hello to Minnie and the kids afterwards.'

Kenny sat down and accepted Bernie's offer of a Scotch. 'I'll get right to the point, mate. You still do a bit of disposal?'

'Only for close friends who I know and trust like yourself, Kenny. Who you got agg with? Anyone I know?'

'No. But rest assured, this geezer's the worst kind of vermin. What's the cost of dismembering the body and getting the parts dropped off at my pal's pig farm?'

'I'd usually charge around fifteen, but ten grand to you, mate. When do you want the job done?'

'Tomorrow. If it's not too short notice?'

'No. That's fine.'

'I've got an address for the geezer, but obviously he

might not be there. I'll give you a bell one way or another. I will track the bastard down quickly, mind.'

'Just call me tomorrow and if you've got him, I'll meet you at the slaughterhouse.'

'Any chance I can borrow one of your van's an' all? I need to bundle him into the back of something. I'll make sure it's spotlessly clean before I return it.'

Bernie took a set of keys off a hook. 'Take the one on the drive.'

'Cheers. Oh, and one more thing, me and my boy are gonna help you chop him up. That OK? We have our reasons.'

Bernie nodded. 'Sure. Less work for me.'

Gary Acorn gingerly got out of bed and started packing his belongings into two sports bags. He'd lost a front tooth, his head ached and his face was battered and bruised.

Lori opened one eye. She felt like utter shit. 'What ya doing, Gal?'

'Taking some of my clothes round to me mum's. My jeans especially are in need of a bloody good wash. Can't wash 'em here now your poxy machine has broken down, can I? She'll give me some of her strong painkillers, too. Me hand's banging.'

'Pick up some gear on the way back, Gal. You've got plenty of money left, ain't ya? That'll help with your pain.'

'Yeah. Will do.'

'How long you gonna be?

'Not long. Couple of hours, tops. You go back to sleep, babe.'

Gary left some of his older clothes in the wardrobe, then left the house without a backward glance. The shit was about to hit the fan big time and he didn't want to be part of it.

Donny walked up behind Tansey as she was buttering bread, put his arms around her waist and kissed her on the side of the neck. They'd finally exchanged presents late last night. Tansey's big surprise was she was pregnant again, twelve weeks, something that Donny could've done without right now. But he'd acted chuffed. What choice did he have? His surprise to Tans was getting down on one knee and putting a diamond ring on her engagement finger. She'd said 'Yes', thank Christ. 'I'm gonna be out most the day tomorrow. Got a bit of business with my dad I have to attend to. Will you be OK looking after the twins?'

'Bloody hell, Donny. You wasn't here all Christmas Day, nor Boxing Day. Today is the only day we've spent together. Can't your business with your dad wait? I barely know the twins yet.'

'Nah. This is important. Once it's sorted, though, I promise I'll be around all the time. Well, until I go back to work. It'll give you a chance to get to know the twins properly.'

'Who has business meetings this time of year?'

'My dad does. Anything to earn an extra few bob,' grinned Donny. He didn't want Tansey knowing what he and his father were really up to.

'OK.'

'Kids, lunch is ready,' bellowed Donny.

Jamie sat silently picking at his food while the twins scoffed theirs like scavengers. He didn't like Beau and Brett at all, couldn't wait until they went back to their other home.

Tansey glanced at Donny, who seemed oblivious that the twins ate every meal like wild animals. She knew it wasn't Beau and Brett's fault, given they'd been brought up by that awful mother of theirs. But in time, they needed to be taught right from wrong and how to use cutlery properly. They were feral in many ways. But after what had happened to Brett, now wasn't the time to speak up. Instead she plastered a smile on her face and said sweetly, 'You enjoying your sausage and mash, Beau? Brett?'

'Yeah,' Beau replied.

'You're a better cook than our other mum,' Brett added.

'You OK, Harry?' asked Tansey. He was too young to understand, but seemed to like the extra company around the house. Jamie, however, had been very subdued since the twins arrived. Tansey ruffled Jamie's hair. It must be hard for him, sharing his home with two hyperactive boys all of a sudden. 'Why you not eating yours, Jamie? You not hungry?'

'No. I feel sick, Mummy.'

Beau nudged Brett under the table and Brett did his best to stifle a giggle. They'd made Jamie eat a live worm earlier and threatened if he told anyone, they would chop his willy off and make him eat that next.

Lori Boswell stared out the window for what seemed the hundredth time. Where the hell had Gary got to? Surely the Old Bill hadn't tugged him and found the gear? No. That couldn't have happened. Gary would always wrap it in clingfilm and shove it up his arsehole.

Clucking badly, Lori suddenly had fear wash over her as she remembered Gary packing some clothes into a sports bag earlier. She stumbled back up the stairs and yanked open the wardrobe. All Gary's stuff had gone apart from a denim shirt, a few discoloured T-shirts, and a pair of tracksuit bottoms. His dealer boots and trainers were nowhere to be seen either.

Lori collapsed to her knees. How could Gary do this to her? She'd lost her sons, thanks to his nonce of a brother, and he'd gone and left her high and dry with no money or gear. What was she meant to do now?

The following day, Donny followed his father's instructions, left home at 7 a.m. and walked towards the Orange Tree pub. He hadn't been walking five minutes when a large white van pulled up beside him. It was his dad.

Kenny Bond had a lot of contacts and it had been easy for him to find out where Jonathan Jones lived, especially as he roughly knew his whereabouts. He had told his son to dress in old black clothes and had done the same himself. Kenny handed Donny a baseball cap, 'Pull that right over your face when I jump out the van. If the nonce is in there, I'll get him out. I want you to drive, so just be ready to put your foot down when I drag him in the back, yeah?'

'Sure.'

Eric Acorn was wide awake. He hadn't been sleeping well at all, not since he'd finally succumbed to his urges. Partly because he kept reliving every moment and masturbating frantically. But also, because he was worried desperately about Brett grassing him up and his own safety.

However, if his special little boy had opened his trap, Eric was sure the police would have hunted him down by now. Or Donny, Gary and Lori. Lori knew his friend Jonathan lived near the chip shop in Hilldene Avenue as he'd told her that. Therefore, as each day passed, Eric was becoming a little more confident that he had gotten away with it. He'd been overcome by lust at the time, but he now missed the twins dreadfully. Perhaps it was time to go back to Lori's? The dust had obviously settled somewhat, he imagined.

Eric jumped as the buzzer sounded. 'Jonathan, you answer that. If it's anyone untoward, tell them you haven't seen me.' Jonathan had loved hearing the story of what had happened with Brett. They'd spoken about it endlessly and in great detail.

Jonathan ran down the stairs in his discoloured Y-fronts and T-shirt. He'd ordered more videos from Holland a few weeks ago and was hoping they'd finally arrived. 'Hello. Who is it?'

'Got a parcel for you, mate,' replied Kenny.

At the sound of Jonathan excitedly unlocking the four bolts he'd put on his front door for extra security, Kenny put on his balaclava. There was nobody around, he'd checked before pressing the buzzer.

Jonathan shrieked as he realized he'd been duped, but was quickly silenced as he was smashed around the right side of his head with a monkey wrench. He fell backwards onto the stairs, spark out.

'Who is it? Are you OK?' said a voice from upstairs. Jonathan lived in a flat above a shop.

Kenny took the stairs two at a time and was repulsed when he laid eyes on Eric. He was even worse than Donny had described. Fat, bald, ugly, with beady little eyes. He had paedo stamped all over him.

'Who are you? Where's Jonathan?' Eric gabbled, while cowering in the corner. Were they being robbed? he wondered.

Kenny walked towards Eric, smashed him in his private parts with the monkey wrench, then stuffed a sock in his fat mouth. 'I'm your very worst nightmare, you filthy, perverted cunt. Now do as I say, or else. Put some clothes on, keep your gob shut and step nicely into the van outside. Disobey me, I swear I will chop that cock of yours off and force you to eat it.'

Tears streamed down Eric's face, and not just because his testicles were in agony. He knew today would be the last in his sad and sorry life. He could feel it in his bones.

Eric Acorn shook like a leaf as the van took him on what he knew would be his final journey. Donny was driving and the other bloke with the balaclava on was in the back with him. He'd already been trussed up like a chicken, his arms and legs tied together.

Kenny rolled Eric onto his back. He took his balaclava off and stared at the man with pure hatred. 'Messed with the wrong kid, didn't ya? Do you know who I am, Eric?'

'No,' Eric wept. 'But I haven't done anything to any kid, I swear. I have a girlfriend called Katie.'

Kenny had massive hands, and his right almost fitted around Eric's obese throat. 'I am Kenny Bond, Brett's grandfather. That little boy was ripped apart by you. That innocent little boy. But I'm not so fucking innocent, you nonce, so me and Donny are taking you to our pal's slaughterhouse, where we shall torture you. Then we will chop off pieces of you, one by one, until you fucking die. And then you will be heading off to my pal Jimmy's farm. His pigs enjoy eating nonces more than they like their swill. More tasty for 'em, Jimmy reckons.'

When Eric screamed in terror, Kenny put gaffer tape over his mouth. 'Stop at the nearest phone box, Donny. I need to ring Bernie.'

*

165

Bernie's slaughterhouse was situated down a tiny lane in the middle of nowhere. Dead animals kicked up quite a stink, so did dead humans, which was why Bernie had chosen this remote spot. He was extra-careful who he dealt with these days, but back in the good old days he'd made a name for himself disposing of human remains on the hush-hush.

After hearing what his father had said to Eric, Donny had been quiet throughout the journey. He wanted Eric dead, of course, but he couldn't do it. He was shaking like a wet dog.

'You all right, boy?' Kenny asked as the van eased to a standstill.

Eric still had the gaffer tape round his mouth. He'd thought he was having a heart attack on the journey and wished he had. Eric hated pain. His dark beady eyes bulged as Kenny undid the rope around his ankles and dragged him out the back of the van. 'All right if me and my boy have ten minutes with this monster alone, Bernie?'

Absolutely terrified, Eric started wriggling on his front like a fat worm.

Bernie nodded. He guessed this was a personal vendetta but would never ask any questions. 'Be my guest. You do what you have to do and give me a shout when you need me.' This wasn't the first body he and Kenny had disposed of together. Before he was banged up, the Charles brothers had upset Kenny by ripping him off for a fair bit of money, and he'd enlisted Bernie's help. But never had he seen Kenny like this. The wild look in his eye gave Bernie the chills, and he'd seen some sights in his life.

Eric Acorn not only shit and pissed himself as he was escorted inside the foul-stinking slaughterhouse, he also started choking.

Kenny ripped the gaffer tape off his mouth and was repulsed when the disgusting beast projectile vomited, chunks of it landing over Kenny's hoodie. He punched Eric in the side of the head. 'I'm gonna cut your bollocks off for that now.'

'Noooo! I didn't do anything. It was my brother. Gary. He likes children, not me. That's why he moved in with Lori. Please don't kill me. I'm innocent. I swear.'

Kenny wasn't deceived; he knew a nonce when he saw one. So while Eric sobbed like a big fat baby, he un-wrapped a skinning knife and tried to hand it to Donny. 'Here, take this – you're gonna chop the cunt's cock and nuts off, boy.'

Donny recoiled, alarmed. 'No, Dad. You do it.'

'Mummy. Mummy. Help me, Mummy,' screamed Eric.

'Shut up, you cunt,' hissed Kenny as he plastered more gaffer tape over the monster's ugly face.

'What was that for?' a shocked Donny asked, after his father slapped him hard around the face.

'Brett's your son. What type of man are you, if you can't do this?' Kenny spat, pulling Eric's filthy tracksuit bottoms and pants down. He placed the knife in Donny's right hand. Fucking do it.'

Donny grabbed hold of Eric's flaccid cock, placed the knife against it and began trying to slice it. All he could smell was shit. He gagged and turned his head away, slicing his finger in the process.

Kenny angrily snatched the knife off his son and finished the job for him. He then slit Eric's throat.

Outside the slaughterhouse, Donny was chucking his guts up. These past few days had been too much for him. Tears rolling down his cheeks, he looked his father square in the eyes. 'I'm so sorry for everything. I knew the boys shouldn't be living with Lori ages ago. How am I ever gonna forgive myself? I wish I was more like you, Dad.'

His face splattered with Eric's blood, Kenny grabbed his son and, feeling choked up, hugged him closer than he had in years. 'None of this is your fault, boy. It's mine. If I was around for you when yer needed me most, like my granddad was for me, none of this shit would've happened in the first place. From now on, no fucker will hurt our boys. I'll die before I see anyone else lay a finger on them and I want you to vow the same.'

The two men stood, arms around each other's shoulders, as they watched three hungry pigs scoff Eric down in minutes.

CHAPTER THIRTEEN

Donny cursed as he overtook yet another slow driver. He was already running late to meet his father. Turning the volume of the stereo up, Donny hurried along to the Eurythmics' 'Love Is a Stranger'. It was an apt song, as love was certainly a stranger at home these days.

Four months had passed since the twins had moved in, and it seemed to have caused no end of bickering between himself and Tansey. Tans was heavily pregnant now, mind. Donny just hoped that she'd lighten up a bit once the baby was born. He dreaded to think what would happen if they had another boy. Tansey hadn't wanted to know the sex, because she'd already convinced herself she was carrying the precious daughter she yearned for.

'Oh, for Christ's sake,' Donny cursed, as he got stuck behind a dustbin lorry. Craning his head, he put his foot on the accelerator to overtake. He then had to slam on the brakes as a black dog ran into the road.

Luckily for the dog, he wasn't hit. But the back of Donny's motor was. Hard. By the van behind him who'd overtaken the bin lorry too.

*

Kenny picked up the newspaper someone had left on the next table and had a flick through. The press were still obsessed with the dosh that had been stolen from a Security Express van in London a few weeks back. In fairness, it was the biggest cash haul in British history. Seven million, they reckoned, and the thieves were still at large. Kenny had a feeling one of the armed robbers was an old acquaintance of his; he chuckled to himself and hoped his old mucker got away with it.

Finishing his mug of tea, Kenny glanced at his watch. Forty minutes late, his braindead son was, and no way was he waiting in this cafe a minute longer. He was frustrated too by his failure to deal with Uncle Pete, the man who'd made his childhood a misery. Reason being, Pete had disappeared off the scene completely. Kenny had asked an old pal of his, Dick the Fish, to do some digging, and it turned out Pete had been sniffing around some young barmaid in Barking, had even moved in with her. What infuriated Kenny the most was that, now it was all over with the barmaid, Pete was at it with his mother again. Pete's new local was the Bishop Bonner in Bethnal Green, so that's where Kenny would head today. His mum might not like him very much, but he'd always have her back. No way was that bastard taking the piss out of her. Or any other bloke, for that matter. Over his dead body.

It was such a beautiful sunny day, Tansey decided to busy herself by doing some spring cleaning. She wanted everything to be spotless for when her daughter was born, including her curtains that were covered in grubby hand marks, probably from those twins.

Tansey had tried her hardest to take to Donny's sons, but there was something about them, Beau especially, that made her stomach churn. She was sure they were bullying Jamie, even though her son swore blind they weren't. He'd become so clingy, wanting to be by her side all the time when Beau and Brett were around. Tansey was positive her poor boy was petrified of them, but Donny wouldn't listen. Apart from the obvious, such as their table manners and cheekiness, Donny could see no wrong in them.

With Donny upstairs in bed, having taken some painkillers after his car accident, and Harry having a lunchtime nap, Tansey got the stepladder out of the garage to take down the beautiful beige curtains she'd had made to smarten up the patio doors at the back of the home.

Jamie was spending the day at a friend's house, which pleased Tansey as he'd done very little during the Easter holidays other than follow her around like a lost lamb. The twins were out the back. For all their faults, they weren't needy, unless demanding food. They were loud, boisterous, but were able to amuse themselves for hours on end.

Singing along to Michael Jackson's 'Billie Jean', Tansey cautiously started climbing the ladder.

Unbeknown to Tansey, Beau was watching her with interest. Brett didn't seem to mind her so much, but Beau hated her with a passion. He'd been earwigging on many occasions when she'd been arguing with his dad, and even though he couldn't understand some of the words she'd called himself and Beau, he'd known she wasn't being complimentary.

'What you looking at, Beau?' enquired Brett. They'd been playing football, but his brother no longer seemed interested.

'Her. Tansey. She hates us, I know she does. I heard her and Dad arguing again this morning. She was saying 'orrible things 'bout us, and Dad told her off.'

'Bitch.'

'Yeah. Let's get our bikes out the garage, Brett. I got an idea.'

Kenny greeted Dick the Fish warmly. Dick must be in his late seventies now, but still looked sprightly enough. His fashion sense hadn't changed: flat cap, shirt, braces, strides and tan dealer boots. 'You ain't changed one iota, Dick. You don't seem to age.'

'Try telling me bones that when I wake up in the morning. Takes me half hour to get outta bleedin' bed. You don't change either, son. Yer don't look no different to that cheeky urchin who used to hang around my stall trying to earn a bob or two.'

'What you having, Dick?' It had been Kenny's idea to get to the pub before it opened, rather than saunter in while Pete was already standing at the bar or something. He doubted Pete would recognize him, as Pete hadn't seen him in the flesh since he was a nipper. But there'd been plenty of photos of him in the press after he'd killed the copper, Harry Harrison, so there was a chance he might, even though that was years ago.

Having been a master of disguise during his armed-robbery days, Kenny had already prepared for his visit. A hooded grey Lonsdale tracksuit, black trainers and black woolly hat should do the trick. He'd even found his old Peacock's gym bag and brought that with him too. He looked like a boxing trainer, especially with his smashed-up hooter.

Kenny got the drinks in and had the same as Dick. A

172

pint of Guinness and a brandy chaser. He sat with his back towards the bar and door.

'So, how you doing, Ken? Sharon and the kids OK? I often see your Aunt Nell out and about, and your mum don't change, does she? Had that same hairstyle since the sixties. Kept herself well, though. Still a pretty lady.' Dick leaned closer to Kenny. 'Too good for you know who,' he hissed. Dick had never liked Pete Terry. Flash bastard with too much to say for himself. He had no idea what Kenny was planning to do, but was hoping he'd give him a bloody good hiding. It was about time someone did.

Kenny chatted about his family, but not Pete. Dick had no idea what he'd been through as a child. He'd never told anybody apart from his nan and granddad, Aunt Nell, Shal and Alan. You kept stuff like that in the family, didn't you.

Unusually for him, Kenny felt a tad anxious. Gut instinct told him that today wouldn't be another wasted journey. He knew any moment; he was going to be in close proximity to that bastard once again.

There were only two other customers in the pub. Old men. Therefore, there was no need for Dick to kick him so hard under the table. Shivers ran down Kenny's spine as he heard that voice, same as he used to when he was six years old, cowering in the corner of the room or desperately trying to find somewhere to hide, knowing 'Uncle' Pete had come home from the pub, pissed.

There was no mistaking those not-so-dulcet tones. None at all.

'This is getting boring now, Beau. Can't we play football again?' puffed Brett. His brother had made him race him on the bike up and down the garden continuously for the past half hour.

'No. Told ya, got a good idea. Keep racing me.'

Beau always called the shots, so Brett didn't argue. 'OK. But why?'

Craning his head to see what Tansey was currently doing, Beau hoped she'd hurry up with whatever it was. 'You'll see why. Soon.'

Kenny knocked back another chaser before glancing around. His jaw twitched furiously. Pete was with another bloke, telling the barmaid a story he obviously thought was hysterical because he was the only one in fits of laughter.

'Thinks he's God's gift to women. Always has done,' whispered Dick.

As Pete glanced towards them, Kenny quickly looked away. Pete was younger than his mother, so seeing as his mum turned sixty this year, he must be mid-fifties. He still had those sharp features. Thin face, pointy nose. He hadn't gone grey, his hair was still brown. But he was shorter than Kenny remembered. Probably about five foot nine. Whereas Kenny always imagined him to be over six foot.

'He's coming over,' mumbled Dick.

'Tricky Dickie. How you doing? Still chopping up those poor live eels?' chuckled Pete. He knew Dick didn't like him and the feeling was mutual. Cantankerous old sod, Dick was.

'None of your bloody business. Trot on. Go on. On your way.'

Kenny felt the hairs on the back of his neck stand up as he felt a hand grip his shoulder. 'Who's your pal? I didn't know you had any,' laughed Pete.

Anger surged through Kenny's veins. He turned around and stared Pete in his evil dark eyes. He reminded Kenny of someone now, somebody famous, but Kenny couldn't think who. 'Get your fucking hand off me. Like, now.'

Pete did as asked. The bloke looked slightly familiar and didn't look like one to be messed with. He had hard features, like an ex-boxer. 'Sorry, mate. No offence intended.'

'I ain't your fucking mate,' spat Kenny.

The look on Pete Terry's face was priceless. So much so, Dick the Fish burst out laughing.

'Right, this is what we gonna do. We race a couple more times, then when I count to five, we race really fast. Fast as we can. Then, when we get near the back doors, I'm gonna knock into your bike and then we both make sure we hit the ladder,' explained Beau.

'But Tansey will fall off.'

'Yeah. And that serves her right for slagging us off.'

Brett chewed his thumbnail. 'But what about the baby?'

'The baby'll be fine 'cause we're hitting the back of the ladder and Tansey will fall on her back.'

'Dad'll go mad at us,' warned Brett.

'No. He won't. As soon as I hit your bike, just aim for the ladder, OK? I'll do the talking afterwards. You just say I hit your bike, which'll be true.'

'OK.'

Tansey had a big smile on her face as she unclipped the second curtain. She'd finally plucked up the courage a fortnight ago to pay her mum's best friend a visit. She'd left a letter there for her mum and today her mum had called her for the third time. It was wonderful to be back in touch. Tansey had told Donny and he was fine with the situation, as long as Matt wasn't involved.

Singing along to Orange Juice's 'Rip It Up', Tansey looked around startled as the twins' bikes collided. Seconds later, she flew off the ladder, smashed her head against the kitchen tiles and was knocked out cold.

Pete Terry felt very uneasy. The man he'd had the altercation with earlier was playing on his mind. Jenny the barmaid had never seen him before, neither had his pal, Tom. They couldn't even see his face properly because of the angle he was sitting. 'Let's make a move down the Working Man's Club eh, Tom?'

'I gotta stay 'ere. Need to pick that bit of dosh up off Robbo.'

Pete finished his pint. 'Do us a favour then, that geezer I mentioned, if he follows me outside, follow him.'

'Will do.'

'He's leaving,' Dick informed Kenny.

Kenny shot out of his seat. 'Oi, Uncle Pete. Don't remember me, do ya?' he bellowed, once outside.

Pete swung around. He was glad to see Tom had followed.

Kenny looked around and pointed at Tom. 'Unless you want a good hiding, I'd get back inside, you. Fucking nose ointment. Oh, and don't even think of calling the filth. 'Cause I hate grasses. I've killed many.'

'I'll be inside if you need me, Pete,' Tom said, before scarpering. He suffered from gout and bad arthritis. The stranger looked evil and if his problem with Pete was personal, he'd stay out of it. Gratefully.

'Get in the car, *Uncle* Pete,' Kenny spat, yanking open the passenger door.

Suddenly it dawned on Pete who this was. 'You're Vera's boy, ain't ya? Kenny?'

176

'Spot on. Now get in the fucking car. Don't worry. I ain't gonna kill yer. We just need to have a little chat about me muvver.'

Feeling his legs start to tremble, a reluctant Pete did as asked. What other choice did he have?

Having been awoken by the twins telling him there'd been an accident, Donny had rushed down the stairs, immediately dialled 999, then called his mum to come over to look after the kids.

Thankfully, Tansey was conscious again now. The emergency services had told him not to move her, so all he could do was hold her hand and whisper words of comfort. 'It's all gonna be OK, babe. The ambulance'll be 'ere soon.'

The twins looked on, their faces full of concern. 'She gonna be all right, Dad?' asked Brett.

'My baby. My little girl.' Tansey pointed at the twins. 'Get them away from me,' she shrieked. 'They did this on purpose. I know they did.'

His face full of innocence, Beau stared his father in the eyes. 'Dad, we didn't. Honest. We had an accident with our bikes. Didn't we, Brett?'

'Go in the garden and play, boys. And you, Harry,' ordered Donny.

'Noooo! Harry, you stay 'ere,' sobbed Tansey. 'They're evil, Donny.'

'Get outside and shut the doors,' Donny repeated to the twins.

Tansey had taken a bad bang on the head, was obviously still disorientated. Beau and Brett's behaviour had improved so much since living with him. They could still be rascals at times, but in a proper little boy way. They were always polite to Tansey too.

'Mummy won't die, will she?' Harry cried.

'No. Course not. Mum's gonna be just fine,' Donny replied.

'No. I won't be. They tried to kill me,' screamed Tansey.

About to stick up for his sons, Donny didn't have a chance to. The reason being, Tansey's waters broke. The baby was on its way. Over six weeks early.

Kenny drove Pete to a little dead end he knew in Bow. There was only garages, most of them unused these days. 'Get out the car,' he spat.

Knowing what Kenny had done to that copper, Pete was in a panic. He knew Vera disliked her son and vice versa, so she'd told him. Therefore, he hadn't thought there'd be a problem once they started dating again. However, he did remember not being very nice to Kenny as a child. But he was only a lad himself back then. He hadn't meant any real harm. 'I dunno what this is all about, lad, but I treat your mum good and proper. The love of my life, is Vera.'

'Yeah, right,' snarled Kenny, giving Pete a sharp body punch in the gut. 'I got eyes and ears, ya know. You've been shacked up with some young tart in Barking. A barmaid.'

Doubled over with pain, Pete tried to catch his breath before explaining. 'Sarah's me daughter. Your mum knows all about her. I've introduced 'em. Ask your mum, if you don't believe me. It ain't common knowledge, mind. I've not long found out meself.'

'Liar,' spat Kenny, giving Pete another hard punch to the stomach. 'Remember doing this to me as a kid, do ya? You always clumped me where the bruises couldn't be seen, didn't yer, big man? How old was I? Five, six – tops?'

Pete lay on his backside, desperately trying to catch his breath. Kenny had a bloody hard punch, and he was sure he'd just broken a rib or two. 'I'm sorry about that. I truly am. I was only young meself. No more than a teenager when I first met your mum. Please forgive me,' Pete panted.

'Never. I was only a teenager when my Donny was born. I didn't torture him, you lowlife piece of shit. You go anywhere near my mother again and I swear I will kill you. You say nothing to her about me paying you a visit either. You end it over the phone with her. Then you stay the hell away. Got me?'

Pete nodded miserably.

'Lie flat on your back,' Kenny demanded.

'What! Why?' Kenny's stony blue eyes had a look of madness about them. 'I'll do as you say, Kenny. I promise.'

'Remember taking your leather belt off and whacking my arse with it, do yer?'

'Erm, no. Did I?'

Kenny looked down at the wimp with hatred. 'Yes, and this is how painful it was.' Kenny then stamped repeatedly on Pete's right kneecap, before doing the same to his left.

Pete cried out in agony. Like a big baby. 'I can't move. You've broken me fucking legs. Please don't leave me. I can't move. I'll die 'ere.'

Knowing he'd been seen in the boozer, Kenny pondered his next move. 'Where's your wallet?'

Tears of pure pain ran down Pete's cheeks. 'In the back pocket of me strides.'

Kenny fished around, found the wallet and tucked it inside his own pocket. He could tell at least one of Pete's kneecaps were shattered, had heard that distinct sound of crunching bones. 'I'm gonna do you a deal. I'll drop you somewhere where you'll be found. On one condition: anyone asks, you say you got mugged. OK?'

'I'll say it. I will. I swear.'

Kenny smirked as he grabbed the tearful Pete by the lapels of his jacket and shoved him in the back of his motor.

Revenge was a blinding feeling.

CHAPTER FOURTEEN

Spring 1985

Kenny Bond ended the early morning call to Aunt Nelly, chuckling loudly to himself. Revenge was a great feeling, even years later.

Pete Terry had spent five weeks in hospital after their altercation. Both his kneecaps were smashed to smithereens and had needed operating on. Turned out Pete had been telling the truth about the bird in Barking, though. She was his long-lost daughter. Not that it mattered one iota to Kenny. Attacking Pete had been a therapeutic way to try to erase some memories of his horrible childhood, and it had worked.

Visualizing Pete hobbling frantically across Whitechapel High Road in a desperate attempt to avoid Aunt Nell, Kenny smirked. Pete had never contacted his mother again. No surprise really. There'd be no more jiving for Pete, not with those dodgy knees.

Kenny took his mug of coffee out to the garden. He was bored shitless lately. There were currently no irons in the fire, only the boat events.

The car scam had gone tits up when the geezer Alan's end had got greedy. He'd also started cutting and shutting for a little firm out of Brixton, then promptly got himself nicked.

The only good thing about having little to do was Kenny had been able to focus on his grandsons. The twins especially. He'd bought them air guns, taught them how to shoot, took them boxing and karate. He was determined that whatever life threw at them in future, they'd be able to handle it.

Beau and Brett were his prodigy, same as he'd been to his granddad. Donny was far too weak to carry on the Bond name with grit and style. The twins, however, were something special.

'Alfie. Please stop screaming. You're going to make Mummy crash if you don't be quiet.' Tansey had tears in her eyes as she barked her orders. Alfie had a habit of making her cry on a daily basis.

When Alfie failed to stop the latest of a long line of tantrums, Tansey turned the radio up full blast. She would much rather listen to Steve Arrington's 'Feel So Real' than the screeches of the son she had failed to bond with.

Tansey blamed the twins. Had something happened to Alfie when she'd fallen off that ladder? Because there was definitely something wrong with the child. He'd been a late crawler and walker, but she'd just put that down at the time to him being born premature.

That wasn't the case now though. Alfie demanded attention from the moment his eyes opened in the morning, never listened to a word she said, had no attention span whatsoever and turned violent during his regular tantrums. Many a time he would try to kick or bite her, sometimes succeeding.

Tansey looked at her red-faced son through the interior mirror. When he wasn't creating havoc, he looked quite handsome. His hair was darker than hers and Donny's, but he had Donny's big brown eyes. However, when he was performing like he was now, he looked as ugly as sin. At times, he actually reminded her of Damien, that awful boy out of that horror movie *The Omen*.

As Alfie's hysterics continued, not for the first time, Tansey wished he had never been born.

'I got you some of that nice boiled bacon you like and the rolls are black as the ace of spades.' The more burnt the roll, the more her husband enjoyed them. 'Want salad in yours? Or tomato?' shouted Sharon Bond.

'Mustard, babe.' Kenny threw the *Sun* on top of the other two newspapers. They were all full of doom and gloom. It had been a terrible month for football. Firstly, the Bradford City stadium fire where fifty-six poor souls had died. Then last night, he and Shal had looked on in horror as a human stampede and a collapsing wall at the Heysel Stadium had resulted in another load of innocent people losing their lives.

Remembering he was yet to watch the latest *Crimewatch*, Kenny switched on the video recorder. *Crimewatch* was a relatively new programme, having started last year, and Kenny loved it. So did Alan and every other crook he knew. Many a time he thought he recognized someone in the 'Wanted' section. Kenny would never grass though, even if he had no time for the bastard the Old Bill were hunting.

'I couldn't sleep, thinking about those poor fans last night. There's thirty-odd dead now, it said on the radio,' Sharon told Kenny as she handed him his lunch.

'I know. But shit happens. You mustn't let it upset you

183

too much. I gotta go out this afternoon. Meeting me drinks bloke. The boat needs stocking up, as we've got a few parties coming up soon.'

'Mum wants to go into Romford, so I'll go for a mooch round the shops with her.'

Kenny didn't reply. He was too fixated by the first reconstruction. A violent attack and burglary on an elderly couple in Cambridgeshire. The poor old geezer had died of a heart attack during the vicious assault.

'Fucking scumbags,' Kenny mumbled as a photo of the man's wife popped up on screen. Her face was black and blue and she was lying in a hospital bed with tubes coming out of her mouth. Her poor daughter was beside herself, while bravely telling the presenter, Sue Cook, how such an awful experience had ruined her and her families' lives.

Then Nick Ross said the two men had accents that suggested they were members of the Traveller community.

It wasn't until the photofit popped up that Kenny spat out his boiled bacon roll. There was no two ways about it. That thin, sour-faced shitbag was none other than his old crooner of a cellmate, Freddie Tamplin.

'Sorry I'm late, Mum. I've had murders with this one again,' explained Tansey. Thankfully, before the journey ended, Alfie had cried himself to sleep.

'Just lay him down next to me, love,' smiled Penny. Unbeknown to Terry or the rest of her family, she'd been meeting Tansey on a Thursday for lunch since before Alfie was born. Penny loved spending time with her grandsons, but Harry was attending pre-school now, so she only got to see him in the school holidays.

The only grandson Penny had no contact with was Jamie. Tansey often showed her photos of her eldest, but reckoned he was a problematic child also and she didn't want to mess with his head.

Tansey asked how her father was, then plastered on a false smile as her mother rambled on about Matt and the kids.

While she had yet to remarry, Matt had wasted no time in proposing to his work colleague, Jayne. They had two children, a boy and girl. It hurt Tansey deeply that her father treated her ex's kids as though they were his own grandchildren and had no interest in his own flesh and blood.

'How's Charlee?' enquired Tansey. Her sister was engaged to a copper, which no doubt her dad was over-joyed about.

'She's good. Very excited. It's only twelve weeks until the big day now.'

As her mum droned on about the wedding plans, Tansey smiled through gritted teeth. She would've loved to see her younger sister get married, but her mum had made it clear that she wouldn't be welcome. Her name was never mentioned indoors. The forgotten, banished daughter. 'Waiter, could you bring us over a bottle of chardonnay, please?'

Penny tutted. She worried about Tansey lately. Her daughter was a permanent bundle of nerves. 'You shouldn't be drinking, love. Not if you're driving with Alfie in the car.'

'I'm only gonna have one or two. Give me a break, Mum. I don't go out very often.'

Charlie Saunders gestured for Donny to follow him into the kitchen. 'Sit at the table, lad. D'ya want a beer?'

'Erm, yes please.' Donny had no idea what this was

about. All he knew was what his nan had told him: 'Your granddad wants to see you to discuss something important.'

Wondering if he'd done something wrong, Donny dubiously sipped his bottle of Holsten Pils.

'Do you remember years ago, I used to tell you that when me and your nan finally retired, we would like to move to Spain?'

'Yeah. You used to say that quite a lot.'

'Well, that time has come. I've never been the same man since I lost a leg and I think a change of scenery would do me the world of good. A lot of me old mates live in Spain – some of them on the run over there an' all.'

'I'm so sorry about your accident, Granddad. It was my fault, bringing trouble to your door.'

'It wasn't your fault. Shit happens in life and it was just one of those things. Wrong place, wrong time. Anyway, that new leg they fitted me last year has given me a new lease of life. No pain like that other bastard thing. I feel almost human again.'

'Thanks, and I'm so pleased you're happy with your new leg. I ain't 'arf gonna miss you and Nan if you move to Spain though.'

Charlie grinned. 'You'll be too busy to miss me.'

'Whaddya mean?'

'You'll be taking over the nursery – as the boss. All I want is twenty-five per cent of the profits, so your nan and I can live in style. The rest, Donny, is yours.'

Unable to believe his luck, Donny sat in his back garden, beer in hand, watching the twins playing football.

Beau and Brett were handsome lads, would break lots of girls' hearts when older, that was for sure. Blond hair, brown eyes. They'd be eight this June. But the thing that pleased Donny the most was their behaviour. They'd come on leaps and bounds since attending the school in Rainham that dealt with kids with behavioural problems and were two of the brightest there. Their teacher, Mr Price, was full of praise for them and had even told Donny they would be more than ready to attend a mainstream comprehensive school when they turned eleven.

'Great volley, Brett,' shouted Donny. 'Great save too, Beau.'

'Cheers, Dad,' the twins said in unison.

Donny shut his eyes. Brett seemed to have gotten over his terrible ordeal, but he never would. Donny could remember everything that happened as though it were yesterday.

A couple of days after his dad had murdered Eric, the Old Bill had turned up with a social worker in tow. They'd already been to see Lori, who'd told them that Eric had looked after the twins alone on Christmas Eve and he must be to blame.

Donny was forced to attend meeting after meeting and had regular nosy parkers turning up at his home before it was decided he'd get full-time custody of the twins. The social workers weren't stupid. They'd seen the state of Lori and her home, and Donny had reiterated that Lori was a smackhead and a danger to the kids.

The police put a warrant out for Eric's arrest, but obviously couldn't find him. His pal Jonathan told the police he'd woken up one morning and Eric was gone, so they assumed he'd done a runner.

Brett was given some counselling, but he didn't like talking to a stranger or reliving the ordeal, so after a couple of sessions that was knocked on the head. Beau was also spoken to, but thankfully Eric had never touched him. Donny had no idea if Brett actually understood the seriousness of what had happened to him, or if he had told Beau.

Lori's mum got in touch about a month after the first police visit to tell Donny that Lori had gone into rehab. That turned out to be a waste of time and money. Within a month of leaving rehab, Lori was back on the gear. Donny was pleased, as when she was briefly clean she'd rung him at work, begging to see the boys. He'd told her where to go.

Donny's thoughts turned to Tansey. Their relationship was a shadow of what it once was. They still slept in the same bed, but rarely had sex anymore. He had to get up at silly o'clock, so would get his nut down early and leave her downstairs guzzling wine.

'Dad, can you be goalie?' shouted Brett.

Donny snapped out of his thoughts. They still lived in the same property in Havering-atte-Bower; he'd had a big extension built. 'You bet I can, and no way will you score against me. Better than Ray Clemence, I am.'

Beau giggled. 'No you ain't. You're shit.'

Donny lifted Beau up and held him upside down. The boys liked football, supported Spurs like he did. 'I am not shit. Gonna save every shot.'

Beau laughed his head off and Brett joined in. They both loved living with their father. It was just a shame Tansey hadn't died when they'd pushed her off the ladder that time.

'Alfie, stop that. I mean it!' Tansey ordered. Her son had just lobbed a fish finger at her.

'No.' Alfie ate half of a chip and then threw the rest at

188

his mother. Even at his young age, he could tell she didn't like him, and he wasn't keen on her. He much preferred his dad.

'I'll kill him, Mum, before long. I swear I will,' Tansey spat, not realizing because she'd barely eaten anything and drunk a whole bottle of wine, her voice was louder than usual.

Clocking other diners looking their way, Penny's face reddened. 'Stop it now, darling,' she said, moving Alfie's plate away from him.

'Nooooo,' shrieked Alfie, kicking and punching the table.

'My goodness. What a brat,' Tansey heard a woman's voice say.

She turned towards the next table where two stuffy-looking old bats were sitting. By now, Alfie was screaming his head off and had thrown himself on the floor. Having also heard the comment, Penny said, 'Leave it, love.' She bent down to try to pick up Alfie, who then wriggled under the table like a snake.

Tansey stood up. 'Leave it? No. Why should I fucking leave it? See, you and all you other judgemental arseholes who are looking at me and my son. He's not normal. But he can't help it.'

'Sit down, Tansey. You're making a fool of yourself,' urged Penny. She had never felt so embarrassed in her life.

Tansey didn't even hear her mother's advice. She was too irate. 'I got pushed off a ladder by my fiancé's evil twins when I was pregnant. That is the result of the accident,' Tansey bellowed, pointing at Alfie.

Penny opened her purse and chucked thirty quid on the table. 'Come on, Tansey. We're going.'

'Nosy fuckers, the lot of ya,' shrieked Tansey.

'Charming,' said a man in a suit.

'And you can shut up too, you prick. I hope you have a kid with disabilities one day. I hope you all fucking do.'

'Tansey. Come on,' Penny urged, dragging the screaming Alfie towards the door.

Tansey picked up the glass of water her mother had been sipping and slung it over the two women who had started the argument. 'Keep your beaks out in future, ya pair of old witches.'

Head held high, Tansey then stormed out of the silent restaurant.

After stocking up the boat with booze, Kenny drove to his pal's car showroom. He'd done well for himself, had Alan. He still had the car lot over in Peckham that sold cheap crap, but also had a cushty site in Wanstead that sold top-of-the-range motors.

'Uncle Kenny!' shrieked five-year-old Ricky.

As his godson ran towards him, a massive smile on his gorgeous, chubby face, Kenny lifted him up and swung him in the air. 'How you doing, Little Man?'

Ricky poked himself in the chest. 'I a big man now. Working with Dad.'

Alan chuckled. He and Julia had been devastated when Ricky was born with Down's syndrome, but they wouldn't change one hair on his head now. He was so intelligent, loving and brought a smile to their faces all day every day. 'This is a nice surprise, Ken. Funnily enough, was gonna bell you later. It's Julia's birthday next month and I was wondering if you and Shal would have Ricky for the weekend? I'm gonna book somewhere nice, surprise her like. I would ask me daughter, but she's away herself that weekend.'

190

Kenny laughed and pinched Ricky's cheek. 'Oh, I dunno about that. All depends if Little Man promises to behave himself.'

'I be good. Promise,' beamed Ricky, pinching Kenny's cheek back. 'Can you take me fishing, Uncle Kenny?'

Alan rolled his eyes. 'He's been obsessed with fish ever since me dad took him over the lake. I can't leave him with Dad though – Steptoe's yard, his gaff, as you know.' Julia's parents had emigrated to Australia seven years ago to be near Julia's two sisters and their grandchildren in Perth. Alan's dad Cliff was a good granddad, but since his mum had died, the house was a shithole. No way would Julia let Ricky stay there, or Cliff stay at theirs.

'Be our pleasure to have him stay, mate. You know Shal loves him as much as I do.'

'But can we go fishing?' repeated Ricky, clapping his hands excitedly.

'Course we can,' winked Kenny, putting the wriggling lad down.

'Right, go do some work if you wanna get paid,' ordered Alan. 'Tess needs your help in her office.' Tess was Alan's secretary.

'You know a few do-as-you-likes, don'tcha?' asked Kenny.

'Erm, only from the other car lot. I wouldn't class any as friends. Want a cuppa or something stronger?'

'Something stronger sounds good.'

As Alan poured the whisky, Kenny filled him in on the *Crimewatch* reconstruction. Alan had seen the programme and was appalled by the crime also. 'I know it was him, Al. Freddie Tamplin. I shared a cell with the shitbag, recognized his ugly mug as soon as that photofit popped up. He was in the Scrubs for similar when I was in there, that's why I took his eye out. You can guarantee that's why he wore tinted glasses an' all. No eye or a glass job's gonna be a bit of a fucking giveaway, ain't it?'

'Listen, I know we're not snitches, but considering the seriousness of the crime, I'd be inclined to ring the Old Bill anonymously from a callbox.'

Kenny shook his head vehemently. 'Nah. No point. I've done enough bird to know where he'll go. He'll be put on the nonce wing for his own safety. Get treated like kings on that wing in comparison to a normal lag. Listen 'ere, when I took that bastard's eye out, I warned him I'd finish him off if he ever targeted old people again. I want you to do some digging, get Mick or someone to ask around, find out where the scumbag lives.' Big Mick ran the Peckham car lot for Alan.

'Will do. But I wouldn't hold your breath, mate. They're a different breed, Travellers.'

Knowing her daughter was in no fit state to drive, Penny insisted Tansey leave her car at the restaurant and pick it up the following day.

Donny was out the front washing his Jaguar XJ6 when a car he didn't recognize pulled up and Tansey and the kids got out. He'd taken the day off work to look after the twins as their school was shut for a teacher training day. 'Where's your motor? You ain't had an accident, have ya?'

Penny stepped out the car. She'd only ever met Donny the once, when he'd come round the house when she lived in Havering-atte-Bower. He no longer looked like the fresh-faced teenager she remembered. He still had a boyish look about him but was broader and taller. 'You go inside with the kids, Tansey. I want to speak to Donny alone.'

'I don't think so,' Tansey hissed. 'I'm not a child. I'm not having you two talking behind my back.'

All of a sudden, the twins appeared at the front door, 'Who's that, Dad?' asked Beau.

Penny studied the twins. Their blond hair was cropped and they had mischief written all over their scrunched-up faces.

'Tansey's mum,' Donny replied. 'Tans, just take the kids inside, will ya? Beau, Brett, you go inside too.'

'Let's talk in my car,' Penny said coldly. Tansey's name was unmentionable indoors and it was all Donny's bloody fault that her one-time close family had been ripped to shreds. Penny explained that her daughter had necked a whole bottle of wine to herself and then made a scene at the restaurant. 'She looks awful, Donny. I can't believe how she's let herself go. How much is she drinking indoors?'

'I dunno. I go to bed at ten most nights 'cause I have to get up so early.'

'Well, you're going to have to keep more of an eye on her. I think she turned to drink when *you* cancelled the wedding last summer. That was the start of it.'

Donny and Tansey had been due to marry last August. The registry office had been booked and a small reception for just close family and friends. Nothing too elaborate, as Donny was saving up to buy them a bigger home. But a series of rows had scuppered their plans and Donny had cancelled the lot. 'Don't be putting the blame on me, Penny. She started drinking when she didn't give birth to the precious daughter she craved. I had no option but to cancel the bloody wedding, seeing as she didn't want the twins to be part of it. Until she accepts *my* sons, there won't be any wedding.'

'You must realize how difficult it is for Tansey. It's not easy for her, bringing up another woman's sons.'

'Well, I've had no problem raising Jamie, and he ain't mine. Relationships only work if there's a bit of give and take, Penny. I treat Jamie as though he's my own, always have done.'

'Alfie's behaviour isn't helping. Have you thought about taking him to a child psychiatrist?'

Donny saw red. 'Don't talk rubbish. The kid's not long turned two. Let me put you in the picture, Penny. Alfie doesn't play up so much when he's with me. Tansey was so sure she was having a girl, when Alfie was born, she didn't even want to hold him. It was me who had to get up in the middle of the night to give him a bottle. She wouldn't even breastfeed him, yet she breastfed Jamie and Harry. She still hasn't bonded with Alfie, so if anyone needs to see a psychiatrist, it's your daughter, not my son.'

Penny felt embarrassed. She'd no idea things were this bad. 'What about some help, Donny? Caring for five young children is bloody hard work. No wonder Tansey is losing her marbles.'

'We have a cleaner.'

'I know. But what about hiring a nanny to help Tansey out?'

Donny shrugged. He could certainly afford one now he was taking over the business. 'OK. If you think that'll help, I'll hire one.'

Tansey didn't fancy cooking, so Donny took a trip to the chippy.

'Can I eat mine out the paper, Dad?' asked Beau. His sausage in batter and chips always tasted better out of the paper.

'And me. I don't want a plate,' added Brett.

Donny smiled. They'd been as good as gold today, the twins. 'Yeah. Course you can.'

'We don't eat food out of the paper in this house,' snapped Tansey, putting two plates in front of Beau and Brett.

Donny looked at his fiancée with distaste. She'd been guzzling more wine; he could tell by her slurring. 'If they wanna eat it out the paper, they can. OK?'

'I'm eating mine out the paper an' all,' said Jamie. He'd been fuming earlier when he'd met his nan and it turned out Harry and Alfie had met her many times before.

'No. You are not. Put your food on the plate,' Tansey hissed.

Still annoyed, Jamie replied, 'Make me.' It wasn't fair. They had two nans and he wasn't even allowed to see one.

When Beau and Brett started to giggle, a furious Tansey stood up, grabbed their food and tipped it onto the plates. 'See what you've caused,' she screamed.

Harry thought the whole thing was hysterical, couldn't stop laughing. Alfie had the giggles too.

'Don't you ever talk to my sons like that again. Look at the fucking state of ya,' bellowed Donny. He stood up and tipped his son's food back onto the paper.

Tansey tried to grab Jamie's food, but he held onto it for dear life. There was a struggle, the paper split and the whole portion of chips and saveloy landed on the kitchen tiles.

When Jamie leapt up, picked up the chips and started lobbing them at his dishevelled mother, the other four boys were roaring. 'I hate you. You're a cunt,' Jamie shouted, before running upstairs to the safety of his bedroom.

There was shocked silence.

'Satisfied now, are ya?' Donny spat at Tansey.

She pointed at the twins. 'Don't be blaming me. It's their fault. They started all this.'

Donny was livid. 'No. They didn't. Go look at yourself in the mirror, Tans. You reckon you look like Leslie Ash. Don't make me laugh. You look more like Leslie Crowther just lately. You need to sort yourself out and fast. Otherwise, you and I are finished.'

Stunned at Donny's cutting words, Tansey let out a racking sob and bolted from the kitchen.

The following morning, Jamie was getting ready for school when the twins sauntered into his bedroom without knocking. 'Whaddya want?' he asked warily. They hadn't picked on him for a while now, but that was only because he steered well clear of them. He spent most of his time in his bedroom, alone.

Beau grinned. 'We thought you were well cool last night, ya know, what you did and said to your mum.'

'Yeah. It was proper funny,' added Brett. 'Especially when you called her a cunt,' he chuckled.

'Well, she is one,' replied Jamie.

'We wondered if you wanted to play football with us after school?' asked Beau. His and Brett's plan was to turn Jamie against his mother even more. That would serve the horrible bitch right for being so nasty to them.

'I dunno.' Jamie was cautious. They had never asked him to play football or participate in any game with them before, so why now?

CHAPTER FIFTEEN

Lori Boswell was a bundle of nerves. Desperate to see her sons again, today was extremely important to her and, having relied on drink and drugs for years as a relaxant, it was torture having to try to control her anxiety without a crutch.

Lori had been out of rehab for just over six weeks now and was as clean as a whistle. This was her second spell in rehab and this time she was determined to succeed.

The local authorities had been very good to her. They'd footed the bill for her latest treatment and her drug counsellor, Rob, had been the force behind putting pressure on the council to move her from that horrid house in Harold Hill, saying that she needed a fresh start to stay clean.

Lori now had a two-bedroom flat in Elm Park. Her mum and her mum's partner Steve had helped her decorate it. The twins' room was sparse at present, but was spotless, and Lori loved the Spiderman wallpaper Steve had hung on the main wall. She couldn't wait for her sons to see it.

Getting clean hadn't been easy for Lori. It had been an

emotional rollercoaster, mainly because what had happened to Brett. She knew that, had she been of sound mind, she would never have allowed that weirdo Eric inside her home. He even looked like a paedophile and had always shown an unhealthy interest in the twins. She could see that clearly now and was finding it hard to forgive herself for letting Brett down. She'd been a shit mother to Beau too. But as Rob kept drumming into her: 'There is nothing you can do about the past. But the future is in your hands.'

Lori paced the carpet her mum had treated her to. When she'd messed up after coming out of rehab the last time, her mother hadn't spoken to her for months. She was proud of her again now though, as this time Lori had sought help for herself.

Chewing her fingernails, Lori glanced at the clock. They'd be here soon. Her mum had offered to be here with her, but Lori knew that would have made her even more agitated. At twenty-five, the main thing she had learned in rehab this time was to face her fears. So what if she had an anxiety attack? It wouldn't kill her. 'What doesn't kill you makes you stronger' was another of Rob's favourite quotes.

Lori breathed deeply to calm herself. She also said a prayer, another thing she'd learned in rehab. 'God, grant me the serenity to accept the things I cannot change. The courage to change the things I can and the wisdom to know the difference.'

'Ooh, he's a bastard that Dirty Den. He treats Angie like shit, Donny.'

Donny rolled his eyes. A new soap, *EastEnders* had started in February and, like his mother and nan, Tansey was addicted to it. What was it with women and soaps?

Did they actually think they were real? 'Yeah, a right bastard.' Donny turned his attention back to his newspaper. There were riots and looting all over the country. HIV was grabbing big headlines too. Aids was a disease only gay blokes got though, so his dad reckoned.

Donny threw the paper to one side and shut his eyes. His grandfather had made good on the promise he'd made: from Monday, the business would be his. Tonight was his nan and granddad's farewell bash. It was being held at his mum and dad's. A marquee had been erected in the garden, a catering company had been hired and there was a band and DJ booked. Much to his surprise, his granddad had insisted he invite Tansey and Jamie to the party. 'Life's too short to hold grudges, lad. I know you love Tansey; therefore I want to leave England on a positive note. She's the mother of your kids, at the end of the day.'

'Dad, can you take me, Brett and Jamie to McDonald's? We want Big Macs,' said Beau.

'And chips,' Brett added.

'And a chocolate milkshake,' grinned Jamie.

'Jamie can't go, Donny. We're meeting my mum for lunch.' Tansey's father had retired from the police force a few weeks ago, so the regular Thursday lunch dates had gone out the window. She now had to meet her mum on the days her dad wasn't around, and today he was playing in a golf tournament.

Jamie dug his hands in the pockets of his Adidas tracksuit bottoms and scowled. 'I don't wanna go out with you and Nan. I want to go McDonald's with Beau and Brett.'

'You can't. Your nan's looking forward to seeing you,' Tansey snapped. She hated this sudden friendship with the twins. They were not a good influence on her son.

'Well, I ain't looking forward to see Nan, and you weren't

bothered about me seeing her when you were taking Harry and Alfie to see her without me, was ya? So you can fuck off.' Jamie loved being pals with the twins and knew his use of the F word would impress them.

When the twins started to giggle, Tansey leapt out of the armchair. Donny grabbed her arm. 'Let's not fight today. If Jamie don't wanna go with you, no point in making him. You can still take Harry and Alfie with you.' His two youngest were currently at the park with Renata, the Spanish housekeeper/nanny he'd hired.

Tansey hadn't touched a drop of alcohol in weeks. Instead, her GP had prescribed Valium to help her cope. Deciding she would pop another pill, Tansey waved her arms in the air. 'I give up! Do whatever! I'm going back to bed.'

'You OK, babe?' Kenny slipped his arms around his wife's waist. Today was going to be tough for her, he knew that much.

'I feel a bit sad again. I am happy for them, Ken. But I'm gonna miss 'em so much. Mum's the only person I go shopping with these days. She's me best mate an' all.'

'Wrong! I'm your best mate.'

'Oh, you know what I mean.'

Kenny held Sharon's face in his hands. 'It's gonna be fine and whenever you're missing 'em, I promise I'll book you a flight and you can be on the next plane.'

'But who will cook for you? And clean?' Sherry was no longer living at home, had moved in with her boyfriend.

'You make me sound like an amputee, Shal. I have got a pair of hands, ya know, and I can cook a mean fry-up. There's also places called takeaways, restaurants and cafes. I won't waste away, honest.' Kenny glanced at his watch.

'Right, I'd better make a move soon. Gonna pop over Nan and Granddad's grave with Nell before we pick misery guts up. Why don't you come with me?'

'No. I'll pop down Mum and Dad's, while I still can.'

The doorbell rang. 'I'll get it. Make us a quick cuppa, Shal, before I go.'

Expecting to see one of the neighbours, Kenny could not believe his eyes. It was none other than that no-good bastard, Pete Terry. Kenny shoved him in the chest. 'You got some fucking front turning up 'ere. Who gave you my address?'

Pete held his hands up in surrender mode. It had taken a lot of guts for him to come here. But he had his mate waiting in the car and guessed Kenny wouldn't want blood on his hands on his own doorstep. 'Nobody, I swear. I got it from your mum's address book ages ago. Your mum didn't know. I was going to pay you a visit, ask your permission to propose to your mum at the time. I'm like you at heart, got old school values.'

'You'll never be like me while you've got a hole in your arse,' snarled Kenny.

Sharon poked her head outside the front door. She had no idea who the visitor was. 'Everything all right, Ken?'

'Yeah. Fine. Go back inside, love.' Kenny turned his attention back to Pete. Credit where due, the geezer had aged well. He was a looker and there wasn't one strand of grey in his brown hair. The outfit didn't fool Kenny though. The grey suit looked like something out of Mister Byrite's, the Crombie a fake from Petticoat Lane and the reek of aftershave was either Brut or Old Spice. 'Whaddya want? Only, I'm a busy man these days.'

'Firstly, I want to apologize for the way I treated you as a kid. I know I clumped you with me belt, which was wrong.'

'You can say that again,' hissed Kenny.

'My dad used to whip me with his belt. I didn't know any different back then, lad. I was still a teenager when I met your mum. A silly drunken one at that. But I'm different now. Older and wiser.'

'Oh for fuck's sake. You're not on *This Is Your Life*. Just spit out why you're 'ere, then piss off back under your rock.'

Pete's eyes welled up. 'I can't get over your mum. Not looked at another woman since Vera. I love her. On my life I do. That's why I came to see you. I want your permission to court Vera again. I promise you, I will never tell her it was you who put me in hospital that time. I stuck to my word, never told a soul, said I was mugged, like you asked me to. I swear to treat your mother like the princess she deserves to be treated as. Honest I do.'

Unable to stop himself, Kenny burst out laughing. His mother might be a lot of things, but with her attitude and gob, she was certainly no princess. A dragon, more like. 'Get on your knees then and beg.'

'Erm, me knees ain't great. Not since what you done, like. I struggle to bend them still and I limp badly.'

'Do it,' ordered Kenny, smirking as Pete began trying to position himself on his gravel.

His knees killing him, Pete felt a right idiot as he looked up at Kenny. He wasn't lying though. He truly loved Vera and would do anything for her. 'Kenny, I'm—'

'Stop right there,' Kenny interrupted. 'If you're gonna beg properly, you need to put your hands in the prayer position.' Kenny was thoroughly enjoying himself now. This was even better payback than smashing Pete's knee-caps to smithereens.

Doing as he was told, Pete said, 'I'm so sorry about the

202

past, son. Please forgive me and allow me to take care of your lovely mum. Surely, we're even now? That hiding you gave me still gives me the heebies.'

Kenny looked down at the prick and for the first time ever, felt pity for him. He reminded him of a starving dog, desperate for a treat. A weak excuse of a man. 'Right, firstly, we'll never be even. You're not fit enough to shine my shoes. Secondly – I ain't your son and if you ever again refer to me as such, I will break yer scrawny neck. And thirdly – you go near my muvver again and I swear I will dig a grave and bury you alive. You understand?'

Pete nodded despondently. 'Can you help me up, please?'

Kenny ignored Pete's outstretched hand. 'One of the things I remember about you the most is while cowering in the corner of the room, you'd spit at me and call me a "Nobody". How wrong were you, eh? Look at the size of me gaff. I got a wonderful wife, children, and grand-children. What you got eh, Big Man?'

'I shouldn't of come 'ere, Kenny. I'm sorry. I'll never bother you again. I promise.'

'Answer my fucking question,' bellowed Kenny.

'Nothing really. I ain't got much at all.'

'I know. Reason being, I've got eyes and ears every-where. You've got a poxy old council flat in Bethnal Green. You're up in court again soon on a robbery charge and you've been knocking off the barmaid in the Nags Head. Linda's her name, right?' Dick the Fish kept Kenny up to date with what was going on in his old manor. Life on the straight and narrow was dull, to say the least. If an opportunity arose to earn some proper readies, Kenny would grab it with both hands. Providing it wouldn't involved getting banged up again, of course.

'Erm, yeah.' Pete was unnerved. Was Kenny having him watched?

'So why lie to me? You told me you haven't looked at another woman since me muvver.'

'Linda means nothing to me. She's just a distraction. I meant every word I said about your mum. I love Vera.'

Seeing Pete struggle to get up for the third time, Kenny grabbed his arm and dragged him up. 'You must think I've just got off the banana boat. As for what my mother saw in you, she must've had shit in her eyes. Either that or you've got the biggest dick going.' Kenny kicked his prey up the arse. 'Goodbye, *Uncle* Pete. Been nice knowing yer, yer two-bob fucking nobody.'

CHAPTER SIXTEEN

Feeling on top of the world, Kenny sang along to 'Brown Sugar'. He loved a bit of the Rolling Stones. Jagger was a legend.

'Can you turn that bleedin' racket down? Nell and me can't hear ourselves think, let alone talk.' Vera Bond hated her son's driving. He drove far too fast in her opinion, which is why she always sat in the back of the car.

'Your wish is my command, Mother,' beamed Kenny. Watching that spiv trying to get back up off his gravel earlier, tears streaming down his boat race, had been one of the highlights of Kenny's life. Talk about what goes around comes around.

Vera watched her son through his interior mirror. He had a smile like a Cheshire cat, which could only mean one thing: he'd been up to no good. She poked him in the shoulder. 'What you looking so bleedin' happy about anyway? Won the football pools, have yer?'

'Nope. Shal's the one does the pools, not me. Look at the weather. Beautiful day. We've got a smashing party to look forward to. The finest grub and booze. What's there not to be happy about?'

Nelly was the next one to eye Kenny with suspicion. He'd definitely been up to something he shouldn't have.

'Well, I suppose there is one thing to be grateful for today.' Vera pursed her thin lips. 'We get to see the back of Maggie and Charlie. Never liked either of 'em. She's up her own arse and he looks like a pervert. Good riddance to bad rubbish.'

Feeling incredibly stupid, Lori sat on her sofa chain-smoking, a bottle of strong cider balanced between her legs. She hadn't had a proper drink since coming out of rehab, but seeing as she wasn't addicted to alcohol, she'd thought sod it. It might help her forget her earlier shame. She'd become so close to her drug counsellor, was sure he'd felt the same way, which was why she'd made a pass at him earlier – only to be rebuffed in no uncertain terms.

When Madonna's 'Crazy For You' came on the radio, Lori turned it off. She'd loved that song. It had reminded her of Rob. How had she read the signals so wrong? Her cheeks burned just thinking about what a mug she'd made of herself. The thought of not seeing Rob again made her feel physically sick. She'd become reliant on his visits and the support he'd given her.

The knock on the door made Lori jump. The buzzer hadn't sounded. Positive it must be Rob returning to check on her and sort things out, Lori flung open her front door.

'Hello, Lori. Long time no see.'

Lori looked at the unwelcome visitor in horror. It was none other than Gary Acorn.

Feeling incredibly anxious, Tansey popped another Valium before leaving for the party. She'd wanted to have a couple of drinks tonight, but Donny was totally against the idea and was bound to be watching her like a hawk.

Donny pulled up outside his grandfather's. If Tansey wanted to leave early, she could take the car and he'd get a cab home later. 'You all right?'

Tansey forced a smile. 'Yeah.'

Donny handed Tansey the car keys. 'Stick them in your handbag, babe.' He turned to their sons. 'And you lot – best behaviour tonight, or else.'

Lori had reluctantly let Gary in, but only because he had puff and booze. It had been yonks since she'd had a spliff and after the day she'd had, she needed one.

'So, what you been up to then? You look really well. I heard you'd moved round this way. Nice flat.'

'You've got some fucking front, turning up here. You left me high and dry after your nonce of a brother raped my son. Or have you conveniently forgotten that?'

'Nah. Course I ain't. Eric's never been seen since. I'm really sorry for what happened and the way I treated you. I was bang out of order. I think I was just scared at the time and embarrassed.'

'Don't bother apologizing now. Chucked you out, your bird, has she?'

'Nah. I left her ages ago. I'm living in Dagenham now. Got a council flat near the Fiddlers.'

'So, what you doing here then?'

Gary smiled. 'I wanted to apologize to you in person. I also miss you, Lori. We had some good times as well, eh?'

'Not really,' snapped Lori.

Gary delved into his pocket, then waved a small see-through bag in the air. 'Oh yes we did.'

Lori looked at the content with longing. Then she

thought of her mum, who was so very proud of her at present. Not for the first time in her life, Lori was torn between the devil and the deep blue sea. It was thinking of Rob that swayed her decision.

'Hello, Tansey. Lovely to see you,' lied Charlie Saunders. He was thankful Donny was yet to marry the sour-faced prat. Shit mother she'd turned out to be as well.

'Hello, Tansey,' Maggie said, her smile false, before turning her attention to the boys.

Donny had told Tansey not to mention anything about the shooting, so Tansey grabbed her eldest son's arm. 'I bet you wouldn't recognize Jamie now. Hasn't he grown?' she said stupidly. The pair of old goats hadn't seen Jamie since the day after Charlie had been shot.

Charlie smiled. 'All right, Jamie?'

'Yes, thanks.'

'Go out the back and grab yourselves a drink. The DJ's about to start. Your mum and dad are over there, Donny,' said Charlie, pointing in Kenny and Shal's direction.

Feeling panicky and desperate to escape, Tansey dragged Jamie towards the marquee.

'Didn't mind me bringing an extra guest, did yer?' Alan Davey grinned as he put a proud arm around his stunning daughter's shoulders.

Unlike his first born, who'd turned out to be a permanently stoned, long-haired waste of space and was currently residing at a kibbutz in Israel with some other losers, Alan and Julia could not be more proud of Louisa. She was intelligent, caring, ambitious and a brilliant big sister to Ricky. 'Tell Kenny about your new job, Lou.'

Louisa explained she'd landed her dream job as a stylist and make-up artist in London.

'That's brilliant, sweetheart. I'm so pleased for you.' Kenny took a wad of cash out of his pocket and handed Louisa four fifty-pound notes. 'Treat yourself to a night out with your pals, to celebrate, like.'

'No. I can't take all that. It's very kind of you, but it's far too much,' protested Louisa.

'Take it, babe. You'll offend Kenny if you don't,' Alan insisted.

'Your dad knows the score,' winked Kenny. 'Where's Little Man, babe?'

'He was sick in the car. Mum was well prepared, put him in an old tracksuit and brought his party outfit separately. She's gone straight to the bathroom to clean him up and change him. Ricky's always travel sick, isn't he, Dad?'

'Sure is. Poor little sod. I can see your mum heading this way, Lou. Before Ricky clambers all over Kenny, I need a word in private. I'll be back in five.' Without waiting for a reply, Alan grabbed his pal's arm and led him to a quiet spot. 'He's been nicked.'

'Who?'

'Tamplin.'

'How d'ya know?'

'Big Mick rung me this morning. He heard it through the grapevine. Then on the way 'ere, I heard on the radio, they'd arrested two geezers in connection with *that* case. How old was Freddie? I think both are mid-thirties.'

'I dunno. But he would be about that age now, I suppose. Bollocks! Spoiled me day, that has. He'll get some cushty short sentence, you mark my words. Ain't like he physically killed the old boy, is it? The poor old sod had a heart attack through shock.'

'Don't let it spoil your day. Things happen for a reason sometimes. You really wouldn't have wanted to start a war with that mob. You know what the pikeys are like. Stick together like glue, mate.'

'Scumbags. The fucking lot of 'em.'

'Lucinda! I thought it was you. What you doing here?'

'Tansey! Oh my God! It's been years since I've seen you. You look great. I love your dress.'

Lucinda had once had a horse at the same stable as Trigger. She was quite posh and the last person Tansey expected to see at Charlie's farewell party.

'My husband and I live down Dark Lane,' Lucinda explained. 'Last I heard, you'd married a policeman.'

'Yeah. We split up. I'm with Charlie's grandson Donny now. We've got two sons together and I've got Jamie from my first marriage. Who did you marry?'

'Glen Richardson, the scrap metal dealer. I didn't know you were with Donny. Charlie and Maggie have never said. Glen and I have two kids, a boy and a girl. Come and meet them and then introduce me to your brood. I'm so excited to see you again.'

Tansey smiled. Perhaps tonight would turn out better than she'd expected.

The singer was amazing. A young handsome blond bloke dressed in a black dinner suit, who sang Sinatra, Dean Martin and Bobby Darin.

The party was buzzing. Charlie had invited around two hundred guests. He and Maggie were up dancing, as were many others.

Donny watched his grandparents, then leaned towards his father. ''Ere, you once told me that Granddad had been a bastard to Nan back in the day. What did he do, Dad?'

'Oh, it don't matter now. The past is the past.'

His mum and nan were up dancing with his sister and Tansey was sitting with her pal. The boys had been well behaved so far, which was a bonus. The little uns were playing with some other kids, and the twins and Jamie were stuffing their faces. 'Nah, go on. Tell me. I want to know.'

'You must never say anything to anyone. Especially not your mother.'

'I won't. I swear.'

'Charlie was knocking off a younger bird. I put the kibosh on it when I found out. She had a kid by him, by all accounts. A boy.'

Donny was stunned. His granddad and nan had always seemed so besotted with one another. 'Jesus wept! Did Nan know? How long ago was this? Does he see his son?'

'It was years ago, long before I got put away. I gave Charlie a clump. Not sure if your nan knew, but the slippery old sod often took his fancy piece away for weekends. They even went to Jersey together. I found out. Gave it to him good and proper. If your mum would've found out, it would've broken her heart. Dunno if he sees the son, but I should imagine he supported the kid financially. I never felt the same about him after that, and he's been wary of me since.'

'I'm in shock.'

'Don't let it spoil your night. As I said, it was a long time ago.'

*

211

With the party in full swing, Tansey felt the odd one out, not drinking. No expense had been spared, even champagne was being given out freely.

'Have a drink, Tansey. Leave your car here,' suggested Lucinda, waving a bottle of champagne in front of her friend.

Tansey looked around to see where Donny was.

What Tansey didn't realize as she had one flute, then another, was that the twins were watching her like two evil hawks.

The twins weren't silly. They urged Jamie to do the grassing.

'My mum's on the booze, Donny. I think she's really drunk,' Jamie blurted out.

The twins and Jamie followed Donny as he stormed over to where Tansey was sitting.

Having now got the flavour, Tansey was on her fourth flute of champers and was too busy talking to Lucinda to see Donny heading towards her like a raging bull. Donny grabbed his fiancée's arm. 'You drinking?'

Seeing Lucinda, Glen and everybody else on the table look her way, Tansey cringed. 'I've had one glass of champagne. Why? Is that a crime?'

'No. But your eyes look glassy and that's because you were told to not drink on your medication.'

At that point, Tansey wanted the ground to open up and swallow her. She'd painted such a wonderful picture to Lucinda of her life with Donny. Now here he was, speaking to her like a child. 'Excuse me, Lucinda.' Tansey dragged Donny away from the table. 'How dare you fucking show me up like that in front of my friend?'

As the argument continued, Beau, Brett and Jamie couldn't stop laughing.

Nelly Bond finished her second helping of food and put the paper plate on the grass. 'Bleedin' handsome that crab. Why don't you have some?'

Vera glanced at her sister with a look of disdain. Size of her and the way she shoved grub down her gullet was enough to put anybody off eating. 'I will later. What was you and my Kenny laughing about earlier?' Vera wasn't stupid, she knew she was often the butt of their humour.

'He was telling me some jokes,' lied Nelly. Kenny had actually been telling her about Pete turning up earlier.

'Really! What were they then?'

'Oh, you know. The usual Englishman, Irishman, Scottish bloke stuff.'

'Nan, Aunt Nelly, meet Andy, my boyfriend,' beamed Sherry.

Andy politely greeted the two women and then was promptly dragged away by Sherry to meet somebody else.

'I never thought I'd see the day Sherry was courting serious,' Nelly remarked. Her niece was loud, liked a drink, was a bit of a handful.

'Well, she don't wanna be marrying him,' said Vera. 'He's a short arse, look at him. She ain't that tall either. They have kids, the poor bastards'll be dwarves.'

After Tansey had called him a 'Condescending arrogant arsehole' then promptly stormed off, Donny hadn't seen hide nor hair of her. He could no longer spot Harry and Alfie either. Surely the stupid cow hadn't driven his car home?

Donny went out the front to check and was livid when his BMW was nowhere to be seen.

'If you're looking for Tansey, she left in tears,' Sharon Bond informed her son. 'Did you have a row or something?'

'Yeah. Were Harry and Alfie with her, Mum?'

'Yes. She said they were both tired.'

Whether it was the three Valium she'd taken or a mixture of the Valium and champagne, Tansey didn't know. But suddenly she felt tired, was struggling to keep her eyes open.

Having already had to stop the car once, just to get out and gulp some fresh air to steady herself, Tansey was relieved she was only five minutes from home. The boys were asleep, thankfully, and she wasn't used to driving Donny's 7 Series BMW. It was too wide for her; she'd already knocked a wing mirror off, which Donny was bound to go ballistic at her for in the morning.

Thinking of Lucinda again, tears of anger poured down Tansey's cheeks. She'd felt that stupid and ashamed, she hadn't even gone back to the table to say goodbye to her old friend.

Her handbag was on the driver's seat, so Tansey tipped it upside down to find a tissue.

It was at that very moment that a car came round the unlit bend at mega speed with its beam on. Blinded by the light, Tansey screamed as she lost complete control of the car and smashed at speed into a clump of trees.

With the party nearing the end, Donny couldn't help but chuckle at the sight of two old birds who'd stacked it while dancing to 'New York, New York' and were having all kinds of bother trying to get back on their feet.

214

It had certainly been a cracking party, must have cost an arm and a leg. There'd been far too much grub, and every kind of seafood you could imagine.

'Did ya try Tansey again?' Kenny asked, as he plonked a beer down in front of his boy.

'Yeah. Still no answer.'

'She's on a wind-up with you, son. Why not stay at mine and mum's tonight with the boys? Give her something to fucking worry about. You ain't even gotta rush back. Stay for breakfast and dinner, then I'll drop you home.'

Donny grinned. 'D'ya know what, that's the best idea I've heard all day.'

Roger and Yvonne Chamberlain were on their way home from a wedding reception in Blackmore, when Yvonne spotted something through the passenger-side window.

'Oh my God, Roger! Stop! There was a car in that clump of trees, looked like it had come off the road. The back lights are still on.'

Roger reversed his car a few yards and put on his hazard lights. This was a very dark and quite narrow road. 'Get out of the car, Yvonne. Stay close to the trees, my love, in case some drunk comes flying around the bend and hits us.'

Roger urged his wife not to follow him as he began breaking off branches, clearing a path to the car. The next thing he heard was a child's anguished screams.

It was 6 a.m. the following morning before the police located Donny. They'd finally managed to get Charlie and Maggie's details out of young Harry, so had knocked there first.

Hearing the pounding on the front door, a heavy-hearted Sharon threw on her dressing gown and stumbled down the stairs. Her mum was standing outside with two policemen and Sharon could not hide her shock. 'Whatever's happened? Is it, Dad?'

'No. It's Tansey, love. There's been a car accident,' explained Maggie. 'Where's Donny?'

'Upstairs – Donny, Donny. Come quick,' bellowed Sharon.

Donny didn't know if he was dreaming when he heard his mother calling him. 'What's going on?' he mumbled.

'The police are here. Tansey's had an accident in your car.'

'Oh no.' Donny bolted down the stairs in only his boxer shorts. 'What's happened? Are my sons OK? Is Tansey all right?' he gabbled.

The policeman looked frightened to death at the prospect of walking into a cop killer's house, but he pulled himself together and informed Donny, 'Tansey and your sons are at Oldchurch Hospital. They were involved in a motoring incident where they hit some trees. We were notified early hours of this morning by a passer-by who thankfully spotted the vehicle. None of their injuries are deemed to be life-threatening.'

'Fuck!' Donny ran back up the stairs. 'Dad, Dad. Get up. We need to go to Oldchurch.'

Seeing his sons lying side by side in the kiddie's ward of Oldchurch literally ripped Donny's heart out. Both had scratches and bruises all over their little bodies and faces. Harry had a big gash across his nose, Alfie a broken right arm. Thankfully, they'd had seat belts on, otherwise it would have been far worse.

'You gonna go and see Tansey now, boy?' Apparently, Tansey was suffering from concussion.

'I don't even wanna look at her, Dad, if I'm honest. She's bound to have been over the limit. One glass of champagne, my arse. I ain't bothered about losing me fucking car, even though it cost a fortune. I'm just relieved me boys are gonna be all right. I'll never forgive her for this. She can go to hell. She ever thinks I'm marrying her now, she's got another think coming.'

Kenny arrived home alone from the hospital, chucked his keys on the kitchen table, then explained to Sharon what had happened.

'Those poor little mites. They must've been in so much pain, Ken, and scared out their wits. She'll be getting a piece of my mind, will Tansey. She could've bloody killed those boys.'

'Tell me about it! Thank God neither are seriously injured. The dopey prat could've broken their necks, backs, paralysed 'em for life. Giving it large down at Oldchurch, Donny was – he'll never forgive her, she can go to hell, all the usual old flannel. Give it a couple of weeks, he'll be dancing to her tune again. Mark my words. How me and you ever produced such a weakling of a son, Shal, I'll never know.'

'Don't be too hard on him. He loves her. She's the mother of his kids. He ain't gonna walk away from her, is he?'

'He walked away from the twins' mother sharpish enough,' Kenny reminded his wife.

'He was only a kid himself back then.' Sharon would never forget what a rock Donny had been to her while his father was in prison. She was no fan of Tansey's, but would always have her son's back.

'No. He weren't, Shal. He was the same age as we were when we were married with him. All I can say is she must be good in the fucking sack, Tansey, 'cause the tart ain't got no other outstanding attributes. She lives the life of Riley an' all. I'd have kicked her sorry arse out years ago if I were Donny.'

'No, you wouldn't. Not if you loved her like Donny does. Look at what life threw at us and we're still going strong. When you truly love someone, Kenny, you put up with anything they do. Even if it's wrong. Well, almost anything.'

Kenny held Sharon in his arms. 'Me and you ain't done bad, have we, girl? Whaddya mean by almost anything, though?'

'Playing away – that's the only thing I don't think I could forgive. It would destroy any love I have for you if I ever found out you'd cheated on me.'

'Bleedin' hell, Shal. That's a bit deep. You know full well I've never done the dirty on ya. I wouldn't dream of it. Anyway, do you honestly think any other old bird would suffer me?' chuckled Kenny.

'Not really, no. Especially after I'd taken a knife to your bollocks and chopped 'em off.'

'I dunno how we got into this conversation, so let's end it. I'm starving. What we got for lunch? Bollocks on toast?'

Playfully punching her husband in the chest, Sharon couldn't help but laugh.

Looking at her handsome husband, Sharon Bond felt the luckiest woman alive.

PART TWO

'Whoever walks in integrity walks securely, but he who makes his ways crooked will be found out.'

Proverbs 10:9

CHAPTER SEVENTEEN

Spring 1989

'I'm nearly there. Are you? Harder, Kenny. Fuck me harder.'

Kenny did as asked, watched her face as she orgasmed, then banged her even harder until he shot his own load, which ended up all over her stomach.

Even though she was supposedly on the pill, Kenny would never come up her. He might be a risk taker in many ways, but not when it came to stuff like this. Kenny kissed her once more, then got out the bed.

'You're not going already, are you? I was going to make us breakfast.'

'I'm meeting Donny for breakfast. Got a few irons in the fire I'm checking out today.'

'You coming back later? I'm happy to cook dinner for us again.'

'Erm, probably. I'll give you a bell this afternoon, let you know for sure. Dunno how long me bits of business are gonna go on for.'

Kenny showered, quickly got dressed, then not for the

first time accidentally referred to her as 'Shal'. He rolled his eyes and put his arms around her waist. 'Sorry, babe. Slip of the tongue.'

'No need to be sorry. You've been married a long time. I understand.'

'Thanks. Right, I'll be off now.'

'Hopefully see you later.'

Twenty-eight-year-old Abigail Cornell smiled as she shut the front door. Sharon could go and fuck herself as far as she was concerned. Kenny was her man now and she had no intention of letting him go. None whatsoever.

The rush hour traffic crawling, Kenny was deep in thought. He'd dug himself a hole and knew quite soon he'd have to dig his way out of it. Sharon had been living in Spain since last November, looking after her mum who had breast cancer.

Kenny had met Abigail, or Abi as he liked to call her, in a nightclub over the Christmas period. He and Alan had been over Walthamstow Dogs, had won a fair few quid, and it had been Al's idea they carry on celebrating in Charlie Chan's.

Alan had spotted Abigail first, reckoned she kept looking over and said she reminded him of Sharon in her younger days.

Kenny was shocked when he laid eyes on her. The likeness, uncanny. They got talking and Kenny immediately knew he was bang in trouble. His and Shal's sex life had been dead in the water for a long time. The way Abi looked at him literally sent shivers down his spine. She made him feel alive again.

Kenny's deep thinking was ended by his mobile ringing. It was Sharon. He chatted to her for over five minutes, experiencing that awful nauseous feeling of guilt he got whenever they spoke lately.

Ending the call with the words 'Love you too,' Kenny took a deep breath. He was nearly at the cafe now, needed to get his normal head back on. Donny was already suspicious, had been asking questions.

He had to knock young Abi on the head. None of his family could ever find out about his betrayal. They would never forgive him. As for Sharon, it would break her heart in a thousand pieces.

Kenny Bond shoved half a sausage in his mouth, wiped up the last of his yolk and brown sauce with crusty bread, then turned his attention back to his newspaper. One article in particular he found interesting, especially seeing as a pal had been telling him about how big ecstasy tablets were about to become in England.

When Kenny had first been released from prison, he'd had a hell of a lot of money squirrelled away, but there was little left now. Due to his warped sense of humour, he'd made a huge cock-up. *The Duchess* had been banned from holding any more tourist trips, due to him talking complete and utter bollocks. Donny had been livid about that, as he'd previously warned him to hire a proper tour guide.

He pushed the *Daily Mirror* Donny's way. 'You're still young. Whaddya know about ecstasy tablets and that illegal rave bash scene?'

'Not much. I'm hardly a teenager, I'll be twenty-bleedin'-nine soon. As it happens though, I do know a geezer who DJ's: Curtis. He reckons the underground scene that started off in Chicago is gonna go off with a bang over 'ere this summer. He's already booked up for numerous gigs. All illegal. Big bucks he's getting an' all.'

'Does he sell E?'

'How should I know? I ain't no druggie. Why you so interested anyway?'

Kenny snatched the paper back. There were too many eyes and ears in Rosie's Cafe for his liking. 'Let's talk later, on the boat.'

'Don't want it,' yelled five-year-old Alfie Bond, purposely knocking his bowl of cereal onto the new kitchen tiles, which resulted in one cracking.

Steam coming out of her ears, Tansey dragged her youngest son off the kitchen chair and smacked him hard on his bottom. 'You naughty boy. Go up to your room and get ready for school.'

'Nooooo,' screamed Alfie, chucking himself on the kitchen tiles, kicking his legs in the air.

'Renata,' Tansey shrieked up the stairs at the Spanish nanny. 'I need you in the kitchen. Alfie's made a mess and will not do as he is told. You'll have to get him ready for school. I need to get Bluebell ready as we're meeting my mum.'

After her car accident with the boys, Tansey had thought her relationship with Donny was well and truly over. He'd even moved out for a while, gone to live at his parents with the twins.

Tansey loved Donny, didn't want to lose him, so had to make sacrifices. She didn't particularly think she had a drink problem, but seeing as it was the cause of many of their arguments, she gave up alcohol. She also tried to be more accepting of his twins.

It festered inside her that Beau and Brett knocking her off *that* ladder was the cause of Alfie's behavioural problems, but even a specialist insisted that probably wasn't the case. He'd explained some children were naughtier than others and would use misbehaviour as a way of demanding attention. He'd also said Alfie was a bright boy with no sign of any brain injury.

When Donny agreed to give their relationship another go, determined to please her man, she'd agreed to move to a new house that had been built down Dark Lane. It had worked out well as the terrible twosome spent lots of time with their grandfather. She still hated Jamie hanging around with Beau and Brett, knew they were a bad influence, but she never said so anymore.

Her relationship with Donny's parents improved and she was pleased they treated Jamie the same as their own grandchildren. Having Lucinda living only a couple of doors away was a comfort too. They'd become great pals, did loads of girlie things together.

The icing on the cake had finally arrived in April 1987, when Tansey's yearning for a beautiful daughter had become a reality. Donny had hated the name Bluebell, but Tansey had gotten her own way, as usual.

Their family was complete. They had a beautiful home and Donny was earning plenty of money. Life couldn't be better. So why did she still feel stressed at times?

Over in Waterloo, Kenny and Donny were sitting on the deck of their boat, *The Duchess*, sipping a well-earned mug of tea. The boat was moored between January and February. It was March now, they had their first booking of the year soon, so had spent the morning watching the crew do all of the work while they put their feet up. 'You know what I spoke to you about in the cafe earlier?' Kenny said.

'Yeah.'

'Well, I'll be straight with ya, but don't be saying anything to your mother or anybody else for that matter.'

'Course not.' They weren't just father and son. These days, Donny classed his old man as his best pal.

'I'm running low on dosh. Your sister's wedding is costing me an arm and a leg.' Sherry was getting married in July to Andy Jolly, son of small-time crook Trevor Jolly. Trevor owned tyre shops which Andy helped run.

'And?'

'An old pal of mine has been in touch. We were banged up together. Good as gold, Phil is. Trustworthy, like. Anyway, cutting a long story short, he reckons he's come up with a concoction for the best ecstasy tablet on the street. If the rumours are true, you and me could make a fortune, Donny. Set ourselves up for life.'

Donny held his hands aloft. 'No way. Not drugs. Anything but drugs.'

Kenny grabbed his son's right shoulder. 'Listen to me; this ain't like the crap Lori got addicted to. Heroin's a killer, boy. These tablets are only taken on a night out. No bastard gets harmed or addicted. Ask your DJ pal, he'll tell ya. Ecstasy is a party drug. Just think of all the extra dosh you'll earn. If we get too busy, which I reckon we will, we can get someone to run the boat parties for us.'

'No, thank you. I like running the parties meself. I want no part of this, Dad, and a word of warning. If you go ahead and Mum finds out, I swear she'll fucking divorce you.'

'Oh my! What a beautiful little girl. She reminds me of a dark-haired Shirley Temple,' said an elderly diner on the next table.

Tansey beamed from ear to ear. With her thick, curly

brown hair and enormous brown eyes, Bluebell was an exceptionally pretty child. Tansey spent a fortune on her daughter's outfits and unlike the boys, Blue, as Donny called her, was a joy to take anywhere. 'Thanks so much. She's a little darling, aren't you, Bluebell. Say thank you to the nice lady, darling.'

Bluebell turned towards the woman. 'Thank you. I be two soon and I'm having a party.'

Both Penny and Tansey chuckled. Bluebell certainly had the personality to match her beauty. She oozed cuteness. 'I've told your dad I'm going to a book club with Linda on Blue's birthday, so I can come to her party,' Penny told her daughter. 'Linda's going to back me up. I'll bring her with me.'

'Oh, that's brilliant, Mum. Did you hear that, Bluebell? Nanny's coming to your party with her friend Linda.'

Too busy munching a fish finger to speak, Bluebell nodded instead.

Beau and Brett Bond now attended a mainstream school in Upminster. It was their first year there and neither liked it much. They hated having to wear the uniform, felt stupid in it. In their old school, they'd been allowed to wear their own clothes.

The lesson today was biology and Brett was feeling more uncomfortable by the second. He had never told Beau what had happened to him, hadn't really understood it himself at the time, and for a while had managed to blank it from his mind.

However, the older he got, the more he was realizing that something really wrong had happened to him. He'd even started having nightmares again, could see Eric's face clearly in them.

When the class clown, Ross Goddard, put his hand up and asked Mrs Horst, 'How are babies made then?' most of the class including Beau began to giggle, as she explained in the best way she could to a classroom full of eleven and twelve-year-olds.

Feeling bile rise to the back of his throat, Brett tried to swallow it. That didn't work though, unfortunately.

Spewing up the chip butty he'd eaten at lunchtime, Brett ran hell for leather out of the classroom and through the school gates. Had Eric tried to get him pregnant?

Having thoroughly enjoyed the Dover sole for her main course, Tansey was about to tuck into her lemon sorbet when her mobile phone rang. It was the school.

Seeing the startled expression on her daughter's face, Penny waited until she'd ended the call before asking, 'What's up?'

'Alfie's in trouble again. The headmaster wants to speak to me and pick Alfie up. How embarrassing. He's such a little bastard. I honestly wish he'd never been born most days. Why can't he be more like Harry?'

'Don't say that, love. You don't mean it. Perhaps you should take him to see a therapist or something? Get to the root of what's wrong with him.'

Tansey chucked two twenty-pound notes on the table. They always ate at nice restaurants these days and Tansey always treated her mum. She lifted her daughter off the chair. 'Come on, Blue. We've got to go.'

Kenny met Alan in the Nightingale in Wanstead. Alan now lived in Essex, had moved from Blackheath as, along with many other businesses, Al's had suffered from Black Monday. He'd been forced to downsize his home just to keep afloat. 'How's tricks, mate? You sounded like you needed this when I rang you earlier.' Kenny pushed a large brandy his pal's way.

'Cheers. I do. Day from hell. Actually, let's rephrase that. The week from hell.'

'Work? Money?'

'Yeah. But it's Ricky I'm upset the most about, mate. He's being bullied at school. Why are kids so fucking cruel, eh?' Ricky was a bright kid, therefore had been accepted in the mainstream system. He'd been happy as Larry in Blackheath, but since moving, there'd been problems. 'It started with name-calling, ya know, mong, spazzie – the usual crap. But yesterday, they actually pushed him and he fell over and grazed his chin.'

'Cunts,' hissed Kenny, his jaw twitching furiously. 'Find out their fathers' names. I'll fucking sort it out. How is he today?'

'He was determined to go back to school even though we wanted to keep him off. Julia's in bits, as you can well imagine. He came home with a smile on his face, mind you. Broke my heart last night when he said to me, "Dad, if I don't go to school, the bullies will think I'm scared and they'll win." I mean, he ain't long turned nine and he's so bloody brave.'

'He gets that from you. I mean it; find out the fathers' names. The little shits won't be so quick to bully Little Man again when I cut their dads' tongues off.'

Alan couldn't help but chuckle. Kenny was a lunatic at times, always had been, and it wouldn't surprise him if he carried out his threat. 'Let's change the subject. What's happening with this Abigail bird?' Alan liked Sharon, didn't particularly agree with what his pal was doing, but after a heart to heart with Kenny, could understand him having an affair. He and Julia weren't exactly at it like rabbits anymore, but still enjoyed a half-decent sex life. Kenny had explained to him how his had been non-existent for the past few years, apart from a once a month roll-around, and Sharon had to be pissed to even want that. When she'd gone to Spain, that was when Abi came along, showering him with attention and making him feel desirable for the first time in ages.

Kenny shrugged. 'I like her. But we both know it can't go anywhere, mate, and she seems to be getting a bit over-keen. But I've never lied to her. Been straight from day one that I'd never leave Shal, and she reckons she's fine with that. I feel so guilty every time I speak to Shal though. She reckons she might be coming home in the next few weeks, so Christ knows what I'm gonna do then.'

'Will you still see Abi?'

Kenny let out a huge sigh, his cheeks puffing out. 'I dunno. It's been so nice to feel wanted by a woman again, Al. The sex is electric, a bit like it was between me and Shal back in the day. But I just know when I look my Shal in the eye, I'm gonna feel a right horrible bastard. Me nut's all over the place, if I'm honest. I just got lonely, I think. I'm staying around Abi's again tonight.'

'Oh, mate. You got yourself into a right pickle. So, is this why you wanted to see me urgently today?'

'Erm, no. I got a new business venture on the boil and I'm looking for a partner. Now, I know you're probably gonna say no, but please hear me out first. It's gonna be a big earner this, Al. Life-changing amounts of dosh, and I know you could do with that right now, just like I could. We ain't gotta get our hands dirty either.'

Alan was intrigued. 'Fire away. I'm all ears.'

Alan listened intently as Kenny explained how the rave scene that had caught on in America was about to take off in the UK and his plan to get in first with the purest ecstasy pills on the market. He laughed as his pal ended his sales pitch with Del Boy's famous one-liner, yet had the balls to add to it. 'I'm telling you, Al, this time next year we could be multimillionaires.'

'Ken, believe me, I could do with the dosh. But I could never do nothing that could potentially land me with a long stretch. Your kids and grandkids would survive if you got banged up. My Ricky wouldn't. I'm his world. He needs me.'

Kenny nodded. 'I get it, mate. If Ricky was mine, I'd say and do the same.'

'Can we go out on our quad bikes, Dad?' asked Beau. He, Brett and Jamie had all got quad bikes last Christmas and they loved racing up and down the lane and across the adjoining fields.

'You and Jamie get the bikes out the garage. I just wanna have a quick word with Brett.' Donny was aware of what had happened earlier because the headmaster had called him to say that Beau had raced after his brother and neither had returned to school. Donny also knew the lesson they'd run out of had been biology.

'I feel all right now,' Brett reassured his father.

Donny didn't know how to speak to his son, the shame burned through him when he thought about what had happened, but he'd known the time would come when they had to talk about it. 'Did that biology lesson remind you of bad things, boy?'

'No. I was just sick.'

'You need to be truthful with me, Brett. 'Cause if it did,

I can make sure you don't have to do that lesson anymore. I'll go up the school and have a chat with your headmaster.'

Brett leapt off the chair, eyes blazing. 'No. Don't you dare do that. You can't show me up. I mean it, Dad. You go up that school, I'll never talk to you again.'

'All right. I just don't want you to keep things bottled up inside. If you ever want to talk about anything, I'm here for you and I promise it'll stay between us.'

'I don't wanna talk about nuffink.'

'OK. But if you do.'

'I won't. Not ever. So stop bleating on about it, Dad.'

Brett tore off on his bike without a backward glance.

After his meet-up with Alan, Kenny had got straight on the phone to an old pal of his, Teddy Abbott. Ted was knocking on a bit now, but there was nothing he didn't know about supplying a bit of couver.

As luck would have it, Teddy's eldest son Tony had been at his house. Kenny hadn't gone into too much detail, but both Teddy's and Tony's ears had pricked up.

'If the E's as good as you say, I can sell shitloads. And I mean hundreds of thousands,' grinned Tony.

'All right. Leave it with me and I'll grab some samples and drop 'em off 'ere tomorrow,' was how Kenny had left it. He'd then headed straight to Abi's. As always, she greeted him with a huge smile, a hug and her luscious lips.

'I've missed you,' Abigail said, stroking her man's handsome face. She had never gone for the pretty-boy look, like some of her friends did. Kenny was craggy, rough and ready, a cockney, a character and a villain. Everything she'd ever wanted, really. 'Have you missed me too?'

Kenny grinned. Being missed, wanted and sexually desired made him feel so good. However, he was careful with his words, didn't want to lead her up the garden path. 'I only saw you earlier, ya nutter.'

'What difference does that make? You've either missed me or you haven't.'

Kenny grabbed her fine buttocks and rubbed his erection against her. 'That answer your question, eh?'

Smiling seductively, Abigail held her man's hand and led him into the bedroom.

Brett Bond lay in bed deep in thought. He was bound to get some stick off the other kids for spewing up in class, but that didn't bother him. If any of the boys laughed at him, he'd just punch their lights out anyway.

It was the biology lessons that worried him the most. But no way could he let his dad tell the headmaster what had happened to him. Talk about ruin his street cred. He couldn't even talk about it to his own twin because he felt too ashamed. 'Beau, you still awake?'

'Erm, sort of.' Beau had been half asleep. 'What's up?'

'I don't like our school and I hate wearing a uniform. Why don't we set fire to something at school and get ourselves expelled? Then we can go to another school, like our old one, where we don't have to wear uniforms. At least most of the lads were cool, not like the dickheads in our class now.'

Beau put his bedside light on and grinned. He had a thing about fire, loved watching things burn. But he'd promised his dad he wouldn't set fire to anything else after accidentally burning Old Man Reeves' stables to ashes last year. Luckily enough, there'd been no horses inside and his dad had footed the repair bill. 'Sounds fun, but what we gonna set alight?'

*

'Not again, babe. You've worn him out, I reckon,' Kenny chuckled as Abigail put his now limp cock in her mouth. He'd already come twice and he'd had a few to drink today. No way would he be able to raise a gallop again until the morning. 'Go and pour us another brandy and bring us in an ashtray. You don't mind me having a cigar in 'ere, do yer?'

Abigail leapt out of bed. She was a non-smoker, hated the smell, especially cigars. However, she would allow Kenny to do anything – literally.

Kenny put his hands behind his head, sighed and thought of Sharon. He always turned his mobile phone off when at Abi's and would bet his bottom dollar Shal had been calling him all evening. She'd started to become suspicious when she couldn't get hold of him on the landline some-times of an evening. She knew his mobile battery often died, so that was his excuse for that. As for the landline, he told her he was out trying to earn a few bob. He hadn't told Shal how low his money was running, but she knew he wasn't exactly flush right now.

'Here we are,' smiled Abigail. 'What you doing tomor-row evening, Kenny? Only my friend is having a birthday party in Chingford. She's got a beautiful home. I'd love you to come with me.'

Kenny took a drag on his cigar. He needed it. 'I'm busy tomorrow night. Got a business meeting with an old pal of mine,' he lied. He couldn't be seen taking her to parties, like a proper couple. Say he got recognized?

'When will I see you again then?'

Kenny looked at Abi's crestfallen face and felt guilty. She was a lovely girl, had so much going for her and at twenty-eight, the world was her oyster. He'd have to nip this in the bud soon. It wasn't fair on her or Sharon. 'I tell you what, I'll pick you up Sunday lunchtime and take you out for a nice bit of grub somewhere. Not locally, though. We'll take a drive out to the countryside or something.'

Abigail beamed. 'That sounds perfect. I might even skip the party, so I feel fresh. Most of my friends will be in couples. I don't want to feel like a gooseberry.'

Kenny lifted her chin and kissed her on the nose. 'You'll never be a gooseberry, you. You're far too beautiful.'

What Kenny didn't realize while uttering those words was that sometimes beauty is only skin-deep.

CHAPTER EIGHTEEN

'Never look a gift horse in the mouth.'

I often thought back to me granddad's old sayings when I had to make an important decision. Thankfully, taking on Teddy and Tony as business partners proved to be a masterstroke. We had a fifty/fifty split on the profits and they did all the dirty work.

The ecstasy tablets were as good as Phil promised me and within a fortnight demand was so high, I rented a disused slaughterhouse that belonged to me old mucker, Bernie O'Callaghan. Obviously, I knew Bernie was as sound as a pound as he'd chopped up a few dead bodies for me in the past, including that nonce-case, Eric.

Phil and his business partner – who looked like some weirdo off of University Challenge *and wouldn't tell anyone his real name, would only be referred to as The Scientist – soon needed more hands.*

Phil assured me the two Chinese geezers he took on were trustworthy. They were known as Peter and Paul, which obviously wasn't their real names.

I was wary of the Chinese 'cause me granddad had

never liked them, so I issued 'em with a friendly warning: 'If I find out you've robbed so much as one pill, I will chop your fucking hands off.'

I tried to distance myself a bit from Abi. I still went round hers and took her out the area for a bit of grub, but I didn't stay round there so much. I couldn't get enough of her still, mind. She was insatiable. The sex was incredible.

Then I got the phone call I'd been looking forward to, yet dreading at the same time. Shal had booked a flight. She was coming home in a week's time.

Me bonce was all over the shop. Not only had I become part of a major drug set-up while my wife had been away, I was also having a torrid affair with a bird who was young enough to be me daughter.

What the fuck was I meant to do now?

Brett Bond had got little stick over spewing up during biology then running out the school that time. One lad had given him a bit of gyp and got a clump in return. But other than that, sod all was said, apart from the headmaster having a word with him, saying it was against the rules to leave the school without permission.

Brett still didn't like the biology lesson. He found it boring. But apart from that one time, all they'd discussed since was plants, animals and even water, which suited Brett down to the ground. None of those subjects brought back visions of what that fat bastard Eric had done to him.

Mrs Horst was talking about whales mating when the class clown, Ross, put his hand up and asked, 'What are johnnies used for by humans, Mrs Horst? Only, I found a pack of three in my dad's drawer at home the other night when I was searching for a pack of cards.'

Mrs Horst was a middle-aged prude, and didn't really understand that Ross was taking the piss, so started talking about human biology.

Brett took deep breaths. He wanted to put his fingers in his ears and rock to and fro while singing 'La-la-la' or something, but obviously he couldn't draw attention to himself. Not after the last time.

Trying to take his mind off the replies Mrs Horst was giving to Ross and the class, Brett took his pack of cola cubes out of his school bag. He looked to his right, where Lisa Howells and Julie Bale were sitting. Those two were always staring at him and his brother, had even asked them out one time.

'What you doing?' Beau asked, as Brett started lobbing cola cubes at Lisa and Julie's heads. 'Listen to Horst. This is well funny,' he chuckled.

To Beau and the rest of the class it might be funny, but not to Brett. He waited until Mrs Horst turned her back to draw a uterus on the blackboard before standing up and chucking cola cube after cola cube at the back of her head.

When one hit her, Mrs Horst clutched her head and swung around. 'Did you throw something at me, Brett Bond?'

Relieved the sexual conversation had now ended, Brett took a deep breath to compose his thoughts once more. 'Yes. Yes, I fucking did.'

Lori Boswell looked out of her window and took in the beauty of the Oxfordshire countryside. She smiled as she watched two foxes playing together. Rehab hadn't particularly worked for her in the past, but this time was different. Reason being, she'd finally met the man of her dreams.

The location of this particular rehab was idyllic, the support workers wonderful. Lori was now seeing life in a different way. Small things made her happy, such as the birds singing of a morning and the beauty of the green fields and trees. She knew deep down she was lucky to be alive.

Allowing Gary Acorn back into her life had been a massive mistake. He was an arsehole of the highest degree who had lost her her children and then come back to drag her into a downward spiral once again. Lori could see that clearly now, but it had taken a near-fatal overdose for her to recognize him for the manipulative bastard he was. That's how she'd ended up in this particular rehab. Her mother had washed her hands of her but, thankfully, the authorities had come up trumps and given her another chance to get herself straight and live a better life.

And a better life was what she now had. The last thing Lori had expected was to meet the man of her dreams in rehab. But she had. Carl Scantlin was forty-three, fifteen years her senior, but the age gap didn't matter one iota to Lori. An ex-lead singer of a punk band back in the seventies, Carl was now a music producer. He owned his own record company and was loaded by all accounts. He was coming to pick her up tomorrow and she was moving straight into his mansion in Epping.

Lori had once thought she was in love with Donny. Then Gary, but that relationship had been through druggie, drunken eyes. Carl had already been in the rehab when she'd arrived, as a heroin-addicted mess. Carl's problem was cocaine and even though they hadn't bonded immediately, when they had started conversing, they had quickly fallen in love.

Lori walked away from the window, laid on the bed and beamed. Life would be different for her from now on. She was moving on. Carl had promised to take her out, buy her a new wardrobe and anything else she might need. She was never going to take drugs again or drink alcohol. She and Carl had made a pledge. Alcohol led him to taking cocaine, so he wasn't drinking anymore either. They had even discussed having children together, that's how serious they were about one another. Carl had a daughter whom he was estranged from.

Picturing her new life, Lori licked her lips. As much as she was in love with Carl, there were two things she wanted more: her sons, and revenge.

After all, Donny Bond was the man who had ruined her life in the first place.

Kenny was munching on an egg and bacon sandwich he'd grabbed from the cafe when his son came storming into the house.

'Mum's been trying to get hold of you last night and again this morning. Where the fuck you been?' bellowed Donny.

Kenny sighed. He was getting a bit sick of his son watching him like a hawk. 'For your information, I spoke to your mother half an hour ago.' Kenny swallowed the last of his breakfast, then paced up and down his lengthy kitchen. 'You've really started to grate on me lately, boy. Are you so unhappy in your own life, you feel the need to check up on me every five minutes?'

'I'm not unhappy,' snapped Donny.

'Well, you could've fooled me. I'm a grown man, Donny. I ain't henpecked and saddled with loads of kids like you. Your mother isn't around right now, so if I want to go out for a few bevvies, then I will. I spent years banged up, unable to do so, if you remember rightly. Perhaps I'm making up for lost time, eh?'

'Where did ya stay last night?'

'Round Tony's. We went to his local in Abridge and I decided not to drive home pissed in case I smashed me motor up like your other half once did.'

'Don't bring Tansey into this. You working the boat with me tonight?'

Kenny's jaw twitched uncontrollably. 'I was. But now you've turned up 'ere shouting the odds, I'm gonna give it a swerve. I ain't a twelve-year-old kid, I'm your father. If it weren't for me, you wouldn't even exist. Show some fucking respect.'

When Donny stormed out of the house, Kenny breathed a sigh of relief. He really hadn't fancied the boat party, had far too much on his mind.

Tonight he would tell Abi that Sharon was coming home, therefore he wouldn't be able to stay over or see as much of her in the future.

It was a conversation he was dreading, as he could sense Abi had fallen for him in a big way, even though he'd warned her not to.

Shal would always be his number one woman. Nothing and no one was worth jeopardizing his marriage for.

Lori Boswell had never had it so good. Carl Scantlin treated her like a queen and his home in Epping was big, modern, and spectacular.

Most days they would venture up the West End in Carl's Ferrari. Money was no object. Lori could choose whatever she wanted from the likes of Bond Street, Harrods or Selfridges, and Carl would buy it for her.

Today, Lori had had her hair cut and coloured at a top salon. She stared at her reflection in the mirror and put on her large blingy Fendi sunglasses. Dressed in an emerald-green designer suit, she could easily pass for a film star.

'You look gorgeous, babe,' beamed Carl. 'Your boys are gonna be bowled over when they see their glamorous mum.'

Lori smiled. She felt nervous, but that was to be expected. It had been years since she'd seen the twins and she couldn't wait to be reunited with them. Now that she was as clean as a whistle, Donny had no right to stop her seeing her sons. She was the one who'd given birth to them after all.

Knowing there was a damn good chance Abi would become emotional and worse even, tearful, Kenny took her to an expensive Chinese restaurant up the West End.

'The food in here is exquisite,' smiled Abi, as she picked at the starters.

Kenny took a large gulp of wine. 'There's something we need to talk about, babe.'

An alarmed expression on her face, Abi put her chopsticks down. 'What?'

'My wife. She's returning to England next Friday, so obviously we're gonna have to cool it a bit.'

'But I will still see you, won't I? You're not dumping me, are you?'

'No. But I won't be able to see you nowhere near as much as I have been. Staying out overnight is totally out the question. I don't really go out of an evening, like, when Shal's at home.'

'So when will I see you?'

'I can try and pop round afternoons, and I'll still take

you out and stuff.' Kenny could tell she was desperately trying to hold back the tears. It made him feel like a right bastard.

'But I'm at work in the week. That only leaves the weekends. Why don't you leave Sharon? You're obviously not happy, else you wouldn't have had an affair in the first place. We're good together, Kenny. You know what we've got is special.'

'Don't start with all that old flannel, Abi. I told you from the start that I would *never* leave my wife. You knew the score from day one.'

'So, what was I? Just a plaything to keep you amused while Sharon was away?'

Getting more flustered by the second, Kenny drank the rest of his wine and topped up the glass. 'Of course you weren't. I like you – a lot. Listen, I know you deserve better than this. You're a beautiful girl who could get any man you wanted. If you want to call *us* a day, I'll completely understand.'

'No. I don't. I love you.' Abi burst into tears.

Kenny felt a right dick. Other diners were now looking their way.

'Are you ready to order your main course?' asked a confused-looking waiter.

'I don't want a main course. I want to go home.' Her evening ruined, Abigail ran sobbing out of the restaurant.

The following morning, Donny was at the farm shop when he bumped into his one-time partner in crime. He hadn't seen Sam for ages. They'd parted ways after getting arrested together and banged up. Donny's dad had ordered him to steer clear, insisting Sam was bad news and a dickhead.

'How you doing, Donny?'

'Yeah. Good. I'm the boss up at the nursery now. My granddad handed it over to me before he moved to Spain. What you up to, workwise?'

'Got a stall down Romford market, selling menswear. I do OK there.'

'Good. Glad to hear it. How's your family?'

'All good, thanks. Are your mum and dad not together anymore?'

Instinct told Donny to play along. 'Erm, nah. Me mum's in Spain with my grandparents at present. Why d'ya ask?'

'I saw your dad a while back in Chinatown in Ilford with a young blonde bird. He didn't see me, and I didn't go over to him 'cause they were all over one another like a rash. Punching above his weight with her, I'd say,' chuckled Sam.

Donny felt nauseous, had to get out of the farm shop. He looked at his watch. 'Shit! I gotta be somewhere. You take care, Sam.'

'Take my mobile number.'

Donny didn't reply. Hands shaking, he leapt in his motor and zoomed off.

'Oh my God! Your poor mum. What you gonna do, Donny? You going to tell her?' Tansey was genuinely shocked.

Donny put his head in his hands. He felt physically sick. How could his dad do this to his lovely mum? Especially when his nan had cancer. 'I can't believe it, Tans. My mum's stuck by him through thick and thin. All those years he was in prison, she never looked at another bloke and this is how he repays her. I wanna kill him.'

'Where you going? Don't do anything stupid,' Tansey pleaded.

Donny ran to his father's house. He let himself in. His dad was dossing on the sofa. Absolutely raging, Donny let fly: 'You no-good, womanizing bastard. And you had the cheek to be appalled about Granddad's affair. At least he was young, not a silly old sod like you.'

Kenny leapt off the sofa, his face as white as chalk. 'What you going on about, ya nutter!'

'You were spotted in Chinatown with your young bit of fluff. All over her like a rash, by all accounts. You make me want to vomit.'

Kenny knew he had to bluff it. On the night he'd met Abi, they'd ended up in Chinatown, alone. 'You've got it all wrong, boy. The bird I was with is Tony's other half. Some geezers were pestering her in there, so I told her to sit with me. Ask Alan if you don't believe me. I'd been out with him all that night.' He knew he could count on Alan to back him up, even though Alan had made himself scarce the minute he saw the way things were going between Kenny and Abi.

'Don't fucking lie to me,' Donny shrieked. 'It all adds up now. Your new wardrobe. The not coming home. You ain't one to doss around mates' gaffs. Got her own drum, Blondie, has she?'

As his son tried to punch him and missed, Kenny grabbed hold of his wrists. 'I would never cheat on your mother. I love her too much. I'll ring Tony. Ask him, if you don't believe me. I'll ring Al an' all. I swear on the twins' lives me and him were over the dogs that night, had a few wins, then ended up in Charlie Chan's.'

'Was he with you, Al, in the restaurant, afterwards?'

'No. He was knackered and had a wife indoors waiting for him. I was starving, was on me Jacks.'

'As if your mates wouldn't back up your bullshit story

anyway. Whoever she is, the slut, it ends now. 'Cause if you carry on with this, I'll find out and I'll tell Mum. I swear I will.'

Kenny took a deep breath. 'Believe whatever you want, Donny. I don't give a fuck. I know the truth. Me, cheat on your mother after everything she's done for me? Never in a million years, son.'

Wondering if he had got the wrong end of the stick, Donny was relaying the conversation to Tansey when the doorbell rang.

'I'll get it,' Tansey said.

'Cuddles, Daddy,' Bluebell grinned.

Donny lifted his daughter up. There was a twenty-first party on the boat tonight and he needed that like he needed a hole in the head. Divvy Dave had agreed to help him, seeing as his tosser of a father had blown it out.

Tansey opened the front door and came face to face with a glamorous blonde whom she'd never seen before. 'Hello. What can I do for you?'

'I've come to visit my sons. Are they in?'

''Erm, I think you must have the wrong house, love.'

Lori took off her sunglasses and gave the woman, who was just as much to blame for ruining her life as that scumbag Donny, daggers. 'No. This is the right house, *love*. I've come to see *my* sons. Beau and Brett Bond.'

Tansey was gobsmacked. Surely this woman – who was dressed immaculately and a real stunner – couldn't be Lori? She managed to find her voice. 'Donny. You have a visitor.'

With Bluebell in his arms, Donny didn't recognize the mother of his sons at first. 'All right. Can I help you?'

Having put her sunglasses back on, Lori took them off again. 'Hello, Donny. Long time no see.'

Open-mouthed, Donny handed their daughter to Tansey. 'Lori!'

'Yes. It's me. I bet you thought you'd seen the last of me, eh? No such luck, I'm afraid. Are *our* sons indoors?'

Donny couldn't believe the change in her. She looked a million dollars in comparison to the skaghead he remembered her as. He would've walked straight past her in the street. ''Erm, the boys are out. You can't just turn up 'ere like this, Lori. Not after what happened to Brett.'

'Can't I? Well, we'll see about that, won't we? Only, my other half has money you could only dream of, Donny. He's hired the best solicitor in Essex. I shall be a mother to my sons whether you like it or not.' Lori pointed. 'That's my bloke Carl, in the Ferrari. Would you like to invite us in to wait for Beau and Brett?'

'No. I gotta work. And you're going nowhere near them boys. Or else!'

'Or else what? Don't work too hard.' Head held high, Lori sauntered back towards the car, leaving Donny astounded and temporarily struck dumb.

Having driven off then returned after Donny left for work, Carl and Lori were now plotted up down the bottom of the Lane. 'You hungry?' asked Lori.

'A bit. You?'

Lori looked at her watch. It was 7.30 p.m. She had no idea what time the twins had to be home by or whether they'd arrived home while she and Carl had taken a detour down the A127. 'We'll give it until eight, then we'll go for something to eat. We can always come back tomorrow morning.'

'OK. But don't forget I need to check a couple of bands out tomorrow night. You'll come with me, won't you?'

Lori squeezed her man's hands. She thought it was well cool he owned his own record company. 'Try stopping me,' she smiled.

About to lean across and kiss Lori, Carl heard a noise. 'That's them, Carl! With another boy.' Lori jumped out of the car. All three lads were on quad bikes. 'Beau, Brett,' she bellowed.

Brett braked and looked around. 'Beau, a woman's calling us.'

Beau turned around. He liked the flash car. The twins and Jamie drove towards the woman. Neither Beau nor Brett recognized her. 'What d'ya want?' enquired Brett. He didn't recognize the man either.

Lori's eyes welled up. 'It's me, Brett. Your mum.'

'You ain't our mum,' stated Beau.

'I am. I promise you I am. Come closer and look into my eyes. I'm clean now. I no longer drink. Ask me anything you want. Go on.'

Beau asked a barrage of questions. All were answered correctly. 'But you don't look like our mum.'

'It is her. I recognize her voice,' Brett told his brother.

Lori beamed. 'Look how grown up you two are. So handsome too. I bet the girls love you.'

'They do. But we don't like them,' Brett snapped.

'Who's he?' Beau pointed to Carl.

'Carl's my partner. He has a fabulous home with a games room, a gym, a swimming pool. You two would love it.'

'We already got a swimming pool,' Brett informed the woman who looked nothing like the mother he remembered.

'What are you doing tomorrow? Would you like to go for a ride in Carl's car? We'll take you out for lunch, then show you the house.'

'We can't tomorrow. Dad's taking us quad-bike racing,' Brett replied.

'What about next weekend?'

Beau eyed the Ferrari. 'Does it go really fast, your car?'

Carl smiled. 'Not 'arf.'

Beau looked at his brother. 'You wanna go for a ride in it in the week? Say Thursday?' He winked.

Getting the gist, Brett nodded. 'Yeah. Thursday'd be cool.'

Lori breathed a sigh of relief. 'We'll meet you here next Thursday morning at say, eleven?'

'Yeah. OK,' Beau replied. He couldn't remember what his mum used looked like, but it was certainly nothing like this. She was always in pyjamas and they hadn't had much food in the house, he remembered that.

'Don't say nothing to your dad, boys. Not beforehand, anyway. He'll only stop you from coming,' warned Lori.

'We ain't grasses,' Beau replied. 'And we're on school holiday, so we can do as we please.'

Lori smiled. With their short blond hair, cute noses and big brown eyes, her boys would break some hearts. They had a confident manner too. 'Can I have a hug before you go?'

Brett shook his head. 'Nah. We gotta get off now.'

'Yeah. We're late,' Beau added before zooming off.

'Can I come with you?' Jamie asked Brett.

'No,' was the blunt reply.

Holding a giant bouquet of roses in his hand, Kenny tried to break the news that Donny was onto them as gently as possible.

'So, what exactly you trying to say, Kenny? Only you seem to be going round the houses a bit. Are you saying that you want to end things? Only I don't appreciate being dumped like a bag of old rubbish. What do you think I am? Some silly slapper?'

Realizing Abi's eyes were glinting dangerously, Kenny tried to soften the blow. 'Don't be daft. It ain't that I don't wanna see ya. But my boy ain't stupid. He's the type to put a tracker on my car and follow me 'ere. My old woman'll go apeshit, and I don't want to cause you any grief. It's not fair on you.'

'Well, you should have thought about that before you started an affair with me. You're obviously not happy in your marriage; otherwise you wouldn't have been playing around in the first place.'

Kenny felt himself squirm. He knew how to handle most situations, but he wasn't a player, therefore had never got himself in this kind of predicament. 'I don't want it to end, honestly I don't. I enjoy every minute I spend with you, Abs. But my boy's threatened to tell his muvver, and I can't allow that to happen. My wife's stuck by me through thick and thin in the past and I can't break her heart. She's a nice person.'

'And so am I.'

'I know you are. You're beautiful inside and out. You'll have no trouble bagging yourself a decent geezer. They'll be queuing up for you.'

'But I don't want anybody else. I want you, Kenny.'

Kenny felt his bowels loosen. Abi wasn't going to be easy to get rid of and he knew it. What the bloody hell had he gotten himself into?

CHAPTER NINETEEN

Over the next couple of days, Kenny Bond became a very worried man. Abi would call him at all hours, wouldn't leave him alone. It was scary shit. One minute she was begging him to reconsider carrying on their relationship, the next she was threatening to tell his wife. He was picking Sharon up from the airport the day after tomorrow. To say he was in shit-street was an understatement.

Explaining the situation to his partner in crime in Rosie's cafe, Kenny was peeved when Tony burst out laughing. 'It ain't fucking funny. This is my marriage at stake.'

'I know. It ain't that I'm laughing at though. I told you the night you met me to drop off some dosh and had her in the car, she had an obsessive look and scary eyes. I bet you wish you'd listened to me now. I can spot a bunny-boiler a mile off.'

'Look, it's her ringing again now. Twenty-seven times she rung me yesterday. I only answered four of her fucking calls. What am I gonna do?'

Tony liked Kenny. He was a shrewd geezer and their current business venture was booming. He could also sense how worried he was. 'First thing you do is ring your

251

phone company and change your number. I've had to do that twice in the past. Don't hurt in our line of business to have a fresh number once in a while anyway.'

Kenny sighed. 'I'm worried if I change my number, she'll track me down. She came across as so normal. Good job, brain, own gaff – and now this. Never fucking again will I have an affair, let me tell ya. My first and last, this. How's me luck, though? Only I could pick a psycho.'

'Does she know where you live? You never told her what you do, did ya?' Tony asked, alarmed. He knew Kenny had been bang into Abigail, as he'd talked about her a lot, especially at the beginning.

'Don't be daft. I told her nothing like that. But she asked me old woman's name and I'm sure I told her Sharon worked with Donny up at the nursery. I thought the woman was sane, like. Perhaps I should visit her again, have it out with her once and for all? I didn't sleep last night. Sharon'll cut my bollocks off, she finds out, I'm telling ya.'

'I wouldn't visit her again. She's obviously unhinged, might stab ya,' chuckled Tony.

'I'm glad you find it so funny.'

'Nah, seriously, mate, get your number changed. Either that, or just blank her calls. She'll soon get bored if she gets no response. They usually do. Having said that, I had one once that turned up at—'

Kenny held his palms up. 'Please don't tell me any more. I really don't fucking want to know.'

'You sure this outfit doesn't look too over the top?' Lori asked Carl. She felt excited, but also as nervous as hell at the thought of spending time with her sons. Her biggest fear was that Brett would ask her about Eric. Her other

252

fear was that the twins would loathe her because they remembered her old filthy house and what a rotten, useless mother she'd been.

Lori was wearing a calf-length multicoloured bodycon dress that clung to her stunning figure. 'You look gorgeous. Stop worrying,' Carl said as they pulled into Dark Lane. It had been his idea they pick the boys up in his Mitsubishi Shogun, in case Donny spotted the Ferrari. He would take the boys out for a ride in that later.

It was times such as this Lori wished she could've had a drink or two to calm her shot-to-pieces nerves. 'Say they don't turn up? They might've slipped up about seeing me to Donny.'

'Calm down. We're fifteen minutes early.' Carl held Lori's face and kissed her on her petite nose. 'It's going to be fine. Trust me.'

'I bloody hope so, Carl. I love my boys, but hate the mother I once was. I don't deserve their forgiveness, if I'm honest, but I would give anything to be a part of their lives again. I know we can't change the past, but I could be a brilliant mum to them in the future. I know I could.'

'I know you could too, and you will be. Don't expect too much from them at the start though. They've got to get to know you all over again.'

'I know.'

Carl looked in the mirror and grinned. 'They're on their way.'

Lori leapt out the passenger side. The twins were dressed immaculately in matching outfits. Black short sleeve shirts, black leather shoes and faded Levi jeans. They looked so handsome, like proper little men. 'You look so smart and grown up,' beamed Lori.

Neither twin smiled or said hello. 'We never got dressed

up for you,' Beau coldly informed his mother. 'We told Dad we were going to a pal's birthday party.'

'Yeah. That's right,' added Brett.

'Oh well, you look great anyway.'

'Where's the Ferrari?' Beau snapped.

'At home. You can go for a ride in it later. That OK?'

Beau and Brett looked at one another and shrugged simultaneously. They then unenthusiastically got in the back of the silver Shogun.

Kenny Bond was sweating buckets as he pulled up outside Abi's flat in Buckhurst Hill.

He'd spoken to Alan and his pal had advised him to visit her one last time. 'Fucking threaten her if you have to. I feel for you, mate. I truly do. What a nutjob she turned out to be,' were Al's exact words.

She'd continuously rung him for the past two hours, so he'd finally answered. 'I need to see you, Kenny. It's important. Pop round mine and then I swear I'll leave you alone,' were Abi's exact words.

Wishing he'd never laid eyes on the bird, Kenny buzzed number seven.

Abi let him in immediately and was waiting at the front door, her eyes red through crying. 'You OK? What's a matter?' Kenny asked awkwardly.

Abigail gestured for Kenny to follow her into the lounge. 'You better sit down,' she wept.

Kenny took a deep breath. He'd once found her so attractive in those baggy dungarees with only a skimpy vest top underneath. Not anymore though. 'Nah, I'm fine standing up. Besides, I gotta be somewhere soon. What's the problem?'

'I'm pregnant.'

Eyes blazing, Kenny's mouth twitched. He'd pulled

himself out of her before he came every time. The bitch was lying and for the first time he could see the actual nuttiness in Abi's eyes that Tony had spoken about. 'Don't fucking lie to me, Abi. I weren't born yesterday. You need to drop this obsession with me now. Yes, it was fun. But now it's over. Accept it and move on.'

'Who do you think you are fucking talking to?' snarled Abigail. 'You got me pregnant, you bastard,' she added, lashing out with her fists.

Kenny grabbed hold of Abi's wrists and slammed her against the wall. 'Don't make me fucking angry, 'cause you really wouldn't like me when I lose my rag. You're pushing your luck now and I ain't putting up with no more. I never spunked up you, not once. So if you are up the spout, it ain't my poxy kid.'

'Yes. It is.' Abigail was bordering on hysterical at this point.

Kenny snarled as he put his elbow across Abi's windpipe. 'This is the last warning I'm giving you. You don't ring me anymore, you don't come anywhere near me or my family. 'Cause if you do, believe me, you're gonna regret it big time. I would kill to protect my family, literally. Under-fucking-stand?'

'You're hurting me,' croaked Abigail.

When he released her, Abi fell to the carpet, holding her throat and gasping. Kenny rolled his eyes. Talk about overly dramatic. 'Did you understand what I said to you, Abi?'

'Yes,' Abi spluttered.

'Good. I'll see myself out.'

'How's your steak?' Lori asked her sons. She'd been amazed when they'd ordered it rare. Their plates were literally swimming in blood.

'Good,' replied Brett. Beau just carried on eating.

The restaurant in Epping belonged to a pal of Carl's. The food was divine, but Lori was struggling to eat her seafood linguine. She couldn't believe how adult her sons were for their age. They'd soon be twelve but acted a lot older. The conversation had been a bit stilted, but Lori had expected that. They hadn't asked her anything about herself yet, which in a way she was glad about. When she asked them questions, they replied with very short answers. But she'd learned today that they both liked football. They also liked boxing, but their big passion was quad-bike racing. For all Donny's faults, Lori had to admit he'd done a decent job of raising them. Far better than she bloody well had.

Beau swallowed the last of his steak, then studied his mother. He had an instinct for weakness, could smell it like flies could sniff out shit. She was quite a pretty lady, and he could tell she was nervous. He turned his attention to Carl. He seemed OK, even though he had long hair.

Carl smiled at Beau. 'Looking forward to a ride in the Ferrari when we get back to mine?'

'Erm, suppose so. How fast can it go, like?'

As Carl and the boys began talking speed – and not the type that she used to take as a pick-me-up – Lori felt a warmth inside her. It was so wonderful to spend time with Beau and Brett after everything that had happened. She'd very nearly died after her last overdose.

'You all right, babe?' Carl enquired.

'Yes, thanks.' Lori smiled. She was more than all right. Her sons and Carl were truly gifts from God. So was life itself. Rehab had taught her that.

For the first time in a while, Kenny Bond curled up in bed and enjoyed a deep and peaceful sleep. He did feel a tad guilty over putting the frighteners on Abi like he had, but it had to be done.

In the beginning, Kenny had thought his feelings for her were real. Now he knew that was lust rather than love. No other woman would ever hold a candle to his Sharon. It was just a shame Sharon was no longer interested in sex. If she had been, he would never have strayed in the first place, he knew that much.

Seconds later, Kenny's phone rang. He looked at it in fright, half expecting it to be Loony Lil. Thankfully, it was Donny.

'Dad, can we talk? I think I owe you an apology.' The more Donny had thought things through, the more he was sure his dad would never cheat on his mum. Sam had always exaggerated stuff. When they'd knocked about together, he'd often lied about shagging birds when he hadn't.

'Yeah. Come down now, boy.'

Donny arrived within a couple of minutes. He needed advice on the Lori situation too. His dad would know what to do. 'I'm sorry for speaking to you the way I did. I know deep down you would never cheat on Mum. I just worry about you, that's all. You know what I think about your new business venture. You gotta keep your wits about yer now you're involved with that, Dad. But you've been going out partying like a teenager with your new best buddy. Tony's single, years younger than you – do you honestly think it's a good thing to be seen out on the piss with him all the time? The Old Bill could be watching you already, for all you know.'

Kenny held his hands up. 'Well, I'm glad you've come to your senses about that bird. As if! But you are quite right about the other stuff. Perhaps I've had a bit of a mid-life crisis 'cause your mother ain't been around. Or maybe it's to do with all those years I was stuck in prison. Who knows? But it stops now. You're right about Tony an' all. We shouldn't really be seen hanging out together, should keep it professional. I can't wait to pick your mum up on Friday. I ain't 'arf missed her, Donny. I don't like being indoors on me own, especially of an evening.'

Donny gave his father a manly hug. 'You should've said. There's always a place for you at mine and a dinner.'

'You gotta lot on your plate at work and home. I didn't wanna bother yer,' fibbed Kenny. The real reason he rarely popped into his son's gaff was because he couldn't stand Tansey. He'd liked her in the early days, but since moving to Dark Lane, she'd changed. A true fucking Queen Bee if ever he'd known one. She doted on Bluebell far more than her sons and was always out larging it with that posh prat, Lucinda. She'd even started talking posh, the silly tart. He and Shal had a nickname for her: 'Miss Uppity'. They only suffered her for Donny's sake. His son seemed blind to her faults. She was a shit mother, an even shittier cook and a gold-digger.

'So, you gonna come back and work on the boat with me?'

Kenny chuckled. 'Yeah. Course. That'll be the only partying I'll be doing in future once your mum gets home.'

'Good. Glad to hear it, and I'm sorry again for doubting you over Mum. I should've known better.'

Guilt flooded through Kenny's veins. 'Erm, seeing as there's no booking on the boat tonight, why don't me and you have a night over Romford Dogs? Dick the Fish rang me with a couple of tips earlier.'

'Renata's off today – her daughter's due to give birth. I'd love a night over the dogs, but Tans'll have the right hump if I sod off out tonight after she's been lumbered with the little uns on her own all day.'

'For fuck's sake, Donny, where's ya balls?' Kenny shook his head in exasperation. 'You're the man of the house, the breadwinner. Tansey shouldn't have had so many kids if she's incapable of looking after 'em. Anyway, you can bring the boys with ya. I'm sure they'll love it. Don't bloody well ask Tansey, just tell her, boy.'

'OK. I will. Dad, there's something else I need to talk to you about.'

'What?'

'Lori.' Donny explained about her turning up at the door, her threats and her new bloke. 'The twins said they were going to a mate's birthday party today, but I don't believe 'em. Jamie never went with 'em and he's been well cagey. I bet they're with Lori as we speak. What am I gonna do?'

'Leave it to me, that's what you're gonna do. I'll get the truth outta the boys and I'll deal with fucking Lori. Don't you worry about that.'

'Go on, number one. Go on, my son,' bellowed Kenny Bond.

'Yes.' Donny punched his fist in the air as Turkish Delight romped home first. His dad had put five hundred quid on the mutt. He'd been more cautious, only bet a twoer. But at 10/1, they were both quids in.

Kenny grabbed his son and did a little jig of delight. He wasn't a regular gambler, but loved a tip or two.

'Dad, I'm hungry,' announced Harry.

Donny lifted his son in the air and swung him around. Tansey had been more than happy to stay at home with Bluebell. The twins were nowhere to be seen when Donny left, so he'd brought Jamie, Harry and Alfie with him. 'Want chicken and chips in a basket?' Donny asked Harry.

'No. Scampi.'

'I'm gonna feed these kids, Dad. You hungry?'

'Peckish. Just get me whatever.' When his son walked away, Kenny checked his phone and smiled. Not one missed call. Finally, the nutjob had got the message.

Little did Kenny know that Abi was currently indoors with a pal, plotting and scheming his downfall.

Another pair who'd been plotting and scheming were Brett and Beau Bond.

Ages ago, they'd decided to strike during the Whitsun holidays and tonight was the night.

'What did you think of Mum?' Beau asked, as they got changed into the old tracksuits they'd hidden in the bushes first thing this morning.

'Don't call her that. Call her Lori. She ain't never been much of a mum to us, has she?' Brett snapped, thinking of Eric.

'All right. What did yer think of Lori then? I reckon she's so desperate for us to like her, we could get anything out of her we wanted.' Carl's mansion had been out of this world. It had every mod con going. Going for a ride in his Ferrari had been well cool, too.

'Yeah. I reckon you're right. Let's play her and him. He seems desperate to be our pal an' all.'

Beau grinned. 'Great minds think alike, bro.'

It was almost 9 p.m. when the twins decided it was dark enough to carry out their plan.

Their curfew was in five minutes, but they were often late, especially when they didn't have to go to school the next day. Their dad never told them off too much. Even on the odd occasion he did, Beau and Brett would play him like a fiddle.

They chucked the sports bag over the school gates, then Beau climbed over. 'You climb up this side and I'll catch the petrol. We don't wanna split the containers and lose any.'

Brett did as he was asked, then climbed over too.

'Hold the other end of this,' Beau ordered his brother, holding out one of Tansey's bed sheets, nicked from the airing cupboard. That would have to be burned, along with their tracksuits and trainers, soon as they were finished here.

Beau put the folded sheet across the large window and started smashing at it with a hammer. It soon shattered and the sheet softened the sound of the breaking glass. 'Gissa leg up. I'll climb through, get rid of the rest of the glass, then pull you in. Hand me the petrol cans first though, and the sports bag.'

Within ten minutes, Beau and Brett had poured petrol onto the sheet, towels and rags they'd collected and were ready to put their plan into action.

'When I say run – run,' Beau ordered, as he lit a king-size match.

The desks were wooden. Beau and Brett had expected them to burn easily, but they stood open-mouthed as the whole classroom caught fire very quickly and all the other windows shattered.

'This is fucking brilliant,' Beau laughed, clapping his hands in glee. He wasn't stupid. They'd both worn gloves.

All of a sudden, a recognizable voice bellowed, 'Beau, Brett, I know you're in here. The police are on their way.'

'Fuck! Run, Brett, run!'

*

On the journey back to Dark Lane both Donny and Kenny were in high spirits. It had been their lucky night. Apart from two races, every dog they'd bet on had come up trumps. 'Did you enjoy yourself, Jamie?' Donny asked. Harry and Alfie were both fast asleep.

Jamie was busy counting his winnings. Donny had given him money to bet with and he'd won twenty-four pound in total. 'Yeah. I loved it. Can we go again next Saturday?'

'We'll deffo go again, but it won't be next week. I've got a hen party booked on the boat.'

'What the fuck!' Kenny's heart sank as he spotted the police car. It was parked outside Donny's. Surely they weren't on to him?

Donny swung onto his drive and leapt out the car.

Tansey flung open the door. 'Thank God you're home. I told you to take your bloody phone with you.'

Donny's complexion paled. 'Whatever's wrong?'

'It's the twins. They set fire to their school.'

'They what!'

Thankful that Jamie hadn't been with the gruesome twosome, Tansey hugged her eldest. 'That isn't the worst news. The caretaker tried to put the fire out and – Donny, he died.'

'Oh God no!'

'Afraid so,' confirmed one of the two police officers. 'The caretaker recognized your sons running from the scene and called the police, but he must have been overcome by fumes. The boys left a bag of clothes behind. We'll need you to come down to the station, identify the items in the bag as belonging to Brett and Beau.'

Kenny sprang to the boys' defence. 'I don't think so. Been at a pal's all day, my grandsons. Definitely won't be their clobber. Got any witnesses, have ya?'

Donny shook his head in total disbelief. 'Are the twins at the station?'

'No,' replied the detective. 'We have officers out looking for them. Have you any idea where they might go to hide? They're in big trouble, so the quicker we find them, the better.'

'You go look for 'em, son. I'll go down to the station, identify their clothes,' Kenny offered. 'I saw 'em earlier – bright green tracksuits they were wearing,' he lied.

The officers glanced at one another. They knew who Kenny Bond was and what he had done. They also knew the clothes found in the bag were not green tracksuits, the lying, murdering bastard.

Knowing full well what his sons had been wearing that morning, Donny glared at his father. They didn't even own green tracksuits and if a man was dead, lying to the Old Bill would only make things worse. 'They're my sons. You go out an' look for 'em – I'll go to the police station.'

'For fuck's sake,' Kenny mumbled.

Beau and Brett Bond were hiding in a park in Cranham. They knew they were in deep shit. As they were about to climb back out the window, they'd heard a big bang. It was loud enough to hurt their ears. They'd had no choice but to leave their sports bag behind. It was Mr Rudge, the caretaker, who'd shouted their names, so they'd put their hoods up and run for their lives. The fire was mental by that point, totally out of control.

'What we gonna do, Beau? We can't stay 'ere all night. We're in enough trouble as it is. Why don't we ring Gramps? He'll give us an alibi.'

Beau put his head in his hands. He reeked of smoke, they both did. 'Nah. Gramps ain't never around lately. He don't care about us no more. He prefers that mongol Ricky,' Beau said bitterly. 'Let's find a phone box and ring Dad. He'll know what to do. He might even give us an alibi.'

'But we ain't got no money on us. Our money was in our jeans.'

'Then we'll reverse the fucking charges.'

Donny didn't want to admit that the sports bag, clothes and shoes inside belonged to his sons, but for once the twins had given him no choice. A man had died, for Christ's sake, been burned alive, and the Old Bill were well aware that Beau and Brett were to blame. He was so annoyed with them, disappointed too. They were good lads deep down. Whatever had possessed them to do such a stupid thing? He could quite easily throttle the pair of them.

When his mobile rang and a woman's voice asked him if he would accept a reversed-charge call, Donny knew it was the twins.

'Dad, we've done something bad. We need your help,' Beau said.

'Where are you?'

Beau reeled off the address.

'Don't move. Stay by the phone box. I'll be there in ten.'

Huddled together inside the phone box, the twins rushed to the safety of their father's car.

Donny sighed. The smell of smoke and petrol was overpowering. Donny turned the engine off, then got in the back.

'Dad, we need an alibi,' begged Brett. 'We—'

'I know exactly what you've done,' snapped Donny. 'It's

been on the news and everything. Why the hell did you do it? You fucking idiots.'

''Cause we didn't like the school. We wanted to go to a different one like our old one,' Beau explained.

'Well, you'll be going to a worse place than that now. A detention centre or borstal. The police know it's yous. They've got you bang to rights. They've got your clothes, shoes, the works.'

Brett began to cry. 'This is all my fault. I made Beau do it. It's 'cause of them biology lessons. I didn't like them, Dad. They made me sick. I hated 'em.'

Even though he was angry, Donny's heart broke for Brett. He hugged him tightly. 'You should've just said. I told you that before. I could've got you outta that lesson.'

As his usual hard-nut of a brother sobbed like a baby, Beau was confused. 'I like biology. It's well funny.'

Donny glared at Beau. 'Shut it, you. You're in enough bastard trouble as it is.'

'Can't you burn our clothes and give us an alibi?' asked Beau.

'I told ya, the Old Bill have got you bang to rights. Don't you understand what that means? There's no way out of this one. The caretaker died trying to put out the fire.'

Beau's eyes nearly popped out of his head. 'Mr Rudge is dead!'

'Unfortunately, yes. Right, this is what we're gonna do. The Old Bill are out looking for you, so I'm taking you straight to the station. Brett, I'm gonna have to explain to them what happened to you in the past. They'll hope-fully go more lenient on yous and a judge'll give you a lesser sentence.'

'Noooo. I can't talk about it.' Brett's sobs were raw, raucous.

'What happened, bruv?' Beau was bewildered.

Donny took a deep breath. 'Do you remember that bloke Eric who lived at yours in Harold Hill?'

Brett put his hands over his ears and began repeatedly kicking the driver's seat.

'I remember a fat man buying us lots of toys and sweets. But I don't remember his name or face.'

'You were the lucky one, Beau. That man did something bad to your brother. He was a pervert, he . . . well he did inappropriate things. The police have a record of it.'

'Like what?' Tears welled in Beau's eyes. He flung his arms around Brett, who still had his hands over his ears and was frantically rocking to and fro.

'Something terrible. That's all you need to know. But you need to pretend to the Old Bill that you knew this all along and that's why you set fire to the school. You couldn't stand to see your brother so upset. OK?'

Beau nodded. He was stunned. Brett had never said anything to him. No wonder he was sick and ran out of the classroom. That evil bastard must have touched his willy and bum.

Donny took Brett's hands away from his ears and gently shook him. 'I know you're upset, but I need you to be the bravest you've ever been for me, boy. The police will have a record of what happened to you all those years ago and we have to play on it. It's the only sympathy vote we've got to play. I'll do all the talking, OK? You two just stick to the story. All you meant to do was light a small fire, so you wouldn't have to do biology anymore. You didn't mean for the fire to get out of hand and you certainly didn't mean for your caretaker to die. Show some remorse and for fuck's sake cry.'

Beau squeezed Brett's hand. 'We will, Dad. We'll do everything you say.'

The following morning, Kenny waited with bated breath at the Gatwick arrivals terminal. Even though they'd spoken on the phone most days, he hadn't seen his wife in almost six months. That seemed like a lifetime.

Thankfully, Maggie was on the mend now. She'd lost her hair and had been really ill after each chemo session, but Sharon had cared for her, cooking her healthy foods, forcing her to go out for short, then longer walks, and eventually Maggs had got her strength back.

Charlie had been about as useful as an ashtray on a motorbike, according to Shal. Unable to cope with his wife's illness, he'd spent most days knocking back the Scotch with some fellow ex-pats down the Rule Britannia. Maggie had always been the strong one in that relationship, a bit like Shal had in theirs, therefore Kenny couldn't knock Charlie, as he had no idea how he'd react if faced with a similar situation. He'd always seen himself as superior to Charlie, but not anymore. How could he, when he'd done the dirty on his own wonderful wife?

Desperate to temporarily forget his wrongdoing, Kenny tried to call Donny. There was no reply. His son was probably sleeping. Donny had still been at the cop shop when he'd called him in the early hours. The twins had held their hands up. They'd had little choice. There was far too much evidence against them.

Donny had explained they'd gone down the child sexual abuse route and Kenny hoped that would considerably lessen their sentencing. They were bound to do some bird, because the caretaker had made a busybody of himself, but Kenny knew the twins would be fine banged up. He'd taught them how to box, taken them to judo and karate. They had his blood running through their veins. They weren't weak like their father; he'd made sure of that. They were Bonds. Proper Bonds, just like him.

Seeing women passing by carrying woven donkeys and men with silly over-sized sun hats on their bonces, Kenny's heart skipped a beat. A couple of divs were wearing T-shirts with SPAIN plastered across the front. This was definitely the flight Sharon was on.

Then he saw her. She'd lost weight, looked tanned. Beautiful. She smiled at him, then ran into his arms. 'God, I've missed you, Kenny,' she cried.

Consumed with guilt, tears streamed down Kenny's cheeks too. This was the woman he loved. The only woman he would ever love. 'Not as much as I've missed you. I love you so fucking much. Don't ever leave me again, Shal. Not ever.'

Even though he'd heard nothing more from the Loony Lil, Kenny turned his mobile off before he got in the motor. On the way home, he broke the news about the twins. Sharon was gutted, as expected, but he reassured her they'd be fine.

He also told her he had a new business venture going with Tony and Teddy Abbott which was bringing in lots of money, but she wasn't to worry as he was only a silent partner – which, in hindsight, he was. Sharon rarely pried into his business dealings, therefore never asked much. He said he wanted Sherry to have the wedding of her dreams, so had needed to pull a rabbit out the hat to afford it.

Having learned to cook better since Sharon had been away, Kenny insisted she put her feet up while he prepared a salmon stir-fry. Then they cuddled up for the evening on the sofa and watched one of Shal's all-time favourite films, *An Officer and a Gentleman*.

When the film ended, Sharon turned her body and kissed her husband passionately. 'Let's have an early night,' she whispered seductively.

Kenny had never felt such a mug in his lifetime as he tried to have sex with his Mrs and his todger was as limp as a sausage that hadn't had enough pork shoved inside it. 'I'm so sorry, babe. I've been up all night, worrying about the twins,' he lied. 'I'm knackered.'

'It don't matter. You lie back. I'll do all the work,' Sharon insisted, kissing Kenny's neck, stomach, belly button, then working her way down to his penis.

As well as looking after her mum, Sharon secretly attended a fat camp in Spain, shedding all that weight she'd put on through the tough times. What with the weight loss and the HRT kicking in, she felt a new woman. Now she was determined to show her husband how much she loved him and finally make up for all the time they'd lost.

Kenny said a silent prayer to get a hard-on. But he couldn't. He knew there and then, this was God's way of paying him back.

CHAPTER TWENTY

'Never lie to your nearest and dearest.
The truth always comes out in the end.'

My impotency was short-lived, thank fuck, and Shal and I soon got our marriage back on track. They say absence makes the heart grow fonder and that was true in my case.

I changed my phone number as a precaution. I'd heard no more from Abigail, but my heart would still nigh on leap out me chest when my phone rang indoors. I knew there was no way she was pregnant, but I had a gut feeling that I hadn't heard the last of her. I told Shal I'd lost my old phone. Thankfully, she swallowed me lie.

I hired a top brief to represent the twins. He reckoned they were looking at between an eighteen-month and two-year custodial sentence. Although Beau and Brett had meant to set fire to their school, no way had they meant to kill the caretaker. They might be arsonists, but they weren't cold-bloodied killers.

The judge looked like a nonce. He had a permanent frown, a huge, pointed nose and cruel, thin lips.

The press and media covered the story, but Beau and Brett's names weren't disclosed because of their age. It was also decided they'd be tried in a youth court, rather than crown.

I attended the trial with Donny. The twins were brave, wanted to speak face to face to the prosecution and judge, rather than appear by video link. They both did good, apologized profusely for their actions, as I'd told 'em to.

The twins admitted they'd spent the day of the fire with their real mum and her new geezer. Our defence played on that. Lori turning up unannounced in their lives. The terrible childhood they'd endured while in her care and the sexual assault Brett had suffered. They didn't go into too much detail over that, mind. Brett had begged me not to let them.

I was spot on about the judge. After taking ages to sum up the case, he gave my grandsons three years in a secure unit in Kent.

Beau and Brett seemed fine about it. So was I, even though I'd expected them to get less. Only Donny was in bits, especially when the twins shouted out 'Dad, don't sell our quad bikes,' as they were led away.

All in all, life was good. My daughter was getting the wedding she'd always dreamed of and I decided to surprise Sharon with a boat party for our anniversary.

My life had always been a bit of a rollercoaster from the day I was born. I was just one of those kids, then geezers, that drama seemed to follow around.

However, nothing could've prepared me for what was to happen in the latter part of 1989. Nothing what-so-fucking-ever . . .

Summer 1989

'Morning gorgeous.' Kenny leaned over and kissed his wife, feeling like the cat that had got the cream. 'Looking forward to tonight? The sun's out.'

'Yeah. I suppose. We're not going to know that many people there though, are we? Julia's gonna be busy, circulating around her friends and family. Don't you do your usual, go wandering off with Alan. I don't wanna be stood there like silly-girl-got-none.'

Kenny smirked. His wife thought the boat party was a surprise bash Alan had arranged for Julia's birthday. Little did Shal know it was actually a surprise for her, to celebrate their wedding anniversary. Not only that, he'd also arranged for them to renew their vows on *The Duchess*. When he'd been in Ford open prison, he'd met Clive, a vicar who'd done a bit of bird for fraud. He'd been slung out of the church, but had agreed to dress up in his dog collar and frock to perform the service this evening. 'We'll know a few people there, trust me. I won't leave you on your own, I promise. Right, I better get up. Got a lot of running about to do today. I'll be home about five at the latest. We got a driver picking us up at six on the dot, so make sure you're ready and wearing that dress we chose together. You look the bollocks in that.'

Donny woke up in a good mood. He was off to visit the twins today. The sun was shining and tonight's party on the boat was bound to be a belter. He couldn't wait to see the look on his mum's face when she arrived with his dad. All the guests would be there then, including his nan and granddad, who'd flown over from Spain.

Donny got dressed and whistled Soul II Soul's 'Back to Life' as he went downstairs.

Alfie was lying on the floor in the kitchen, kicking his legs and thumping his fists against the tiles.

'What's a matter with him now?' Donny asked Tansey.

'Wants chocolate and Coca Cola for breakfast. You better have a word with him and look after him tonight, Donny. I don't want him showing us up.'

'Postman's been, Mummy.' Harry handed his mother three letters.

'For you.' Tansey handed them to Donny.

Spotting one of the letters was from Lori's solicitors, Donny ripped it open. His earlier good mood soon evaporated. 'I don't fucking believe it,' he bellowed, punching the kitchen tiles.

'Whatever's wrong?'

Donny's face was etched with rage. 'The court has only granted that junkie slag permission to visit my sons once a fortnight. I can't believe it. What is wrong with these arseholes? That'll mess with the boys' heads. They barely know the useless prat. I mean, how can they even consider giving her permission to visit them when she went behind my back and spent the day with them? That very same night they burnt the bastard school down. Surely, they must know she's a terrible influence on 'em?'

'Oh, no.' Tansey sighed. She hadn't been to visit the twins. Donny's dad and Jamie did, and Donny liked to have one visit a month alone with them. 'Why don't you tell the twins to tell the staff at Compton House that they have no wish to see Lori. They can't force them to see her, surely?'

Donny paced up and down, feeling totally helpless.

'Perhaps it's time me dad paid her a visit?' As he said it, he felt sick to his stomach, but what choice did he have?

Compton House was set in its own grounds in Swanley in Kent. A rather depressing-looking old building, it had once been used as an orphanage.

The inside of the property was much more upbeat. There was a TV and games room and the gaff was painted in bright colours. The boys had to get up at 7 a.m. sharp for breakfast, then they'd do school lessons, have a lunch break, then more lessons until 3 p.m. There were lots of outside activities too: football, cricket, and they often held fun sports days where they would participate in egg-and-spoon races, tug of war, and suchlike.

Donny thought it sounded more like a holiday camp, but as long as his sons were happy there, he didn't care. The twins said the food was shit and a couple of the staff were horrible. But other than that, they loved it.

Visiting was only allowed on a Saturday for three hours. Up to five visitors were allowed per child and any belongings or treats that were brought in were searched thoroughly before the lads were allowed to have them in their rooms.

Beau and Brett were in extremely high spirits today. Danny Drew, AKA Danno, was fourteen and the main lad in Compton. The twins turned twelve recently and now Danno's sidekick Meathead had been released, Danno had chosen *them* as his new sidekicks. Tall and streetwise for their age, Beau and Brett looked and acted far older than their years. 'Ya know that film *Scum* we watched with Gramps that time, Dad?' Beau said. 'Danno is like Carlin. He's the Daddy in 'ere.'

'Be careful you don't get yourselves in any more trouble.

You don't want time added to your sentence,' warned Donny.

'How's Jamie doing? Still missing us?' Beau grinned.

'Jamie's doing all right now. He's palled up with a lad at school. Darren's into motorbikes, scrambling racing. Jamie's been driving me mad for a bike, but Tansey ain't too keen. She's worried he'll come off it and break bones.'

Beau frowned. He'd liked it more when Jamie was moping about in his bedroom. 'Darren who?'

'Brooks. Nice enough lad. He's been round the house a few times.'

'Didn't take Jamie long to forget about us, did it?' snarled Beau.

'Don't be daft. He still talks about you all the time. He even wanted to come with me to visit yous today. He can hardly mope about for three years, can he?'

'S'pose not. He ain't our brother anyway, eh, Beau? We only started hanging about with him 'cause we felt sorry for him. He can do what he likes from now on for all we care.'

After going through a difficult time after the fire because of having to speak about the whole Eric trauma, Brett had now managed to put it to the back of his mind once again and toughen himself up. Beau had asked him what had happened and Brett had replied, 'I can't really remember. But he touched me and stuff.' Brett did remember the excruciating pain he'd been in and realized Eric must have stuck his cock up his backside, but he would never tell Beau that. He'd been so young at the time; he honestly couldn't recall much else.

Donny looked at his watch. Visiting time would soon be over. He leaned forward. 'I need to talk to you about something important.'

'What?' enquired Brett.

'I had a letter this morning from a solicitor. Your mother's been granted permission by some do-gooding ponce of a judge to visit you. I know you ain't gonna wanna see her, so you tell the guvnor in 'ere that. Just tell him she's a junkie, was a shit mother and it'll only dredge up bad memories for you both.'

'But she ain't a junkie no more. She's normal now and lives in a great big house with her boyfriend. He has lots of cool cars on his driveway and took us for a ride in his Ferrari,' Beau informed his father.

'Yeah. We like Carl, and Mum seems all right now,' added Brett.

To say Donny was livid was putting it mildly. 'A ride in a fucking Ferrari doesn't make up for you being half-starved to death as kids. If it wasn't for me, you would never have been fed or clothed. All she ever did was put your lives in danger, having all her smackhead mates round the house. You might be too young to remember it well, but I recall every shitty thing she did. When I bought you new clothes, she even flogged them to her mates in exchange for her daily fix.'

'But Mum weren't well then. She told us that. She's better now,' Beau argued.

'I don't give a damn if she's better now. I don't want her visiting yous and that's final.'

'But we want her to visit us. She writes to us and we said we wanted to see her,' Beau admitted.

'After everything I've done for you two, this is how you repay me?' snarled Donny.

In the lengthy letters the twins had received, their mum had explained how she'd gone off the rails after their father had walked out on her and them to be with Tansey.

She'd apologized profusely, explained she was only young and couldn't cope alone. She'd said their dad had broken her heart and she would do anything to make up for the past. She'd even promised that when they got out of Compton, she and Carl would take them on holiday abroad. They could choose where they wanted to go.

'You got one last chance, boys. You either refuse to see your mother and her wanker of a bloke. Or, your quad bikes go up for sale first thing tomorrow.'

Both Beau and Brett had been angry to learn that their father had walked out on them as little kids in favour of being with Tansey, and especially Jamie. How could he leave them to raise another woman's son as his own? They were his flesh and blood. Jamie bloody wasn't. There were two sides to every story and now they were beginning to understand their mum's.

'Well?' Donny spat. He was furious Lori had been writing to the boys, poisoning their minds.

Beau and Brett glanced at one another. It was Beau who replied. 'Sell the quad bikes. We don't care. Mum and Carl will buy us better ones when we get out.'

'Don't forget it's a late one tonight, Kev. Just wait at the usual spot and we'll be there when we'll be there,' winked Kenny. His driver knew the score, had his suit in the boot and would join them, once he'd parked up.

'I ain't gonna last five minutes in these heels,' Sharon complained, holding onto her husband's arm for dear life. 'As for this dress you made me buy – that's the last time I let you take me out shopping. I feel so over-dressed, like a fat fucking fairy.' Since returning from Spain, Sharon had put on a good half a stone, which was a whole dress size on her short frame. The dress was a tight-fitting, ruched at the front, burgundy satin number. It was classy, calf-length, and Sharon felt ridiculous in it.

'You look beautiful, babe. Honest you do.' Kenny rarely went shopping with his wife. He left that particular pleasure to his daughter. But tonight was so special, he hadn't wanted her to come home with a black outfit as she usually did these days, for her sake as much as anything. She would hate to renew her vows looking like she was dressed for a poxy funeral, and he had a pal videoing this evening and taking photos.

'Are we early?' Shal asked. There was nobody else walking towards the boat.

'Yeah.'

'Let me take these shoes off then, Ken, and put me flats on. I can change 'em again once I'm on board.'

'No, Shal. We're almost there. Come on. Just walk, will ya.'

'They're coming!' bellowed Donny.

In total there were around a hundred guests on board, including the kids. Kenny had wanted to keep it small and personal, so had only invited a few blasts from the past, close friends and family.

'Stand up, Vera. They're coming,' urged Nelly Bond.

'I've already seen 'em get married once. That was enough. Bleedin' vow renewal! Never heard such cobblers in all my lifetime. They've said 'em once,' complained Vera. She'd been quite looking forward to a knees-up, but not having to sit through a load of old shit first.

Kenny was buzzing. He'd hired a company to turn the boat into a temporary wedding venue, with an aisle down the middle. He'd hired professional caterers too, and a Rod Stewart impersonator. Sharon loved a bit of Rod.

'Surprise,' yelled everybody, beaming and clapping as the DJ played Slim Whitman's 'Happy Anniversary'.

'What the 'eck!' Sharon was bemused, didn't know what the hell was going on. 'What's happening, Ken? Why's all the family 'ere? And the kids? Oh my God! There's me mum. And Dad! Julia won't want all our mob 'ere.'

'The party ain't for Julia. It's a surprise anniversary bash for you, darlin'.'

Their official anniversary wasn't until next Friday. Sharon was gobsmacked. It wasn't even a special one. They'd got hitched in 1960. 'You know its twenty-nine years next week and not thirty, don'tcha?'

'Course I do,' chuckled Kenny. He got down on one knee. 'I want you to marry me all over again, Shal.'

'You what! Get up. Everyone's looking at you.'

'There's a vicar 'ere. He's gonna renew our vows. I wanted to do something special after the tough year you've had.'

'Oh, Kenny. You big softie.' Tears brimmed in Sharon's eyes as her husband got up and held her in his arms. 'Of course I'll marry you again, ya daft ha'p'orth,' she blurted out.

Vera pursed her lips. 'Soppy bastard.' She poked her sister, who had tears rolling down her fat cheeks. 'I wouldn't bother crying if I were you, Nell. I'd bet my house on it he's been at it with a bit of stray. Like father like son.'

Nelly looked at Vera in disgust. 'Why can't you ever say anything nice about people?'

Vera knew she was right. The apple didn't fall far from the tree in the Bond family. And she should know. She'd dated more American servicemen during the war years than she'd had hot dinners at the time. They'd never found out about each other. She was far too clever to be caught out. She'd bet her house on it Kenny would, though. He wasn't as bright as he thought he was. Took after his arsehole of a father.

The renewal of vows was short yet beautiful. 'They say when you meet *the One* you know, and I knew from the first night we met, Shal, that you were the woman I was gonna marry. And what a journey we've been on, eh? I know I can be a nightmare to live with at times, but you've stuck by me through thick and thin. You're funny, loyal, me sidekick and I love you to the moon and back,' Kenny said in earnest.

Murmurs of 'Aah' and 'Bless 'em' were whispered. Apart from Nelly, who blurted out 'Shut up, you!' as her sister tried to mouth something awful to her again.

Sharon wasn't one for being the centre of attention, never had been. Unlike her husband, she didn't have a speech in mind. 'What can I say? Erm, we've certainly been on a rollercoaster, Kenny. And you're right about being a nightmare to live with. No other woman would put up with yer, that's for sure. At one point, my car knew its own way to that bloody Wormwood Scrubs.'

Everyone chuckled at that.

'But for all your faults,' Sharon continued, 'I wouldn't change a hair on your head. You're my first, my last, my everything.'

Unusually for him, Kenny was overcome by emotion. He must've been mad to risk chucking away what him and Shal had, and he was damn sure he'd never make the same mistake again. He handed his wife an envelope. 'That's the second part of your surprise.'

'What is it?'

'I'll open it, Nanny,' shouted Bluebell, much to everyone's amusement.

Inside were two tickets to fly to New York on Wednesday for a seven-night stay at the luxurious Plaza Hotel. Having always wanted to visit New York and go shopping there, Sharon burst into tears and flung her arms around Kenny's neck. 'Today has been the best surprise ever. I love you, Kenny Bond,' she whispered in his ear.

As ordered by Kenny, the DJ then played Nat King Cole's 'Unforgettable'. That had been their first dance at their actual wedding.

Tansey squeezed Donny's arm. 'We really should book our wedding soon. I want a day to remember and, now we've moved, there's no reason for us not to.'

Still livid over his visit to the twins, Donny sighed. 'Not today, Tans. All I can think of is those ungrateful bastard sons of mine at the moment. After everything I've done for 'em. Talk about throw my loyalty back in me face! I'll tell you something now: I ain't visiting 'em next week, nor the week after. Bollocks to the pair of 'em.'

Another woman feeling the romance was Sherry. She snuggled up to her fiancé. 'This'll be us very soon and we still can't agree on our wedding song. Let's decide on one today.'

'All right. But none of that sloppy shit you keep picking. My mates'll never let me live it down,' chuckled Andy. He'd wanted the Madness tune 'It Must Be Love', but Sherry wasn't having none of it. She wanted Fern Kinney's 'Together We Are Beautiful'.

'What a beautiful ceremony,' Nelly said out loud. 'Makes me wish I'd have got married, days like this.'

'It don't me. Rotten no-good cheating bastards the lot of 'em,' spat Vera. The only two men she'd ever loved were Kenny's dad and Pete Terry. Both had made promises to her, then left her in the lurch. Never again would she trust anything that had a penis swinging between its legs. She'd use men in future, for whatever she could get out of them.

Catching the man in the grey suit with the big mop of grey hair and a quiff glance her way again, Vera locked eyes with him and smiled. He grinned back and, even from a distance, she was sure those pearlies were his own. He looked familiar, but for the life of her, Vera couldn't place where from.

Most importantly though, he was very handsome and looked like he had a few bob.

The company Kenny had hired quickly took down all the white decor, removed the chairs and the aisle, so *The Duchess* was ready for the party.

Having got over the initial shock, Sharon was roaring at some of the photos Kenny had had blown up of them and plastered all over the boat walls. 'Look at us in that one, Mum. Kenny looks as skinny as a rake with his little sparrow legs, and he's sunburnt.'

'That was taken in the Isle of Wight just after your nan died. Your Aunt Glad lived there. Remember?' asked Maggie.

'Yeah. I'm so glad you could make tonight, Mum. It's made my day.'

Maggie hugged her daughter. 'I wouldn't have missed it for the world. Now go and talk to your friends. We'll have plenty of time for a catch-up later. We're not flying home until Wednesday either.'

Sharon was amazed there were friends there that she hadn't seen for years. Quite a few had attended her and

Kenny's actual wedding, including Pauline, her old best mate from school who'd been one of her bridesmaids.

Seeing Julia standing alone, Sharon excused herself from present company and made her way over to her. 'I bet you were in on this. I honestly didn't have a scooby-doo, thought it was your birthday party. I even brought your present with me.'

Julia chuckled. 'Guilty as charged.'

The boat set sail with DJ Del playing the Hues Corporation's 'Rock the Boat'.

'Let's go up top and look at the sights. We can hear one another talk then,' Sharon suggested.

A waiter urged Sharon to take another glass of champagne off his tray. 'All right. But that's the last for a while. Already had two. I'll be tiddly before the party's properly started.'

It was a lovely calm evening. Even though her husband and son owned *The Duchess*, Sharon rarely stepped foot on it. 'Where's Ricky?'

'He so wanted to come, bless him. But we couldn't risk it because he's so travel sick. He's murder in the car if we go on a longish journey. I was worried the poor little sod would be ill all evening.'

'Ahh, bless him.'

'He's OK. Alan promised him that we'll take him out on Kenny's boat another time and if he's not ill, he can have his own party on it one day. He's made a nice friend at school now: David. He's having a sleepover at his tonight.' Julia rolled her eyes. 'They're camping in the garden, looking for owls and squirrels. David has lovely parents, so I'm not at all worried. They adore Ricky.'

'Lovely. How's Brad and Louisa doing?'

'Brad's currently bumming his way around Thailand. We

rarely hear from him unless he wants money. Alan despairs of him, Sharon. He's forbidden me to send him any more cash, but I'm his mum and I hate to think of him struggling. Louisa is doing great, thanks,' beamed Julia. 'She's got a wonderful reputation now as a top make-up artist, often travels abroad with wealthy clients. She would've come tonight, but she's at a party on another boat on the Thames. I think she's got her eye on some bloke who'll be there.'

The conversation ended when Harry and Alfie came ambling up the stairs. 'Nanny, why you and granddad only just get married?' enquired Harry.

Donny appeared, grabbing his son's hands. 'I told you you're not allowed up 'ere in case you fall in the oggin.'

'It's OK,' smiled Sharon. 'I'm coming now.' She stroked her grandsons' hair. 'It's party time, boys. And Nanny wants a dance with both of you.'

By the time darkness set in, Sharon was having one of the best nights of her life. Kenny had ordered DJ Del to mainly play sixties and seventies music: 'I Will Survive', 'Young Hearts Run Free', 'Band of Gold' were just a few of the classics that got the dance floor rammed.

Then all of a sudden, Sharon squealed with delight as a bloke looking just like her music idol took over the proceedings and introduced himself as Rud Stewart. He started his set with 'Do Ya Think I'm Sexy', then sang all Rod's classics, including Sharon's favourite, 'Maggie May'.

Having taken her high heels off early on in the evening, Sharon stood on tiptoes and swung her arms around Kenny's neck. 'This is the best surprise I've ever had. Where did ya find the singer from? He's brilliant. Sounds so much like Rod.'

Thrilled his wife was having such a blinding night,

Kenny stroked her cheek. 'You got Al to thank for that. Rud's a pal of his. He drinks with him over West Ham. His real name is Michael Dean, by the way, so don't go throwing your knickers at him, will ya?' he chuckled.

A bit tipsy, Sharon punched her husband hard in the chest. 'As if! There's only one man for me, Kenny Bond.'

Unaware that the man of her dreams had today renewed his wedding vows, Abigail Cornell stared at her sideways reflection in the mirror, then turned to her best friend, Annie. 'How many months do I look?'

'Four at least. Maybe even five. Are you nervous about Monday?'

'No. Why should I be? He started the affair. Not me. He was all over me like a rash, the using bastard.'

'Do you reckon his wife will kick him out?'

'From how he described her, I would be amazed if it's not the end of his marriage.'

'Oh well. Not your fault, like you said. As for the way he dumped you, then threatened you, he deserves everything coming his way.'

Smiling, Abigail studied her bump in the mirror once more. 'Too right he does. I'll give him Kenny fucking Bond.'

'What time do you want me to pick you up on Monday?'

'Ten OK?'

'Yes. That's fine. How long is the drive to the nursery from here?'

'Not long. About half an hour, if that.'

Annie smiled. 'This'll be another story for the book you keep promising to write one day.'

Abigail chuckled. 'Too right it will.'

*

'Ain't No Pleasing You' was blasting out the speakers when Kenny and Donny decided to go up on deck for a breather. It was a clear night, the Thames and its surroundings all lit up looked spectacular. They saw the *Marchioness* pass them. There was a big party going on board there too. The partygoers on the deck waved and Donny and Kenny waved back. 'Listen, just forget about the twins tonight and enjoy yourself. They didn't mean what they said. I'll pay Lori a visit and have more than a stern word. OK?'

'OK.'

'Also, why are you running around like silly-boy-got-none watching what Harry and Alfie are doing? All Tansey's done has parade Blue around all night, like she's some china fucking doll, and rabbit to that posh prat of a mate of hers.'

Kenny hated the name Bluebell, thought it was ridiculous enough to get the child bullied at school. He'd never dug Donny out on it, though. It had been Tansey's choice, obviously. But Harry and Alfie's had been Donny's. He had named them after Kenny's beloved granddad and uncle.

About to reply, Donny heard a loud bang. 'What was that?'

'Dunno. It came from that way.' Kenny was pointing towards the direction of Southwark Bridge, that they'd not long passed.

Minutes later the captain's mate appeared, his face as white as a ghost. 'We've gotta turn back. Stop the party and get the lifeboats out. The *Marchioness* has gone down.'

'Down where? We only just passed it,' Donny replied, perplexed.

'It's sunk.'

CHAPTER TWENTY-ONE

'Actions speak louder than words.'

I'd been through some horrors in my lifetime, but a lot of those were my own doing. Nothing could've prepared me for this.

The captain turned The Duchess around and we chucked our lifeboats into the river, hoping they would help. Unfortunately, they didn't. They floated off in the opposite direction.

The Hurlingham was the closest boat, they arrived first on the scene. By the time we got there it was total mayhem and the Marchioness was nowhere to be seen. Watching terrified partygoers scrambling onto lifeboats and trying to swim to safety was a scene I would never forget.

What had been such a blinding evening had now ended in tragic circumstances. Shal was sobbing, so was Maggs and me Aunt Nell. Lots of the blokes had tears in their eyes too. A truly heartbreaking scene had unfolded before our very eyes.

The most hysterical though, was Julia. 'Louisa, Louisa. My baby girl. Louisa,' she shrieked, falling to her knees.

Alan tried to console his wife. They weren't even sure of the name of the boat their daughter was on. But Julia was inconsolable, had convinced herself Louisa was on the Marchioness.

Watching the tragedy unfold was all I could do. We were stuck in the middle of the Thames. For the first time in my life, I felt helpless. Truly helpless.

I held my sobbing wife in my arms, not realizing our world was about to be ripped apart too. In the most unimaginable, fucked-up manner you could think of.

By the time Kenny and Sharon got to bed, daylight had broken.

'You asleep, Ken?'

'Nah. I feel shattered though, completely drained.'

'Me too. Those poor people in the water. I can't get the image of them out of my head. Phone Alan, see if they've found Louisa yet.' The survivors had been taken to Westminster Pier by the rescue teams. She and Kenny had accompanied Alan and poor Julia there, but there'd been no sign or news of Louisa.

Kenny rang his pal's landline, but there was no reply. He hadn't had his mobile with him at the party. 'They must still be up there. We just gotta pray Louisa wasn't on that boat. Alan said Julia couldn't remember the name of the boat Louisa was on earlier. It was only when the *Marchioness* sunk that she started freaking out, saying that was the boat. All we can hope is that paranoia got the better of Julia and she was wrong,' added Kenny.

'I prayed earlier. I can't blame Julia for freaking out, though. I'd be the same if it was Donny or Sherry.'

'I know. Good job Little Man weren't with 'em. He would've been so upset.'

'Ring Cliff, Ken. See if he's heard anything.'

Alan's dad Cliff had been on the *Duchess* with them. 'I can't ring him this early. He might've only just got to kip. I hope me muvver never invited Cliff in hers and sunk her vampire gnashers into the poor bastard. I saw her dancing with him at one point.' Kenny's driver had dropped his mum, aunt and Cliff home.

'They looked extremely cosy most of the evening. Nell came and stood with me in the end. I think she felt like a gooseberry. Turn the radio on, Ken, so we can catch the news.'

Not surprisingly, the news was all about the tragic events they'd watched occur. Dead bodies were still being pulled out of the Thames and it was now being reported that a dredger, the *Bowbelle*, had hit the *Marchioness*, which had resulted in the boat sinking in less than thirty seconds.

'Jesus wept! No wonder there was no sign of that boat,' Kenny mumbled.

Sharon burst into tears. 'Turn it off, Kenny. I can't listen to any more.'

Kenny must've dozed off because he was awoken by the ringing of the landline. It was his mother. 'Are Alan and Julia with you?' she enquired.

'No. Why'd you ask?'

'Cliff's been on the phone. He can't get hold of 'em and he's worried.'

Kenny sat bolt upright. 'We left 'em at Westminster Pier. They were waiting for news on Louisa.'

Louisa is fine. She weren't on that boat. She's been in touch with Cliff this morning.'

'Thank God for that. Louisa is OK,' Kenny mouthed to Sharon.

'You got Cliff's number? Can you ring him? Only I don't know what to bleedin' well say. I've only known the man five minutes.'

'Give me his number and I'll call him now.'

An hour later, an extremely worried Kenny was on his way over to Alan's gaff. Louisa no longer lived there, but still had a key, so was meeting him there. As was Cliff a bit later.

Shal was still crying when he'd left home, but thankful Louisa was safe and well. Donny was shell-shocked by events, but had agreed to stay with his mum until his nan and granddad got there. Charlie had booked a five-night stay at the Ritz as a treat for Maggie, but understandably, they weren't in the mood for shopping or going to the theatre now. They just wanted to be with their family.

As Kenny pulled up outside Al's, a concerned-looking Louisa ran outside to greet him. 'Dad was meant to pick Ricky up at ten and he didn't turn up. Something's happened to Mum and Dad. I know it has. I think we should call the police and report them as missing.'

For obvious reasons, Kenny had never been a fan of the Old Bill and wasn't surprised they were as much use as a chocolate teapot.

The young PC they spoke to on the desk suggested Alan and Julia might've been so tired, they'd booked into a nearby hotel and were still sleeping. He also said it was too early to file a missing persons' report. They had to be missing at least twenty-four hours to do that.

Kenny let Louisa do all the talking. He didn't want to give his name. Realizing Louisa was getting more distraught by the second, trying to convince the copper that her parents would never fail to pick up her Down's syndrome brother, Kenny grabbed her arm. 'Leave it, babe. We'll pick up Ricky, then I'll go an' look for your mum and dad meself. No point wasting precious time 'ere.'

Kenny pulled up outside Ricky's friend's gaff. 'Try to act lively. Like sod all's happened,' he urged Louisa.

'I don't think I can act normal, Kenny. I can't stop crying.'

'Just stop crying until you get home, girl. I'll keep Little Man in the car with me and take him straight home to Shal. I've already called her. She'll take good care of him. As soon as I drop him off, I'm gonna drive back to Westminster Pier and try to retrace the journey your mum and dad would've driven home.'

'Oh my God! You don't think they're lying dead somewhere in Dad's new car, do you?'

'No. Course not,' lied Kenny, fearing the worst. Crashing the motor was his obvious concern. But back in the day, he and Al had been ruthless bastards and made a hell of a lot of enemies. Surely too many years had passed for Al's disappearance to be down to any form of skulduggery though?

Apart from spewing up his breakfast on the journey, Ricky believed Kenny's fibs and was happy as Larry as he would be staying over.

Sharon looked and seemed much brighter when Kenny

291

dropped Ricky off and he ordered her not to watch or put on any news. Reason being, he'd had it on in the motor and the death toll was rising all the time.

Kenny then zoomed off and started his search. A bad car accident it had to be, surely? Julia hadn't been drinking on the boat, but had certainly been in no fit state to drive home.

Alan had swallowed a skinful, but must've sobered up somewhat after leaving Westminster Pier.

Obviously, if they'd smashed their car up in London or any other that saw a lot of traffic, the Old Bill and emergency services would know by now, so Kenny concentrated on the country lanes that they might've driven down near Epping, peering through any partings in the trees for a sign of their car.

It was a fruitless search that went on until darkness fell.

CHAPTER TWENTY-TWO

The following morning, Kenny was up at the crack of dawn. Him and Alan had been together since their school-days. Al was the best mate he'd ever had and could've wished for. Where the hell was he? And more importantly, was he still alive? Because as time ticked on, the outcome of Al and Julia's disappearance was looking bleaker and bleaker.

Yawning, Sharon came downstairs in her dressing gown. She'd tossed and turned all night, was too scared to sleep because of the awful images that kept floating in her mind when she did succumb to tiredness. 'Did you sleep? Silly question, I know.'

'Fitfully. I got an hour or two, I think. You?'

'I did go off an' had a terrible nightmare. You and Donny were drowning and I was holding me hands out to you, but you couldn't reach 'em. Any news?'

'Nothing. I rung Louisa. Not heard a dicky bird. Her and Cliff are going back to the cop shop this morning to report 'em missing. Ricky still asleep?'

'No. He's in the bath. He knows something's up, Ken. Keeps asking why his mum and dad haven't called. What's happening today? And what we gonna do about New York? We can't go away if Alan and Julia are still missing.'

Kenny sighed. 'I know. I'm gonna carry searching again today. That's all I can do. They can't have just disappeared off the face of the earth, Shal.'

'I'll come with ya.'

'You can't. Little Man's travel sick. I need you to look after him.'

'All right. I ain't staying 'ere though, Ken. I'd rather be up the nursery.'

'OK. I'm meeting Donny for lunch at one in the Top Oak. He's all over the place an' all. Is Sherry—'

The conversation was ended by the appearance of Ricky, looking like a dwarf wearing Kenny's dressing gown. 'Auntie Shal, Uncle Ken, I do like being 'ere and staying with you, but I ain't got no clean clothes. Are Mum and Dad picking me up today? 'Cause if they ain't, I'll be stinky.'

Abigail woke up full of excitement. She'd barely slept knowing today was the day. She knew what Sharon looked like and that she worked today, as she'd driven her cousin up to the nursery last Monday to buy some plants. Abi hadn't got out of the car, but she'd heard a tall, skinny lad call Sharon's name. Abi hadn't got a close up at her, but from what she'd seen, Kenny's wife was nothing special. She'd been wearing jeans and a vest top. She wasn't fat, but neither was she skinny. She was just an average-looking middle-aged woman. Not a patch on herself. No wonder Kenny hadn't been able to keep his hands off her. Abigail was very proud of her perfect figure and was well aware how pretty she was. Wherever she went, men would always stare at her.

Annie turned up at ten, bang on time.

'How do I look?' asked Abigail. Even though her stomach was big, she'd obviously made a special effort. She'd had her hair cut and coloured on Saturday afternoon. Yesterday, her cousin had painted her nails, toenails and plucked her eyebrows. The outfit she'd chosen was casual, but stood out. A plain black T-shirt, bright pink leggings and flat glittery black sandals. She'd pondered about wearing her stilettoes, but knew if Sharon clumped her one, she'd be bound to topple arse over tit.

'You look great. I love your highlights.'

'Thank you.' Abigail turned sideways. 'And how does my baby bump look?'

'Big. I reckon you're having a boy,' Annie smiled.

Abigail chuckled. 'Little Kenny Junior.'

'You ready to make a move?'

Abigail was buzzing. 'As ready as I'll ever be.'

Kenny hadn't a clue as to the exact route Alan or Julia would've driven home. Their gaff was out in the sticks, so there were a lot of ways they could've driven. However, he studied his A–Z and drove down as many routes as possible.

'Oi, you dopey prick. Don'tcha know how to drive?' bellowed a bald meathead out the window of a white transit van.

Having already had a few rows for slowing down to peer through trees and gaps in bushes, Kenny had had enough. He hit the accelerator, overtook meathead, slammed his foot on the brakes and blocked the one-way country lane.

Meathead leapt out of his van and was stunned as Kenny came at him like a raging bull and gave him the headbutt of all headbutts, smashing the back of his head against the van. Dazed, he slumped down the side of his van, then onto the ground. He held his head. 'What the fuck!'

'See you, you in-a-rush cunt, I happen to be searching for a mate of mine.' Kenny then proceeded to kick seven bells out of the overweight, tattooed, shaven-headed bell-end before marching back to his own car and zooming off at top speed.

His jaw twitching furiously, Kenny took deep breaths and glanced at his watch. This searching lark was doing his head in.

Swinging the car into a sharp U-turn, Kenny drove towards home. When he lost it like he just had, he needed his family around him, Sharon especially.

Abigail was full of adrenalin. 'Is Sharon around?' she asked the tall, lanky guy.

'Nah. She'll be 'ere this afternoon. What is it you're after? I can help you with whatever,' replied Dave.

'I just need to speak to Sharon about something personal. Do you have any idea what time she'll be here?'

Dave shrugged. 'About one or two. She's taken Ricky over the park.'

'OK. Thanks. I'll pop back later.'

'Who shall I say was looking for her?'

'Oh, just a friend.'

Abigail smiled as she walked back to Annie's car. Kenny adored her. She knew that. All he needed was *that* push and they'd be able to be together. Their love was meant to be. She could feel it in her bones.

After a trip to the park and Burger King, Sharon turned up at the nursery just after one, with Ricky in tow.

'A friend of yours was looking for you earlier. She's coming back this afternoon,' Dave informed her.

'What friend?'

'Dunno. Never seen her before. Pretty girl, younger than you, and she's pregnant.'

Sharon racked her brains. She couldn't think of any friend who was currently pregnant, then promptly forgot all about it when her daughter turned up. Sherry had calmed down a lot since getting engaged. She seemed the happiest she'd ever been, which was a weight off both Sharon and Kenny's shoulders. She'd been a bit of a party animal at one point.

Sharon closed the office door and was just about to phone her mum when Divvy Dave barged in. 'Your mate's back to see you.'

Sharon came face to face with two women she had never seen in her lifetime. 'Hello. How can I help you?'

Abigail studied Kenny's wife. She had a pretty face, nice hair, but her body was lumpy and left a lot to be desired. 'Hello, Sharon. I'm Abigail. I am so very sorry to drop such a bombshell on you, but I didn't know who else to turn to. Kenny's no longer answering my phone calls and I'm carrying his baby.'

The colour drained from Sharon's face. 'Is this some kind of bloody joke? Because if it is, it truly isn't funny.'

Sherry appeared by her mother's side. 'What's up, Mum?'

'I'm not joking. I wish I was,' replied Abigail. 'Kenny and I had a five-month affair. I met him at Charlie Chan's nightclub. He was with his pal, Alan, when we first met.'

'No. No. You've got it wrong. Not my Kenny.' Sharon said vehemently. 'You're lying. Kenny would never cheat on me. I don't know who you are or what you're after, but you can't pull the wool over my eyes. I know my husband better than anybody.'

'My dad ain't like that. He would never cheat on my mum,' bellowed Sherry. 'Piss off, ya nutter. Go on. Do one,' she ordered, pushing the pregnant bird in the chest.

Abigail stared Sharon in the eyes. 'I swear on my baby's life, your husband and I had an affair. Ask him if you don't believe me. How else would I know you were in Spain looking after your mum who has breast cancer? And how else would I know he has a mole near the tip of his penis?'

Still thinking Abigail was some kind of lunatic, Sherry asked, 'Has Dad got a mole on his cock, Mum?'

Sharon was that stunned, she couldn't speak. She could only lock eyes with Abigail, who was pretty, slim, young and beautiful. Everything she'd once been. But she didn't blame this dirty little tramp who her husband had not only shagged, but also knocked up. She blamed *him*. Never in a million years would she ever have believed Kenny would cheat on her. She'd stuck by that no-good bastard through thick and thin. No wonder he'd thrown her a big party, renewed their vows and organized a flashy trip to New York. Guilt surprises. That's what they were.

'Well? Has Dad got a mole on his cock or not?' Sherry reiterated.

'Yes. Yes, he has,' mumbled Sharon.

Absolutely furious, Sherry drew back her right fist and punched Abigail so hard, she flew backwards and landed in a large pallet of geraniums.

Dave ran over. 'What the fuck! You've squashed all the flowers.'

Annie helped her friend up. 'Don't be blaming Abi. It

was Kenny who chased her, not the other bloody way around. Touch her again, I'll call the police. Abi's pregnant, for goodness' sake.'

'Why you fighting, Sherry? 'Cause Uncle Kenny got a mole on his cock?' enquired Ricky.

When her daughter grabbed Abi by her long blonde hair and dragged her to the ground, Sharon ordered Sherry to stop. 'Dave, you look after Ricky for a bit. I gotta go somewhere.'

'What the hell's going on? I thought you two were friends?' Dave asked, directing his questions at Sharon.

It was Sherry who answered. 'None of your bastard business. Keep your trunk out and get on with your work.' Absolutely disgusted with her father and heartbroken for her mother, Sherry asked, 'Is *he* at home? Dad.'

'He's in the Top Oak.' Sharon pointed at Abigail. 'Get in my car. We're gonna confront *him* right now. Then we'll find out the fucking truth.'

Unaware his wife was on the warpath of all warpaths, Kenny was scoffing pie, chips and peas.

'Get it down your gullet, son. You need to keep your strength up,' he urged Donny, who had barely touched his food.

'Still no news on Alan and Julia?'

'No. Not gonna be good news now, is it? Gonna go searching for 'em again this afternoon.'

'I'll come with yer.'

Spotting his wife walk in the boozer, Kenny was about to smile, when he spotted who was behind her. He dropped his knife and fork in shock and his complexion turned a light shade of grey.

'What's up?' Donny asked. He had his back to the door.

Kenny clocked Abi's protruding gut and felt physically sick. He was done for and he knew it.

Sharon clocked the confusion and horror on Kenny's face. He was guilty all right. She picked up his plate and tipped the remainder of his lunch over his head. 'Got anything to say for yourself, you slippery bastard? How could you? How could you do this to me after everything we've been through? You disgust me. She's young enough to be your daughter, you fucking pervert.'

Donny leapt out of his chair. 'Someone care to explain what the hell's going on?'

The pub wasn't packed, but every single customer in it was glued to the entertainment. This was better than *EastEnders*.

Kenny stood up, brown sauce dripping from his forehead. 'I can explain. It ain't what you think.' He pointed at Abi, and if looks could've killed, she would have dropped dead on the spot. 'She's a nutjob. Don't believe anything she says. The woman's a fucking psycho. Needs sectioning.'

'Please don't lie, Kenny,' Abi said calmly. 'The very least you owe your wife and children is to be truthful with them.'

Apart from being clumped and having strands of hair pulled out, Abigail was thoroughly enjoying the drama.

Realizing this was the bird his dad had been spotted out with, the one he'd confronted him over, and his father had denied any wrongdoing, Donny laid into his old man. 'This her, is it? The tart you were reefing 'round in Chinatown? You lying cunt!'

'Enough!' bellowed the assistant manager. Mondays were the quietest day of the week. There was never any trouble. 'I mean it. Get out, the lot of you. You're all barred.'

Sherry had inherited her father's temper. Unable to stop herself, she picked up her dad's pint glass and threw it at him. It smashed him right in the face.

'That's it. I'm calling the police.'

Kenny wanted the ground to open up and swallow him. There were a couple of geezers in the boozer he knew. 'Cunt!' he yelled, spitting in Abi's face, before bolting from the pub. He could barely see, had an eye full of Guinness.

As everyone followed Kenny outside, Donny grabbed hold of the back of Abigail's hair. 'Slag. You've broken my mum's heart. You'll pay for this. I'll make damn fucking sure of that,' he hissed.

'How dare you blame Abi? If anyone's to blame, it's your womanizer of a father. I was there the night they met. *He* did all the bloody chasing,' Annie informed Donny.

'I'm telling ya, she's lying.' Kenny's jaw twitched repeatedly. 'Why don't my own family fucking believe me?' Denial was all that Kenny had left. No way was that nutter's baby his. He'd made sure he never come up the bitch. Not once. He wasn't that stupid.

Sharon looked at her husband with pure hatred. Had their whole marriage been a sham? 'You're the liar, Kenny. Not that little tart.' Sharon pointed at Abi, before walking up to her husband and poking him in the chest. 'I thought it was weird you pulled out all the stops for an anniversary that weren't even fucking important. As for your New York trip, you can shove that where the sun don't shine. And don't you dare bastard well come back to the house. Not tonight. Not ever. I'll pack your clothes and leave 'em outside the door in bin bags. Our marriage is over. For good.'

*

Beau Bond had the raving hump. When Danny Drew had welcomed himself and Brett to be right-hand lads, Beau had been elated. But it wasn't working out quite as planned.

Danno wasn't treating them with the respect he had his last sidekick. He was treating them like lackeys, making them do stupid things to prove themselves. Beau wasn't no fool, he'd had a gutful of Danno already. 'He's mugging us off, Brett, I'm telling ya. He's treating us like we treated Jamie at first. He must be laughing at us behind our backs. I can't believe he asked us to drink our own piss. The geezer's a fucking bully.'

Brett shrugged. 'So, what we gonna do about it? We can't tell him we don't wanna knock about with him no more. He'll just get some older lad on the firm, then they'll make our lives a misery.'

Beau had a lot of anger in him at present. Not only had he been horrible to his dad, although his dad had deserved that, he'd then worked himself up into a frenzy yesterday morning, when he'd heard the staff discussing the boat sinking on the Thames and then his dad hadn't turned up to visit him as usual. He'd rung home and Tansey had said his dad was ill in bed. 'What you reading?' Beau asked, his tone ratty.

'It's a letter from Mum. She's coming to visit us next Sunday.'

'Fuck Mum. She didn't wanna know us for years. We got more important things to worry about than her. Danno, for starters. I ain't putting up with him treating us like clowns anymore. We need to take him out.'

'Take him out where?'

'Beat him up. We ain't gonna take him to the pictures, are we, ya div? There's two of us and one of him. It's the only way. Then all the other lads'll lose respect for him and we'll be the main men.'

'Don't call me a div, Beau, 'cause I ain't one. When we gonna do it then?'

'Today. In PE. Mr Hardy always leaves us alone for a minute or two while he gets the cones and footballs out. We'll do it then.'

Kenny Bond took off his navy T-shirt and cleaned his face as best as he could. He could barely see out of his right eye; that's where the glass had hit him. It was stinging, bloody painful. Heart aching, Kenny shook his head in despair. He loved his wife more than anyone or anything in the world. Now he'd lost her, all because of shoving his schlong up some stupid whore, who'd turned out to be the fruitcake of all fruitcakes.

Picking up his mobile, Kenny rang Tony. 'You at home?'

'No. Basildon. Why?'

'I need your help, mate. How quickly can you get home?'

Tony never asked what was wrong. He and Kenny never spoke business on their mobiles. It wasn't worth the risk in case the Old Bill were listening in. Anything important, one would ring the other from a phone box and they'd chat in their own private code made up of innocuous-sounding words and phrases so nobody would cotton on.

Tony could tell by the tone of his business partner's voice some serious shit had gone down. He could only pray their lucrative business venture hadn't or wasn't about to come on top. 'I'll leave 'ere now. See you in a bit.'

There were currently thirty-six lads residing at Compton House aged between eleven and sixteen.

'All right, lads?' Danno slapped the twins on their

303

backs. Not gently. Hard. He actually wasn't that keen on Beau and Brett Bond. They were cocky little bastards, Beau especially. But they were tall, looked up to by lots of the other lads, which was why he'd taken them on board. The twins had the potential when they were a bit older to take over his status in Compton and no way did Danno want that.

Beau and Brett smiled falsely. 'Fine,' they replied in unison.

Danno grinned. He got a kick out of taking the mickey out of them. It served them right for being so flash. They had a massive house with a swimming pool in the back garden. They were always bragging about racing their quad bikes too.

Raised by an unstable mother on a shithole council estate in Deptford, Danno had grown up with nothing. His mother was addicted to weed and prescription drugs, and his dad had left her when he was only eighteen months old, never to return. It grated on Danno immensely that Beau and Brett had a loving father who gave them anything they wanted.

Danno had purposely stabbed a lad he disliked at school, just to get away from his mother, his older dollop of a sister and her brat of a child. He hadn't meant to paralyse the lad, mind. He'd only stabbed him once, in the lower back, but had somehow managed to sever his spinal cord, hence he'd got a four-year sentence.

Nevertheless, Danno was much happier in Compton House than he'd ever been at home. He got three meals a day and for the first time in his life was a somebody, rather than a nobody. The other lads were scared of him, wanted to be his buddy, and that made Danno feel powerful. 'How d'ya fancy playing a trick on Hardy later?

You know how he loves that little sports car of his. I'll tell you how to hot-wire it. You two can drive, can't ya? Even if you only move it round the back to the other car park, it'll be well funny watching him search for it. I'll keep watch, be ya lookout, like.'

Beau smirked. Danno was a bit of a lump, but he wasn't that tall. He was ugly as sin too, had a big nose and curly brown hair. 'Yeah, sounds a laugh,' lied Beau. There were cameras everywhere. How thick did Danno think he and Brett were? He had seriously underestimated them.

Hardy blew his whistle. 'Outside on the grass and do your warm-up exercises, lads. I'll grab the cones and the balls and be out in a tick.'

Danno ran out in front of the twins and was stunned when first Beau walloped him in the side of the head, then Brett punched him in his lower back. He bent over in pain. The punch in the back had proper hurt him.

Knowing they only had a couple of minutes before Hardy came out, Beau and Brett went full throttle at Danno, punching and kicking him as hard as they could.

The other lads were loving it. Most of them hated Danno. He bullied them, but they would never have the guts to stand up to him like the twins were.

'What the fucking hell ya playing at? You'll regret this,' Danno bellowed as he fell in a heap on the grass.

'Nobody mugs us off,' Beau spat, stamping on Danno's ugly face with the studs of his football boots.

'Go on, do him,' shouted one of the younger boys.

Brett kicked Danno in his pot-bellied gut, before jumping up and down on it. 'As if we were gonna drink our own piss, ya div.'

'Hardy's coming,' shouted Little Lee. He loathed Danno with a passion.

305

Brett swung back his right foot and kicked Danno bang on his nose. It literally splattered across his face, blood spurting everywhere.

Beau bent down and gobbed in Danno's ugly mush. 'We're in charge now, yer fat prick. Grass on us, you're dead.'

Sharon Bond sobbed her heart out on the journey to her once idyllic marital home. She wasn't capable of driving, so Sherry drove her car. 'I'll never speak to Dad again. I can't believe he's done this to you, Mum. If Andy ever cheated on me, I'd stab him straight through the heart. I swear I would. I haven't got a father anymore. No-good shitbag. I hate his fucking guts. As for that whore Abi, I'll give her Abi when she's had that bastard baby. I'll smash the living daylights outta the cocky-looking slut.'

'What hurts me the most is, he was at it when he knew your nan had cancer. He knew how worried I was, how could he be so callous? Talk about when the cat's away, the fucking arsewipe!' wept Sharon. 'All them years I stood by him when he was inside. I didn't as much as glance at another man. I wasn't even away for six months and he had his moley fucking schlong stuck up *her*.'

Sherry pulled up outside her mum's house. 'Let's chuck all his belongings out straight away. We'll cut his clothes up and I'll get the electric saw out and chop his beloved golf clubs in half. We'll trash the fucking lot. It'll make us feel better.'

Fiercely wiping her eyes with the palms of her hands, Sharon's lip wobbled again. She was so angry and hurt. 'Dirty, cheating whoremonger. How could I not know? To have an affair is bad enough, but to do it with a bird half his age and knock her up. I hate him for that more than anything.'

Sherry hugged her mum. 'Come on, let's get you inside. Donny'll be round soon with the locksmith.'

'Your eye feel any better?' Tony had given Kenny some eye lotion to rinse any crap out of his eye.

'Nah. It's killing me. I can barely see. I think when the glass cracked, a shard must've gone in me eye.'

Tony sighed and handed Kenny a black towel. 'You should go to the hospital, get it properly checked. Told you that Abi had a psychotic look about her, didn't I? I bet you wish you'd never clapped eyes on her now.'

'My marriage is in tatters. Me life is in tatters and I'm blind in one eye. I really don't need your "I told you so's" right now, mate. Just be quiet and drive me up the hospital, please. I need to think.'

Two hours later, Kenny left Whipps Cross Hospital like a man possessed. He hated Abi with a vengeance. She'd hadn't just ruined his marriage; she'd trashed his whole life.

He still couldn't see properly out of his right eye, even though two tiny shards of glass had been removed. Everything looked blurry. He'd been given and ordered to wear a patch, but no way was he walking around like a poxy pirate. He'd suffered enough humiliation for one day. News travelled fast around Essex. He was bound to be the talk of the bastard county by this evening. 'Do a right 'ere. I'm going round that slag's flat. I'll give her Abi-fucking-gail, the bunny-boiling slapper.'

Abigail was sitting on the sofa sharing a bottle of red wine with her friend.

'What time do you reckon he'll turn up?' asked Annie.

'It could be any time. His daughter's a bit of a lunatic, isn't she?'

'A bit of lunatic is putting it mildly. His daughter is off her head, Abi.'

'I know. But, she doesn't scare me. She can hardly glass a pregnant woman, can she?' Today had been rather stressful, but Abi had also found it fun. She knew Kenny was bound to go ballistic when he first turned up, which she knew would be sooner rather than later. Abi was also in no doubt Kenny's marriage was well and truly over. She'd seen the look on Sharon's face.

'You sure you're OK? You took a bit of a tumble earlier.'

'I'm fine,' smiled Abi. She was actually more than just fine. She was ecstatic. She'd always dreamed of a life with Kenny and now there was nothing stopping them being together.

'Sit down, boys,' bellowed Mr Greaves. A tall, broad man with a bicycle moustache, bad breath and yellow teeth due to his love of chain-smoking, he was the governor at Compton House and wasn't a bloke to be messed with.

Greaves handed out corporal punishment as often as a kiddy fiddler handed out penny sweets. Most of the lads were terrified of him, especially the younger ones. But not Beau and Brett. They'd learned how to play the system after their first caning. It had bloody well hurt, and they hadn't been able to sit comfortably for days afterwards, but they hadn't let Greavesy know that.

Greaves lit up a cigarette, took a deep drag and swung around on his chair, full circle. 'I'll get straight to the point, shall I?'

'Yes, sir,' the twins said in unison.

'This afternoon, there was an unfortunate incident on

308

the playing field. Daniel Drew sustained serious injuries to his nose, face and stomach and had to be taken to hospital. I take it you were aware of this?'

'Yes, sir,' replied Brett.

'Yea, sir,' added Beau.

Mr Greaves stood up and smashed his large wooden cane, which was the size of a walking stick, against his desk. 'Speak up when I'm talking to you.'

'Yes, sir,' Beau and Brett bellowed.

Greaves walked around the other side of his desk and waved the tip of his cane in front of the twins' faces. 'A little birdy tells me you two were responsible for this unfortunate incident.'

Beau looked Greavesy straight in the eyes. 'Nothing to do with us, sir. We were over the other side of the field.' Beau knew none of the lads would've grassed. They'd all told Hardy that Danno had fallen over.

'Beau's telling the truth, sir. We were nowhere near the incident,' added Brett.

'Hmmm,' murmured Greaves, before smashing his cane so hard against the desk, his glass ashtray flew off the edge and smashed. Ignoring his little misdemeanour, Greaves shoved his face firstly in Brett's face, then Beau's. 'If I find out you two are lying to me, there will be serious consequences. Do you hear me?'

Beau wanted to recoil as spittle flew from Greaves' foul-smelling gob and landed on his chin. Instead, he confidently held the governor's gaze. 'You won't find out we're lying, sir. Our dad brought us up to tell the truth.'

'The whole truth and nothing but the truth,' sarcastically added Brett.

Greaves looked at the lads he referred to in private as the 'Terrible Twosome' with pure disdain. They were as guilty as sin, but as bright as buttons, which is why he despised the pair of them with an absolute burning passion.

'Quick, hide the wine and the glasses.' Abigail popped a strong mint in her mouth. She knew without even answering the buzzer, it was *him*.

Annie grabbed her handbag and ran into the bedroom as planned. Abi had told her to hide in there and only come out if things became too overheated.

'It's me. Open the fucking door,' Kenny bellowed. He stormed up the stairs and as Abi opened the door, he grabbed her by the throat and marched her backwards into the lounge. 'Do you realize what you've done today, you nutjob? Yeah, course ya did, 'cause that was your plan all along, weren't it? You're a fucking head-case,' he hissed, slamming her back against the wall.

'Don't hurt the baby,' gasped Abigail. Kenny's eyes looked manic. She'd expected him to be furious, but knowing she was carrying his child, she certainly hadn't expected him to be violent.

He'd loved her deeply when they'd been a couple, she knew that much. 'Kenny, please stop,' croaked Abi. His hand was gripping her so tightly she was struggling to breathe.

Kenny could've quite happily throttled her there and then. But he'd done enough bird to last him a lifetime and this nutter wasn't worth losing his freedom over. He loosened his grip on her. 'You ever go near, or contact my wife or kids again, I'll fucking well kill you. Understand?'

Tears streamed down Abi's face. Their reconciliation wasn't exactly going the way it had in her daydreams.

Kenny glanced at her protruding stomach. 'D'ya think I'm fucking stupid? Not once did I come inside you. Well, only up your skinny arse, and that don't count. No way does *that* kid belong to me,' he spat, prodding her bump.

Abi immediately clocked the look of confusion in his eyes. 'I need the toilet, Kenny. I'm busting,' she gabbled.

'Not so fucking fast. Holding both her wrists together with his right hand, Kenny ripped open Abi's baggy white shirt with his left. He stared at the false bump in disbelief. It was made of foam with a bit of soft fleshy-looking plastic on top and was strapped around her like a fucking dildo. 'Jesus wept!' Kenny leapt up, picked up a vase full of fresh flowers and aimed them at the wall.

Abi screamed as the crystal vase smashed above her head, water saturating her blouse, pieces of crystal drawing blood from her skin.

Annie ran out of the bedroom. 'Leave her alone, you bastard!' The sight that greeted Annie's eyes was startling. Abi had convinced her she was genuinely pregnant. 'Oh, my God! Abi, what have you done?'

'I'm sorry, Kenny. Please don't go,' Abi begged. 'We could be so happy together. I know we could. We were happy once, wasn't we?' she wept.

Annie felt embarrassed. She'd thought it a bit odd when Abi had wanted to crack open a bottle of wine earlier, but had put that down to shock. She looked at Kenny. 'I had no idea. I'm sorry.'

Kenny glared at Annie. 'It's a bit late for fucking sorrys. Your screwball mate needs sectioning.'

When the love of her life turned and walked away, Abi screeched. 'Kenny. Come back. I love you. I will always love you. Kenny!'

Thirteen-year-old Jake Gardner was in big trouble. His older brother paid him and his pal Michael to walk his retired greyhounds after school, and he was under orders *never* to let the newest addition off her lead.

Martha had nigh on pulled his shoulder out the socket today, so Jake had let her off the lead and she'd bolted. 'Gray's gonna kill me. Martha, Martha,' bellowed Jake.

'I think I just heard her bark over that way,' said Michael, pointing. 'It sounded like her anyway.'

With the other two greyhounds now safely on their leads, Jake and Michael ran in the direction the bark had come from. As they neared, both stopped in their tracks.

Michael grabbed his mate's arm. 'Oh, God! Do you reckon anyone is inside it?' There was a smashed-up red sports car lying on its roof.

'I don't know. Martha, there you are. Come here and go on your lead. Good girl,' enticed Jake.

Not taking a blind bit of notice, Martha stayed next to the car, barking madly. As Jake neared and made a grab for the dog, the stench hit him first. Then he saw it, gagged and fell backwards. It was a terrible sight; the worst thing Jake had ever seen.

A decapitated human head with its eyes pecked out.

CHAPTER TWENTY-THREE

'Always treasure the ones you love. Like I did with
your nan. Only you never know what you've got
until it's gone.'

*Although I'd prepared myself for bad news, the tragic
untimely deaths of Alan and Julia hit me like a ton of
bricks.*

*Their Porsche 911 was found at the bottom of an
embankment in Epping. It had shot through some trees
and rolled several times, before landing on its roof, decap-
itating poor Julia. The coroner's report said Alan had been
alive for some time after the crash and that was like a
knife in my heart. How must my best mate have felt?
Helplessly trapped in a car with his wife's headless body
next to him.*

*Ricky, Louisa and Cliff were all inconsolable, so I took
charge of arranging the joint funeral, running on autopilot
the whole time. It was a terribly sad affair. There wasn't
a dry eye in the church as I tried without much success
to give a eulogy. I kept breaking down and the vicar
had to read out the heartfelt words I'd penned about me*

and Al growing up together and being more like brothers than pals.

Shal, Donny and Sherry attended the funeral together. None of 'em came to the wake afterwards, which I was relieved about as they weren't talking to me anyway.

Aunt Nelly was the only support I had that day. Me mother was there too, but as usual didn't have a good word to say about me. I also clocked at the wake that she'd got her sharp manicured nails into Alan's dad. Poor old Cliff didn't know what he was letting himself into, that was for sure.

'Bad luck comes in threes' the old saying goes. First the Marchioness *sank*, then I lost me wife and me best pal, all in less than a week.

Having lost everything that truly mattered to me, I went off the rails for a while. I moved into a flat on a new estate and was permanently out on the piss with Tony. I weren't shagging birds or shit like that. I was just trying to deal with me grief in the only way a single, unwanted, unloved geezer could. I even snorted cocaine on a few occasions, but that just made me feel more depressed, once the high had worn off.

I missed my kids, being a family man. But most of all I missed Sharon. Even when she'd been out in Spain, we'd chatted at least once a day on the phone. I'd ring her every morning, sometimes consumed with guilt.

It was Aunt Nelly who finally snapped me out of the rut I was in. 'Look, at the state of you,' she said to me when I visited her after a heavy weekend session. 'You look terrible. I know things have been tough for you, boy, but the bottom of the glass ain't the answer. You'll never win back Sharon's respect or the kids', the road you're heading down. When was the last time you had a shave, for gawd's sake! Your granddad'll be looking down in disgust. So will your nan. They raised you to be a winner, Kenny, not a bloody loser,' added me aunt.

That telling-off did wonders for me, so I took up Aunt Nell's kind offer of staying at hers for a week to get me nut straight. While I was there, Aunt Nell gave me another piece of valuable advice: 'Your granddad would never run away from a problem, boy. He'd get to the root of it, deal with it, then fight tooth and nail for what was his.'

It clicked then. I knew exactly what I had to do . . .

PART THREE

'A fool thinks himself to be wise, but a wise man
knows himself to be a fool.'

William Shakespeare

CHAPTER TWENTY-FOUR

Spring 1992

'Shal, he's in again.'

'Who?' Sharon asked, knowing full well who.

'Your fancy man. Go out there and serve him. Go on,' urged Tina.

Sharon glanced out of the office window, already feeling flustered. He was a looker, all right, Ray Weller. But why would he be interested in a menopausal middle-aged fat frump like her when he could have his pick of much younger women? 'You serve him,' Sharon told Tina. Everyone's eyes were on her whenever Ray came up and asked for her to arrange a bouquet for his mum or aunt, and Sharon felt ever so embarrassed. It made her feel like a teenager again, until she scolded herself and gave herself a reminder that she'd be fifty next year.

'If you don't go out there, I'll send him in 'ere,' threatened Tina. Tina Pickett had been working at the nursery over two and a half years now. She was forty-five and had also chucked her husband out after finding out he'd cheated on her. Hence her and Sharon getting on like a house on fire. Tina had been with Sharon the night she'd met Ray. Sharon hadn't wanted to go to Palms nightclub, had only agreed to because it was Tina's birthday.

Taking a deep breath, Sharon walked out of the office. It was a chilly spring day, had been raining heavily earlier. She felt like a tramp in her scruffy Barbour wax jacket, trackie bottoms and wellies.

Divvy Dave stood grinning at Sharon like a Cheshire cat. 'Go unload those garden ornaments that came in earlier, you,' Sharon ordered, before turning to Ray and smiling. 'Hello again. What can I help you with today?'

'I'd like a similar bouquet to the one you made up for me dear old mum the other day. These ones are for Aunt Betty. Oh, and I wanted to ask you, are you free tomorrow evening?' grinned Ray.

'Erm, I don't know. I think so. But I'm not sure,' gabbled Sharon. She was totally out of touch with the dating scene. Apart from Kenny, she'd never properly dated or slept with another man in her entire life.

Ray chuckled. 'I don't bite, you know and I'm a decent geezer. Well, that's what me mum tells me anyway,' he joked. He could sense Sharon's nervousness and he liked a hint of shyness and vulnerability in a woman. Sharon was a very pretty lady, had a bit of class about her. Far more his type than all those half-cut mini-skirted old dragons that chucked themselves at him on a regular basis.

Sharon blushed. Kenny's affair had knocked the stuffing out of her, made her confidence dip to an all-time low. Even though she was dead nervous, finding herself sought after by a handsome man was the most excitement she'd had in years. 'Erm, yes. I've just remembered. I am free tomorrow. It's the following Sunday I'm going out.'

'Well, in that case, would you do me the honour of allowing me to take you out for a meal?'

'OK. If you like.'

Ray winked. 'I do like. Very much.'

'Have a good day, boys, and make sure you're back by seven.'

'Thanks, Mr Hardy,' Beau and Brett replied in unison.

In the last six months of their sentence, youth offenders were allowed out for family days. It was a way of integrating them back into the real world ahead of leaving Compton House.

Dressed in faded jeans, long red stiletto boots, a black T-shirt and expensive red leather jacket, Lori looked and felt the trendy mum as her boys approached her. She beamed. 'Look at you two. So smart and handsome. You're as tall as me with these four-inch heels on. Look,' she said, standing in between them.

Kenny had visited her and Carl recently to issue a few threats, the gist being that if the twins were messed about by them, they'd have him to answer to. Lori hadn't been scared, she'd held her own, and by the time Kenny left, they'd all been on surprisingly good terms. Kenny had even praised her on his way out: 'Good on you, Lori. You've got a good man there and a beautiful home. It takes a proper person to get their act together like you have. Don't mess it up.'

Lori had been secretly thrilled by Kenny's compliment. She was in a good place now, but it had been an awfully tough journey getting there. She could never truly forgive Donny, or Tansey. But she respected Kenny. He was a very good grandfather to her sons. Beau and Brett adored their gramps.

'Nah. We're taller,' Beau replied, snapping Lori out of her thoughts.

'So, what we doing today then?' asked Brett. 'You said you had a surprise for us,' he reminded his mother.

'I have. It's Carl's best pal's daughter's sixteenth birthday, so they're having a big party in the garden this afternoon. There's a DJ and barbecue. There'll be lots of pretty girls there too.' With their height, good looks, blond hair and brown eyes, even though her sons were only fourteen, Lori just knew the girls would flock to them. They looked older and wiser than their years.

Beau grabbed Brett in a friendly headlock. He'd started to get urges this past year or so, couldn't wait to touch a girl properly. 'We gonna fondle some titties, bro?' he whispered.

'Yeah,' Brett replied, trying to sound enthusiastic. He had urges too. Not for girls, though. When he masturbated, he thought of the new posh boy at Compton, Alex Mariner.

Alex was blond, tanned, tall and handsome. No way would Brett ever disclose his feelings to anyone though. They wouldn't understand, especially Beau.

'I'm gonna come,' groaned Kenny Bond, seconds before shooting his load in Karen Bamber's mouth.

Karen spat Kenny's sperm on his chest and licked it off seductively, just as he liked her to. 'Why don't we spend the day together? It's meant to brighten up this afternoon. We could take a drive down to Leigh-on-Sea, have a nice pub lunch and bring our supper home from the cockle sheds. Kayleigh won't be home until tomorrow lunchtime.' Kayleigh was Karen's twelve-year-old daughter and spent every other weekend at her father's house in Colchester.

Kenny held Karen in his arms. Apart from Tony nobody

knew he was seeing her; Ricky thought they were just friends. At thirty-seven, Karen was twelve years younger than him. She worked as a primary schoolteacher and was a lovely person inside and out. She had a pretty face, gorgeous long chestnut-brown hair and was decent in the bedroom department. Quite wild, in fact. Most importantly, she was brilliant with his godson, who he looked after a lot lately.

There was one major problem though. Kenny was still in love with Sharon, which is why he didn't see Karen that much. Two or three times a week, tops. He would only ever stay round at her flat in Grays when her daughter was at her father's, and she would pop round to his once or twice a week for a takeaway and a bunk-up. She never stayed over at his, which kind of suited Kenny. He knew Karen's feelings for him were much deeper than his for her and he didn't want to lead her up the garden path. He'd be fifty later this year and the only present he wanted was reconciliation with his wife.

'Well?' Karen prompted. She knew her feelings ran deeper than his did. She also knew he wasn't over his ex, whom he was yet to divorce. However, they had a good thing going and Karen was hopeful that, in time, Kenny would get over Sharon and perhaps they'd move in together. She'd love another child, a little brother or sister for Kayleigh, but whenever she broached the subject, Kenny would tell her in no uncertain terms he didn't want any more children. He'd also told her all about his thing with Psycho Abi, so the last thing she wanted was to come on too strong and put him off. With men like Kenny, playing it cool was the key to success.

'I'd love nothing more than to spend the day with you, down at Leigh,' lied Kenny. 'But business calls, babe. Tony and me gotta go and see a man about a dog.' Kenny leapt out of bed. 'I better get me arse in gear. OK to jump in the shower first?'

'Of course. Unless you want to share a shower?'

Kenny chuckled. He had no wish to have sex again. 'Leave it out. I'm an old man. You'll send me to an early grave, you will.'

Karen smiled as she watched Kenny's pert arse walk towards the en-suite. He might be older than her, but she adored the ground he walked on. She also knew, after seeing him with Ricky, what a brilliant father he would be.

Hearing Kenny singing in the shower, Karen grabbed the packet of condoms they'd used last night and put them in her drawer.

Sharon left work early and went to her favourite boutique with her daughter. Debra's in Chigwell sold the most exquisite outfits. Designer clobber of the highest quality.

Sherry had an eighteen-month-old son, Damien, and was four months pregnant with her second child. She was thrilled her mum had bagged herself a date for tomorrow evening. 'This is nice, Mum. Bright blue suits you.'

Sharon turned her nose up at the bat-winged dress. She was absolutely petrified she'd accepted Ray's offer, wished she'd asked for his phone number, so she could tell him she couldn't make it after all. What was she meant to talk about? It suddenly seemed very daunting, going out with a strange man. She felt physically sick. 'I don't think I can go, Sherry. Will you come to mine tomorrow, answer the door and say I'm not well for me?'

'No. You need to move on, Mum. Dad cheated on you. Never forget that. This Ray sounds lovely, just the tonic you need.'

Sharon sighed. 'OK, we'll look at black dresses then. Nothing skin-tight, though. I'll look like a beached whale otherwise.'

'Sharon! How are you?' beamed Debra, the owner.

'I'm fine, thanks. Yourself?'

'All good, thank you. What can I help you with today? Are you shopping for a special occasion?'

'A first date,' blurted out Sherry.

Sharon glared at her daughter, then turned back to Debra. It was common knowledge she and Kenny were no longer together; however, she didn't want people to think she was at it with another bloke. Kenny had been extremely generous since they'd split up. Then again, he'd always been a very generous man. He'd signed the house over to her and he still paid all the bills.

'Take no notice of my daughter. It's only dinner with a male friend.'

Debra smiled. 'Follow me. I have some amazing new stock in.'

The first thing the twins noticed when they arrived at the party was that most of the guests looked weird and there were only soft drinks. Carl's best pal, James, had longer hair than their mum. It went right down to his arse.

'James is a hippy, so are a lot of his friends. It's an alcohol-free house. James and his wife are both recovering alcoholics. They've been clean for years,' explained Lori. Neither she nor Carl had touched drink or drugs since leaving rehab. Lori would sometimes have nightmares about her drug-taking, the past coming back to her subconscious to haunt her, and she couldn't believe she had once been that person. For that reason alone, Lori had never bothered to build bridges with her mother. She didn't want any reminders of her sordid past. She was reminded of it when she looked at Brett sometimes. Not that he ever mentioned his terrible ordeal. Lori could only hope and pray her son had been too young to remember it properly.

Putting her arms around her handsome boys, she smiled. 'Seen any girls you like?'

'Nah, and the music's shit,' complained Brett. He and Beau couldn't stand Take That. They liked hip-hop and garage.

Beau didn't reply. He was far too fixated by the older girl in the long green strappy dress. She was swaying to the music seductively, bare-footed, and kept staring at him with a half-smile on her face.

Beau smiled back. He'd love to fondle her tits.

Kenny pulled up in the pub car park, the afternoon sun glinting against his shiny black Mitsubishi Shogun. Tony was yet to arrive, but he knew his business partner had something tasty up his sleeve. He could sense the excitement in Tony's voice earlier.

Kenny put the front seat back, opened the window and closed his eyes. Apart from the boat parties and flogging counterfeit clobber, business had been dull of late. He craved for something exciting to turn up that earned him bundles like the ecstasy pills had.

Around eighteen months ago, one of their main men had got nicked with a car-load of tablets. They were well hidden, behind a false panel that had been concealed by the interior panels, but the Old Bill knew exactly what they were looking for. The sniffer dogs had found them in seconds.

Mal, the guy who got arrested, was as trustworthy as they come. He got a ten stretch and Kenny promised him a huge amount of dosh on his release. In the meantime, Kenny was giving a nice fat envelope to Mal's wife every month to keep her and the kids sweet. Hush-hush money, so to speak.

Phil was the one who'd pulled the plug after Mal's arrest. He and his partner had shit a brick. 'We've had a good run and we've all raked in a lot of wedge,' he'd told Kenny. 'I'm walking, as is The Scientist. Greed is one of the seven deadly sins and, if you want my advice, you should call it a day too.'

Kenny had never been good at taking advice, especially off geezers. He'd listened to Al most of the time, but Sharon was the only one whose advice he'd truly taken heed of. However, instinct told him it was time to call it a day. Their pills were the best and they were supplying most of Essex. The Old Bill would break their balls to find out where they were coming from.

The sound of Tony pulling up beside him ended Kenny's reminiscing. 'What's occurring?' he asked.

Tony grinned. He'd kept his eyes and ears open regarding the quality of pills on the market. There'd been sod all to touch theirs since Phil and The Scientist pulled the plug. 'You'll never guess who I bumped into this morning.'

'Nah. Go on.'

'The Scientist. Tracy dragged me to Lakeside and he was there with his old woman.' Tracy was Tony's new girlfriend.

'He must live pretty local then. Did you get his name?' Kenny still didn't know any of the real names of the lads Phil had employed.

'Nah. But I got him back on board. He's gonna contact the ting tongs. It's time we got back to business, Kenny lad. We've had a long enough break now.'

Kenny grinned broadly. He had no intention of getting his own hands dirty, but as his grandfather had drummed into him as a kid: 'Never look a gift horse in the mouth, son. You can never have too much money.'

'Want to go for a walk? I'll show you my special place,' grinned the barefooted girl in the green strappy dress.

Beau gulped. Her name was India, she was twenty and the elder sister of the girl whose party it was. Beau knew she was coming on to him. The way she was looking at him was sending shivers down his spine. Even the big braces on her teeth hadn't put him off. He was scared, though. He wasn't used to mixing with girls of his own age, let alone older ones. 'Erm, OK. I'll just let me brother know where I'm going.'

'Hurry up then. Meet you round the back of the marquee,' grinned India. She was sex mad, had already slept with over forty lads. She couldn't get enough of it.

'You all right? I'm Jethro, by the way. Your brother has gone for a walk with my sister.'

Jethro was older and dressed weird in rolled-up cream cheesecloth trousers and a matching baggy shirt. He was very good-looking though, had a mop of curly dark hair and bright blue eyes. 'I'm all right, apart from being bored shitless. I thought there'd be booze 'ere.'

'Come for a walk with me. I hid some cider and joints earlier, man. Got to be better than hanging out here, eh?'

Brett locked eyes with Jethro. Was he into boys too? 'OK then. Lead the way.'

'Whit woo,' shouted Donny Bond. His mother was standing in front of her full-length hallway mirror looking very glamorous in a black chiffon catsuit and red patent stiletto pointed shoes. He'd had to shout as the music was so loud. Candi Staton's 'Young Hearts Run Free' was belting out of the front room.

Spotting Donny behind her, Sharon jumped. 'Frightened the bleedin' life out of me. I wish you wouldn't creep up on me like that.'

'What you all dolled up for?'

'Don't ask.' Sharon turned the music down. She knew she could trust her son implicitly. Even though he was back on good terms with Kenny, Donny would never go tittle-tattling behind her back.

Donny grinned. 'You got a geezer on the go or what?'

'Oh, don't you start. I've had your sister on my case all day. She's just left, thank Christ. You know that bloke that they take the mickey out of me over at the nursery?'

'Ray?'

'That's the one. He asked me on a date this morning, put me on the spot. I got in a right kerfuffle, boy. I didn't know what to say, so ended up blurting out yes. I was so embarrassed. I mean, why would he want to take me out? He's a nice-looking man, could have his pick of younger women. And I've put on so much weight since I split with your dad. At least a stone.'

Donny put his hands on his mum's shoulders and smiled. 'You're a good-looking woman. Pretty, funny, with a heart of gold. Don't put yourself down. You going out with him tonight?'

'No. Tomorrow. You won't say nothing to your father, will you? You know what he's like. I doubt he'd be happy for me.'

'Course I won't. Don't you worry about Dad. He made his own bed. You enjoy yourself tomorrow and I wanna hear all about it on Monday. You can spare me the gory details, mind.'

Sharon playfully slapped her son's arm. 'Stop it! As if! We're just going out as friends.'

'Not that old chestnut,' Donny chuckled.

'Let me get changed and I'll make us a cuppa.'

'I'll put the kettle on.' Donny chewed at his lip as he turned on the tap. He'd heard a lot about Ray Weller through the grapevine. A highly respected self-made millionaire who was no man's fool. His old man wasn't going to like it if he found out. In fact, he'd blow a fucking fuse.

Beau literally didn't know if he was coming or going. Within seconds of walking down to a secluded area that had a small stream running through it, India had stripped off and was now swaying stark-bollock naked in the clear water. 'Take your clothes off and get in,' she ordered.

Having never seen breasts or a vagina in the flesh before, Beau could feel his erection growing so rapidly, he thought he was going to come in his pants. No way was he stripping naked though. He was far too embarrassed to do that. 'Come over 'ere and give me a kiss,' he retorted.

India climbed up the small grassy bank, put her arms around Beau's neck and her lips on his mouth.

Not really knowing what to do, Beau stuck his tongue as far as he could down India's throat, then roughly grabbed her breasts.

'Ouch. That hurt. You're not really nineteen, are you? I reckon you're sixteen or seventeen. You can tell me the truth. It doesn't matter,' India said, rubbing Beau's hard-on. He had a throbbing erection. That was all that mattered to her.

330

'I'm seventeen,' lied Beau.

'Are you still a virgin?'

'Nah.'

India lay on the grass and started playing with herself. Beau's eyes were like organ stops as he watched her. His cock was pulsating nineteen to the dozen.

'Fuck me. Hard,' demanded India.

Beau couldn't believe his luck. He'd have been happy just to touch her tits and finger her. He ripped off his shoes, jeans and pants, positioned himself between her parted legs and rammed his prick inside her. He came rapidly. In ten seconds flat.

Another one lying about their age was Brett. Jethro was eighteen, so Brett had told him he'd be seventeen soon.

Brett and Jethro were both lying on their backs, sharing a joint and staring at the sky. 'Wicked clouds, man. Look, they're moving,' said Jethro.

Feeling a bit too stoned, Brett handed the joint back to Jethro. 'I don't want no more. I'm 'ere with my mum, a recovering junkie. She'll go mental if she thinks I'm stoned. Pass me that cider again.'

'They're all in recovery here, man. But we're young, still got our lives to lead. Just because they're unable to have fun anymore, doesn't mean we can't.' Jethro propped himself on his elbow and rubbed his hand across Brett's thigh.

'What you doing?' Brett snapped, embarrassed he'd immediately got a bit of a hard-on.

'Just checking you like me, man. I sort of knew you did. I can always tell.'

Brett sat up. 'I ain't a poofta, if that's what you're trying to say.'

'Not saying that. Let's call it sexually curious,' Jethro replied, unzipping Brett's jeans.

Whether it was the drink or drugs, Brett did not know, but within seconds of Jethro putting his cock in his mouth, Brett came like a steam train.

It was a mental feeling, the best ever. But once it was over Brett wanted out of the seedy situation. He leapt off the grass. 'I ain't a queer, you cunt. You tell anybody I am, I'll fucking well kill ya.'

After the deaths of Alan and Julia, Louisa had insisted she wanted to take care of her younger brother in their parents' home. Their deaths were reported as 'accidental'.

It had been Alan in the driver's seat of a motor that didn't even belong to him. He'd part ex'ed it earlier that week and was thinking of keeping it. Kenny reckoned Al must've fallen asleep at the wheel; nothing else made sense – he was a decent driver.

The newer car lot was sold to property developers shortly afterwards. Kenny had sorted that sale for Louisa, which had enabled her to pay off the rest of the mortgage. The other car-lot in Peckham was only rented anyway.

Kenny pulled up outside his best mate's old gaff. It depressed him every time he visited. Louisa had given up her career to care for Ricky and the home was now like a shrine to her parents. There were photos of Alan and Julia in every room, apart from the khazi. Al had been so proud of his daughter working her way up as a top make-up artist. This wasn't the life he'd have wanted for her. Kenny had tried to tell Louisa that, time and time again, but until recently, when she'd met a bloke after a rare night out, she'd refused to listen.

Ricky was twelve now, hated school and was becoming

increasingly unhappy living with his big sister. Little Man was a proper little man's man, had begged Kenny to let him live with him numerous times. But that wasn't his call, it was Louisa's.

Louisa was crying as she ran outside to greet Kenny. 'You're right. I've tried my best, but it breaks my heart to see Ricky so unhappy, Kenny. He's so much happier when he's with you. I did what I thought was right, but perhaps that was wrong? I miss my old life, my work, socializing and being free.'

Kenny held the sobbing Louisa in his arms. 'It's fine to feel that way. Let it all out, girl. I get it and so would your mum and dad. They'd want both you and Ricky to move on with your lives and be happy. You know it was your dad's wish for Ricky to live with me anyway.'

'I know. But that was when you were with Sharon. Will you be able to manage on your own? I still want to see Ricky regularly. I want him to stay for sleepovers and take him out for days and stuff.'

'Of course. And believe me, I'll manage just fine. Shal's mum and dad's old bungalow is up for sale in Dark Lane, so I'll buy that. Ricky'll have me and Shal to care for him then; he can split his time between all of us. Me and Shal are getting on a lot better these days anyway. Hopefully soon, we'll be a proper family again,' winked Kenny. 'Where is he, Little Man?'

'Packed a bag earlier and left home again. He's at my granddad's. Do you want to pick him up and tell him the news? I'll pack some of his belongings for him.'

'Yeah. Sure.' Kenny stroked Louisa's cheek. 'You're doing the right thing, ya know, sweetheart. Your mum and dad would be proper proud of you.'

CHAPTER TWENTY-FIVE

'Tans, I got a mega busy day tomorrow. I need you to take Alfie to see his shrink. I ain't gonna be around until later this afternoon.'

'I can't! Bluebell's got her photo shoot. You know she has.'

'You're gonna have to rearrange it. I don't ask you to do a lot, do I? The therapist, shrink or whatever you bastard well call him must think Alfie's only got one parent as it is. It won't hurt you to show your face for once.'

'I'm sorry, Donny, but no. This is the best modelling agency in London. I can't mess them around. This is a fantastic opportunity for Bluebell to get her foot in the door, and she'll be heartbroken if I tell her she can't go. All the top models started around Blue's age, you know.'

Donny slammed his fist against the kitchen table. His daughter would be seven next month and, in his eyes, far too young to be taking up modelling. There could be all kinds of nonces in that game, getting off on his daughter's angelic looks. 'You must think I was born yesterday, Tans. You're doing this for you, not Blue. It'll give you bragging rights among the Chigwell massif. You can't kid a kidder, girlie.'

'Don't talk such rubbish,' snapped Tansey. 'And as for referring to my showjumping friends as the "Chigwell massif", how very childish. I have our daughter's best interest at heart, Donny. Unlike you, obviously.'

'Well, it's a damn fucking shame you don't take such interest in our sons. When do you ever do anything with them, eh?'

'The boys are into cars, bikes, racing, boxing and football. What do I know about any of those things? That's your field, not mine.'

Donny glared at his long-term fiancée. No wonder they were on their way to having a crack at the longest engagement in the Guinness Book of Records. 'Shame we never had five daughters instead of five sons. You'd have your work cut out then, wouldn't ya, Little Miss Selfish.'

Already in a tizz about her date that evening, the last thing Sharon needed was Kenny turning up. He often turned up unannounced, usually with the excuse of picking up some more of his tools. Sharon knew this was just an excuse to see and spend time with her. She'd normally put the kettle on and offer Kenny something to eat, but with her date looming, today she didn't have time. 'I'm busy. What do you want?'

'Ricky, you can come in now and show Auntie Shal what you're wearing.' It had been Ricky's idea to get a T-shirt printed to announce his news, so they'd stopped at the arcade in Romford on the way.

Ricky missed his dad terribly, but he loved his Uncle Kenny and being around him. Listening to all the stories about his dad and Uncle Kenny when they were younger made him feel close to his father. Unlike his sister, who

335

treated him with kid gloves, Uncle Kenny spoke to and treated him like an adult.

Grinning like a Cheshire cat as he'd finally got his biggest wish, Ricky ran into the kitchen and pointed to the front of his T-shirt, which read: I AM GOING TO LIVE WITH?

Perplexed, Sharon asked, 'What's going on, Kenny?'

Ricky giggled, then turned to reveal the back of his T-shirt, on which was printed: MY UNCLE KENNY AND AUNTIE SHARON XX

Already stressed beyond belief, Sharon glared at Kenny. 'You haven't told him we're back together, surely? 'Cause we bloody well aren't.'

'No. Course not,' spat Kenny, annoyed that Sharon's response to Ricky's over-excited 'announcement' had put an immediate dampener on his mood. 'Louisa has agreed to Little Man living with me and I'm gonna put in a bid for your mum and dad's old bungalow, as I thought you'd want to be involved too.'

'I do! Of course I do.' Sharon walked over to Ricky and kissed his crestfallen face.

'You do want to see me lots, don't you, Auntie Sharon?'

'Yes. Always. It's great news and I mean that.' Sharon wasn't overjoyed that Kenny might be moving back to Dark Lane though. The more time she spent with Kenny, the more she knew she still loved him. But she could never forgive him, and needed to move on with her life. 'I'm not being rude, but I'm going out tonight and need to get ready. Can we celebrate this good news tomorrow? I'll cook a roast for us all, if you like?'

'Yes, please. I like your roasts,' Ricky grinned.

'Where you off to then?' Kenny enquired. He knew his wife well enough to know something was amiss.

'Out for a meal with the girls,' Sharon lied.

'Where to?'

'A Chinese. I don't know which one. Tina booked it. What is this, Kenny, five thousand questions? Only, what I do and where I go isn't really any of your business anymore.'

'Come on, Ricky. We're leaving.' Kenny stormed out of his old marital home with a face like thunder. Sharon was jittery and far less overjoyed about the news than he'd thought she'd be.

That could only mean one thing. She'd found herself another geezer.

Brett Bond was bored rigid listening to his brother's explicit account of his time spent with India the previous day. Hearing all the intimate details was making him want to vomit, because it triggered memories of having his todger sucked by Jethro. Feeling confused and dirty, he was desperately trying to push those thoughts away. 'Can you shut up about India now? You've told me everything that happened about ten times.'

Beau chuckled and grabbed his twin in a friendly headlock. 'You're just jealous 'cause you never got your end away. There's plenty more Indias out there, bruv. Your time will come. Like I did, ya know. Come. Three times. She couldn't get enough of me, I'm telling ya.'

'So you keep saying. I'm made up for you, honest I am, but please, let's talk about something else now.'

'You don't reckon she was lying when she said she was on the pill, do ya? I reckon I'm too young to be able to get her pregnant though, don't you?'

'How would I know? What you doing now? You ain't playing with yourself, are ya?'

'No. Me cobblers are itchy.'

'Scratch 'em on your own bed then, ya dirty git.'

Wondering if itchy cobblers were normal after coming three times, Beau did as his brother asked.

'Oh, God! That's him pulled up. I'll ring you later.' Sharon's nerves were at breaking point as she ended the call to her best pal, Tina. She wasn't at ease with this dating lark, had already drunk two glasses of wine in an attempt to calm herself down.

Ray rang the doorbell and wolf-whistled. 'You look stunning. I booked my favourite Italian, but if you don't fancy it, I can always cancel and we can eat somewhere else.'

'No. Italian is fine. Wait in the car. I'll be out in five minutes.'

Feeling like a silly schoolgirl once again, Sharon poured another half glass of Chardonnay and downed it in one. She was common and old. Why the hell did Ray want to take her out?

With his plans for a celebratory takeaway with Sharon scuppered, Kenny took Ricky over Aunt Nell's instead.

Nelly was pleased Ricky would be moving in with Kenny. The lad needed a father figure in his life. 'Want seconds, boy?' Apart from fish and chips, which she ate of a Friday, Nelly wasn't keen on takeaways, so had rustled up a shepherd's pie when Kenny said he was on his way over.

'Yes, please,' grinned Ricky. That was another thing he liked about being with Uncle Kenny. They always ate good food. His sister liked salad and Ricky didn't. 'Rabbit's food', he called it.

'He hates that school he goes to, so I'm gonna pull him outta there. He's too bright to spend his days surrounded by notrights. I'll get him a home tutor,' explained Kenny, much to Ricky's delight. Mainstream school hadn't worked out for him as he'd gotten older, so his sister had sent him to a special needs one. They treated him like an infant there, making him dance and paint stupid pictures. He'd be glad to see the back of the dive.

'What about when you're out and about? He can come 'ere when I'm not at work,' Nelly suggested.

'Thanks. I don't go out much of a night now, but that'll be handy when I have to. He's not travel sick anymore, are you, boy? So he can hang out with me during the days. I'll teach him all me tricks,' winked Kenny.

'Can I eat this in the front room? I wanna watch *Beadle's About*,' asked Ricky.

Nelly put the TV on and put Ricky's shepherd's pie on a tray for him.

As soon as the boy was out of earshot, Kenny opened up about Sharon. 'She's definitely going out with a geezer tonight. Acting all weird and jumpy, she was. The thought of another bloke even kissing her makes me lose the plot, Auntie. I wanna fucking kill him, whoever he is. She's still my wife, on paper.'

Nelly squeezed her nephew's hand. 'Don't be doing anything rash. You've got Ricky to think of now. Sharon will always love you, Kenny. Why don't you talk to her rationally, tell her how you feel? If she'd really wanted a clean break, she'd have divorced you by now.'

'D'ya reckon?'

'Of course. You need to have a proper heart-to-heart though. Talk through what made you play away in the first place. You told me how lonely you felt at the time,

339

explain that to Shal. Get everything out in the open, including any other bits of fluff you've been with since.'

'I don't play about no more. I did have a bit of a thing going with some schoolteacher, but it was nothing serious. She was a decent woman, not a nutter, so I don't need to worry about her.'

'Well, my advice is to tell Shal about her. You don't wanna risk another affair coming out the woodwork. Best to be up front. 'Cause no way if Shal takes you back will she forgive you twice, Kenny. Trust me on that one.'

'Tell me more about yourself, Sharon. How long have you and your husband been separated?' enquired Ray. Wanting to impress, he'd pushed the boat well and truly out. His favourite Italian was in the West End, so he'd got his Rolls-Royce out of the garage and had his chauffeur drive them. Their table was in a romantic corner spot. Champagne on ice awaited them and a bouquet of roses for Sharon. The food was exquisite.

Sharon was a bit taken aback by the effort Ray had gone to. She and Kenny might've always had money, but she had no airs and graces about her, was a typical South London girl at heart. The restaurant was too poncey for her liking, as was the roller and the chauffeur. She'd have felt far more at ease if Ray would've greeted her in a pick-up truck and taken her to a pie and mash shop. 'Kenny and I split up a few years ago. He cheated on me with some young bird.' Sharon gulped at the champagne. Ray was a gentleman, good-looking, but she felt totally out of her depth. She wasn't used to opening up to strangers, only ever talked about Kenny to friends and family.

'I'm sorry to hear that. Kenny must be kicking himself now. I know I would be. You're a lovely lady, Sharon, inside and out. Genuine women like yourself are hard to find. If a man is lucky enough to find a diamond like you, he should never let them go. Why have a beef burger when you've fillet steak at home?'

Sharon blushed. 'What about you? You been married?'

'Many moons ago. I was young and naive at the time. Sascha was your typical gold-digger. Five years older than me. I caught her cheating too, with my best pal at the time.'

'Oh no. That's awful. Did you have kids?'

'A daughter, Carly. She's twenty-one now. Done well for herself, works in the city for a Dutch bank.'

'You got any other kids?'

'Nah. I would've liked more, but I was cautious of women after what Sascha did. Too old now. One's enough at my age. The music's about to start. Ruby's singing tonight. She's got an amazing voice, sings jazz and blues.'

When a large black lady appeared and belted out Ella Fitzgerald's 'Cry Me a River', Sharon started to relax. It had been ages since she'd been taken to a posh restaurant, so she might as well make the most of it.

'I'll order us another bottle of champagne, shall I? Or would you prefer a cocktail, Sharon?'

'Best I stick with champagne. I'm not good when I mix my drinks.' Sharon already felt extremely light-headed and the evening had barely started.

By 8 p.m. Beau couldn't bear the itching anymore, so asked to see the doctor.

'The doctor won't be happy being called out on a Sunday evening. What's wrong?' asked Mr Poulter, one of the live-in staff.

'There's something wrong with me dick and balls. They won't stop itching.'

Poulter raised his bushy eyebrows. 'Have you been in close contact with any girls recently, Bond?'

'Erm, yeah. I had a little fumble with a girl yesterday. We didn't do that though,' he lied.

'Drop your trousers and pants. I'll take a look.'

Feeling embarrassed, Beau did as asked. He'd been scratching himself to shreds all day, wouldn't sleep if he didn't get to the root of the problem.

Poulter took a magnifying glass out of his drawer and crouched down, so he was level with Beau's private parts. 'Aha,' he said. 'Crabs.'

'You what! My dad eats them. Big things with claws in shells.'

'Crabs also come in a smaller form. Also known as pubic lice. I can see them crawling all over your pubic hair.'

Beau felt ill. 'How d'ya get rid of 'em?'

'There's a shampoo you can get, but we haven't got any here. Shaving your pubic hair should do the trick.'

'You got a razor?'

'Yes. But as you well know, you're not allowed to use it without supervision.'

Beau had never felt such a fool as when Poulter reappeared with a bowl of water, carbolic soap, a plastic razor, then sat opposite him, watching him desperately trying to shave his pubes without cutting his cock off.

'Do you want me to help you?'

'No. I bloody don't.'

'Don't take that tone with me, Bond. You've only got yourself to blame. You need to be choosier when fraternizing with the opposite sex. If you lie down with dogs, you catch fleas.'

Beau thought of India with hatred. Catching crabs off

342

the slag, then having to shave in front of Pervy Poulter, was enough to put him off girls for life.

'You OK, Sharon? Would you like a glass of water or a black coffee?' asked Ray.

'Nope. Fine with this,' slurred Sharon, unsteadily lifting her champagne flute. 'Ooh, I love this song. Let's dance.'

The song was 'My Baby Just Cares for Me'. Ray felt awkward as he took Sharon in his arms. She'd hardly eaten, was clearly the worse for wear and could barely stand, let alone dance.

'Oops, sorry,' Sharon said as she bumped into the couple dancing next to them.

'I think we should make a move in a minute, Sharon. I'll give my driver a call; get him to meet us out the front.'

'No. I'm enjoying myself. Liven up, Ray, for gawd's sake.'

Clocking other couples looking their way, Ray wanted the ground to open up and swallow him. He was all but holding Sharon up. Even her arms were limp. 'Let's sit down. You need a black coffee.'

Throwing her head back, Sharon laughed and playfully pushed Ray away. 'You bloody sit down, ya boring fart.'

Ray walked back to the table to call his driver, but before he had a chance to, he heard a commotion. He spun around. Sharon was lying in a heap on the dance floor.

The manager appeared out of nowhere. 'Would you like me to call a cab for you and your lady friend, Ray?'

'No. It's OK.' Ray chucked a wad of cash on the table to more than cover the bill, then approached Sharon, who was trying but unable to get up.

'She's lost one of her shoes. It's over there,' pointed a posh bald-headed chap.

Ray grabbed the shoe, then hauled Sharon to her feet. Her legs buckled under her, so he had no option other than to chuck her over his shoulder like a bag of spuds.

All eyes were on Ray as he did the walk of shame out of the restaurant.

Sharon Bond leaned over the edge of the bed and retched into the plastic orange bucket. She had nothing left to come up, only bile. From the moment her eyes had opened around 4 a.m., she hadn't stopped vomiting. As for her head, that was pounding like a herd of elephants had stampeded all over it.

Sharon had very little recollection of the previous evening. She wasn't usually a big drinker, was mortified she'd acted like some old lush. She could recall the food being served and knew she must've fallen over as she had bruises and scabs on her knees. She also had a terrible vision of being sick in the Rolls-Royce.

Ray had rung her earlier to check she was OK. She hadn't picked up, had cringed as she'd listened to the answerphone message. He must've helped her up the stairs as she'd been incapable of climbing those alone. To say she was embarrassed was an understatement. No way did she ever want to speak to or face Ray Weller again. She very much doubted he'd want to see or speak to her either, unless it was to give her the valet bill.

Feeling shameful, Sharon put her head back under the quilt and swore she would never again drink alcohol or go on another date. Why did Kenny have to cheat on her? Her life was all but over. She was nothing more than a fat, menopausal, washed-up old drunk. She hated herself, big time.

CHAPTER TWENTY-SIX

It had been Kenny's idea they find new premises to make the pills. Somebody must've grassed or opened their big gob in the past for the Old Bill to be all over Mal's motor like a rash.

Tony found a similar set-up in Ingatestone. It was remote, down a quiet lane, but this time the land was owned by a pal of his father's, Reggie Hammond.

'Stay in the car, boy. I won't be long,' Kenny ordered Ricky.

The Scientist, the Chinese and Tony were already inside the building. Kenny stormed in, still in a raging temper. Not only had Sharon cancelled, via Donny, the Sunday roast she'd promised to cook for him and Little Man, she wasn't answering the phone to him either.

Donny had tried to reassure him that Shal had got pissed with her mates and was recovering, but Kenny weren't having none of it. Shal had probably had that geezer stay over and lied to their son. Either that, or Donny was lying for her.

'All right, mate? Whaddya reckon then? Nice quiet spot, ain't it?' asked Tony.

'Yeah,' snapped Kenny. 'Right, stop what you're doing, you lot, and listen to me. That includes you an' all, Bruce Lee.'

'Ken,' hissed Tony.

The Scientist and the Chinese all turned around.

'I just wanna get one thing clear. Phil – I knew and I trusted him. You lot – I don't know ya from Adam. If any of you think you can pull a fast one and have me an' him over' – Kenny pointed at Tony – 'then you can think again. 'Cause if I find out any cunt has thieved off me, or grassed, I'll burn 'em alive. Now do we understand one another?'

The Scientist glared at Kenny. The Chinese glanced at one another, shrugged, then mumbled 'Yes' one by one.

'Crack on, lads,' Tony said, grabbing Kenny by the arm and dragging him out of the building. 'What the fuck's wrong with you? We've worked with 'em before. You can't go round threatening 'em like that for no good reason.'

'I can and I will. The filth knew exactly where to look for those pills last time. Anyway, we ain't worked with 'em all before. I don't remember him, the Bruce Lee looka-like.'

'I can't talk to you while you're in this mood, Ken. Who's upset yer?'

Kenny smashed his fist against the wall of the building. 'Long story. You free for a drink later? I could do with one or ten.'

'Yeah. Gotta meet a geezer in Wanstead at teatime. I'll call you after I'm done.'

Having spent two days beating herself up in bed, Sharon Bond stepped under the shower and immediately felt better as the hot water cleansed her pores of that poison, alcohol. Tina had popped round last night. Ray had gone up the nursery yesterday. Sharon was so glad she wasn't there. Sod facing him any time soon. She'd told Tina all she could remember. Tina had found it hilarious. She bloody didn't though, was still burning up with shame every time she thought about it.

'Mum, Mum.'

Sharon quickly dried herself and put on her dressing gown.

'How you feeling?' asked Donny.

'Better than I was, thanks.'

Donny knew his mother had got drunk and was thoroughly embarrassed about making a show of herself. 'Good. I need you up the nursery today. Divvy Dave and Jeanette are off sick,' he lied. The sooner his mum got out of the house, the better she would feel.

'Not today, Donny. I don't feel up to working yet.'

'Yes. You do. You're not the first woman to get sloshed and make a tit of herself, and you certainly won't be the last. Get your arse in gear. I'll give you a lift. You've got fifteen minutes.'

'Who you been on the phone to?' Sharon asked her son. She'd been annoyed on finding out he'd lied to her. There was sod all wrong with Divvy Dave or Jeanette. But being back at work, arranging flowers, was therapeutic. She just prayed Ray Weller didn't roll up again. She couldn't avoid him for ever though, would apologize and hope that was the end of the matter. Her nerves had been shot to pieces, especially when she'd got in that Rolls-Royce. Honesty was the best policy. She'd tell Ray the truth.

'The twins' guvnor. They're allowed to stay at mine

Saturday night 'cause it's their birthday. I gotta take 'em back Sunday evening.'

'Aww, lovely. They'll be coming home for good soon, won't they?'

Donny smiled. He couldn't wait to have his sons back where they belonged. 'Yep. Another three months and they'll be working up 'ere. No point in 'em starting a new school. They were born to graft. Take after their old man.'

The office door burst open, Tina's face a picture of excitement. 'Ray's just pulled up, Shal.'

'Oh, shit. Tell him I'm still off sick. Me car ain't 'ere.'

Donny chuckled. 'Mum, go and face the geezer. He obviously still likes ya. Go on. Front it out.'

'Good luck,' Tina said. 'And don't forget to find out if you were sick in his roller.'

Feeling ridiculous as she knew Donny and Tina would be peeping through the blinds watching her, Sharon reluctantly walked out the office. At least she felt comfortable today in her jeans, trainers, T-shirt and padded black gilet. 'Hello, Ray.'

Ray grinned. He had lovely blue eyes that twinkled when he smiled. 'How you doing? Feeling better, I hope.'

'Look, I'm really sorry for showing meself up and you. I'm gonna be honest, I was so nervous. I was with Kenny since I was a teenager; I ain't cut out for dating at my bleedin' age. I dunno what I was thinking. Please don't tell me what I did or didn't do, as I can remember very little and would rather leave it that way. I'm mortified enough as it is. I've a feeling I might owe you a valet bill for your roller though. There's money in the office. So sorry if I puked in it.'

Ray burst out laughing. 'You did puke, as you so daintily put it, but not in the roller. We stopped the motor and you chucked up on a grass verge. Therefore, you owe me nothing. Well, only another date, so I can get to know you properly this time. Whaddya say?'

Sharon was astounded. No way had she expected Ray to want to take her out again. 'Erm, yeah, but not yet, if you know what I mean. You're a lovely man, Ray. You truly are. But I need to sort me head out first. I'm not into Rolls-Royces or fancy restaurants. I'm a pie and mash girl at heart.'

Ray grinned. 'I'm a pie and mash boy too. No more drivers or rollers, I promise. You choose where we go on the next date. I mugged meself off too. I hate that bastard Rolls-Royce. I rarely get it out the garage more than twice a year. I was just trying to impress you, I guess.'

Sharon smiled. This was more like it. 'I'll call you soon, Ray. I promise.'

Tansey wasn't having a good day. Her housekeeper was off sick. Alfie had refused to go to school this morning, then had smashed the window in his bedroom when she'd tried to get him dressed. Then her washing machine had broken mid-cycle.

'Mum, someone at the door,' shouted Harry. He'd been off school too, with mumps.

As soon as Tansey saw her neighbour's face, she knew that her day was about to get even worse. 'What's wrong, June?'

June pointed to the end of Dark Lane. 'You better ring Donny, love. It's the gypsies. A load of 'em have pulled on that field we're adjoined to. I dunno what else to do. George is away playing golf.'

Karen Bamber checked her appearance one final time. She always liked to make a special effort when Kenny was coming round.

Karen was meant to be at work today, but had thrown a sickie. She wasn't exactly ill, but her inability to sleep of late was getting her down. She'd only seen Kenny once in the past ten days and was missing him. Kenny was a gentleman, treated her with respect. The total opposite of her daughter's father. What an immature waste of space he'd turned out to be.

It had been a nice surprise earlier when she'd called Kenny and he'd offered to pop round. He said he'd had a poxy couple of days, so Karen had decided to cheer him up. She'd popped out and treated him to his favourite meal: pie, mash and liquor. Then all being well, they'd spend the afternoon making love.

Donny pulled up in Dark Lane. 'What's going on?' he asked Dennis, another Dark Lane resident.

'Fucking pikeys. They reckon they've bought the land, Donny. I can't see it meself, but they reckon they're having some groundwork done, then moving massive mobile homes on there.'

'I went and spoke to 'em. Polite enough, the old man was. Swears blind he's bought the plot of land,' added Frank, another neighbour. 'Introduced himself as Bobby, said he bought the land for himself and his kids to live on. Lots of chavvies running about over there, Donny. I mean, I ain't got nothing against Travellers, but our lovely gaffs ain't gonna be worth two-bob if we wanna sell up. Who in their right mind would buy a property with a bunch of didicois living a spit's throw away?'

'We'll have to nail everything down,' piped up June. 'My George hates the robbing bastards. They used to thieve out of his yards back in the day.'

Donny shook his head in despair. 'I'll ring me dad. He'll sort it.'

Kenny turned his phone off outside Karen's gaff. Donny had said Sharon would ring him this afternoon and he wanted her to suffer, like he had been.

Karen opened the door, smiling. 'Give me a hug. I've missed you.'

Kenny held her tightly. He needed a bit of TLC. 'Let's go a bed.'

'But I got us pie and mash. It's still hot.'

'Fuck the pie and mash. We can warm that up later. Come on.' Kenny grabbed her hand and dragged her off to the bedroom. 'It's you I need, not grub, girlie.'

Karen chuckled. That was another good thing about Kenny. He was so bloody passionate, like a man possessed at times.

Tansey could not help but glare at Donny. As if her day had not been bad enough. Now Donny was informing her that on Sunday, they would be having dinner with his junkie of an ex and her bloke. 'I'm not going. You're having a bloody laugh, ain't ya? Why would I want to spend time with some scumbag of a woman who had no time for your sons when they were young?'

'Please, Tans. Do this for me. I don't wanna go either, but its Beau and Brett's birthday and it's their wish that me and their mother build bridges. What else can I do but go along with it?' Donny flung his hands upwards.

'Have you forgotten it was thanks to Lori that Brett got brutally raped as a young child?'

'Keep your voice down in case the kids hear,' urged

Donny. 'Nah. Course I ain't. I'll never forgive her for that. I hate her, ya know I do. But I don't wanna lose the boys. They've become quite fond of Lori, probably because of the flash gaff and cars Carl owns. She's using the boys, getting the twins on side just so she can play games with me. If I don't play the game back, I'm worried they might move in with her and Carl. That would rip my heart out.'

'Well, if they're that disloyal to you, they're not worth it. Never forget you took them from a life of misery and gave them everything. Perhaps, too much? I always said you spoiled them.'

'Oh, and Bluebell don't get spoiled, does she? I am asking you one fucking favour, Tans. Two hours this lunch'll last for, tops. I know you've never liked the twins, but they're my sons and I will always love 'em. Lori's got into their nuts, coming across as the perfect mother now she's clean. She blames me for her ending up on drugs in the first place.'

Tansey sighed. She was on a loser with this one and she knew it. 'All right. We'll go to lunch with the junkies. But two hours, no more, and I mean that with every bone in my body, Donny.'

Having heard the gypsy news, Kenny Bond was livid. He'd rung the council first and the dumb tart on the end of the phone had taken over an hour to finally inform him they had no idea who that particular piece of land belonged to.

Kenny then rang his pal, who had bought the land and built the houses on Dark Lane in the first place. Their conversation soon turned into a massive barney when the guy admitted he didn't know who the adjoining acres belonged to.

'No wonder you fucking sold up last year. Worthless,

these properties are now. Did you get wind we'd end up with a load of pikeys next door to us?' ranted Kenny.

His pal denied all knowledge and apologized profusely. In a rage, Kenny hadn't accepted the apology gracefully. 'If you don't help me get this sorted somehow, I swear, you're dead to me and I mean that literally, ya cunt.'

Like a man possessed, Kenny marched up to the end of Dark Lane, alone. He'd told all the others to stay put, including his son. He was still the main man of Dark Lane, even though Sharon had slung him out.

Kenny was appalled as he clapped eyes on the numerous trailers, kids running riot, tethered horses and yapping dogs. It was worse than he could have imagined; already the place resembled the shithole of all shitholes. 'Oi, who's the owner of this land?' he bellowed at a group of men who seemed to be measuring up the ground.

A stocky dark-haired bloke walked over to Kenny. 'I am. What can I do for ya?'

'Who'd you buy this land off?'

'A pal.'

'Does your pal have a name?'

'None of your business, and for future reference, I don't like being addressed with an "Oi".'

Kenny sized up the bloke by locking eyes with him. The geezer had the look of an ex-boxer, his nose gave that away. His eyes were a piercing blue with a steely look. 'I got a house in Dark Lane, so has my son. You're gonna have to put up a proper fence to separate yourself from us.'

'You wanna fence put up, erect one yourself.'

'Don't mess with me, mate, because believe me, you'll regret it. Kenny Bond's the name and I take no prisoners, me.'

'Everything all right, Dad?' asked a lad in his mid- to late-twenties.

'Yeah, fine. Kenny Bond's one of our new neighbours,' Bobby said, his gaze still holding Kenny's.

Having heard the back-end of the conversation, Billy Tamplin grinned at Kenny. 'You any relation to James Bond?'

'Fuck off,' spat Kenny. Good job he never had a shooter on him, because he could've quite easily blown them all away there and then.

'Look 'ere, we don't want no aggravation. We're moving 'ere for a quiet life. You stay away from us and we'll keep out of your way. Deal?' Bobby held out his right hand.

Kenny snarled and ignored the gesture. 'You keep your kids, dogs, horses and your fucking selves off our land. Got that?'

'Loud and clear. Oh and the name's Bobby by the way, and my family take no prisoners either. You wanna start a war, you ignorant shitcunt, then that's up to you.'

Kenny would usually knock any man sparko who called him that, but there were six blokes standing behind Bobby. He couldn't mug himself off, was way too outnumbered. Neither would he forget that insult, mind. Kenny pointed a forefinger at Bobby. 'Keep away from us, or else,' he spat, before turning and walking away.

'Go fuck your grandmother,' shouted a voice.

Kenny swung around, his face twitching with fury. 'What did you say? Who said that?'

'I did. Whatcha gonna do about it?' smirked Johnny Tamplin.

'I'll fucking come back and blow the lot of ya off the face of the earth, you keep pushing my buttons. Dirty cunts, the lot of ya.'

As Johnny and Billy went to lunge towards Kenny,

Bobby grabbed hold of both. 'Leave it for now. Go on, Kenny. Off you trot. Nice meeting ya.'

Kenny spat on the ground before walking away, his face like thunder.

Still fuming, Kenny dropped Ricky off at his aunt's, then met Tony in a wine bar in Woodford. Tony's dad knew a lot of Travellers and was doing some digging.

'I got you a large Scotch, thought you might need it,' Tony said.

Kenny grabbed the glass and downed the drink in one.

'Chin up, mate. We've already got a load of orders in. We'll be back in business properly by the weekend. All that lovely dosh rolling in'll take your mind off the other shit.'

'Your old man find anything out yet?'

'Yeah. The land belonged to an elderly Traveller, Joe something. He sold it to Bobby Tamplin. He's meant to be OK, Bobby. Proper family man. Grafts hard. Got good morals. He ain't one to upset, though. Hard as nails. Ex bare-knuckle boxing champion.'

'Tamplin, you say?'

'Yeah.'

'I know that fucking name. He's the brother of that scumbag Freddie who I shared a cell with. Robbed old folk, that cunt did. He better not be living on that land, I'm telling yer. I'll blow his brains out and gladly do time for that piece of shit.'

'Calm down, mate. No good working yourself into a frenzy and kicking off. They've legally bought the land. What can you do?'

Kenny's jaw twitched manically. 'Those houses on Dark Lane will be worth fuck all now. I've just put a bid in for the father-in-law's old bungalow an' all.'

'Well, you might get it cheaper. Changing the subject, there's a right sort at the bar who can't take her eyes off you. Spotted top she's wearing.'

Kenny looked up. The bird was certainly attractive, but he wasn't interested in any woman, other than Sharon. 'I think she's got a bloke, you know, my Shal. I'm gonna hire a private detective, find out who the fucker is.' Kenny chucked a twenty-pound note at Tony. 'Get some more drinks in, mate. Same as before, but get us a pint of Guinness an' all.'

As Tony walked up to the bar, the woman he'd pointed out walked over to Kenny. 'You don't remember me, do you?'

'Erm, you look a bit familiar as it goes. Where do I know you from?'

'Abigail. I was her mate. Annie. Remember?'

'Yeah. Course. How's she doing?'

Annie stared at Kenny with hatred. 'She disappeared years ago, about ten days after she confronted your wife. Bit of a coincidence that. Didn't the police speak to you? They did me.'

'Er, yeah, at the time they did. I thought she'd gone away to clear her head and would've turned up by now though.'

'Don't lie! You don't fool me. I know what Abi did to you was wrong, but she didn't deserve to die. She loved you.'

'What's this all about then?' Tony put the drinks on the table.

Kenny stood up. 'I don't need this shit and I don't have a clue where your nutty mate is. I'm going to pick up Ricky, mate. I'll bell yer tomorrow.'

'What about your drinks?'

Kenny waved a hand, then bolted from the pub.

'That's it. Run away. You're as guilty as sin, I can see it in your eyes. I'll be going back to the police, you know,' shrieked Annie.

Kenny sat in his car and for the first time in his life, struggled to breathe. He held his chest. Was he having a heart attack?

CHAPTER TWENTY-SEVEN

'Evie, make some more tea for the men, please,' shouted Bobby Tamplin. Evie had only been sixteen when they'd married, him seventeen. Their love for one another was still as strong to this day and what a wonderful family they'd created. All their kids were good uns, their grandkids little belters.

'Mum, I wanna work with the men,' announced five-year-old Bobby-Joe, Evie's youngest son.

'No, darling, 'cause the men are plumbing and laying concrete and stuff. You choose the cake and biscuits you think the men'll like.'

'But that's a girl's job.'

'No. It ain't. Not in our family, ya cheeky monkey,' laughed fifteen-year-old Jolene. She and her twin Tammy totally adored their little brother. Bobby-Joe had been born with Down's syndrome. A happy boy with a big smile and hearty chuckle, Bobby-Joe had been named after their father to give him the best chance in life. Their dad had once been a decent amateur-boxer before becoming a bare-knuckle fighter. No one messed with him. He was very well respected.

'You take the trays of teas out, girls. I'll bring the cakes and biscuits,' said Evie.

Bobby Senior grinned as the three women in his life approached. His Evie wore her curly brown hair up in a bun and was still as pretty as the day he'd met her. You'd never think she'd had six kids either. Only a size ten, a tiny little thing in comparison to him.

As for his girls, Tammy and Jolene, they'd been so wanted and prayed for. After three boys, he and Evie had thought they weren't destined to be blessed with daughters, then two had popped out at once.

Bobby worried about his girls something chronic. Stunning, they were. Worryingly pretty with their long, wavy dark hair, smouldering brown eyes and beautiful figures.

'The girls are cooking Joe Grey tonight, Bobby. I got a couple of crusty loaves to go with it. Gotta teach 'em all me cooking skills now, ain't I?' Evie slyly winked at her sons. 'Seeing as they'll be married themselves soon.'

Knowing how their mum loved to wind his dad up, Billy joined in. 'Yeah. Not long now before they have chavvies of their own. Gotta be able to cook proper food for the chavvies.'

'They might even have twins themselves,' added eighteen-year-old Sonny.

'Shut up, the lot of ya. My princesses ain't fleeing the nest for a while, are ya, girls?'

'No, Dad. We're too young,' Tammy reassured him.

Jolene rolled her eyes. 'And we don't even have boyfriends.'

'You will soon, though. Bound to jump the broomstick in the next year or two,' Johnny insisted.

'Enough now. Wind me up any more and you'll give

me a bleedin' heart attack. Now orf you go. Us men got work to do.'

'Don't work too hard,' said Jolene and Tammy. They both playfully punched one another's arms, laughing. It was a standing joke that at least half a dozen times a day, they'd say a sentence in unison.

'Keep your eye on the chavvies, Bobby,' Evie ordered. Their grandchildren were playing quite a distance away.

'They're fine. Don't worry. We been checking on 'em regularly.' Bobby picked his shovel back up and smashed it into the ground. He imagined the turf was Kenny Bond's head. He might have acted unbothered when that arsehole turned up giving it large the other day, but on the inside he'd felt like a raging bull. His boxing name had been Bobby 'The Bull' Tamplin.

What had enraged Bobby the most was the way Kenny had spoken to him, looked at the precious bit of land he'd grafted all his life to buy as though it were something nasty he'd stepped on.

Bobby knew what Kenny had been thinking. Dirty, scummy, thieving gyppos. However, Bobby and his family were anything but. They were an extremely respectful family who had never chored a thing off a soul in their lives. Both Bobby and Evie had raised their children well, had threatened to chop their fingers off if they ever went out choring off gorgers or anybody else for that matter. Bobby owned two salvage yards, one in Aveley, one in Purfleet. He employed four women and twenty-four men, including his sons who helped him run his thriving business.

There were good and bad in every community and the Traveller community was no different. Truth be known, he'd bought this plot of land to move away from the damage his youngest brother, Freddie, had caused to

360

the family name, and the Franklins. They were a bad lot, those Franklins and he'd known Danny and Josh had designs on his daughters. Over his dead body would his princesses end up as part of that family. He'd rather they marry gorgers. Not that he wanted them to marry at all. If he had his way, they'd stay at home so he could protect them for ever. Their boobies had grown at an alarming rate this past year and he hated seeing them with make-up on their faces. Evie took the mickey, would sing Tanya Tucker's 'Delta Dawn' to him. 'You'll be calling the pair of them your babies at forty-one, Bobby. We can't wrap them in cotton wool. They're teenagers. Of course they're going to want to wear certain clothes and experiment with make-up. It's what fifteen-year-old girls do.'

'Dad. I'm bored. Can I work with you?'

Bobby picked up his youngest son and swung him in the air. Bobby-Joe was another reason he'd wanted to move. He hadn't wanted his son hanging around with those scallys on the Traveller site they'd lived near to. Bobby-Joe was special, needed protection, and Bobby would move heaven and earth to protect his family. Always.

'How's your week been, boys?' Donny was on the way back to Dark Lane with the twins.

'Beau's had better weeks,' Brett smirked. He'd thought it was hysterical his brother had caught crabs off India and had to shave his pubes off in front of Pervy Poulter.

'Why? What happened, Beau?'

'He had the itches,' Brett informed his father. 'I think he had ants in his pants.'

Beau elbowed his brother in the ribs. 'Take no notice, Dad. He's just being a dick. So, is Tansey coming to Mum's tomorrow?'

'Yep. We're all coming.' Donny hadn't originally wanted to accept the invitation; his dad had talked him into it. 'If Lori's offering an olive branch, then take it. It'll make like easier in the long run. Those boys'll get married one day, have children of their own. Best you bury the hatchet now, son. You haven't got to be best friends. Just be polite and keep it amicable,' was his father's advice.

'Carl's gonna do a barbecue. They got a wicked garden. It's double the size of ours and it's got a hot-tub as well as a swimming pool.'

'Nice,' mumbled Donny. He was dreading it.

It had been Beau's idea that his mum invite his dad over so they could all celebrate his and Brett's birthday together. It was bound to kick off, especially with that miserable cow Tansey. Beau smirked. At least it wouldn't be boring.

'Changing the subject, you spoken to Granddad lately?' enquired Donny.

'Yeah,' the twins replied in unison.

'Did he tell yer Ricky's living with him now?'

'No. Why's that then?' enquired Brett.

'His sister weren't coping too well, by all accounts, and I think Ricky started playing her up a bit. Be kind to him, please.'

'Course. Why wouldn't we be?' questioned Brett.

Donny glared in his interior mirror at his sons. 'Let's be honest, you haven't always been nice to him in the past.'

'Leave it out, Dad,' Beau replied. 'We were only kids back then. We ain't now. If Gramps has took Ricky on, then he becomes family and we'll look out for him as one of our own.'

'Too right we will,' added Brett.

Knowing by the twins' serious expressions they'd meant every word, Donny smiled. They'd gone into Compton House as kids and would be leaving as men.

Kenny left the private hospital feeling like a bit of a weirdo. Since leaving Sharon and moving to Chigwell, he'd only visited his GP surgery once and that was to register with them because he was still having a bit of gyp after those shards of glass went in his eye.

However, the other night had been a proper scare for Kenny. As he'd driven to pick Ricky up after meeting Tony, he'd felt clammy, had palpations like no tomorrow. Even his hands and feet had been shaking.

His GP had examined him, taken his blood pressure, which was a bit high, and given him a form to have a CT scan. It had come back fine, thankfully. He'd admitted he'd been under stress recently and the doctor's diagnosis was that he'd suffered a panic attack. He'd never heard of such a thing, felt a right wally as the doctor explained it, then gave him a prescription for an anxiety drug called diazepam.

Kenny's phone rang. It was Karen, asking him how he'd got on and trying to persuade him to pop round. She'd offered to accompany him to the hospital, but he didn't want her thinking they were some proper couple. It wasn't fair on the woman, giving her false hope.

Unbeknown to Karen, he'd stayed at Sharon's last night in the spare room. They'd shared a takeaway, watched a film, had a lovely evening. Ricky had enjoyed it too. 'I can't come round now, Kal. Ricky's only got another hour or so with his tutor. I need to get home for him.'

'Just pop in for half an hour. I've bought you something. It's nothing special, but I'm sure you'll love it.'

Kenny felt bad. Karen had been a rock to him too. He'd banged on endlessly about Sharon and how he'd messed up his marriage, and she always listened and tried to advise him. He glanced at his watch. 'All right. But I can only stay forty-five minutes, tops.'

'You heard any more from lover boy?' Tina asked Sharon. It had been busy at the nursery this morning. This was the first chance they'd had to talk. Donny had expanded the business recently. They were selling sun-beds and all sorts. It was more of a garden centre now and lots more work.

'He rung yesterday but I couldn't answer it 'cause Kenny was there. I'll ring him back later or something.'

'How you getting on, you and Kenny?'

'Yeah, all right. It's nice to have a bit of company in the evenings. We watched *Thelma and Louise* last night. I love that film. Tomorrow, we're gonna get a takeaway and watch *Fried Green Tomatoes*. That'll be a bit soppy for Kenny, I reckon,' chuckled Sharon. It was because of the gypsies moving onto the adjoining land that Kenny had insisted he stay in the spare room for the time being. He was worried it might kick off and wanted to be on hand in case it did.

'Not gonna get back with him, are ya?'

'Nah. I think he'd like to try again, mind. He hasn't actually said that, but he's dropped a few hints. I could never trust him again though, could I? It's been lovely having Ricky around too. He's such a character, comes out with the funniest things, bless him. I get lonely on me own at times. Especially in the evenings.'

'Once a cheat, always a cheat, Shal. You're better off going out with Ray, giving him a chance.'

'Yeah,' Sharon said, none too enthusiastically. It was difficult moving on when you'd spent so many years with the same man. She and Kenny knew one another inside out and she could never imagine getting undressed in front of Ray, even though he was an attractive man. She was a bit old-fashioned in that respect. For all she knew, Ray could turn out to be a bloody pervert in the sack.

'Speak of the devil,' said Tina.

Sharon looked up. It was Ray.

It was a warm June day and all Tansey could hear through the open window were whoops of joy coming from the garden. Jamie, Alfie, Harry and Bluebell all loved having the twins home. It was a shame she couldn't feel the same. They were devious little shits, Beau especially. However, she had to put on a happy act for Donny's sake.

Donny stood behind his fiancée and put his arms around her waist. 'Love their big brothers, eh? I might have a swim meself in a bit. Fancy a dip? I thought we might all have a game of volleyball in the pool.'

Tansey turned around. 'Yeah, OK. I invited Darren to the barbecue tomorrow. An extra mouth to feed won't matter, will it?' Since Beau and Brett had been away, Tansey's relationship with her eldest son had gone from strength to strength. So had Jamie's overall behaviour.

Donny looked at Tansey quizzically. 'Nah. But why would you invite Brooksy when we're having a family day out?'

Tansey liked Jamie's friend. He was polite and, unlike the twins, a good influence on her son. Whenever the twins were around, Jamie seemed to play up, act loud and flash. He wasn't like that when he was around Brooksy. Obviously, Tansey had said nothing to Donny, but she was dreading the twins' release. They were old enough now to go wherever and get into all types of mischief and she would much rather *her* son be out on his scrambling or quad bike with Darren Brooks. 'The twins will be out soon, Donny. Thought it would be nice for them to get to know Jamie's friend. He's been a great support to Jamie while Beau and Brett have been away.'

Happy with the explanation, Donny smiled. 'Yeah. You're right. Brooksy's a good lad. I'm sure the twins'll love him.'

After spending a couple of hours frolicking about in the pool, the twins and Jamie scoffed their lunch and decided to go out on their quad bikes.

'Let's go and check those gypsies out,' said Beau. 'See what they're all about.'

'Dad said we ain't allowed on their land no more,' Brett reminded his brother.

'So! When have we ever listened to Dad? We know that slip road that gets us in on the other side of those fields. We won't get too close to 'em or nothing, and if we get caught we'll just act dumb. We've always driven on that land anyway. It can't all belong to them.'

'I wanna check 'em out,' grinned Jamie.

Beau winked. 'Follow me then.'

When they got within sight of the Travellers' land, Beau said they should get off their quad bikes and walk the rest of the way. They'd been pally with a Travelling lad in Compton House. He'd only done nine months, but unlike most of the other lads in there, Beau had loved listening to his stories. There was something about the way gypsies lived that enthralled him. They did their own thing and didn't give a shit about the authorities. 'There's dogs and horses.

We don't want our bikes to scare 'em. Let's be respectful,' Beau ordered. Whatever he said, Brett and Jamie would always agree with. That was the way it was.

There were six trailers on the land and a group of men sitting on the grass, drinking beers. There were also kids running around.

'That young boy's a mongol like Ricky,' Jamie said, as they approached.

'Shut up!' hissed Beau and Brett in unison.

The men watched them approaching. They all looked hot and sweaty, like they'd been grafting hard. Beau took charge as always. 'All right, gentlemen. Me and my bruvvers live in Dark Lane, but we've always used these fields to ride our quads. We know you've bought some land 'ere, so we don't wanna take no liberties. What parts can we ride our bikes on still?'

Young Bobby-Joe ran over to Beau. 'You look same. Like my sisters,' he said, pointing at Brett.

Used to young Ricky, Brett talked to Bobby-Joe as he would anyone. 'Yeah, we're twins, mate.'

The men looked at each other, then one stood up. 'Bobby's the name and it's my land. You're welcome to use whatever you want to ride your bikes. Just stay away from the chavvies, trailers, dogs and horses. Ride over that way,' he pointed.

Beau grinned. 'Thanks, mister. I'm Beau, this 'ere is Brett and that's Jamie.'

Having done a bit of research on Kenny Bond since their altercation, Bobby guessed these were his grandsons. He'd been told about the twins. 'What's your surname?'

'Bond,' replied Brett. 'Our dad's Donny.'

All of a sudden the trailer door opened and out walked two girls. Beau's mouth opened wide. He'd never met identical girl twins before and these were the prettiest girls he'd ever seen.

Jolene locked eyes with Beau. He was so handsome, as was Brett, but instinct told her that Beau was the more dominant twin . . .

It wasn't often Beau was lost for words, but he couldn't say anything. It was as though Jolene was looking via his eyes into his soul and he was doing the same to her.

The following morning, the twins were up bright and early to open their presents. Gramps had bought them the mobile phones they'd asked for. Their dad had got them aftershave and trainers, and given them money to buy some new clothes.

'I can't stop thinking about that girl,' Beau admitted to Brett. 'Do you fancy the sister?'

'We don't even know 'em.'

'So? You must know if you fancy her or not?'

'Fancy who?' enquired Donny.

'Jolene and Tammy. They're twins, like us,' Brett explained.

'Where did you meet 'em?'

'On that land at the end, Dad,' replied Brett.

'The man said we can ride on there still,' added Beau.

'I don't care what the fucking man said. You steer clear of that family and their land. Understand me? Gramps'll go apeshit if he knows you've been mixing with that mob.'

'OK,' agreed Brett.

Beau said nothing. All he could think about was seeing Jolene again.

'You sure you're gonna be OK today? We can always cancel if you're not feeling it, see the boys alone.' A laid-back bloke, Carl had no issues with Lori inviting her ex over. He could sense Lori was anxious though.

'I'll be fine. It'll be nice for the boys, that's the main thing.'

'You gonna tell 'em our exciting news?'

Lori smiled. 'Of course.'

'You're a bit dolled up, Tans. It ain't half hot. Why don't you put a pair of shorts on? You'll be sweating in those jeans,' warned Donny.

Tansey had chosen her outfit carefully. She was determined she'd look far classier than that ex-smackhead, hence her designer jeans, vest top, stilettos and Louis Vuitton clutch bag. 'I'm fine in this, thanks. Not that I want to go at all.'

'I know. Shall we make a move then?'

'Yeah. The quicker we get this over with, the better.'

'You had a phone call, geezer called Ray,' Kenny informed his wife.

Sharon felt the colour drain from her cheeks. When she had spoken to Ray yesterday, it'd been left that she would call him. 'Did you answer it?'

'No. Why would I do that? I'd like us to be honest with one another from now on though, Shal. If you're dating a geezer, just tell me.'

'What, like you told me, when you were dating your young bit of fluff?'

Kenny raised his hands. 'Point taken. None of my bloody business.'

Sharon softened slightly. 'Ray is a friend. I went out with him for a meal recently. That's all.'

'Do you like him?'

'He's a nice man, but I don't feel ready to move on. Not sure I ever will, to be honest.'

Kenny felt relieved. 'Me neither.'

'You not got another bird in tow? I thought you would have by now.'

'No. That psycho was enough to put me off women for life. Well, apart from one and she's stood right in front of me. How 'bout I take you out for lunch today? We can eat that beef tomorrow. We'll take a nice ride out into the country, if you like?'

Pleased that Kenny had remained single, Sharon smiled. 'Yeah. All right. I'll go get changed.'

The first shock for Tansey was the size of the gaff. It was enormous, set in large grounds, and the cars on the drive were outstanding: Ferrari, Aston Martin, Porsche, as well as two smart four-wheel drives. Carl was obviously no man's fool. 'Jesus! She's done all right since her council gaff in Harold Hill,' Tansey said, half-forgetting the twins were crammed in the back alongside Jamie, Harry, Alfie and poor Darren, who nobody seemed to be speaking to.

Beau nudged Brett and smirked. It had been a bummer this morning when he'd ridden his quad bike over the gypsies' land and Bobby had informed him he'd dropped his wife and daughters off at Dagenham Sunday Market first thing. Beau had been gutted, as he'd hoped to see Jolene again before returning to Compton House. However, Tansey's reaction to his mother's gaff had cheered him up no end. That's another reason he'd arranged this visit. He knew Tansey was a 'Keep up with the Joneses' type as he'd heard his father accuse her of it numerous times when speaking about Lucinda and her horsey pals.

'This'll kick off,' Beau whispered in Brett's ear.

Brett didn't reply. He wasn't struck on Tansey, but he didn't love his mum as much as Beau seemed to either. He still had nightmares over what had happened to him on *that* Christmas Eve, could still see Fat Eric's face, almost smell his sweaty breath, and he would never forget the pain either. His mum had left him with *that* man. It was her fault. He'd heard his dad say that in the past. End of.

'Gorgeous roast that was, Kenny. So succulent that beef. The roasties were the business an' all.'

Kenny smiled. 'Succulent's a posh word for you, sweetheart. Did you learn that off Ray?'

Sharon chuckled. 'No. I bleedin' well didn't. If you must know, I got so pissed when I went out with Ray, I don't even remember what I ate. I didn't feel comfortable. I'm not into that dating lark, am I?'

'So, it was a proper date then? What's he do for a living, this Ray? What's his surname?'

'Oh, I can't remember his surname or job. Nothing special,' lied Sharon. She knew Kenny only too well. If he got wind of who Ray was, he'd be bound to pay him a none too friendly visit.

Sharon didn't want no trouble. Ray was a nice man and didn't deserve that. The poor bloke had done sod all wrong.

The second shock for Tansey was how stunning Lori actually was. There were no signs of her past, her face was wrinkle free. She had a long black summer dress on and huge designer sunglasses. Her home was amazing too. Very modern. Gold discs hung on the wall, next to the biggest widescreen TV Tansey had ever seen.

'This is my movie room,' Carl explained.

Tansey felt awkward. 'Erm, it's nice, isn't it, Donny?'

'Yeah. Pukka.'

'Let's sit out by the pool. Too nice to be stuck indoors. What would you like to drink? We don't have any alcohol, I'm afraid,' smiled Carl.

Even though he was knocking on a bit, Carl came across as a nice guy. Tansey had no idea how he'd fallen for an ex-smackhead, but he had, and it grated on her to think how well Lori had done for herself. Especially considering what a terrible mother she'd been. Those twins had been dragged up, not raised. 'I'll just have water, please.'

'I'll have Coke. The liquid type, of course,' Donny joked.

Not finding the pun at all funny, Carl glared at him as he poured the drinks.

The garden was huge, the swimming pool double the size of theirs. Tansey sat uncomfortably as Donny and Lori spoke about the twins. Carl got busy with the barbecue and the kids were all splashing about in the pool. 'You OK, Darren?' Tansey asked. She was fuming with Jamie. He'd barely given his friend the time of day since they'd picked him up earlier, and it was clear the twins didn't want him there.

'Want to open your presents, boys?' Lori shouted out.

The twins leapt out of the pool and were urged to follow their mother. 'Come on. Let's show some interest,' Donny whispered to Tansey.

Two brand-new top-of-the-range quad bikes were hidden underneath the canvas.

'Ah, they're wicked. The nuts. Cheers, Mum,' grinned Beau. 'Can we ride 'em now?'

'They're blinding,' Brett added, leaping on one.

'Thank Carl. He chose them,' smiled Lori.

'They've got quad bikes at home, ya know full well they have,' Donny reminded Lori.

'So! They now have some here too. Once they leave Compton, they'll be spending lots of time here.'

'Where's my present?' asked Alfie.

'It's not your birthday, son,' replied Donny.

'But I still want a present.'

'Stop that, Alfie. Now!' Tansey ordered, as her son began one of his tantrums.

'Whatever's wrong with him? Does he always behave like that?' Lori coldly asked Donny.

Tansey was fuming. 'You're a fine one to talk. The twins didn't even know how to use a knife and fork when they first moved in with us.'

'Leave it, Tans,' warned Donny.

'I was a normal loving mother before you decided to steal the twins' dad,' retorted Lori.

'Let's not argue, please,' said Carl. 'Food's nearly ready. The salad and bread are in the kitchen.'

Beau put his arm around his mother's shoulders. 'Well said,' he smirked.

Having persuaded Sharon to stop on the way home at a rural beauty spot, Kenny found Aunt Nelly's advice was in the forefront of his mind as he plonked himself on the log next to Sharon.

The birds were singing, squirrels scarpering up trees and there were even deer lurking. Two had bolted past as they'd pulled up in the car. 'This is the life, ain't it?' Kenny said.

'Yeah. So peaceful.'

Kenny squeezed his wife's hand. 'Where did it all go

wrong for us? All those years together down the drain. I'll never love another woman the way I love you.'

'That's big of you. I think it went wrong when my mum had breast cancer and you couldn't keep your John Thomas in your trousers and ended up shoving it up some tart not much older than our daughter.'

Kenny let out a deep breath. 'Don't say it like that. You make me sound like a nonce, and you know that ain't me. I was out of order. Bang out of order. I'll hold me hands up to that. But our relationship was stale long before you went to Spain and I met that nutter, Shal. Please don't think I'm trying to shift the blame, 'cause I'm not. I'm the one who strayed and I'll never forgive meself, especially for hurting you the way I did. But, there were times you made me feel so unloved and unwanted. The worst part being, on the odd occasions you initiated sex on a weekend, you had to be sloshed to do so. That made me feel like total crap, even though I went along with it. How would you feel if I had to be pissed to shag you?'

Sharon's eyes welled up. 'I'm sorry I made you feel like crap. I didn't mean to. A woman's body changes over the years, Ken. Well, mine did anyway. I went through the change early. It started when Donny got nicked, then put away. It's not you I went off. I still think you're as handsome as the day I met you. The problem lies with me. Once I went through the change, I had no sexual urges anymore. Perhaps I should've been more honest? But it's not an easy subject to talk about. My mum never spoke about periods and the change in front of my dad. It's embarrassing.'

'But me and you can talk about anything, Shal. I wish you'd have told me. We'd have joked about it, then worked it out. I honestly thought you didn't fancy me no more.'

'Oh, Ken. I'm sorry.'

'Me too.'

'Do you think if I'd have told you the truth you'd have still strayed?'

'Never in a million years. I'd have found the best specialist in the country. We'd have sorted it. We always do.'

'I bought some HRT back from Spain with me. A private doctor prescribed it. I stopped taking it once we split up, though. I'm sure it made me put on bloody weight an' all.'

'You don't need HRT, or any other drug for that matter. You're perfect as you are.'

Kenny stroked Sharon's hand, regretting all that had happened, and wished to his heart he'd been strong enough to stay true.

The atmosphere was like ice. The food was good, but Tansey wasn't hungry. She couldn't wait to leave.

'Why you being horrible to me, Jamie?' asked Darren. He wished he hadn't come and couldn't wait to leave either.

'I'm not. Just wanna spend time with me brothers on their birthday. I ain't seen 'em, have I? Anyway, it was me mum who invited you, not me.'

'Don't be so nasty,' Tansey told her son. She could see the twins smirking, guessed they were the reason behind Jamie's rude behaviour.

'Ain't this nice? All celebrating our birthday together. Like one big family,' grinned Beau.

'Mum, I want a wee-wee,' announced Bluebell.

'I'll take her, Mum. I need one too,' said Harry.

'Tell the boys our news,' prompted Carl.

Lori smiled. 'You're going to have another brother or sister soon.'

Neither twin was impressed. They had enough brothers as it was and a sister. They rather liked being their mum's only children, Beau especially.

'Say something then,' chuckled Carl. He still had a difficult relationship with his only daughter and couldn't wait to become a dad again. It was a gift from God, a second chance.

'Congratulations,' Donny said. The silence was deafening.

'I dunno what to say,' Brett mumbled.

'Me neither,' added Beau. Another screaming baby was the last birthday present he'd wanted.

'I wouldn't be happy if I were the twins either,' piped up Tansey. 'They must have so many memories of their awful upbringing until they moved in with me and Donny.'

'Tans!' Donny glared.

'Well, it's the truth.'

Lori put her plate down, walked over to Tansey and wagged a forefinger in her face. 'How dare you come into my home and insult me? Who the hell do you think you are? A whore and a relationship breaker, that's all you are.'

'For crying out loud. Leave it, the pair of ya,' Donny pleaded.

Tansey stood up, her eyes blazing. 'At least I never left my kids alone with a paedo—'

Those words were the final straw for Lori. She grabbed hold of Tansey's hair and slung her fully clothed into the swimming pool.

*

'Haven't we had a top day?' Kenny said to Sharon.

'Yes. It's been nice.'

'Done Beau and Brett the world of good doing a bit of bird. I couldn't have been more proud of 'em when I told them about Ricky and they said they'd always have his back.' Kenny knew it was wrong to have favourite grand-children, yet the twins were his. Not that he'd ever admit that to anyone. He could see so much of his younger self in Beau and Brett. They were extremely bright and with his guidance in the future, would definitely go far in life.

'They've certainly grown into fine young men. So hand-some too.'

'Take after their gramps,' winked Kenny. He slung a casual arm around his wife's shoulders. 'It's me fiftieth soon and I need to sort something. How 'bout we go away? Just the two of us. Anywhere in the world. You can choose our destination.'

'Not promising anything. But I will think about it. I could do with some sun.'

'That Ray geezer, did you have a fumble with him?'

'No. Not even as much as a kiss.'

'Swear on your life.' Kenny had a jealous nature when it came to *his* woman, couldn't help himself.

'On my life, I did sod all with the man. But what about you, Kenny? You must've dabbled with other women since that loony. Be truthful. If you've had a couple of one-night stands or more. I'd rather know. No more lies, please.'

Kenny chewed on his lip. Part of him wanted to heed Aunt Nell's advice and tell Sharon about Karen. But he was too worried that, if he did, Shal would be fuming. Not that it was a proper relationship he and Karen had been in. But it was far more than a one-night stand. Surely Shal would feel he'd betrayed her all over again? They were still legally married, after all. 'There's been no one else, babe. I swear on my life.'

'OK. I believe you. But believe me also, Kenny. I ain't no mug. If I ever find out you've lied to me over this when I've given you a chance to come clean, that would not only be end of our marriage, it would also be the end of any friendship between us too.'

Kenny's jaw began twitching. But then he thought of Karen. He'd always been straight with her from day one, told her he still loved Shal. Karen wasn't a nutjob like Abi. She was a single mum, a schoolteacher. A decent woman, who he was sure would never cause him any grief. So he said nothing.

What Kenny didn't realize was, Karen could be quite devious when she wanted something badly.

CHAPTER TWENTY-EIGHT

'A bird in the hand is worth two in the bush.'

I thought Shal would choose New York for my fiftieth, as it had always been a dream of hers to go there. But she didn't. She reckoned it would remind her of the torrid time we'd been through the last time I booked it, so she opted for Vegas instead.

Separate beds, but a shared room was what Sharon wanted, so I booked us into a lovely five-star hotel.

We had a blast that week, laughed more than we had in years. We visited casinos, theatres, did lots of shopping. We also had a few day trips. One on a boat, another to Death Valley. We even flew over the Grand Canyon in a helicopter.

It did us wonders to spend some time alone, get away from the run-of-the-mill. By the time we left Vegas, I felt we were soulmates all over again.

I didn't bother taking my mobile abroad with me, wanted a break from that an' all. When I got home and switched it on, there were numerous messages, mainly from Karen.

Even though Shal and I weren't officially back together, I knew it was time to put poor Karen out of her misery. So I decided to visit her sooner rather than later, come clean so to speak.

I could never have envisaged what would happen next. Not in a million years . . .

There were no lessons at Compton House during the six-week summer holidays. Therefore, the governor decided to bring the twins' release date forward. He loathed the way they sauntered around like they owned the place. They also ruled it. The other lads looked up to them like they were twin messiahs. Who did they think they were? The bloody Krays?

Donny picked up his buoyant sons on a hot Saturday morning. They looked so tall and handsome as they greeted him warmly, their short blond hair glistening in the sun. 'Can we stop at a cafe for a fry-up, Dad?' asked Brett.

'Yeah, sure. That all your clobber, is it?' Donny loaded their bags in the boot.

'There's another two bags there,' pointed Beau. 'They'll have to go in the back.'

'I bought a people carrier the other day, so we can go out in comfort as a family,' Donny informed them.

Beau and Brett glanced at one another. They were a bit old for family days out. 'What we got for dinner later?' enquired Brett. That was the thing he'd missed the most: a decent bit of grub. Not that Tansey's cooking skills were much cop, but the housekeeper's were.

'Renata's off today, so we'll have a takeaway later. Yous can choose what we have. I've booked a restaurant for lunch tomorrow.'

'We can't come, Dad. We promised Mum we'd see her and Carl. They're picking us up at twelve.'

Donny hadn't had any more contact with Lori since the barbecue had gone tits up. 'Oh well. You do what you've gotta do. I've got a party tonight on the boat, so you're gonna have to amuse yourselves anyway.'

Beau thought about Jolene. He'd only ever seen her once, even though he'd tried to hunt her down since. 'As soon as we get home, we're taking our quad bikes out.'

'Are we?' Brett asked, surprised.

'Yeah,' grinned Beau. He'd masturbated himself half senseless thinking about Jolene. He had to see her again. The sooner the better.

Karen Bamber draped her arms around Kenny's neck. 'Thank God you're OK. I know you said you wouldn't be around for a while, but I thought you'd have your phone with you. You never go anywhere without it.'

'Sorry. I didn't mean to worry ya.' Kenny pecked Karen on the lips and released her grip. 'Shall we go in the front room? I need to talk to you about something.'

'OK. But let me give you your present and card first. I know you're going to love your pressie.'

Karen knew Kenny was a boxing fan, had treated him to a large framed signed photo of Muhammad Ali. 'Ahh, that's the nuts, Kal. Thank you.'

'Open your card as well.'

Kenny felt a right bastard. How was he meant to come clean with her now? But he had to.

Happy Birthday Best Friend, were the words on the front and Karen had written a funny poem inside. 'That's brilliant,' chuckled Kenny, feeling more of a shitbag by the second.

'Glad you like it,' smiled Karen. 'Little Miss Attitude's at her dads, so I thought we'd get a takeaway and watch a film later. You staying over? Or have you got to get home for Ricky?'

While he and Sharon had been in Vegas, Ricky's sister and granddad had been taking care of him. He and Shal had bought him loads of presents back, but weren't due to pick him up until tomorrow. 'I can't stay long. Gotta pick Ricky up,' lied Kenny. He hadn't even told Karen he'd been staying at Sharon's.

'Oh. That's a shame. You can stay a while though, surely? You look sunburnt. Where did you go last week?'

Kenny sighed. He had to put the poor cow out of her misery. 'I went to Las Vegas with Shal. Only as friends. But we got on well and even though we aren't currently back together, I've gotta give my marriage another go, babe. You're a top lady, you are, Karen. I'll never forget your kindness to me and if you're ever in any trouble or need help in any way, I'll be there for you like a shot.'

Crestfallen, Karen burst into tears. 'Just leave, Kenny. Please.'

Feeling awful, Kenny said, 'I'm sorry,' then did so, without taking the Muhammad Ali photo with him. That must've cost Karen a few bob. He just hoped she'd kept the receipt.

Beau's luck was in. As he, Brett and Jamie rode across the fields, he spotted Jolene and Tammy sunbathing outside an enormous new mobile home. 'They've got bikinis on,' Beau said excitedly. 'We'll walk the rest of the way. Get off the bikes.'

There were four new mobile homes in total. The trailers that had originally been there were gone. 'All right?' Beau felt a bit tongue-tied. The sight of Jolene in a skimpy bikini was too much for him. It was weird, because even though she and her sister were identical, he could tell which one was her. She had the red bikini on. Her boobs were massive.

Jolene sat up, huge sunglasses covering her eyes. 'We're all right. You all right?'

Realizing his brother was lost for words, Brett took over the conversation. 'Your new homes are well cool.'

'We live in that one,' pointed Tammy.

'With our brother next door. He watches us like a hawk, so don't you boys be getting any funny ideas,' Jolene grinned.

'We're gentlemen,' Beau retorted, a twinkle in his eyes.

'That's what all the lads say,' Jolene replied. Tammy giggled and a woman appeared with a tea towel in her hands. 'Go cover yourselves up, girls,' she ordered. 'Your father and brothers will blow a fuse they see you talking to boys half naked.'

'Sorry. It's our fault,' apologized Beau. 'We only came over to say hello. Are you Mrs Tamplin?'

'Yes.'

'Your husband said it was OK for us to ride our bikes on the land as long as we stay away from your homes and animals,' Beau explained.

'I'm sure that includes our daughters then. Orf you go.' Evie waved her tea towel in the direction of their bikes.

'Mum,' Jolene hissed, as soon as the boys were out of earshot. 'They were only talking to us and they were polite.'

'Boys all have one thing on their minds and they're gorgers. Don't be encouraging 'em,' ordered Evie.

When her mum walked back inside, Jolene turned to her sister. 'Beau is so hot. I really do like him. Do ya think he likes me?'

'By the size of the big bulge in his shorts, I'd say yes.'

Jolene burst out laughing and playfully punched her sister on the arm. 'Stop it, Tammy. You got a filthy mind, you.'

'I've had that latest bid accepted on your mum and dad's old bungalow,' Kenny informed Sharon. 'Got it for thirty-five grand less than the original asking price.'

'Not surprised with a load of gyppos living a spit's throw from it. You gonna move in there with Ricky then?'

'Well, that's up to you. There's nothing more I want than to give our marriage another go. Whaddya reckon? We've been getting on so well lately, just like old times. You know how much I love you, Shal.'

'Let me have a think about it. I don't wanna rush into things and you still haven't told me where you're earning all this money from. I couldn't be dealing with police raids and all that palaver. You must be up to no good.'

'Honestly, babe, it's nothing serious,' Kenny fibbed. 'It's just a little earner I've got going on with Teddy and Tony. I'm the silent partner, me. Have very little dealings with any of it.'

'I still need time to think things over. I also think you should buy the bungalow, in case things don't work out between us. If they do, you can always rent it out.'

Knowing Shal was warming to the idea of a marital reconciliation, Kenny grinned. He'd heard no more from Karen, which was another good thing. 'Great idea. Me mum and Aunt Nell ain't getting younger. One day it might be suitable for them to live in.'

'Aunt Nell, yes. But not your mother, thanks, Ken. I'd go grey within a month if she was me bleedin' neighbour.'

Kenny chuckled. 'Me and you both.'

*

It was another week before Beau clapped eyes on Jolene again. He hadn't had much time to stalk her, as he and Brett were now working up the nursery. 'Where you off to? Wanna ride?' Beau grinned.

'Romford. Shopping.' Jolene glanced around to make sure her mum wasn't watching before getting on the back of Beau's bike. 'We got a cab meeting us at the bottom of the lane. You can drop us there.'

'Get on mine,' Brett urged Tammy. He'd been pretending to Beau that he fancied Tammy just to shut him up.

The feel of Jolene's arms around Beau's waist felt awesome. 'Fancy some company in Romford?' he asked.

'Do we want some male company or not, Tammy?' shouted Jolene. She knew her sister liked Brett. They'd talked of little else when alone this past week.

'Be rude to say no,' Tammy smirked.

'Get the cab to wait while we take our bikes home and grab some dosh. We'll pay for it,' Beau said.

'Best you get your own cab in case our dad or brothers come home and spot us. We'll meet you at twelve at Maccy D's,' Jolene said.

Beau grinned. 'Cushty.'

It was weird walking around Romford with another pair of identical twins. Everyone was staring at them as though they were aliens. 'Wanna photo?' Beau asked a notright-looking couple.

Jolene chuckled as the couple looked away and quickened their pace. Beau reminded her of a Traveller. He was cheeky, oozed confidence and he was generous. He'd insisted on paying for a dress she liked. Brett was generous too, had paid for Tammy's sandals.

When Beau held Jolene's hand, Brett felt obliged to hold

Tammy's. 'It's too hot to walk around 'ere. How 'bout we get some cider and go over Raphael Park?' suggested Beau.

'Get some mints then 'cause our dad will kill us if he thinks we've been drinking,' Jolene replied.

Beau squeezed her hand. 'Your wish is my command.'

Beau had never met a girl he'd got on so well with before. He and Jolene had so much in common. They had a similar sense of humour. There was an age gap of ten months, Jolene would soon be sixteen, but that didn't matter to either of them. 'So you had boyfriends in the past?' asked Beau. He and Jolene were sitting alone, backs against the tree. Brett and Tammy were chatting over by another tree.

'No. Me and Tammy got asked out a lot, but we always said no. What about you? You had girlfriends?'

'No. Brett and me got put away. It was all boys there.'

'Why did ya get put away?'

'We burned our school down.' Beau grinned. He decided not to mention poor old Mr Rudge ending up like burnt toast.

Jolene burst out laughing. 'We never went to school. Our aunt taught us to read and write.'

Beau stared at Jolene's eyes. They were big and brown, just like his. 'I really like you. Will you be my girlfriend?'

'Yes. But we'll have to keep it a secret. My dad and brothers are protective over me and Tammy.'

Beau stroked Jolene's cheek then leaned in for their first kiss. It was electric.

'This'll be my last sprog, Mum. I absolutely hate being pregnant,' Sherry announced, rubbing her huge bump.

When her mother didn't answer, Sherry waved the

newspaper in front of her face. The front page screamed the headline RIOTS. It had been a summer of rioting in the UK.

'Earth to Mother. What's up with you today? You're on a different planet.'

Sharon sighed. 'It's your dad. He wants us to give our marriage another go.'

'You're not going to, surely?'

'I might. It's so hard, love, when you've been together as many years as me and your dad have. We know each other inside out.'

Sherry's relationship with her father had never been the same since she'd found out he'd cheated on her mum. 'You want your head tested if you forgive him. After what he did! What about Ray?'

'I don't feel comfortable with Ray. Not like I do your dad.'

'But you've barely given the man a chance. Ray's good-looking, wealthy and clearly besotted with you. What's not to like?'

'I couldn't sleep with another man, Sherry. It wouldn't feel right.'

'Well, it's up to you. But if Andy cheated on me, I would *never* take him back.'

Later that evening, Sherry's words popped into Sharon's mind. 'Who's Karen?' she asked Kenny when he got out the shower.

Kenny felt the hairs on the back of his neck stand up. 'Karen's Tony's cousin. Why?'

'Because I answered your phone and Karen cut me off.'

'She might've thought you were Old Bill or something. I'll call her back later.' Kenny made a mental note to pretend to lose his phone in the next few days. He'd get a new one with a new number.

'I've thought about what you asked me, us getting back together.'

'And?'

'I'm willing to try again, see how it goes. But I need you to be honest with me, Kenny. If you were seeing this Karen or anyone else, you need to tell me now. No more secrets.'

Not willing to chance Sharon changing her mind, Kenny held his hands up. 'I swear on my life, babe, I ain't been seeing no birds. Karen's been doing a bit of work for me and Tony. I even introduced her to Ricky, took him round to hers. I wouldn't be doing that if I were knocking her off, would I? You're the only woman for me. Please believe me.'

Sharon rolled her eyes. 'All right. I do.'

Brett was bored. Beau had not stopped banging on about Jolene all evening. He'd had his first proper kiss today, had felt pressured into kissing Tammy as Beau and Jolene couldn't prise themselves away from one another. He'd felt nothing. No excitement whatsoever.

'I can't wait to see Jolene tomorrow. You excited about seeing Tammy again? Ain't it weird we met twins and fancied 'em? It's like fate, I reckon.'

'Yeah,' mumbled Brett. He still thought of the posh boy at Compton House, Alex Mariner, whenever he masturbated. He certainly wouldn't be thinking of Tammy to perform such a deed, he'd never be able to come if he did.

'Can I tag along tomorrow?' asked Jamie. He'd been bored all day and felt left out.

'No,' Beau said bluntly. 'You can't hang around us like

a gooseberry. You need to find yourself a girlfriend, then you can come out with us.'

'All right,' Jamie replied miserably. He didn't even have Darren to knock about with now. His old pal refused to speak to him anymore.

Beau put his hands behind his head. 'I wanna buy a bit of land one day and live in a mobile home. That life would suit me.'

'You'll be saying you wanna get married next,' Brett replied.

'I do. And I will. I'll have a bet with ya I marry Jolene.'

Brett held out his right hand. 'Go on then. Hundred quid you don't.'

Beau grinned. 'Make it five hundred.'

As Kenny inserted his penis inside her, a fleeting vision of Abigail popped into Sharon's mind. She tried to push it away, but it was difficult knowing *her* husband had shoved his todger up that slag.

'You OK?' asked Kenny.

'Yeah,' Sharon lied. She had to try, couldn't not have sex. That had been the reason Kenny had strayed in the first place.

'I love you, Shal,' groaned Kenny.

'I love you too.' It was at that point Sharon shut her eyes and thought of her shopping list for tomorrow's dinner.

CHAPTER TWENTY-NINE

'Act in haste, repent in leisure.'

Me and Shal soon got our marriage back on track. It was as though we'd never been apart, yet better. Me granddad always used to say: 'You never know what you've got until it's gone'. Ain't that the truth? Well, it certainly was in my case.

Shal still worked part-time up the nursery, while I did me own thing. But we spent lots of time together with Ricky and the younger grandkids mainly.

Life was good, until I found out Beau and Brett were courting the Tamplin girls. Travellers were a breed of their own, tended to stick to their own. I knew it was bound to end in tears.

I spoke to the twins, tried to drum some sense into 'em, but Beau especially was having none of it. He was smitten with Jolene, the silly little bastard.

There was nothing I could do to stop them seeing the girls. They were fifteen, not five. Working lads, not silly schoolboys.

I could feel it in my bones that this wasn't going to end well. But I didn't expect it to end in death. Not one. But two deaths . . .

Spring 1993

'Jolene, Tammy, get in 'ere now,' ordered Evie Tamplin.

'Calm down, love. I'll do the talking,' advised Bobby Tamplin.

Young Bobby-Joe grinned at his sisters. 'You're in trouble.'

'What have I told you about hanging around with those gorger twins,' Evie bellowed. 'One of Billy's friends spotted you earlier with 'em in Romford.'

'So?' Jolene spat. She was sick of having to sneak around to see Beau. She was so in love with him, wanted to scream it from the rooftops.

'I'll give you *so*. You're not going out anymore. Not without one of your brothers to chaperone ya.'

'We like Brett and Beau. They're twins. They get us,' Tammy replied.

'I'm gonna marry Beau and there ain't nothing you can do to stop me,' announced Jolene. She'd finally said it; it was out in the open.

'Calm down, Evie. You bashing the saucepans up ain't gonna solve this. Neither is shouting and bawling. Sit down and let's have a rational conversation. You sit down too, girls.' He wasn't as anti-gorger as his wife. All he wanted was for his precious daughters to be happy. He'd seen how the Travelling lads behaved in the pubs. Lots of them were at it behind their wives' backs, with gorger women. He didn't want that for his girls, would kill any man that cheated on them. 'Are you courting these boys? Or are you just friends?'

'I'm courting Beau and Tammy's courting Brett.'

'Me and Brett are not serious like Jolene and Beau are though. We're more close friends,' Tammy added truthfully. There wasn't the same spark between herself and Brett as there was with her sister and Beau. She didn't want to marry him, would personally prefer to marry a Traveller.

'Are they respectful towards you?' asked Bobby.

'I like them,' Bobby-Joe piped up.

'You shut up. Children should be seen and not heard,' berated Evie.

'Of course they're respectful. We wouldn't hang out with them otherwise,' Jolene informed her parents. Apart from kissing and cuddles she wouldn't do any more with Beau, not until they got married, and he respected that.

'You're not marrying a gorger. Your brothers won't allow it,' warned Evie. 'It's not ethical.'

'Beau'll be sixteen soon. I want to marry him,' Jolene replied. In their community, it wasn't seen as unusual to marry young. Her cousin had got married last year and she was only seventeen.

Bobby held his hands up. 'All I want, Evie, is our daughters to be happy. If Jolene has chosen Beau to be her husband and he treats her respectfully, then the least we can do is get to know the lad better.'

Evie glared at her husband. 'You should be introducing 'em to single Travellers, decent lads.'

'A lot of the Travelling lads are whoremongers, Evie. You don't see what they get up to in the pubs. Even our Billy's got an eye for the women.'

'He better not have. Crystal will kill him,' spat Evie.

'Why don't we invite Beau and Brett over for dinner?' Bobby suggested.

Evie pursed her lips. Bobby was the man in their home and what he said stood. 'OK. But I'm not happy about it, not one little bit.'

Jolene smiled at Tammy. She couldn't wait to tell Beau the good news.

Kenny Bond was not having a very good day. The Scientist had disappeared, nobody knew where he was and his phone had been disconnected. They had a big order for ecstasy pills this week, which the Chinese were now going to make. He just hoped they knew what they were doing. They said they did.

Kenny picked up the *Daily Mail*. 'State of Liverpool Street station. Bastard IRA again,' he moaned.

'I was reading about that Stephen Lawrence. A racial attack, they reckon it was,' Sharon said. She and Kenny were getting along just fine again now. She'd told Ray she was giving her marriage another go and he no longer came to the nursery. She hadn't seen him since last summer.

Kenny answered his phone and began spewing profanities.

'Who's that? What's a matter?' asked Sharon.

'Donny. He's got agg with the twins. I've told 'em time and time again to steer clear of those pikey girls. Now they've been invited to dinner by the old man. Beau's been telling Donny he wants to marry the girl, the silly little sod.'

'He's not even sixteen yet.'

'Tell me about it. But they marry young, those gyppos, then breed like flies. Over my dead body will a grandson of mine end up part of that family.' Kenny had never forgotten that scumbag, Freddie Tamplin. Neither had he forgotten the altercation he'd had with Bobby and his sons.

It wound him up even now. They had kept themselves to themselves since, mind, but their presence had sent all the house prices in Dark Lane plummeting. Micky Fallon had had his house on the market for over a year now and still couldn't sell it, even though he'd dropped the price twice.

'Where you going?' asked Sharon.

'To try to talk some sense into my thick grandsons yet again.'

'Don't blow your top.'

Kenny sighed. He felt like bashing their thick heads together to knock some bloody sense into them.

'You all right, love?' Tansey asked Jamie. He didn't knock around with the twins so much now that they had girl-friends. Tansey felt sorry for her son. He was a bit of a recluse of late, spent most of his spare time in his room alone, playing video games. He'd even lost interest in his quad bike.

'Yeah. I'm fine. I'll answer the door.'

Kenny stormed into the lounge. 'Where are they?' he asked Tansey.

'Arguing out in the garden. I'm staying out of it.' Tansey actually hoped the twins married the Travelling girls. It would get them out from under her feet. 'I'm meeting Nan for lunch on Friday. Why don't you come, Jamie? You've not seen her for ages.'

'Yeah. All right. I'm going up to me room for a bit.'

Tansey sighed. Jamie had now left school and showed no signs of getting another job. Donny had given him a start up the nursery, but he hadn't liked it. It was a shame he didn't have a girlfriend too. Not a Traveller, mind, Tansey wouldn't have that.

*

Kenny shook his head in disbelief. 'You're playing with fire, the pair of ya,' he warned. 'You're a good catch, can't you see that? You start having dinner up there, getting to know the parents; they'll have you up the aisle, those girls jumping the broomstick in no time.'

'I don't wanna marry Tammy,' Brett informed his grandfather.

'Thank fuck for that,' Kenny replied.

'Well, I'm gonna marry Jolene. I really do love her,' Beau insisted.

'You're not even sixteen yet. Use your noddle. You really wanna be lumbered with a load of ankle-biters by the time you're twenty-one?' Donny asked.

'Well, you was,' retorted Beau. Unlike that crab-infested slag India, Jolene was a decent girl. Beau was that desperate to have sex with her, he'd marry her tomorrow if he could. It was so frustrating, wanting her so badly, that he was masturbating every single night.

'At least wait until you're eighteen, see if you still feel the same then,' suggested Donny.

'I was inside with Bobby's younger brother Freddie,' admitted Kenny. 'Believe me, lads, he was a degenerate, rotten to the fucking core. Robbed, then beat up pensioners. You really wanna be part of that family?'

'There's good and bad in all families, Gramps, and Bobby's more like you. He's a grafter. He's got a Down's son too, ya know, like our Ricky. He's a good dad, man and person. Jolene can't speak highly enough of him,' argued Beau.

'I give up,' hissed Donny. 'I seriously do. Let 'em get on with it, Dad. Bound to be me and you caught in the firing line when it all goes Pete Tong. Which it will. I'd bet me house on it.'

*

'Wear trousers, not jeans,' Beau told Brett. 'We want to make a good impression, don't we?'

Brett pretended to agree. He did like Tammy, she was good fun. But he didn't fancy her at all. He still kissed her sometimes as he didn't want his brother to become suspicious. At least, having Tammy as a girlfriend, he didn't have to worry about his true feelings. He'd only had sexual urges for boys so far. But that didn't mean he was gay, did it? He was confused about his sexuality to say the least.

Beau splashed himself with aftershave. He looked the part in his expensive tight grey trousers and crisp white shirt. Brett wore a different-coloured shirt and slacks. They never dressed the same anymore, were too old for all that lark.

'You nervous?' asked Beau.

'Not really. We've already met their mum and dad. Why? Are you?'

'Yeah. I'm determined to smash it though, come across well.' Beau glanced at his watch. 'Let's make a move then.'

Beau was even more nervous when he arrived at the Tamplins'. The brothers were there, none looking too friendly, apart from young Bobby-Joe who greeted them warmly.

Beau handed Evie the huge bouquet. 'Thank you for inviting us over. It's very kind of you.'

Evie put the flowers on the side. 'It wasn't my idea to invite you.'

'Mum,' hissed Jolene.

'Come and sit over 'ere, lads,' said Bobby. 'This is my eldest son, Billy, and this is me second eldest, Johnny.'

Beau and Brett held their right hands out, but neither man accepted their handshake.

'Have some manners, boys. Beau and Brett are our guests,' glared Bobby.

'Your guests,' spat Billy.

'If you're gonna be rude, then just go back to your own trailer, Billy,' Jolene barked.

'So, whaddya do for a living then?' asked Johnny.

Beau did most of the talking, explaining what their work involved. 'We won't be working for me dad forever, though. We wanna set up our own business, don't we, Brett?'

'Yeah.' It was the first Brett had heard of that idea.

'Nothing wrong with working with family. We work for our dad. But we don't arrange pansies,' Billy informed the gorgers. He didn't like them at all, was fuming with his sisters for having such bad taste.

The door opened. 'Sorry I'm late. I'm Sonny.'

Brett locked eyes with Sonny and felt a strange sensation. He instantly knew he was nothing like the other brothers. He dressed nicer and his eyes lit up when he smiled. He had big puppy-dog eyes, a lopsided grin and thick light-brown hair with a floppy fringe.

Brett stood up. 'I'm Brett. Nice to meet you, Sonny.'

'Where you been, Jamie?' asked Tansey.

Jamie picked up Alfie, who was demanding his attention. 'Out with Brooksy. I bumped into him earlier and apologized properly. We're pals again now. I'm going to a party with him tomorrow night.' He grinned.

Tansey was thrilled. 'That's great, love. He's a nice boy. Make sure you don't fall out with him again.'

'I won't. D'ya reckon Donny will give me my old job back, Mum?'

Tansey smiled. 'I'm sure I can twist his arm. Leave it with me.'

The meal was smashing. Evie was a great cook. Steak and onion pudding with new potatoes and lots of vegetables.

'That was handsome. Thank you, Mrs Tamplin,' said Beau, pushing his plate away.

'Just call me Evie. I hate Mrs Tamplin, makes me feel like a bloody schoolteacher.'

'Sorry,' Beau replied. The atmosphere was better now Billy and Johnny had gone back to their own trailers. Sonny was sweet as a nut and little Bobby-Joe, hilarious.

'Mum's warming a bit,' Jolene whispered in her sister's ear.

'How old are you, Sonny?' enquired Brett. He'd been studying Sonny as he'd been telling a story. His tone was different from his brothers' too. He still sounded like a gypsy, but his voice was soft, not harsh.

'I'm eighteen.'

'You married with kids?' Beau asked.

'Nah. Too young for all that yet,' Sonny chuckled.

Brett smiled. He knew who he'd be thinking about while banging one out in future and it wouldn't be that posh lad from Compton House.

After scoffing two helpings of blackberry and apple pie, it was Tammy's suggestion the four of them went out for a walk. 'That's OK, isn't it, Dad?'

'Yeah. But I expect you to look after my princesses at all times you're with 'em, lads.'

'Of course,' replied Beau.

'And you be respectful. They been raised with good

morals, my Jolene and Tammy. Their mother saw to that,' added Bobby.

'We would never take liberties. My dad raised us with good morals too. He wanted us to be gentlemen,' Beau replied.

'Hold your grys. You've asked about our family, but we ain't heard much about yours yet. Your grandfather was very rude to my Bobby when we first moved 'ere. Spoke to him like we were trash,' Evie said, hands on hips.

'Not tonight, love. We can talk about this another time,' urged Bobby. He liked the twins, thought they were decent, hard-working lads with morals.

'No. It's fine,' Beau replied. He knew grys meant horses in Romany, through Jolene. 'I hope I'm not saying anything out of order by this, but Gramps – sorry, I mean me granddad, once shared a prison cell with your brother Freddie, Bobby. Put it this way, they didn't exactly get on.'

'Don't mention that man's name in my home,' hissed Evie.

'Who, Gramps?' Brett asked, alarmed. He glanced at Sonny, who rolled his eyes.

'No. My bruvver. Excuse my language, but he's the shitcunt of all shitcunts. I washed my hands of him years ago,' said Bobby. 'I also knew your grandfather took his eye out.'

'How? With his fingers?' asked Bobby-Joe.

Beau started fidgeting. He hadn't known Gramps had ripped Freddie's eye out. 'I'm sorry if I've spoken out of turn. But our gramps is a good man. He's always had our backs, ain't he, Brett? Taught us right from wrong. He also took on his best pal's son, when they—'

'I know all this,' interrupted Bobby. 'I also know he killed a gavver. The problem is though, 'cause we're Travellers, your grandfather sees himself as better than us. That ain't the case, lads. I work hard, take care of my family, and if you and my Jolene are going to have a future together, you need to wise your gramps or whatever you call the bloke up. 'Cause I is a family man, just like him.'

'Can we go out now, please?' snapped Jolene.

Beau clasped Jolene's hand. 'Your dad's right. I'll talk to Gramps tomorrow. Get a meeting sorted with you both, Bobby.'

Bobby smiled. He liked Beau especially, and he could tell by the way that Beau and Jolene looked at one another that it was true love. He still looked at Evie that way now, would rather cut his own penis off than ever cheat on her. He also knew Donny wasn't a threat. He was ruled by his old woman by all accounts. Bobby liked living here, so did his family. He didn't want to start a war, was done with violence. But Kenny Bond was capable of starting one, he knew that much. And if he did Bobby would pay him back *tenfold*.

'Bye, Evie,' said Beau and Brett in unison. 'Thank you for the smashing dinner,' added Beau.

'That's OK. Look after my daughters or you'll have me to deal with.' Evie still wasn't happy that the boys weren't from the Travelling community, but they were polite enough and seemed genuine.

'Apart from my elder brothers acting like dicks, it weren't too bad, was it?' Jolene squeezed Beau's hand, once out of earshot.

'No. It was great.' Beau waited until they were far enough away from the mobile homes to take Jolene in his arms. He kissed her passionately before asking, 'Did I do you proud?'

'Of course. But I knew you would. You could charm the birds out the trees. That's why I loves ya.'

'I love you more,' grinned Beau.

'Where's my kiss?' Tammy playfully punched Brett's arm. They were more like mates than boyfriend and girlfriend, but Tammy liked practising kissing, so she could get it right for when she fell in love like her sister had.

Brett put his arms around Tammy's waist, shut his eyes and as he snogged her thought of her brother. Sonny.

CHAPTER THIRTY

Kenny Bond wasn't in the best of moods. They'd had another load of complaints over the latest batch of ecstasy pills; so much so, some of their biggest punters wanted no more and were saying they'd try elsewhere.

With Tony by his side, Kenny stomped inside the premises. There were eight Chinese in total, including the new one who was a ringer for Bruce Lee. Kenny pointed at the pair who'd worked with them from the start and were known to him as Peter and Paul. 'Who's in charge of what's being shoved into these pills? Only we're getting complaints after complaints and losing business like no tomorrow.'

'It ain't good enough, lads. The people we're supplying are livid,' Tony barked. 'No bastard is coming up properly on the poxy things. They're just feeling nauseous, then fucking tired. I thought you knew The Scientist's recipe. You promised us you did. Me and him ain't geezers to mess with ya know,' he added, pointing at Kenny. Apart from knowing Phil and The Scientist were using chemicals including formaldehyde, ammonium chloride and mercury, neither Kenny nor Tony had a clue what else went into the bastard pills.

The Bruce Lee lookalike pulled his mask down. 'We do our best. Try different recipe. We get it right soon. My cousin very good at this. He in Hong Kong visiting family. When he come back to England, he get recipe right.'

'When's he coming back to England?' enquired Tony.

'Soon.'

'Soon ain't fucking good enough,' spat Kenny. 'Can't he come back this week?'

'No. His mum dying. My aunt. He wait for her to die.'

'Well, Mum better fucking croak it soon, else we're all out of a job,' glared Kenny. 'You better get this right and I mean proper soon. Otherwise I'll be digging graves for the lot of ya.'

'Kenny! Enough! Come on, let's go and leave 'em to it,' hissed Tony.

As they left the premises, Tony shook his head in despair. 'Don't threaten 'em like that, mate. They're trying, I think – to get it right. Phil and The Scientist always worked alone with what went into the pills, didn't want their intelligence ripped off, I suppose. They fucking knew what they were doing though, eh?'

'Hmmm,' replied Kenny. 'Makes you wonder if The Scientist's disappearance had anything to do with that mob. Perhaps they thought they knew the recipe? My granddad hated the Chinese, said he would never trust 'em as far as he could throw 'em. We could be working with a fucking Triad gang for all we know. D'ya reckon they're Triads?'

'How should I know? Come on, we've said our piece. Let's not spoil our weekend. Life's too short.'

'We haven't heard anything form that modelling agency, have we?' Tansey said to Lucinda.

'Nope. We definitely got conned there. I knew we were onto a loser as soon as I saw those ropy offices. They looked as though they'd never been cleaned.'

'I thought your friend said it was the best child-modelling agency in London,' laughed Tansey. They'd paid five hundred quid to have Bluebell and Dolly's photos taken at the awful-looking premises in Whitechapel.

'She isn't my friend anymore, that prat,' chuckled Lucinda. 'Oh well, Glen wasn't keen for Dolly to model anyway.'

'Same with Donny. Funny though, eh?'

Lucinda rolled her eyes. 'Only us! Tell me about Jamie's girlfriend then. I'm so glad he's back at work and in a happy place now. I know how worried you were about him.'

Tansey smiled. It was amazing how her son had changed in a few weeks. He was hanging about with Darren again and both boys had met girlfriends who were also friends. 'Her name's Clare. She lives in a nice house in Upminster. Me being nosy, I had to drive past it. Her parents sound nice and she has a little brother. Jamie seems smitten with her. I'm so glad he'd away from those twins, Lucinda. It's a relief to me they met those gypsy girls.'

'I bet. How's Harry and Alfie doing?'

'Harry's doing well at school. He's no trouble, him. As for Alfie, he keeps costing us housekeepers. They can't seem to handle him during school holidays like Renata does.' Renata was at retirement age now, but had agreed to continue working for Tansey, providing she took all the children's school holidays off to visit her family back in Spain.

'Shame. He can't help the way he is, bless him.'

'I know he can't. We've been informed he may well be autistic. They're going to test him for that, among other

404

things. It would explain a lot, I suppose. I just worry about his future.'

'Bless you. Perhaps they can give him some form of medication to help?'

'Hopefully. It just feels good to find a specialist that actually takes Alfie's issues seriously for once. All we've been told in the past is "Some children are naughtier than others", "Boys will be boys" and "There's nothing wrong with him, apart from he's hyperactive."'

'You'll get him sorted, Tans. Changing the subject, weather's meant to be nice on Sunday, so Glen's cooking a barbecue. Come with the kids. Glen's family will all be there, and I know his sisters-in-law and brothers all loathe me. They're so bloody common, the lot of them.'

Tansey chuckled. 'Of course I'll come. But I'm going to need you to return the favour soon. Donny wants to arrange a bit of a party at ours for the twins' sixteenth birthdays. Unsurprisingly, they haven't got many friends, so it will probably just be family. Donny's, naturally.' Tansey rolled her eyes. 'The old slapper of a grandmother with the beehive that went out of fashion in the sixties is bound to be there. So is Sherry, the common minger. I could really do with your support that day.'

Lucinda grinned. 'You got yourself a deal, girlfriend.'

Beau and Brett were sunbathing outside Jolene and Tammy's home, while playing a game of cards. It was their day off from the nursery and it had been Beau's idea to take the girls out for something to eat later. Neither Jolene or Tammy worked. It was their dad's duty to support his daughters until they found husbands of their own. The girls spent their days helping their mum cook, clean among other chores.

Apart from the two elder brothers, who clearly still didn't approve of them, Beau and Brett had won over the rest of the family. Evie was still a bit wary, but was polite enough now. It had been Tammy's decision that she and Brett remain friends, a decision that was a relief to Brett. They got along even better now, like best mates. Tammy had even confided in Brett recently that she had her eye on a Travelling lad, Jimmy Dean. She'd told nobody else, not even her sister. That's how close they'd become as pals.

Beau dealt the cards. 'Our dad's planning our sixteenth. He said we can have the boat for a party down the Thames, but me and Brett ain't sure. We got friends, like. But not loads.'

Jolene and Tammy squealed with delight. 'Oh, you gotta do it. I would love to have a party on the Thames.'

'Yeah. You must. That'd be wicked,' added Tammy, and we got loads of cousins we can invite to make up the numbers.'

Beau smiled at Jolene's excitement. 'All right then. A boat party it is.'

'Cushty. I meant to ask you, Dad asked me last night if you'd sorted out a meet with him and your granddad yet? I think Dad's keen for us all to get on, which is great, eh? You know, a handshake.'

Beau glanced at Brett, before answering. When he'd asked Gramps to meet with Bobby, he'd been told, 'You can fuck right off. You wanna involve yourself with a family of pikeys, that's your call. But you can count me out, and your father. I'd rather pull me teeth out with pliers.'

'Well?' prompted Jolene.

'Gramps has been busy. I ain't had a chance to ask him yet, but I will,' lied Beau.

*

'Whatever's the matter?' Kenny asked. He'd arrived home to find his wife in floods of tears.

'It's Mum. Her cancer's back. She needs a double mastectomy, she's coming back to England to have the op. I said she could stay here. I can look after her then.'

'Yeah, course.' Kenny dreaded the arrival of Maggie. She'd never forgiven him for cheating on Sharon, hated his guts now. Kenny took his wife in his arms. 'I'm so sorry, sweetheart, I truly am. But your mum will be fine. She's a fighter.'

The following Sunday, Maggie and Charlie Saunders arrived back in the UK. Sharon picked them up from the airport early hours of the morning, then had to listen throughout the journey home to her mother berating her decision to take Kenny back. Her parents had been in the UK when she'd first found out about Kenny's affair. But rather than upset them, her mum especially, due to her recovery, she'd not told them until they were back in Spain a month or so later.

Knowing Kenny knew about his own affair, which had resulted in a child he had no contact with, Charlie stuck up for Kenny. 'It's Sharon's decision, love, and they're happy again. It was one mistake and Kenny's obviously truly sorry for it. Please don't cause a bad atmosphere, just concentrate on your op, then getting yourself better.'

'One mistake! Good job we weren't still in England when I found out. Nobody hurts my baby. I'd have chopped his wandering cock off. The dirty bastard, going with a girl half his age. He's a pervert, that's what he is.'

'Mum, please don't spoil my happiness by making Kenny feel uncomfortable in his own home. That's really not fair on me.'

'It's your home. Not his,' Maggie reminded her daughter.

'I know. But you know what I mean. Please be polite, for my sake if nothing else.'

'I'll try.'

'Maggie, Charlie. 'Ere let me grab those cases,' Kenny was surprised at how well Maggie looked, considering her cancer had returned.

Charlie shook Kenny's hand. 'You all right? I'd say good to see ya, but under the circumstances, that doesn't quite seem the right thing to say.'

'Maggie's a fighter. I'm sure she'll be fine.'

Maggie gave Kenny daggers. 'You're a doctor now, as well as a womanizer, are you?'

'Mum,' hissed Sharon.

Kenny rolled his eyes at Charlie. This was going to be a long couple of months, or however long they were staying for.

Kenny was just about to carve the beef when his phone rang. It was Ted who lived four doors away. 'Two women have just knocked on my door asking for you, Ken. One said she needs to see you urgently. They're outside mine in a little red car.'

The hairs on the back of Kenny's neck stood up. Who could this be? And what the hell did they want?

'Where you going?' enquired Sharon.

'That was Ted. He needs a hand with something. I'll only be five minutes.'

'Don't be any longer – dinner's nearly ready.'

Kenny bolted along the lane. He looked inside the red car and could barely believe his eyes. It was none other

408

than his ex, Karen Bamber. She opened the window. 'Hello, Kenny. Long time no see.'

Kenny didn't recognize the other woman. 'What ya doing coming 'ere? What's a matter?' he gabbled, nerves already shattered.

'I need to speak to you. Not here, obviously.'

'What about?'

'I'll tell you when I see you, but it's important.'

Kenny sighed. 'All right.'

'Come to mine in the morning then. Say about eleven. I'm still at the same address.'

'Yeah. OK.' Kenny ran back to his house. Perhaps Karen had some agg with someone or needed to borrow some money? Those were the only things he could think of. Oh well, he only had to wait until tomorrow to find out.

'Mum, Carl, this is Jolene and this is Tammy,' grinned Beau.

Lori stood up and hugged both girls. 'It's so lovely to finally meet you and I can see why my boys talk about little else. You're so beautiful.' Lori and Carl had a daughter of their own now, Hope. She was being looked after by Lori's mum today. They had finally made peace and were back on good terms.

'Lovely to meet you both,' Carl smiled.

Brett winked at Tammy as he pulled back a chair for her to sit on. He'd wanted his mum to think she was his girlfriend and Tammy was happy to play along.

'Everyone's looking our way,' chuckled Carl.

'I'm not surprised. It's not often you see two stunning pairs of identical twins,' beamed Lori. She was so proud of the hard-working young gentlemen her boys had become. She was also relieved that what had happened to

Brett as a child hadn't affected his ability to have a relationship. Hopefully he couldn't remember his awful ordeal.

'The lamb shank looks good. What do you like to eat, girls? There's no rush to order, by the way.' Carl put down the menu.

'I'm starved. Could eat a scabby gry,' said Tammy.

'I'm that starved, I could eat an even scabbier one,' replied Jolene.

Seeing their mum and Carl's confused expressions, Beau and Brett both laughed. 'Gry means horse in Romany,' explained Brett.

Lori smiled politely. Since getting clean and meeting Carl, not only had she gone up in the world, she'd kind of reinvented herself, the way she spoke included.

Jolene and Tammy might be pretty girls, but their turn of phrase left a lot to be desired. So did their dress sense.

After a rotten night's kip, Kenny made a limp excuse to Sharon about having to meet up with Tony, then headed towards Karen's gaff. His luck must be well and truly poxed. Maggie hadn't stopped having a pop at him since the moment she'd laid eyes on him again and Karen turning up out of the blue was the icing on the cake.

Having not thought about Karen for ages, Kenny tried to calm his frayed nerves on the journey. Unlike Abi, Karen was sane, a schoolteacher, a good mum to her only daughter. He had remembered telling her that if she had any grief in the future, he would always be there for her, so perhaps it was that? He'd since changed his phone number. But why the hell would she turn up at his home? That was double worrying.

Heart in his mouth, Kenny knocked on Karen's door. 'How you doing? Sorry I couldn't speak properly to you

410

yesterday. But what with your mate in the car and me neighbour looking on, it was a bit awkward, to say the least.'

'That's fine. You don't have to explain. I would have spoken to you on the phone, had you not changed your number. You always said you'd help me in a crisis,' Karen said coldly.

'Yeah, sure. Sorry about me old number. I lost me phone. That's why I had to change it. So, what's the problem?'

Karen gestured Kenny to follow her. She opened the door of a small room. There was little inside apart from a tiny chest of drawers and a cot, with a baby asleep inside it. 'I thought it was about time you two became acquainted. Kenny, meet your son, Jake.'

'Goodbye, Jolene,' Lori hugged the girl, before hugging her sister. She could tell Beau was the more besotted of her sons. 'It's been a pleasure to meet you both,' gushed Lori.

Brett thanked Carl, then gave his mum an awkward hug. 'Cheers for the meal. See you soon.'

Beau gave his mother a massive hug. 'Thanks so much. Jolene loved you,' he whispered.

With a false smile on her face, Lori waved as she and Carl left her sons and their girlfriends to finish their desserts.

'You OK?' Carl asked, once outside the restaurant.

'No. Not really. I had to get out of there. I felt I needed a drink for the first time in ages.'

'Why?'

'Why do you think? Those girls aren't good enough for my boys, Carl. Beau and Brett could get any girls they wanted. Why choose those two? They're as common as muck. Awful pedigree. Even their clothes were nasty and tarty.'

'I get where you're coming from, but I wouldn't worry about it too much. The boys are only young, probably just having fun. As for the attraction, perhaps it's because the girls are also twins?'

'Beau and Jolene seem besotted with each other. They marry 'em off young in the Traveller community. No way is she marching my Beau up the aisle any time soon. Over my dead body.'

Kenny Bond was in a state of shock. A father again at his age was unthinkable alone. As for the predicament he'd gotten himself into, the whole situation was a nightmare. 'How did it happen? I know you weren't on the pill, but I never came up you, not once. Then I started wearing dunkies.'

'I don't know how it happened, but it obviously bloody did. There's your proof, lying in the cot.'

Kenny cursed himself. 'He's definitely mine, yeah? I mean, is there any chance he could be someone else's?'

'No chance at all. I don't usually leap into bed with men like I did with you. I hadn't slept with anybody for ten months before you and I haven't slept with anyone since.'

'Jesus wept,' mumbled a shell-shocked Kenny.

When Jake started to cry, Karen went into his room and Kenny put his head in his hands. No way could Sharon ever find out about this. It would be the end of them for good if she did.

'Do you want to hold him?' asked Karen.

Kenny didn't particularly want to, but felt horrible saying no. 'Go on then.' Any doubt Kenny had that the child wasn't his left him when he stared at Jake. He looked just like Donny as a baby, the spitting image of him.

Kenny studied his son for a couple of minutes, then handed him back to his mother. 'What exactly do you want from me, Karen? I can give you money, obviously. But I can't give you me. I'm happy with Sharon. We're back on track.'

'I'm not a bitch, would never come between you and Sharon. I want a nice place to raise Jake. A house with a decent-sized garden would be a start.'

'Why didn't you let me know about Jake earlier?'

'Oh, I did try to tell you, but you didn't answer my calls. Shortly after the last time I rung you, you'd changed your phone number.'

'Oh yeah. Sorry. I forgot. I'll pay the rent on a new gaff for ya. What else do you need?'

'Money every week, to feed and raise Jake. I'll also need money to support myself as I don't intend on being a working mum. A newer car would be nice too. Mine's knocking on a bit now, keeps breaking down. I'd also like you to see Jake, even if it's only once a week. I don't want him growing up thinking he hasn't got a father.'

Panic growing by the second, Kenny couldn't stop his jaw from twitching. 'Look, I'll do everything you ask on one condition. You tell nobody that I'm his dad. Have you told anyone?'

'Only my best friend, Tara. She was the one with me yesterday. My mum knows too. Other than that, I promise I haven't told a soul.'

'Jake can't have my surname, ya know. He can't even know my surname when he's older.'

'That's fine. He has my surname anyway.'

'You wanna look round and find yourself a gaff to rent.

Or do you want me to? You're gonna have to stay over this side of Essex or go further out.'

'I'd like a house in Loughton. That's a nice area to raise Jake. I'll find somewhere, then let you know. I'm also going to need a contact number for you. If you give me your mobile, put me in under a man's name and I'll text you if and when I need to. You can ring me back when you're free that way. Oh, and I need a new phone myself. I dropped mine in water the other day when I was bathing Jake.'

Rather reluctantly, Kenny gave Karen his number. He could hardly say no when she knew where he lived.

Kenny stood up, took a wad of money out of his pocket and counted out five hundred quid. 'That's to get a new phone and whatever Jake needs. I've gotta be somewhere in a bit, so I need to make a move.' Kenny didn't have to be anywhere, but his head was mashed and he needed some time alone to clear it. Perhaps he'd stop at a boozer, neck a couple of brandies. That might help.

'Thanks.' Karen snatched the money. 'Jake needs quite a lot of things. I'll give you a list next time you're round here and perhaps you can get them for me?'

'Can't you get 'em if I give you the dosh? I don't know anything about baby stuff.'

'My car isn't working. I told you it keeps breaking down. Could you get me a new car this week, Kenny? I don't know much about cars. Then I can get all Jake's bits myself.'

'OK. I'll be in touch in the next few days.'

'Can you get me a sporty-looking car? It doesn't have to be new. But something not too old with low mileage.'

Kenny sighed. Karen had changed from the warm, loving woman that he'd once known. She was cold, businesslike almost. She also had him over a barrel. He knew it and so did she. 'I'll be in touch in the next couple of days,' Kenny said.

'Will you have my car by then?'

'Erm. I'll try. I'll have a look round for one tomorrow.'

'Great. Thanks. Speak soon then.'

'See ya.'

When Kenny left the flat, Karen bounced her son up and down in her arms. 'Well, that wasn't too bad was it, Jakey.'

Karen had once been head over heels in love with Kenny, which was why she'd so desperately wanted his child. With Kenny using the withdrawal method, there was little chance of her falling pregnant. That's why she'd put the frighteners on him. She'd told him there was still a chance of conception, as a pal of hers had conceived using the withdrawal method, so to be on the safe side they'd be better using condoms.

Kenny had fallen for her little white lie and had turned up on his next visit with a box of Durex, that he'd then left at hers. At the time, Karen had hoped if she did fall pregnant, Kenny would settle down with her. That's why she'd taken extreme measures. She'd stabbed each and every condom with a sterilized needle. Not just once, quite a few times.

It took a few months, but her cunning plan worked. Karen hadn't known she was pregnant with Jake when Kenny ended their relationship. She found out a couple of weeks later and in time, tried to contact Kenny. But not only did he ignore her calls, he then changed his phone number.

That was when Karen's feelings had changed. Instead of continuing to place Kenny on a pedestal, she'd grown

415

a backbone, forced herself to see him for what he truly was. A user and a liar.

'Even if I do get back with Shal, I'll always be there for you, Karen. You've been such a rock to me and I'll never forget your kindness. You ever have any grief or need me for anything, I promise I'll be there like a shot for yer,' were Kenny's exact words. Yeah. Righto!

Karen sat on the sofa, lifted her son up and laughed as he smiled. What was good enough for Sharon and her kids was now good enough for her and Jake. They would have everything they needed; she would make damn sure of that.

Her knight in shining armour might've turned out to be a lying tosspot in tin foil, but at least he was a wealthy one . . .

CHAPTER THIRTY-ONE

'That's the last of the meat, Donny. I'll go pick the seafood up in a bit.'

'Can I have a hotdog now?' pleaded Ricky, jumping up and down.

'No. You bleedin' well can't. We ain't even got the barbecue on yet and you've not long stuffed a big breakfast. You can come with me, help me carry the seafood. Time you started earning your keep.' Kenny winked at Donny.

'No. You earn your keep,' Ricky chuckled, playfully punching the godfather he totally adored.

'Weather's been kind to us eh, boy?' said Kenny. It was hot already, not a cloud in the sky.

'Sure has. You picking Nan up?' enquired Donny.

'Nah. Cliff's picking Mum and Aunt Nell up.'

'My sister not coming 'cause she's in the Big Apple,' Ricky informed Donny.

'Yes, Little Man. I told Donny all about your sister's new job,' sighed Kenny.

'You OK, Dad? You seem fine to me, but Mum was a bit worried about you yesterday. She said you haven't been yourself and not been sleeping well.'

Of course Kenny hadn't been himself. In less than a week, Karen had cost him over twelve grand in total. He could hardly tell his son that though. 'It's having your nan living with us. She's doing my nut in. Pecking at me all day long like a fucking woodpecker.'

'I thought it might be. Don't worry, I won't say nothing to Mum.'

'Cheers, lad.' Kenny's phone beeped. He'd put Karen in his phone under the name Kevin. It was her again. She knew they were having a barbecue as an early birthday celebration for the twins today. What the bastard-hell did she want now? Not more money, surely?

'I don't like Vera much,' Ricky announced on their way to pick up the seafood.

'Why's that then?' enquired Kenny. He'd given Karen a quick call and thankfully she hadn't wanted to stripe him up for anything else. He'd bought her a two-year-old white Volkswagen Golf Cabriolet and she hadn't a clue how to take the roof down.

''Cause she's horrible to Granddad.'

'In what way?'

'She won't go inside his house, says it's dirty. And she wouldn't get in his jeep, 'cause she says that stinks too. So Granddad had to buy another car just to take her out in.'

'How d'ya know all this?' In fairness, what with Cliff being an ex-rag-and-bone man who now spent his days tinkering about with car engines, Kenny wasn't surprised. Cliff's old Land Rover had never had a valet, was full of odds and sods and filthy. And his gaff resembled Steptoe's yard.

''Cause I heard 'em talking when I stayed with Louisa and Granddad while you were in the Big Apple.'

Kenny smiled. He had no idea where Ricky had heard America referred to as the 'Big Apple' but once he found a saying he liked, Ricky tended to use it constantly. 'Don't you worry. I'll have a word with your granddad later, find out what's going on.'

'I don't like Vera's hair either. She looks silly.'

Kenny chuckled. 'Me neither. Perhaps we should find a big pair of scissors and chop it off, eh?'

Ricky clapped his hands together. 'Yes.'

Tansey was in the kitchen washing and preparing the salad when the gruesome twosome came storming in. 'I thought this was meant to be a barbecue for *our* birthday and only family were invited,' bellowed Beau.

Tansey turned the tap off. 'It is, apart from Lucinda. She's coming soon to help me prepare the food, so it would have been rude not to invite her husband and children, wouldn't it?'

Beau glared at Tansey. 'So how comes Jamie is bringing his bird?'

'Because I told him to. His friend couldn't make it and I didn't want Jamie to be standing all alone. You'll be busy circulating and your family isn't Jamie's, is it?'

'You saying you invited Brooksy an' all?' Brett spat.

'Yes. At first. But as I said, he had other plans, so I told Jamie to invite Clare instead,' gabbled Tansey. Both boys looked angry. Very angry. Even more evil than usual, if that were possible.

'Well, you can fuck right off. If Clare's coming, then so are Jolene and Tammy,' insisted Beau.

'No. They can't! Look, speak to your dad. He won't be long. He's only popped out to get more beers.'

'Fuck you and fuck Dad,' retorted Beau. 'Come on,

419

Brett. Let's go an' tell the girls they're invited.' Beau pointed at Tansey. 'And best you tell the old man, if they ain't welcome, then we won't be 'ere either.'

When Donny arrived home with Harry and Alfie, who'd insisted accompanying him to choose what crisps they wanted, he couldn't believe what he was hearing. 'Out in the garden, boys,' he ordered. Bluebell was down at Lucinda's playing with Dolly.

Tansey knew Donny was livid, could see it in his eyes. 'Don't you be blaming me. Unlike the twins, Jamie has none of his own family here. I didn't want him to feel like an odd one out.'

'Nah. You've just been gagging to ruin things ever since I arranged this. Reason being, you can't stand Beau and Brett.'

'Oh, don't be so ridiculous. I didn't know they were going to kick off then storm out, did I? I never even told them Clare was invited. Jamie did.'

'And how did you think they would feel, Tans? It's their party, but only *your* son's girlfriend is invited. I can't believe you've been so fucking stupid. Well, I've got no choice now other than to welcome the gypsies with open arms. All thanks to you. Wait until I tell me father. He'll go mental. Not at me. At you, ya devious bitch.'

Open-mouthed, Tansey was dumbstruck for once, as Donny stormed off. Who did he think he was? Speaking to her like that. Some party this was going to be.

Kenny walked the tiny distance to his son's house with his wife by his side. 'You go inside, babe. I'll have a cigar out 'ere first.' Kenny wasn't a cigarette smoker anymore, but still liked a big fat expensive cigar, especially at parties, or when stressed.

'You OK? You've been acting weird all week,' Sharon informed him.

'I'm fine. I just want a moment out 'ere to think of Alan. He would've been the first 'ere today. Loved the twins, he did.' Kenny wasn't lying. You expect your grandparents to die, as they're so much older than you. But not your best pal, especially at such a young age and in tragic circumstances. He still struggled to get his head around what had happened to Alan and Julia. Horrendous, with a capital H.

Sharon squeezed Kenny's arm. 'I understand. I'll bring you a large brandy out in a minute.'

Kenny craned his neck when an old classic car pulled up. He then did a double-take as Cliff got out, followed by his mum and aunt. 'Not got your Land Rover anymore, Cliff?' he enquired.

'Course I have. Bit dirty to take your mum out in though. Vera came with me to choose this, didn't you, love?'

'Yes. I weren't getting in that other bleedin' thing.' The car Vera had insisted Cliff buy was a 1960s Jaguar Mark II. She'd loved the sixties, hence her keeping up with the fashion from then and her beehive. The car suited her image and Vera loved being driven about in it.

Kenny shook hands with Cliff, whom he was determined to have a quiet word with later, hugged Aunt Nelly and then politely kissed his mother on the cheek. She didn't do hugging, his mum, had always been as hard as nails, unable to show him any affection.

Donny appeared, looking flustered. 'Dad, we've sort of got a problem.'

'What?'

Donny explained what had happened with Tansey and the twins.

Kenny shrugged. Jolene and Tammy coming to the barbecue was the least of his current problems. 'It's your house. Invite who you want, boy.'

'Lovely! Hold onto your handbag for dear life, Nell. The gypsies are coming.' Vera pursed her lips. 'Come on, Cliff. Find me a seat and get me a drink. And I don't want no uncomfortable chair, thanks very much.'

Beau and Brett sat outside Bobby's trailer chatting to him, Evie, Sonny and young Bobby-Joe. Thankfully, the older two brothers weren't around. Jolene, especially, had been thrilled when Beau had told her that his dad had rung him, inviting her and Tammy to the barbecue. Beau obviously hadn't told her why. Reason being, he wanted the girls to feel welcome.

'Take ages to get ready girls, don't they? I'm glad I was born with a cory,' announced young Bobby-Joe.

'Don't be talking about your cory in front of your mother, ya dirty boy,' scolded Evie.

Bobby senior, Sonny, Beau and Brett all burst out laughing.

'Baking, I is,' Sonny said, taking off his T-shirt.

Brett tried to avert his eyes from Sonny's toned stomach, but couldn't help keep having a crafty glance. Fit as a butcher's dog he was. 'You not got anything on today, Sonny?'

Bobby replied for his son. 'No. We need to find him a woman, don't we, Evie?'

'Too fussy is his problem.' Evie rolled her eyes.

'Nah. Having a lazy day. Been working too hard all week,' Sonny replied.

'Come to the barbecue too,' Brett blurted out.

Beau nudged his brother with his knee. It was a miracle his old man had invited the girls, without them turning up with a brother too.

Sonny locked eyes with Brett. 'Nah. I'm fine, honest. Cheers for the invite though, mush.'

Jolene appeared. 'How do I look?'

Beau smiled, but inside winced at the same time. Tight frayed denim shorts that were right up her arse. A bright red bikini top, showing off her pierced belly button, and high red stilettos wasn't the type of attire his family would appreciate. Tammy was dressed similar, but had a denim mini-skirt on instead. 'You look gorgeous,' Beau replied honestly. And she did to him. But he knew his family would see her as some little slapper, even though the most she'd let him do to her was tit her up.

Kenny collared Cliff as he went over to the bins filled with ice to keep the beers cool. 'Heard any more from Louisa, Cliff?'

'Yeah. She's loving LA. Met a lad out there too. An American model.' Cliff rolled his eyes.

'Good luck to her. She needed a change of scenery. I'm glad she's happy. That's what Alan and Julia would've wanted.'

'I know. And I'm glad Ricky's happy with you and Sharon too.'

'Your grandson's a pleasure to have living with us, Cliff. No trouble at all, mate. So, how's it going with me muvver? You two an item these days, like?'

'It's just nice to have a lady friend in my life again, Kenny. Since my Lily died, I've been lonely at times. Your mum's certainly a character and I do enjoy her company. She has expensive taste, mind. Wants me to take her on the Orient Express for her birthday. Arm an' a leg job, that is.'

'You gonna move in together at some point or what?' Kenny knew his mother was partial to a bit of cock but couldn't exactly ask Cliff outright if he was getting his leg over.

'Goodness, no. You know me, lad, I love living amongst tut and messing about with cars. I still do repairs you know – only for friends, mind. Your glamorous mum wouldn't put up with me. Once a rag-and-bone man, always a rag-and-bone man,' chuckled Cliff.

'You're just friends then?'

'Yes. Of course. Very good friends. I'm way too old for all that nooky lark, boy. Christ Almighty!'

About to warn Cliff not to book the Orient Express and wise him up in the kindest way possible, Kenny's jaw dropped as his favourite grandchildren approached him with two birds in tow that looked and dressed like lap dancers.

Beau put a comforting arm around his girlfriend's shoulders. 'Gramps, meet Jolene. The girl I'm gonna marry one day.'

Unlike Donny, who was crestfallen over his eldest sons' choice of girlfriends, Tansey adored Jamie's. A pretty girl with an infectious laugh, Clare was warm and friendly. She was only tiny, around five feet, Tansey reckoned. But she had cute dimples and it was clear to see she was as besotted with Jamie as he was with her. She hung onto his every word.

Lucinda leaned towards Tansey. 'I can't take my eyes off the two Travelling girls. So common, aren't they? Thank God your Jamie has good taste.'

As pleased as punch, Tansey smiled. Jamie was a credit to her now and she couldn't be any more proud of him.

Bored, it was Tammy who suggested Brett steal some alcohol and the four of them drink it in private. She didn't feel comfortable being surrounded by so many gorgers and knew they were all gossiping about her and Jolene. Judging them, without even bothering to get to know her and her sister.

'Don't drink no more, Tammy. You go home drunk and Mum and Dad won't let us go to the boat party,' Jolene warned her sister.

'Oh, shut your trap. When did you become so boring?' questioned Tammy, as she took another sip of the neat vodka. She actually knew when her sister had become boring, since she'd fallen for Beau. Beforehand, Jolene was the wilder out of the two of them, the instigator in any trouble they'd get themselves into.

Brett laughed as Tammy ordered him to open his mouth, then poured some vodka down his throat. If he did fancy girls, she would definitely be his girlfriend.

'Hello,' said Ricky. He liked Jolene and Tammy. They'd been really nice to him earlier and he'd been interested in hearing about their little brother, Bobby-Joe. So much so, he'd decided he wanted to meet him.

'What you got behind your back?' asked Beau. He felt embarrassed now at feeling jealousy towards Gramps' relationship with Ricky once upon a time. But in fairness, he'd only been a kid himself back then.

Ricky grinned as he pulled out a pair of garden shears. 'Uncle Kenny said earlier that I should cut off Vera's silly hair, so I stole these from the shed. I don't like Vera. She's horrible to Granddad Cliff.'

Beau and Brett both burst out laughing. Gramps had never opened up to them much about his childhood, but they knew from their father he'd had an unhappy one and had been raised by his grandparents. 'Hide that bottle. We'll finish it off later,' Brett said, grabbing Tammy's hand.

Beau leapt up and ruffled Ricky's hair. 'Too right. We can't miss this.'

Vera was sitting alone when her great-grandsons strutted over to her to introduce their trashy-looking girlfriends. Vera loved Donny in her own way, but had never had time for those twins of his. They had Kenny's blood running through their veins all right. Full of mischief and untrustworthy.

'Nanny Vera, this is Jolene and this is Tammy,' grinned Beau.

Vera immediately knew Beau was taking the mickey. He'd never referred to her as Nan in his lifetime. 'Nice to meet you,' she said coldly, craning her neck to see what was taking Cliff so long. She spotted him chatting to Kenny and another man. A reason to scold him later. As for Nelly, she was stuffing her face again with yet another plate of food, while chatting to Sharon.

It was Jolene who distracted Vera, pulling her up about a comment she'd heard her make as she and Tammy had walked past her earlier. 'We don't chore by the way, me and me sister.'

'I beg your pardon?' Vera stopped tapping her foot to the music and glared at the awful girl. She couldn't even understand her, she spoke that fast.

Beau, Brett and Tammy had to turn their backs as they clocked Ricky going to town with the shears. The back of Vera's beehive was dropping on the grass in chunks.

426

'I heard ya. Your handbags. You told that fat woman you were sitting with that we were gonna chore 'em,' Jolene replied in earnest.

'Erm, excuse me, young lady. But *that* fat woman just happens to be my wonderful sister.'

How Jolene kept a straight face as more of Vera's hair fell onto the grass, she did not know. The one thing she did know was the judgemental old battleaxe deserved it.

As she was about to tear the woman off a strip, two little girls ran over and started picking up Vera's hair. Ricky wasn't silly. He scarpered.

'Nanny Vera. Your hair is falling out,' announced Bluebell, showing her clumps of it in her hands.

Startled, Vera looked at the child in amazement, before touching the back of her hair. Most of it was gone. Vera stood up and seeing all her wonderful blonde hair on the floor, immediately came over all funny. 'Me hair. Someone's cut me fucking hair off,' she raged.

Seeing his lady friend in distress, Cliff dashed towards her. 'Whatever's wrong, love?'

Both sets of twins were creased up with laughter. So was young Ricky, who was hiding behind a bush.

Her unique hairstyle having been her pride and joy for years, the shock was too much for Vera. Her knees gave way and she fainted.

Bobby Tamplin glared at Tammy. 'Are you drunk, girl?'

'No. She's not,' lied Brett.

Tammy was cracking up as she told the story of Vera's hair. 'Serves her right for calling us thieves. The old rabbit's crotch.'

'You have been drinking. Sonny, make your sister a strong coffee.' Evie wasn't amused. In their community it was a usual occurrence for the men to roll home drunk, but not the women. Especially girls.

'I only had a couple of vodkas and that's 'cause I didn't feel comfortable. They was all horrible to us,' elaborated Tammy.

'Whaddya mean? They were horrible. What did they say?' Bobby Tamplin clenched his fists.

Sensing trouble on the horizon, Jolene steered her sister inside their trailer, before explaining the situation to her parents. 'Apart from the old lady who got her come-uppance, nobody was horrible to us. They were nice and friendly.'

'I should bloody hope so too,' Evie spat.

'I wouldn't allow anyone to be nasty to the girls, Bobby. They'd have me and Brett to deal with if they were,' said Beau.

'I should think so too. Welcomed you two into our family, haven't we?' Bobby snapped.

'I don't want 'em going on that boat party. Say they gets drunk and one of 'em falls over the side,' said a worried Evie.

'I can promise you faithfully there will be no booze on the boat. Gramps won't allow it. He'd lose his licence,' Beau replied.

'Tammy's being sick,' announced Bobby-Joe.

'Tammy drunk some vodka, OK. But none of us did. We're all sober,' insisted Jolene. 'And I promise she won't drink nothing on the boat. None of us will.'

Not impressed, Bobby stood up and waved his index finger at Brett and then Beau. 'I never want a repeat of this, understand? You take my girls out, you bloody look after them. 'Cause if either comes home drunk again, that's it! I'll put the kibosh on the whole thing.'

'Of course. I understand,' said Beau.

'Yeah. I'm sorry too,' added Brett. He wasn't, thought Tammy had been hilarious today when sozzled.

'Get orf now, the pair of ya.'

Jolene squeezed Beau's hand. 'It'll be OK. I'll talk 'em round,' she whispered in his ear.

Beau walked away, his shoulders slumped. He'd done his utmost to impress Jolene's parents; now all his hard work had been undone.

CHAPTER THIRTY-TWO

'Act like a proper man at all times. Especially in public. Always remember, what's seen cannot be unseen.'

The week following the barbecue, I didn't know if I was coming or going. That was when it truly hit home. I had a baby, a son, by another woman.

Part of me wanted to come clean with Sharon, spill me guts and beg her forgiveness. But Shal was no pushover. No way would she suffer a double betrayal, especially when she'd given me plenty of opportunity to confess to any sexual misdemeanours before we'd got back together. But me being the muggins I was, had lied. How I wished I'd been straight with her now. There was nothing going on romantically between me and Karen. But the guilt of having to lie to my wife about where I was going and what I was doing, began eating away at me like a cancerous tumour.

I needed alibis, regularly, so I told Tony what had happened. He urged me to tell Shal, but I just couldn't. She had enough on her plate with her mum's cancer returning. I couldn't add to her grief, neither could I face

430

losing her again. Truth be known, I needed Sharon far more than she probably needed me.

Me and Tony were having major problems with the Chinese too. They still couldn't get the pills right, but thankfully, the geezer they promised would be their saviour had finally turned up from China. He was in charge of making next weekend's batch. So me and Tony were hopeful we'd soon get some of the custom back we'd lost. There were lots of little firms in Essex banging out ecstasy now. We had big competition on our hands.

Beau and Brett were well excited for their boat party, but I was dreading it. They didn't want any family there, apart from me, so Tony had agreed to help me out on the night. Donny was a bit put out, but understood the twins didn't want their street cred ruined.

I told my grandsons in no uncertain terms that no alcohol was to be sneaked onto the boat. The bar would be open, the drinks free, but soft drinks only. I was laying on grub for 'em too.

Obviously, I didn't have an inkling of what I was letting meself in for. If I had, there'd have been no party.

My luck was obviously poxed. Well and truly . . .

Beau Bond studied himself in the mirror. His new hairstyle suited him, longer on top and slicked back. It made him look older, more sophisticated. 'How do I look?' Designer short-sleeved black shirt, tight black strides, black Gucci belt with the famous red-and-green trim and black suede loafers worn with no socks.

'Like you're going to a funeral,' chuckled Brett. 'Only kidding! You look good, bruv.' Brett had chosen a similar outfit, but his shirt and strides were grey. 'Do my clasp up for me.' The identical thick white-gold chains were their birthday present from their father. That's what they'd asked him for. Their Rolex watches were their favourite presents, though. Gramps had bought them.

'Ready?' Beau asked. The weather had thankfully been kind. It had rained all day yesterday, but today was dry and warm.

Brett put on his Ray-Ban sunglasses. 'Yep.'

The twins ran down the stairs, then sauntered into the kitchen. 'We're off now, Dad.'

Donny smiled. The twins loved their clobber and he couldn't be more proud of them. They looked so handsome and smart. Memories of picking them up from Lori's as kids, filthy dirty, dressed in tatty old clothes flashed through Donny's mind. No wonder they were fastidiously clean and shopped up the West End now they could afford to. From a terrible start in life, they'd come so far.

'You all right, Dad?' asked Brett.

Donny stood up, grabbed both the twins round the neck and hugged them. 'I can't tell you how proud of you two I am. Don't let me down tonight. No boozing beforehand. Your grandfather'll be reporting back.'

'Mind the barnet, Dad,' said Beau.

'We won't get boozy and let you down,' promised Brett.

'Good lads. Now go an' have a blast. Love ya both.'

'Love you too,' replied the twins in unison.

A party with no booze wasn't exactly enthralling, so it had been Brett's idea to score some ecstasy pills. He and Beau had taken them before, while in Compton House, and they'd had a right giggle on them.

Brett didn't know anybody that sold ecstasy, but Jamie did. A lad he'd gone to school with was a dealer.

Jolene and Tammy studied the blue tablets. They'd never taken them before. 'What do they make you feel like? asked Tammy.

'Happy. They make ya wanna dance all night long,' explained Brett.

'They don't make ya look out your nut, do they?' enquired Jolene. 'My mum and dad'll kill us and you if they think we've taken drugs. Especially after her coming home drunk last weekend,' she added, poking her sister in the arm.

'If you take 'em as soon as we get on the boat, they'll have worn off by the time we get home,' Brett replied. 'If you don't wanna take 'em though, you don't have to.'

'Whaddya reckon?' Jolene asked her sister.

'Yeah. Let's take 'em. I fancy a good old dance,' grinned Tammy.

'Why don't you just take a quarter or half each, see how you feel on that and if you ain't keen on it, don't take no more,' Beau suggested. He didn't want to risk upsetting Bobby Tamplin again.

'Yeah. That sounds a good idea. Let's do that, Tammy. A half'll be enough for me to try. Best to be safe than be sorry.'

The boat was due to set sail at seven from Waterloo. Beau and Brett arrived early so they could greet their guests. They didn't know most of the people who were coming, could only think of forty-odd themselves to invite. Jolene and Tammy had invited the rest and assured them they would turn up.

'Oh no. How embarrassing. We can't have them pictures up of us. We'll look like right numpties,' complained Brett.

There were numerous photos of himself and Beau as kids plastered all over the boat and a big HAPPY SIXTEENTH BIRTHDAY banner.

Kenny shrugged. 'Don't blame me. That was your dad's idea. He got the photos blown up.'

'We'll be a laughing stock. Help me take 'em down, Brett,' Beau said.

'Ahh, you were so cute,' chuckled Jolene.

'No. We weren't. We were little bastards,' replied Beau. 'Get that banner down an' all, Brett. Next thing, we'll be expected to cut a cake with sixteen candles.'

'Your dad got you a big cake,' Kenny joked.

'Don't you dare bring it out 'ere in front of all our mates.'

'Come on, Tony. Let's leave 'em to it,' Kenny replied. 'Who are you?' Kenny asked, as a big black bloke appeared.

'That's Samson, our DJ. Show him how to work the equipment, Granddad,' Beau ordered.

Brett grinned. 'All right, Samson?'

'Yeah, man. Sweet.'

Kenny sighed. Gut feeling told him he wasn't going to enjoy this party one little bit.

As the guests started to arrive, Kenny's gut feeling returned with a vengeance.

'They're all gyppos,' Tony whispered in his ear.

'Bound to be trouble. Always is with them. We better be on our toes,' Kenny stormed off to find his grandsons. He asked for a word with them in private.

'What's a matter?' asked Beau.

'I've got a boat full of fucking pikeys, that's what's the matter. If there's any damage done, your old man will be giving me your bastard wages until we're square.'

'And what makes you think there'll be damage?' asked Brett.

''Cause he's racist against Travellers,' replied Beau.

'I'll give you fucking racist if it all goes Pete Tong,' spat Kenny. 'I can't believe you've done this to me.'

'Chill out, will ya?' Beau spat back.

'Get out me sight, the fucking pair of ya,' ordered Kenny.

Samson specialized in drum and bass with a bit of garage thrown in for good measure.

'What a fucking racket,' Kenny moaned to Tony.

'It ain't too bad. This is what the youngsters are into, Ken.'

'Half of these ain't that young. That little firm of pikeys over there to your right, they've gotta be nineteen or twenty. You can tell they've been boozing an' all.'

'It'll be all over by eleven. Just grin and bear it, Ken.'

Beau and Brett spoke to their pals, then decided to pop their pills. Beau took Jamie to one side. He'd brought Clare with him. 'Did you get a pill for yourself?'

'Nah. If it was just us I might've, but Clare's very anti-drugs.'

'She's got you right in the palm of her hand, eh?' grinned Beau. 'Where's your mate Brooksy? I thought he was coming with his bird.'

'He's not well,' lied Jamie. Brooksy didn't like the twins.

Jolene walked over to Beau. 'Me and Tammy are going to the bog to take our pill.'

Beau kissed Jolene on the forehead. She looked absolutely stunning in her tight-fitting cerise satin dress and stilettos. 'Just take half at the most yeah, babe.'

*

435

The two sets of twins weren't the only one who'd taken ecstasy pills. Some of Jolene and Tammy's cousins and their pals had too.

When Samson began blasting out a more commercial set of tunes, which included Inner City's 'Good Life', Frankie Knuckles 'Your Love' and Adeva's 'Respect', Jolene and Tammy went wild along with many others who were dancing. Tammy leaned towards her sister. 'I love you, Jolene. Ain't these pills good? Let's take the other one in a minute.'

'Nah. Half's enough for me. I feel brilliant. I love you too.'

Knowing the girls had also come up on theirs, Beau and Brett grinned at each other. 'Gramps don't look too happy,' Brett told his brother.

'Fuck him. Miserable bastard.'

'I'm having the best night ever. I love you, Beau Bond,' Jolene grinned, throwing her arms around her boyfriend's neck.

Beau passionately kissed Jolene. 'Blinder, ain't it? Good job we got those pills though. Would've been well boring otherwise. I love you more by the way,' he chuckled.

'Where's Tammy? She with Brett?'

Beau shrugged and glanced around. 'Nah. Brett's over there talking to two of the lads we were in Compton with.'

'I'll go find her. But first I must go see Jimmy. He's my favourite cousin in the world,' gushed Jolene.

Beau smiled. Ecstasy gave you the love all right. Even your worst enemy was your best pal when you were on one.

*

436

Tammy clung onto the basin and stared into the small glass mirror. She'd felt great until she'd swallowed that second pill, whole. Now she looked and felt terrible. Her heart was beating too fast and sweat was pouring down her face which had totally ruined her make-up.

'Hurry up. There's a big queue out 'ere,' shouted a voice.

Tammy splashed some water on her face and unsteadily unlocked the toilet door.

'You all right, Tam? What's a matter?' asked her cousin, Kirsty, who happened to be in the queue.

'I don't feel well. I need some air and some water.'

'You don't bloody look well.' Kirsty put an arm around Tammy's waist. 'Come on, we'll get you on the deck.'

Her palpitations worsening, Tammy was struggling to put one foot in front of the other. Then everything went blurry and she collapsed, convulsing.

'Help. Someone help me. Where's Jolene?' screeched Kirsty.

Seeing a crowd gather, Kenny ran over. 'What's a matter with her?'

'I dunno. I think she's having a fit. She needs an ambulance. How we gonna get her off the boat?' a bloke replied.

'Jesus wept!' Kenny didn't know which twin it was, but it was definitely one of Bobby Tamplin's girls. She was having some kind of funny turn, literally frothing at the mouth. Kenny bolted off to speak to the captain, explain there was a major problem.

Jolene barged her way through the crowd and kneeled by her sister's side. Tammy looked so ill and her body making all kind of weird jerky movements. 'Tammy, Tammy, can you hear me?'

Tammy's eyes were open wide, a terrified expression in

them. Jolene burst into tears. She had never seen her sister look like this before.

Beau and Brett looked at one another, panic-stricken. 'D'ya reckon it's the E that caused it? Did she take the other pill?' asked Brett.

'I don't fucking know, do I? We're in shit-street, that's all I know. What are we meant to say to her father?'

Kenny ordered Samson to cut the music, then grabbed the mike. 'Party's over. We'll be docking in a few minutes and an ambulance'll be waiting there for us. Just get your bits together, leave the boat orderly and let the paramedics do their thing.' Spotting his grandsons, Kenny grabbed both of them and marched them out of earshot. 'Had that girl taken anything?'

'I dunno. I don't think so,' lied Beau.

'Don't fucking lie to me. This is serious. Your pupils look massive, the pair of ya. I weren't born yesterday. You've all taken something, haven't ya?'

'Nah. We ain't,' replied Brett.

Knowing they were both lying, Kenny grabbed their heads and smashed them together.

'Fuck. That hurt,' Brett complained.

'Now listen to me good and proper. I'm trying to help you 'ere 'cause they'll test that girl, then the Old Bill'll be involved an' all sorts. What did she take?'

'An E,' Beau replied.

'Who got it for her?'

'We did,' Brett replied. If they were going to be in trouble, they would be in trouble together.

'Bollocks!' cursed Kenny. 'Right, you act dumb. You say nothing to nobody, OK?'

Beau and Brett nodded.

'Did her sister take one an' all?'

'Yeah. They only took half each, but I reckon Tammy might've took the other one later 'cause Jolene didn't want it,' Beau explained.

'Beau, you must speak to Jolene, beg her to keep her trap shut. You'll never be allowed to see her again if this gets back to the family. Not only that, it'll cause the war of all wars. Me and your old man can do without that. Best you fucking pray the girl pulls through an' all.'

'What if she don't?' asked Brett.

'I don't wanna even think about that. What did these pills look like by the way?'

'They were blue, with a stamp on the front that looked like a crown,' Beau replied.

Kenny's face drained of colour. That was his stamp. Those were his pills.

By the time the boat cleared and the paramedics got on, the situation wasn't looking good at all. Tammy was still frothing at the mouth, her body making odd movements like a puppet on a string. Her eyes looked vacant and she certainly wasn't able to speak.

Jolene was beside herself, couldn't stop crying. To see her beautiful sister lying there like that broke her heart.

'Has she taken any drugs?' the paramedic asked.

'Not to our knowledge,' Beau replied. 'If this is down to drugs, someone must've spiked her drink. Her sister said she's never taken drugs, has she?'

'No. Never. Neither of us have,' wept Jolene. She'd spoken to Beau first, saying her parents must never find out she and Tammy had willingly taken those pills. Jolene guessed her sister had taken the other whole one as she'd looked in her clutch bag and the see-through bag had been inside minus the pill. Jolene had chucked that away to get rid of any evidence. Her family would never forgive her if Tammy didn't recover. As for what her dad and brothers would do to Beau and Brett, that didn't bear thinking of. It wasn't their fault what had happened. They were just as upset as she was. If tests proved Tammy had taken ecstasy, then they had to stick to their story and insist she'd been spiked. That was the only way.

'This is a nightmare, mate,' Tony whispered to Kenny. He was horrified to learn their pills were the probable cause of this.

'We wanna hope no more are dropping like flies as we speak. Otherwise, we're in deep shit. As for them chinkys, I'd like to throttle 'em with me bare hands. I knew they didn't know what they were bastard well doing. I've said it before and I'll say it again, I bet they did The Scientist in after thinking they knew the right recipe. They knew they'd be on a lot more dosh if they ran the show.'

'You could be right. You don't need me to come to the hospital with you, do ya? I can jump in a cab from 'ere.'

'Nah, nah, nah. This is *our* little problem, mate, not just mine. You was the one who wanted to continue, said the Chinese would get it right. Well, this is the outcome. The do-as-you-likeys are bound to be well happy when they turn up at the hospital to visit their seriously ill daughter. I'll need some back-up.'

'OK. I got your back, Ken. Always. You know that, mate.'

Jolene laid her head on Beau's shoulder, tears streaming down her face. She no longer felt or looked like she'd taken anything untoward, had looked in the mirror in the toilets. A relief that was, as her parents were on their way here.

The London Hospital was where Tammy had been rushed to. She'd been resuscitated in the ambulance on the way. It was like a bad dream; Jolene had to keep pinching herself to check she was actually awake. Life without her twin sister didn't bear thinking of. They'd spent every single day of their lives together, were best friends as well as sisters.

Beau held his girlfriend tightly. 'Let's say another prayer for Tammy, eh?' He felt so guilty, but knew it wasn't entirely his fault. The girls had said the party would be boring with no booze and even though it was Brett's suggestion to get some pills, Tammy had been up for it too. Little did he know it would end like this. Never would he take another drug again in his lifetime.

Kenny Bond glanced at his grandsons. He could truly throttle the pair of them right now, but at least they didn't look smashed anymore. Brett did a tiny bit, but Beau didn't at all. It was clear to see how in love Beau and Jolene were, but no way would they last now. Not after this. They were only kids anyway, they would move on and get over one another. They'd have to.

'You all right, mate? We gonna gel after the family arrive?' whispered Tony.

'Yeah. The boys are coming with us. I ain't leaving them 'ere,' sighed Kenny. He'd promised Beau and Brett he would say nothing to Donny about them buying the pills and taking them themselves, providing they made sure Jolene kept schtum and Tammy, if the poor girl ever recovered. 'Who keeps ringing ya, Tone?'

'It's Timmo. I better get it. That's the third time he's rung.' Paul Timms was one of their big Essex buyers.

Tony walked away, then returned a minute later, his face ashen. 'Ken, 'ere a minute.'

Kenny followed his business partner. 'Please don't tell me anybody else has keeled over.'

'Two. One collapsed in Faces, the other in Hollywoods. One of 'em's dead.'

The hairs stood up on the back of Kenny's neck. Sharon still didn't have a clue how he was earning a living and she would kick him out tomorrow if she got wind of this. 'Fuck this for a game of soldiers, Tone. We leave 'ere, drop the twins home, go to the premises where the pills were made and we burn the lot to the fucking ground. They've only gotta find fingerprints and tug one of them cunts in and we're both for the chopping block.'

Tony sighed. 'I'll ring me old man. He'll know what to do.'

'Nah. Don't speak to anyone else on that phone. We both get rid of our phones tonight an' all, mate. This is our problem and we'll deal with it ourselves.'

About to reply, Kenny was grabbed by the neck and his head slammed against the corridor wall. 'My sister don't get better, you're dead, cuntsmouth. So is your son, your gorger grandsons and the rest of your family.'

'Stop it, Billy!' ordered Bobby Tamplin. 'We don't even know what happened yet. Tammy getting better is all we should be concentrating on right now.'

Any man laid a finger on him, Kenny would usually knock seven bells out of, but he didn't retaliate. The guilt was already eating away at him. That could just as easily be Beau and Brett lying in intensive care, fighting for their lives, and it was all his fault.

Evie was sobbing her heart out, being physically supported by Sonny. 'My baby. I wanna see my baby,' she wept.

Bobby locked eyes with Beau and Brett. 'Get out of my

sight, you two. Don't you ever come near my daughters again, d'ya hear me?' he bellowed.

'No, Dad. It ain't their fault,' shrieked Jolene.

'Boys, come on. We're going,' Kenny said.

'Nah. I ain't leaving Jolene,' Beau argued.

'You'll do as I say,' Kenny replied, through gritted teeth.

As Billy and Johnny lunged at Beau and Brett, both Kenny and Tony intervened. The scuffle that followed was broken up by Bobby. 'Get out of our faces now, Bond, and yer can take those two little shitcunts with ya. If my daughter don't recover, believe me, you'll know all about it. I'll kill the fucking lot of yous.'

CHAPTER THIRTY-THREE

'Live every day like it's your last. 'Cause you never
know when your time's up.'

*I couldn't believe what had happened, especially when,
five days later, Tammy's life support was switched off.
Ecstasy had left her brain-dead. Sixteen years old. A tragic
waste of life.*

*That same week, four other youngsters collapsed. Two
died, one survived and another was put in an induced
coma. One lad, Barry, was only fifteen. His parents released
a photo of him to the press, lifeless in a hospital bed,
covered in tubes. They did so to warn others the danger
of taking drugs.*

*I'd never felt such a cunt in me life. I had massive
amounts of blood on me hands and so did Tony. Our little
blue tablets with the crown print were all over the news.
Youngsters being urged not to take them.*

*The Old Bill got involved, obviously. They questioned
Beau and Brett at length. The twins stuck to their stories.
Jolene must've done the same, insisted her sister's drink
must've been spiked. We'd have heard differently otherwise.*

Beau was in bits, couldn't eat, sleep, work or function properly. He missed Jolene dreadfully, was banned from seeing her by her family. I didn't blame the Tamplins. Had the boot been on the other foot, I'd have done the same.

Worried about comebacks, I rented a couple of caravans off a pal in Clacton. I didn't want to put Shal and Ricky in any danger. I insisted Donny take his kids there too, much to Tansey's displeasure.

Only me, the twins and Jamie stayed in Dark Lane. The Old Bill wanted to question us again. Tammy's death had seen to that. They also wanted a list of all the guests who'd been on board.

The whole thing was a fucking nightmare. I needed to search for a way out of the massive bastard black hole I'd dug for meself.

But I couldn't see a way out. Not with the gypsies anyway. They'd seek revenge, I knew that much.

The clock was ticking . . .

Kenny got out of his motor and followed Tony into the woods with his Staffordshire bull terrier, Bertie. They'd both been like cats on a hot tin roof this past week or so. Tony had also been questioned by the Old Bill regarding Tammy.

'What's occurring?' Kenny asked when they were well away from the motors. When they'd burned down the premises where the pills were made, the Chinese had already done a disappearing act, taking all the ingredients and equipment with them. Kenny and Tony had got rid of their old phones, purchased new ones, but were too shit-scared to talk anywhere but in person in the woods.

'We've got more blood on our hands. A girl from Southend. Twenty-six.' Tony's face was etched with worry. Sleep hadn't been coming easy to him. He was concerned one of the dealers might grass; especially now a juicy fat reward of fifty grand had been dangled like a carrot. Kenny had never dealt with the actual dealers. Only he had.

'For fuck's sake. The girl ain't brown bread, is she?'

'Dead as a dodo.'

'Jesus wept! When is this nightmare gonna end?'

'I dunno, mate. But I'm living on a knife edge at present. Now they've shoved out that reward for information, I'm terrified some cunt'll snitch. Me old man's made a few calls, put the frighteners on, so to speak. At least you know your name ain't in the frame. It's me in the firing line.'

'Not with the gyppos. They'll be gunning for me and mine. I'm telling ya, once the dust settles, I'm gonna hunt those Chinese cunts down and feed 'em to me mate's pigs.'

'And how ya gonna find 'em? We don't even know their real names.'

'Ready?' Beau asked Brett.

'As ready as I'll ever be, I suppose.'

'We got no other choice, Brett. We'll be fine. Turn the music up a bit and I'll call him. Just act normal, OK?'

Brett nodded, then did as asked.

'Jamie, we need your help down 'ere, bruv,' bellowed Beau. He knew Jamie was feeling guilty, that's why he was spending so much time in his room playing on his games console. So he should be, thought Beau. It *was* Jamie's fault he'd lost Jolene and Tammy was dead. He'd bought the poxy pills off a so-called pal.

Dressed in black Adidas shorts and a grey vest top, Jamie

came down the stairs with a dirty mug and plate in his hand. 'I thought you went down your granddad's. How comes you're back?'

'Gramps was busy,' lied Beau. 'Listen, we got a plan. I gotta get Jolene back, so Brett's agreed to take one for the team. He's gonna lie and say he gave the E to Tammy, which'll leave me in the clear. We ain't good writers, me and Brett, so we need you to write a letter for us.'

Jamie was confused. 'That ain't a good idea and it won't get you Jolene back. The Tamplins will kill Brett if he says that.'

'Nah. They won't. We know what we're doing. Pen and paper's on the kitchen table.'

'Why have I gotta write it? You two can write.'

'We can't spell properly. You know we can't. This is the least you can do for us, seeing as it was you who got them pills.'

Jamie sighed. Beau was right. He'd given the twins the name of his old school pal who'd sold the tablets to him, but they were yet to pay him a visit. Jamie wouldn't want to be in his shoes when they did, that was for sure. 'Whaddya want me to write?' Jamie picked up the pen.

Beau glanced at Brett. 'Let's start with – Dear Mr and Mrs Tamplin . . .'

Tears streaming down her cheeks, Evie Tamplin began decorating her daughter's trailer by hanging pure white sheets up the walls. She'd be coming home soon, her baby, and Evie wanted everything looking perfect for her. She'd already dotted numerous candles around the trailer. Obviously, the flowers would have to wait until the date of Tammy's homecoming was confirmed.

'Where's your mum?' Bobby asked Jolene. His family had

been ripped to shreds and for once he didn't know how to handle things. The grief was overwhelming and each family member was dealing with it in their own manner. Evie was jointly blaming him and Jolene for entertaining the gorgers in the first place. Billy and Johnny wanted to throttle the twins with their bare hands. Sonny was saying very little and young Bobby-Joe was in a terrible state.

'I dunno, she won't talk to me,' sobbed Jolene.

Bobby sat on the edge of Jolene's bed. She'd moved back in with him and Evie, couldn't face being inside the trailer she'd shared with Tammy. 'You can't keep staying in bed. I'm worried about you. You gotta eat too; need to keep up your strength.'

'Please let me see Beau. None of this is his fault. Or mine. I swear, Dad.'

Bobby shook his head vehemently. 'No, love. That ship has sailed and once your sister's laid to rest, we'll be moving. Far away from here. Do us all good to have a fresh start.'

'No! I ain't moving nowhere. I'm gonna marry Beau whether you like it or fucking not,' shrieked Jolene.

'Right, read 'em both back to us,' ordered Beau.

The letters Jamie had been told to write were odd. Brett was going to be in deep shit when the Tamplins received theirs. Why couldn't the twins see that? 'You can read. You read 'em.'

'You've got weird slanted writing. I can't read that,' replied Beau.

Jamie picked up the first letter.

Dear Mr and Mrs Tamplin,
    I am so sorry for the loss of Tammy and I can't

*live with the guilt anymore. This is why I have to tell
you the truth.*

    *It was me who crushed up an E and put it in
Tammy's drink. It was meant to be a laugh, nothing
more. I really liked Tammy which is why I now can't
forgive myself.*

    My life is over now too.

'Now read the other one,' Brett demanded.

Jamie sighed. These stupid letters were bringing Tammy's
death back to him. He'd been petrified when he'd seen her
convulsing on that boat.

Dear Mum,

    *I'm so sorry for what I've done, but it was me who
gave Tammy the ecstasy pill. I bought it off a mate
of mine, crushed it up and put it in her drink.*

    The guilt is too much for me to bear.

    *I hate myself and will never be able to forgive myself
for what I've done.*

'That's it,' said Jamie. 'You wanna sign it, Brett? I still
think you're making a big mistake though, especially telling
the Tamplins. Why you lying to your mum an' all? It don't
make sense.'

'It will now,' hissed Beau, grabbing Jamie in a headlock.
''Cause you're gonna sign it, Jamie. From you.'

Jamie's eyes widened. 'No. I ain't. Don't be daft. Stop
winding me up, you're hurting me neck.'

With his free hand, Beau took the meat knife off the
rack, and held it to Jamie's throat. 'Sign the fucking things,
else I'll slice your head off.'

Brett winced. He'd only gone along with this idea because

he'd felt pressurized into doing so. But it was wrong. So very wrong. Yet he couldn't defy orders. There was no way of backing out now – not unless he could get Beau to agree.

'Ain't it awful, Donny? All those youngsters dropping like flies on that bad batch of ecstasy pills. Broke my heart, the photo of that lad in the paper. What must his parents be going through? I hope whoever is responsible for those kids' deaths rots in hell,' exclaimed Sharon.

'Yeah. It's terrible,' mumbled Donny. He actually felt physically sick every time he spotted an article in the news-paper about it. Reason being, his dad was acting shady and he was sure it had something to do with those pills. Were they his?

'Who's that keeps messaging ya?' asked Sharon.

'Dad. He's spending the day with the twins.'

'And why would he be telling you that?'

'Probably hooked up with a bit of skirt, more like,' spouted Maggie.

'Leave it, love,' Charlie urged his wife.

'Well, forcing us to stay at this shithole. Bored rigid, I am. I might not have long left! What a waste of me precious life this week's been.'

'For goodness' sake, Mum! Don't talk so morbidly,' scolded Sharon. 'You know why we're here, 'cause of what happened with the gypsy girl. The kids are loving it. Let's just make the most of it, eh?'

Seeing those little blue pills pop up on the news yet again, Donny leapt up. 'I'm gonna head down the nursery, check all is OK and we ain't being robbed blind.'

'Can you check up on Jamie too?' asked Tansey. She wasn't too worried, had only spoken to Jamie this morning.

He'd been hanging out with Clare a lot and seemed content. What had happened on that boat certainly had sod all to do with her son.

'Tape his mouth up. Use that,' Beau ordered, handing Brett the black duct tape.

'This ain't funny no more, lads. Seriously. You're scaring me now. Stop it, please.' Having been the butt of the twins' jokes when younger, Jamie knew what a warped sense of humour they had, Beau especially.

Brett's hands were shaking as he tried to tape Jamie's mouth up and a petrified Jamie fought to stop him. 'Enough, I said. What the fuck you doing? What's wrong with the pair of you? You're my brothers.'

'This ain't right, Beau. There must be another way,' pleaded Brett.

'Shut it, you div. You know there ain't.' Beau grabbed the tape and ordered Brett to hold Jamie down. 'We're not blood related, are we?' Beau hissed, before shutting Jamie up completely. 'Get the rope now, Brett. Time's knocking on.'

The garden in Dark Lane was very secluded. Jamie tried to wriggle and fight, but couldn't escape the twins as they marched him in the garden like a captive soldier.

Beau grabbed one of the garden chairs. 'You tie yourself to that with the rope,' he ordered.

Jamie shook his head furiously, weird noises coming from his nose and mouth. Pure panic had now set in; it was a struggle to breathe. Were the twins going to leave him tied up in the garden to teach him a lesson for buying those pills? Surely they wouldn't do anything worse? They'd never get away with it.

'Strap his legs tight to the chair, like this,' Beau directed Brett.

'I can't, you do it.'

Jamie had never felt such fear as when his legs were strapped to that chair by Beau. He was helpless. He thought of his mum, Clare, Alfie, Harry and Bluebell, and stared at the twins with pleading eyes. He suddenly didn't recognize them, especially Beau. He'd loved them, treated them as brothers. How could they turn so evil?

'Right, that's tight enough. Now help me drag the chair,' Beau said.

Brett thought of all the good times the three of them had spent together. The races on their quad bikes and the laughs they'd had in general. 'Please, Beau. Let's untie him. This has gone too far already.'

'We've gotta do this, and you know *why*,' snapped Beau.

'Well, at least explain it to him. He deserves that much.'

'Fucking hell. Next you'll be wanting us to pray for him an' all. OK, Brett. Let's do this your way. Sorry about this, Jamie lad, but you got hold of the pill that killed Tammy and someone has to pay the price. I ain't losing Jolene over this. Neither are *my* family going to war with the gypsies. So, on that note, I bid you farewell.'

Tears streamed down Jamie's face as he frantically waved his arms, like an injured bird desperately trying to fly.

Tears in his own eyes, all Brett could say was, 'So sorry, Jamie. I truly am.'

'Now, lug this chair with me. Time's fucking ticking,' ordered Beau.

Brett helped his brother lug the chair to the edge of the swimming pool.

Jamie's eyes bulged with terror as it dawned on him what the twins were about to do. They were going to drown him and make it look like suicide. In a final attempt to save his life, Jamie put his trembling hands into a

452

praying position and looked at the twins with pleading, tearful eyes. He was too young to die, had been at his happiest since meeting Clare.

Brett grabbed his brother's arm. 'We can't do this. We'll get found out. I know we will.'

'Stop acting like a fucking tart,' snapped Beau. He crouched and looked Jamie in the eyes. 'I am sorry about this as I did sort of become fond of yer. But if you don't pay for what happened, then me and him are gonna pay the price.' Beau pointed at Brett. 'Blood is much thicker than water. We should know. Your cunt of a mother's always hated us. Not that this is payback for her. But I will have a crafty chuckle at every tear the bitch cries.'

Beau stood up. 'After three,' he said, not a hint of emotion in his tone.

'One, two.' Beau ripped the tape off Jamie's mouth and pocketed it. 'Three.'

The chair was heavy, made of cast iron. It sank to the bottom of the pool with Jamie strapped to it. Neither resurfaced.

Unable to get hold of his father because his phone was off, Donny arrived home just after five and unwrapped his fish and chips. The twins and Jamie could order a takeaway if they were hungry later. He'd decided to kip at home tonight. He needed to have a serious chat with his old man. He could no longer avoid the subject of those poisonous ecstasy pills. Especially now his own family had been forced to stay in Clacton.

Opening a bottle of Bud, Donny decided to eat in the garden. He loved the outdoors, especially after being stuck in that bloody caravan. Donny stuffed a handful of chips in his mouth, then bit into his wally. He was ravenous.

'What the hell's that?' he muttered, as something in the swimming pool caught his eye. It was a trainer, in fact there were two. White Adidas ones. They were either the twins' or Jamie's, Donny thought as he fished them out.

Thinking no more of his find, Donny finished his meal and went inside to get another beer. That was when he spotted the letter with MUM on the envelope. Instinct told him to rip it open, read it, and as he did so his blood ran cold. 'Please God, No! Jamie, Jamie,' he yelled, as he leapt fully clothed into the pool.

Seconds later, he spotted the chair with Jamie strapped to it. He felt for a pulse. There wasn't one.

'Enjoy that, lads?' enquired Kenny.

'Handsome,' Beau grinned, munching the last of his steak and kidney pie.

'Thanks, Aunt Nell. I can't eat all mine, but it was lovely,' added Brett.

'There's plenty left. Anyone want seconds?' asked Nell.

'I'll have another bit, please,' Beau piped up. It was amazing how a murder could work up one's appetite.

'You want some more, Cliff?'

'No thanks, love.' Cliff looked at his watch. Vera would skin him alive if she knew he'd met up with her family behind her back, but he'd only done so for her sake.

Vera hadn't been outside the door since her beehive had been partially chopped off. She was beside herself, tearful and extremely angry. She'd vowed never to talk to Kenny again, or Beau and Brett, reckoned they'd conspired and were all in on it. Cliff hated bad feeling and he was also extremely fond of Kenny, which is why he was trying to get to the bottom of what had really happened.

'It was Ricky,' laughed Beau. 'We never told him to do nothing, did we, Brett?'

Brett pushed his half-eaten plate of food away. He was dreading going home and pretending they'd found Jamie drowned. He was hoping they could stay at Gramps' tonight, so he wouldn't have to deal with the police interrogation until the morning.

Kenny explained that Ricky had spoken to him in the car about taking a pair of scissors to Vera's hair. 'I thought he was joking, Cliff. He don't like her much though, says she speaks to you like shit.'

'Of course she doesn't,' blushed Cliff. 'That's just your mum's way, Kenny. Her sharp tongue don't bother me. She's spirited, like a lot of us who survived Hitler's bombs.'

'Oh well, as long as you don't spunk all your money on her, Cliff,' Kenny said bluntly. 'Don't be wasting your hard-earned lolly on the Orient Express. Take her up the bingo hall instead. She'll be just as happy.'

'Who wants some apple pie and custard?' asked Nelly.

'I'm full thanks, Auntie,' replied Kenny. 'You all right, Brett?' he enquired, noticing how white his grandson suddenly looked.

'Yeah. Just full up,' Brett lied. He couldn't believe what he and Beau had done earlier. He'd liked Jamie and kept having flashbacks of the terror on his face. How could Beau act so normal? 'What time we leaving Gramps? I'm ever so tired.'

Nelly put her hand on Brett's forehead. 'He looks like he might be coming down with something. Temperature feels OK though.'

'Let's skip dessert and I'll buy us all a quick drink in your local, Aunt Nell, before we leave,' suggested Kenny.

The day's events catching up with him, bile crept into the back of Brett's throat before he slung his half-eaten dinner up all over Aunt Nell's kitchen lino.

'You fucking dickhead. What happened to acting normal?' Beau seethed, pushing Brett out the front door.

'Sorry. I couldn't help it. I just feel bad.'

'Well, don't. It was either him or us, wasn't it? Shush now,' Beau ordered as Gramps and Cliff approached.

'Bye, lads. Hope you feel better soon, Brett,' waved Aunt Nelly. 'Been a lot of that sickness bug going around. Get yourself an early night, boy.'

Brett waved. 'I will, Aunt Nell.'

Kenny switched his phone back on. His battery had been low. 'Bye, Auntie,' he shouted, honking his hooter. 'Where you off to, Cliff? Home? Or the Working Man's Club?'

'Drop me at your mum's, Kenny. I wanna try and sort all this hairdo palaver out before I enjoy a pint or two. I'm sure Vera'll mellow when she finds out it was Ricky and he acted alone. Well, I bleedin' well hope she does anyway.'

Kenny's phone rang. 'Slow down, Donny. Whaddya mean? All right, well stay calm. Yeah, the twins are still with me. We're on our way.'

Beau nudged Brett. 'What's up, Gramps?'

'I dunno. But your dad sounded in a right panic. He ain't in Clacton. He's back home.'

'The Old Bill are 'ere. Christ knows what's happened,' Kenny said, as he pulled up outside his son's gaff.

'I wonder if it's to do with Tammy?' Beau replied.

'No idea, but we'll soon find out. You all right, Brett?'

'Yeah.'

The twins followed Gramps inside the house. 'Dad, we're home. What's happened? Why are the police 'ere?' Beau shouted out.

'I'm in the kitchen, boys.' As his sons walked in, Donny stood up and hugged them, tighter than he ever had before.

'What's happened?' asked Kenny.

Tears streaming down his cheeks, Donny ordered the twins to sit down. 'I'm so sorry, boys, but I've got some terrible news. Jamie's taken his own life. He's dead.'

'Nah. He can't be,' Brett mumbled.

'No. He's not, Dad. He's gone to meet Clare. We only see him this morning,' added Beau.

Donny handed his sons the letter meant for Tansey. Jamie's handwriting was slanted, extremely distinct.

Tears streamed down Beau's face. 'No way, Dad. Not our brother. He never said he spiked Tammy's drink to us.'

'Where did he do it? How?' wept Brett. Unlike Beau's, his tears were genuine.

'He tied himself to a garden chair and drowned in the pool. The police need to ask you some questions. You were the last to see him.'

'I can't believe it. Where is Jamie now?' shrieked Beau. 'Is his body still 'ere?'

Kenny held Brett in his arms. 'Let the tears out, boy. Better out than in. I can't believe it. What a shock, Donny. I take it you found him?'

'Yeah. I haven't even told Tansey yet. I need to tell her in person, not over the phone. I'll have to drive back up to Clacton.'

Kenny shook his head in despair. 'Poor Tansey. She's

gonna be devastated. He was a good kid, Jamie. Always treated him as me own grandson.'

'Can we ask you some questions now, boys? We won't take long,' asked a police officer.

'I'll answer any questions you need me to,' replied Beau.

Thinking how brave Beau was, Donny put a comforting arm around his shoulders.

'I've already told the officers, Jamie has been holed up in his bedroom since your party. The guilt must've been eating away at him. Two lives ruined and two families' lives ruined. All over a bloody ecstasy pill. It beggars belief.' Donny shook his head miserably. Tansey would never get over this. Not in a million years.

'That was the police, Evie. We can bring our girl home on Tuesday.'

For the first time since Tammy had died, Evie smiled. 'I want the vigil to be perfect, Bobby. I want you and the lads to make the biggest bonfire. I want you to get me loads more candles to light and I want the best flowers and lots of 'em. I know Tammy didn't die in her trailer, but she didn't die in that hospital either. She never woke up there. Tammy loved that trailer, so I want us to act as though that's where she took her last breath.'

'OK, love. Whatever you want.'

'I want us to order a massive coffin an' all, as I want to put lots of her belongings in it, including her favourite jewellery and records.' Tammy had been named after the singer Tammy Wynette and, like her parents, had been a big country and western fan. 'And I'm going to dress her up and do her make-up. You can leave all that to me.'

'OK, love,' Bobby repeated. He'd known Evie was going overboard when she'd put all the white sheets up in the trailer. His family had only ever done that in the past if the deceased had taken their last breath inside. But he wasn't about to argue. If this was Evie's way of coping, he was happy to go along with her wishes.

'She's going to have a wonderful send-off, our girl. The best, Bobby.'

Bobby squeezed his beloved wife's hand. 'She sure is. And I was thinking, after we say goodbye to our Tammy, I'm gonna put this land up for sale. Let's move away. Far away.'

Evie punched her husband hard in the chest. 'We ain't going nowhere, Bobby. I like living 'ere. And we need to find out who killed our baby. And when we do, I expect you to go all out for revenge. I won't ever leave this land. In fact, I want to make it a shrine to my Tammy—' With that she broke down again.

Her wails of grief pained Bobby's heart. He led her into his arms, stroking her hair, both lost in grief for their beautiful girl. 'All right, love. Whatever you decide suits me.'

Whoever did this to their family would pay the gypsy way.

Tansey was fuming. A caravan park in Clacton was not her ideal holiday destination. Most of the other parents and kids on the site were poor and common and she couldn't wait to return to her lovely home.

The kids had been enjoying themselves. Until today, when Alfie had created havoc in the swimming pool, biting another boy's arm. The other lad's mother looked like a bloated, tattooed loudmouth off the *Jerry Springer Show*, so Tansey had been given no other option other than to grovel, profusely apologize and then drag her children off to perform the walk of shame with her.

Now, to add insult to injury, Donny had sodded off all day, having told her he'd only be gone a couple of hours, and his phone was switched off.

Deciding that, no matter what Donny said, she would make him drive her and the children home first thing tomorrow, Tansey leapt up as headlights appeared. She'd put the kids to bed ages ago and was back in her own caravan. Sharon, she could suffer, and Maggie to an extent. But Charlie was a bigoted male chauvinist who grated on her immensely. Ricky, she liked. Her sons and Bluebell seemed to adore him too.

Having necked a bottle of wine to deal with her annoyance, Tansey flew off the uncomfortable sofa bench as Donny let himself in. 'Where the bloody hell have you been? You inconsiderate bastard. I've been stuck here all—'

'Sit down, Tans,' Donny interrupted. His face was a whiter shade of pale, his eyes brimming with tears.

'Whatever's wrong?'

Donny sat next to Tansey and held her in his arms. 'I'm so sorry. But I couldn't tell you on the phone. I had to tell you in person.'

'Tell me what?'

Tears streaming down his cheeks, Donny shook his head in despair. 'It's Jamie. He topped himself earlier. In our swimming pool.'

Within seconds, Tansey's screams of unadulterated pain woke most of the campsite up.

It was just after 10 p.m. when Beau wandered the short distance to Gramps' house.

'You all right?' Kenny asked. 'Silly question, I know. Let's go in the garden, get some air. Poor Jamie. I can't stop thinking about him.'

'Me neither. Loved him to bits. We might not have been blood brothers, but we were proper brothers.'

Once out the back, Kenny lit up a cigar and wandered down towards the garden bench that was situated under the trees at the back. Once seated, he said, 'Don't lay it on too thick.' He was always careful in case his gaff was bugged. Same with his motor.

'OK. Sorry.'

'How's Brett?'

'OK-ish. In bed. He'll be fine tomorrow. I'll make sure of that.'

'You sure?'

Beau gave a half-smile. 'Gotta be, ain't he? We can't undo what we've done. He's tougher than you think.'

'Good.' Kenny took the lid off the bottle of Cognac. It had not only been a long day, it had been a long fucking month for him.

Firstly Karen springing a son on him. The Chinese bollocksing up his business venture. Tammy then croaking it had just been the proof that all bad things come in threes. 'Wanna swig?'

Beau took the bottle and nearly choked as he downed a gulp. He cleared his throat, got his composure back, then asked, 'Can I try a cigar, Gramps?'

'Don't push it. Just have a puff of mine.'

'It's all gonna be OK, ya know. Don't worry about Brett. I know how to handle him. I didn't exactly enjoy today, but it had to be done, didn't it?'

Kenny ruffled Beau's hair. Donny had never quite cut the mustard, but Beau did. He was the next *him*. Would carry on the Bond name with pride, just like he had for his grandfather.

'When shall I post the letter to the Tamplins? Tomorrow? I need Jolene back, Gramps. I love her like you love Nan.'

'I know you do, boy. Post the letter tomorrow, but you gotta leave it then. The Tamplins need to digest stuff, bury their daughter. If you and Jolene are meant to be, it will happen. You gotta be patient though. They need time to grieve.'

Beau took another puff on the cigar and another swig of Cognac. He was a man now, not a boy. Gramps had seen to that.

Kenny slung a casual arm around his grandson's shoulders. The twins topping Jamie, forcing him to write suicide letters first, had all been his idea. Same as the visit to Aunt Nell's with Cliff. The twins had needed an alibi. A watertight one.

It had been the only plan Kenny could think of to get them all out the shit. Jamie wasn't their flesh and blood, after all. He didn't have the Bond gene running through his body.

Beau handed the cigar and Cognac back and winked at the man he idolized. 'It's all gonna be fine, Gramps. I promise you.'

Kenny winked back. 'I know it is, kiddo. You are *me* to a tee.'

CHAPTER THIRTY-FOUR

Evie was polishing the twins' trailer for the umpteenth time when Bobby arrived home with bunches of wildflowers. There were candles and vases dotted all over the gaff. Tammy would be home tomorrow evening and Evie was determined her vigil would be absolutely perfect.

'How early did Eli say he could have the flowers 'ere on Wednesday?' That was the day her beautiful daughter would finally be laid to rest.

'They'll be 'ere by seven at the latest.' Bobby had spent over two grand on floral tributes from his family. Eli and his wife were fellow Travellers, owned a florist over in Tilbury, and Bobby knew they'd do his family and daughter proud.

'How d'ya think it's looking?'

'Lovely. Will look even more beautiful once all those candles are lit. You done our girl proper proud, Evie.'

'Thanks.' Evie forced a smile. Keeping herself busy was the only thing keeping her going at present.

'We got post,' Bobby announced, handing his wife four envelopes. Unlike gorgers, it was rare for his family to

463

receive post. So much so, he only checked the mailbox he'd installed at the entrance of the bumpy road that led to his family home once a week.

Evie could barely read, neither could Bobby, but she ripped open the envelopes. It was clear to see the first three contained sympathy cards. She opened the fourth and a strange feeling washed over her. The handwriting was joined-up, slanted, but she spotted Tammy's name immediately.

Evie's grandmother Rose had been able to read tea leaves and had always insisted Evie had physic powers too. 'This letter. It's important. We need Jolene to read it to us, Bobby. Immediately.'

'I'm not in the mood for talking. Just leave me alone,' begged Jolene. She was dreading the vigil and the funeral. Nobody missed Tammy more than her. They'd spent virtually every minute of every day together for as long as she could remember. Beau was the one she needed to help her through such an ordeal. Not her parents.

'We need you to read a letter. It's about your sister. It's important, I knows it is,' insisted Evie.

Wondering if it was from Beau, Jolene shot out the bed. She snatched the letter out of her father's hands and did her best to understand the words.

'I knew it! I told you Beau and Brett were innocent. It was Jamie. He spiked her drink. Jamie killed Tammy.'

Yawning, Kenny sauntered downstairs in his dressing gown. The twins were sitting at the breakfast table. 'How are you feeling this morning?'

It was three days now since Jamie's death and they were yet to hear a dickie-bird from the Tamplins. Expecting a visit any day soon, Kenny was staying at Donny's with his grandsons.

'We still can't believe we're never gonna see our brother again, can we?' piped up Beau.

'Nah,' mumbled Brett. 'Poor Jamie,' he said genuinely.

'I know how you feel, boys. But you're doing good. We gotta keep strong. That's what Jamie would've wanted.'

Kenny had no doubt the Old Bill would see Jamie's death as a cut-and-dried suicide. They'd popped round again on Saturday to ask the twins a few questions, then had swiftly left.

Kenny had made sure Beau and Brett had watertight alibis and there'd be no witnesses to say otherwise. Donny's garden, like all the others down Dark Lane, was secluded. The neighbours either side were both away – one family was in Greece, the ones on the other side were at their caravan in Lowestoft.

Kenny gestured the twins to follow him. 'Let's get some fresh air. You're looking a bit pasty, the pair of ya.'

Once down the bottom of the garden, Donny ruffled Brett's unbrushed hair. 'How you doing?'

'He's all right,' replied Beau.

'I'm asking him, not you,' snapped Kenny. Unlike his brother, Brett genuinely did look pasty-faced.

'Yeah. I'm OK,' lied Brett. He was struggling to sleep, kept getting flashbacks of Jamie's terrified expression every time he closed his eyes. He knew he had to hold it together though. He didn't want Beau or Gramps to see him as weak, because he wasn't. He could still see that pervert Eric's repulsive face in his nightmares at times. He'd dealt with that, so would deal with this. He had no bloody choice anyway.

'Not been talking openly in your bedroom, have yous?'

Kenny had always suffered from paranoia and would never put it past the Old Bill to bug Donny's house too. If the filth had any inkling he was involved in the production of *those* ecstasy pills, Kenny knew they'd do their utmost to put him away forever. Most of Harry Harrison's old cronies would've retired by now, but once a cop killer . . . It never went away. There'd always be some newbie baying for his blood.

'D'ya think the police will want to speak to us any more about Jamie?' asked Brett.

'Nah. I'll ring 'em today and ask for Tansey's letter back. That should be the end of it.' The police had asked for a sample of Jamie's handwriting, so Beau had given him an old schoolbook of Jamie's. Obviously, the handwriting was the same – slanted, distinct.

Pleased that Brett seemed to have perked up a bit, Kenny ruffled his hair once more. 'Never forget, it was Jamie who bought those dodgy pills. If he hadn't, Tammy would still be alive. None of this is your fault, you gotta get that in your nut.'

Brett nodded. 'I have. What's done is done. How's Dad doing?'

'He's all right, but Tansey's in a terrible state, as you'd expect. Your dad had to call an ambulance for her on Saturday. She couldn't breathe properly. She's now been sedated. I've told your dad, nan, Maggs and Charlie all to stay put at the caravan until we've sorted this shit out with the Tamplins. The kids are happy there and I want 'em all kept outta harm's way.'

'Me too. I can't say I'm upset Tansey's had a meltdown though,' smirked Beau. 'Serves her right. She's always been a cunt to me and Brett.'

Kenny locked eyes with Beau. Even he was shocked by

the lad's lack of compassion at times. 'There's no need for that. That woman's just lost a son. Tansey might not have been the perfect stepmother, but believe me, she treated you better than your real mother when you were little. Now, go pack some clothes and shoes, the pair of yer. Smart and black. We're staying at mine from today. The Tamplins must've received Jamie's letter by now.'

A spit's throw away, Jamie's letter had caused mayhem.

'I want him dead, Bobby. Nothing less will do,' spat Evie.

The eldest sons, Billy and Johnny, paced up and down their parents' trailer. 'We should take Donny out an' all. He's Jamie's father,' bellowed Johnny.

'No. He ain't,' shrieked Jolene. 'You know nothing. Jamie is Tansey's son. Not Donny's.'

Billy smashed his fist against the trailer wall. 'How do we even know Jamie wrote the letter? We should take the fucking lot of 'em out.'

Jolene ran towards her loudmouth of a brother and punched him hard in the chest. 'You lay one finger on Beau and I'll kill you too. I swear I will.'

'Stop it! Stop arguing,' screamed young Bobby-Joe, tears running down his plump face. 'Tammy be home soon,' he reminded his warring family. He missed his big sister so much, couldn't wait to see her again, even though she was dead.

'I love Beau and if we can't be together, I swear I'll run away with him, and you'll never find us,' threatened Jolene.

Sonny put an arm around his distraught sister's shoulders. 'It's gonna be OK. I'm on your side,' he whispered in her ear. He actually liked Beau and Brett, got on well

467

with the pair of them, and could see that Jolene and Beau were in love.

'This needs to be sorted. Today!' bellowed Billy. 'How can Tammy rest in peace if we don't do her justice beforehand?'

Bobby glared at his eldest. Billy had always been a hothead, acted on impulse before using his brain. 'I'm the head of this family and I dish out the orders. You do nothing, understand me? Nothing! Now get back to your own fucking trailer. You too, Johnny. I will deal with this. In my own way.'

Billy and Johnny glanced at one another. They knew better than to defy their father's orders. Especially when he had *that* evil glint in his eyes.

The visit Kenny had been awaiting came late afternoon. He'd been keeping vigil, had a strong feeling today would be the day, and wasn't surprised when Tamplin's Shogun swung onto his drive, with Bobby the only person inside it. The two eldest sons were dickheads, Kenny had sensed that the first time he'd properly met them. Mouthy, irresponsible. Especially in a situation as delicate as this one.

Kenny raced out into the back garden. The twins were lounging on sunbeds, their shirts off.

'Look smart. Act smart. Bobby Tamplin's 'ere, alone.' Kenny had a Colt 45 hidden under the floorboards, just in case the whole clan had turned up. Instinct told him now to leave it where it was. Bobby wasn't that stupid. 'You answer the door, Beau.'

Quickly pulling on his shirt, Beau looked the part. Dressed in a short-sleeved black shirt, smart black strides and polished black shoes, Beau did as asked with a sombre expression on his face.

'Where's your grandfather?'

'In the kitchen. How's Jolene? I really miss her, Bobby.'

With a face like thunder, Bobby stormed inside the house. Kenny was dressed in black too, and Brett. Were they taking the piss?

'I got a letter supposedly from Jamie. Where is he?'

Thankful he could finally let out the emotions he'd been trying too hard to keep inside, Brett burst into tears. 'Jamie's dead. He drowned himself in our swimming pool.'

At first Bobby had thought he was being told a load of old fanny. That was until some gavvers had turned up on the doorstep, handing Jamie's schoolbook back and another letter he'd also written to his mother.

'Jamie came clean to the twins the day before he topped himself,' Kenny lied. 'Apparently he hadn't meant to spike Tammy's drink. He'd crushed the pills up and put it in Beau and Brett's for a laugh.'

'Some laugh that turned out to be. I'm fucking burying my baby girl.'

'Jamie said he did it 'cause we'd moaned Gramps wouldn't let us have no alcohol on the boat,' Beau explained. 'I felt a bit strange that night, so I reckon I must've drunk some ecstasy too. Brett didn't, so we think it must've been his drink Tammy picked up by mistake. We were all drinking Coke. Please let me see Jolene, Bobby. I really do—'

'Not now, Beau,' snapped Kenny. 'You two go upstairs for a bit. I want to speak to Bobby man to man.'

When the twins left the room, Kenny poured two large glasses of brandy and handed one to the crestfallen man. Just for a moment he looked broken. Kenny's heart actually went out to the poor bastard. He couldn't have dealt with losing a child in such tragic circumstances.

'I truly am sorry for your loss, Bobby. If I'd have known Jamie was involved with drugs, I would never have allowed him on that boat, or the twins to knock around with him. But I don't think he was. He told Beau and Brett it was a one-off and I'm inclined to believe that. I know none of this brings your Tammy back, but Jamie never meant to harm her. It was a prank, a stupid fucking prank, that ended in the deaths of your daughter and my grandson.'

Bobby tilted his head. 'But he wasn't your grandson, was he?'

'Not my flesh and blood, no. But I'd always treated him as such. Donny raised Jamie from a baby. I loved him like he was one of me own. I tell yer something though, Bobby. Had Jamie not opted to take his own life, I would've handed him over to you on a plate. As much as it would've ripped my heart out to do so, I'm a man of morals. I swear on the twins' lives, I would've done the right thing.'

Bobby downed his drink in one, then slammed his glass against the wooden table. 'If I find out they were pals of yours dressed up as gavvers and you've packed Jamie off to another part of the country, I swear I will kill you, Kenny.'

'Fair enough. But you ain't gonna find that out. I gotta go with my Donny to arrange the boy's funeral tomorrow. Tansey's in bits, been hospitalized through the shock of it all. Go see the gavvers. You got the letter on you that Jamie sent yer?'

'No.'

'Well, take it to the Old Bill, if you think I'm trying to pull the wool over your eyes. It was Donny who found the lad. He saw his trainers floating on the top of the swimming pool, dived in, but it was too late to save Jamie. He'd strapped his legs to a wrought iron chair, was as dead as a dodo at the bottom. He weren't a bad kid, Bobby, obviously couldn't live with the carnage he'd caused.'

'So what happens now? My family are in bits. My eldest sons are gunning for revenge. Now that's been taken away from us.'

Kenny topped both their drinks up. 'Well, I dunno about you. But, I don't want to start a war between our families, Bobby. We're already lost two members, one from each. The twins got the name of the lad who sold the pills to Jamie. I can give you that and the lad's address. The boy's only local, lives in Upminster. I don't know Jamie's real dad's details offhand, but I can find those out for you too. All I ask is you keep my Donny out of any repercussions. He had nothing to do with this, wasn't even on the fucking boat.'

Bobby put his head in his hands. 'I can't think straight at present. I'll take the name of the lad who sold the pills though. I don't want a war either. My family like living 'ere on my land. Or they did anyway. Evie wants to make part of it a shrine to Tammy.'

'That's a lovely idea. We won't be doing the same for Jamie. I loved the lad but he was the one to blame. I'm a big believer of an eye for an eye, which is why I would've handed him over to you, Bobby.'

'What a fucked-up situation. My Jolene truly loves your Beau an' all, I thinks.'

'Beau loves Jolene too. Talks about little else. I fear we'll never be able to keep them apart. They'll just end up eloping together if we forbid them to see one another.'

'I know. I fear the same. It's not their fault what happened, is it? Let me talk to Evie and the rest of my family. But first, we've got our Tammy's vigil and funeral. I'll pop round to see you again later in the week.'

'Perhaps we could arrange a meet for both our families? Not yet, of course. We'll need to get Jamie's funeral out the way first too. Beau often speaks of your Bobby-Joe. Reckons he would get on like a house on fire with our Ricky. I adopted Ricky when his parents got killed. A lovely, bright lad he is.'

'So is my Bobby-Joe.'

When Bobby stood up, Kenny dubiously held out his right hand and was relieved when Tamplin shook it.

'I really am sorry, Bobby. I mean that from the bottom of my heart. If you need any help, ya know, with the kid who sold Jamie the drugs, or even his real father, I'll be there by your side.'

'Thanks. I appreciate that. I'll be back in touch soon.'

Kenny shut the door and couldn't keep the grin off his handsome face. A war had been avoided, thanks to his quick thinking. His dear old granddad had taught him well.

CHAPTER THIRTY-FIVE

One month later

Kenny met Tony in their usual spot. Both got out of their motors and, with Tony's Staffie alongside them, walked into the woods.

'I take it you've seen and heard what happened?' asked Tony.

'Couldn't miss it. Been on every news programme, radio and front page of most of the papers. Baffling, ain't it? But bloody good news for us.'

'It ain't just good. It's fucking blinding news,' chuckled Tony.

An ecstasy factory had been raided in Southend. No names had been released yet, but apparently five geezers had been caught red-handed making the pills. The beauty of the whole thing was, the Old Bill had announced on national TV that they believed this factory and the people working inside were responsible for numerous deaths. The police chief had then reeled off a list of names, including Tammy Tamplin.

'D'ya reckon they're bluffing, the filth? I wouldn't put

anything past 'em.' Kenny's jaw twitched. His paranoia had set in since he'd heard the news. It somehow seemed too good to be true.

'No, mate. They ain't bluffing. I know one of the geezers that's in custody. Well, I know his brother better, to be fair. Grant Archer. His brother Jason was one of the lads nicked in the factory.'

'You sure?'

'Positive. Grant popped round to see me and the old man yesterday, wanted the number of a good brief.'

'I can't believe it.' Kenny grinned, slapped Tony on the back. Firstly, a reprieve from the gyppos and now this.

'I reckon me old granddad's looking down on us. Either that or I was a better man in me previous life than I was in this one.'

Tony chuckled. 'You were never no saint, ya fucker. Trust me on that one.'

'You've cheered up a bit,' Sharon remarked when her husband arrived home, full of the joys of spring. He'd been out walking around in a trance most of the weekend, having one of his funny turns where he constantly looked out the window. Sharon had no idea what he was expecting to see. Aliens landing on the driveaway, perhaps?

'I feel better after a bit of fresh air, babe. A nice walk always seems to clear me nut.'

'They named them blokes while you were out. The ones responsible for Jamie's death and Tammy's. I wrote down a couple of names, but I didn't catch the rest.'

Kenny looked at the piece of paper. *Jeffrey Payne, Andrew Dennis and Simon Something*, Sharon had written.

'Bastards. They'll get years for that, babe.'

'And so they bloody well should. I'm dreading today,

474

Kenny. I honestly am. I doubt me and Evie will have sod all in common. I bet she's off with me too.'

'Nah. I doubt it. But even if she is, just bite your tongue, Shal. It'll only be the grief talking.'

Kenny and Bobby had met up a few times since Tammy's funeral. Not at one another's gaffs but on neutral ground at the Huntsman and Hounds. Beau and Jolene had got back together, but Beau had yet to be invited round the Tamplins' again. The two eldest sons still weren't happy about the situation. But as Bobby kept saying, 'Time's a healer.'

Today would be the first time Sharon and Evie were crossing paths, and both Kenny and Bobby were hoping it would go well. Kenny actually quite liked Bobby. He was nothing like that scumbag brother of his that Kenny had the misfortune of sharing a cell with. Bobby lived for his family, grafted hard and had good values. Well, apart from making the kid from Upminster who'd sold the pills to Jamie disappear off the face of the earth. But that was understandable.

'Who keeps texting you?' questioned Sharon.

'Only Tony. He knows one of the geezers they've arrested for those pills.'

It was actually Karen texting him. She was getting right on his nerves lately. The meek little schoolteacher had somehow turned into a fucking piranha. He'd pay her a visit later.

Sharon still had no idea Karen existed or that he had a son with her and that's the way Kenny intended it to stay.

'You look nice, babe,' smiled Kenny.

Sharon hadn't had a clue what to wear. She knew very

little about gypsies, and how the wives dressed. She'd gone for a smart/casual look. Cream trousers, a baggy leopard-print chiffon top and beige sandals with a kitten heel. 'I'm gonna give Mum a ring, then pop down to Donny's while you're getting ready. Pick me up from there.'

'OK. Pick you up at quarter to one.' Much to Kenny's dismay, Sharon's parents had gone back to Spain to sell their property. It was Maggie who was insistent she and Charlie move back to England.

With Maggie still sniping at him constantly, no way was Kenny putting up with them moving back in with him and Shal. So he'd kindly told them they could live rent-free in their old bungalow, the one he'd bought, until they found a place in England. Not for all the tea in China would he sell the gaff back to them though. Maggie was never going to forgive him for cheating on Sharon. The further away from Dark Lane she moved, the better.

Dressed in a pair of light grey slacks, black leather shoes and short-sleeved black shirt, Kenny hooted outside Donny's at the arranged time.

Kenny was still close to his son, but tended to see him at his own gaff or they'd go out for a beer together these days. *The Duchess* had been sold. Neither himself nor Donny had any interest in sailing down the Thames anymore. The *Marchioness* sinking had been bad enough, plus losing Alan. Tammy's death had been the final straw.

'How's Tansey?' Kenny enquired the second Shal got in the motor. That was another reason he avoided his son's house. He was no fan of Tansey's, far from it. But seeing the pain in her eyes and listening to her racking sobs tugged at his heartstrings. It made him feel a right bastard.

Jamie was yet to be laid to rest. Twice, Tansey had cancelled the funeral days beforehand, saying she wasn't well enough to attend. Yet she was well enough to visit the funeral parlour on a daily basis and spend hours there talking to her dead son.

'She didn't come downstairs. I told Donny he and the boys were welcome to join us, but even though Harry and Alfie wanted to come, Donny didn't want to. Bluebell's out with Lucinda and Dolly. I'm dreading Wednesday, Kenny. I really am.'

Nobody was dreading it more than Kenny. That was when Jamie's funeral was set to finally go ahead, and Donny had put his foot down, insisting that under no circumstances could Tansey cancel the proceedings again. Kenny held his jaw to stop it twitching. Brett was dreading it too. Only Beau didn't seem to be bothered. 'Tansey's gonna have to snap out of it soon, love. Jamie weren't her only son. She's got three other kids who need their mum.'

The Jobber's Rest pub was in a rural part of Upminster. Sharon had hoped on the journey that the twins would already be there, but her luck was out and they weren't.

Bobby Tamplin stood up, shook Kenny's hand, then formally introduced his wife to Kenny and Sharon.

'Lovely to finally meet you both,' Sharon smiled, her voice full of hesitation. Evie had a kind face, but her eyes told a different story as she gave both her and Kenny daggers.

'Let me get yous both a drink. What you having?' Kenny asked.

'Lemonade,' Evie snapped. 'And before we go any further, I've only come out today for his sake.' She pointed at

Bobby. 'And because of my Jolene. I ain't happy about this situation. Not one little bit. Especially after everything that's happened. My eldest sons are livid. They—'

'That's enough, Evie,' Bobby interrupted.

Not about to be shut up, Evie stood up. 'My Billy and Johnny are furious that me and Bobby have allowed Jolene to have anything to do with your grandson again. But I already lost one daughter and my Jolene loves Beau and I can't lose another. So I have to suffer it.'

Sharon kicked Kenny hard in the ankle, before glaring at Evie. 'If it makes you feel any better, I don't want to be here either.' She pointed at Kenny. 'I'm only 'ere for his sake. I'm not happy about your daughter courting my grandson. But like yourself, for Beau's sake, I'm willing to suffer it.'

The women sat in stubborn silence.

Kenny and Bobby glanced at one another, but said nothing. A knife wasn't going to cut the atmosphere between Sharon and Evie. A pickaxe, perhaps?

The youngsters' arrival helped thaw the ice somewhat. Beau, Brett, Jolene, Ricky and Bobby-Joe had spent the morning down Dagenham Sunday Market and came into the pub laden with carrier bags.

'Look what Beau bought me,' Jolene said, showing her parents numerous skimpy outfits.

Ricky had now met young Bobby-Joe a few times and had taken on the role of another older brother. The closeness between the two was a joy and even Evie couldn't stop smiling at that.

'Where's Sonny?' asked Brett. Usually when they met at the pub, Sonny always joined them.

'Got himself a woman at last,' replied Bobby. 'No before time, eh, Evie?' he chuckled, trying to keep the atmosphere as jovial as possible.

'Yes! I fixed him up. Lovely girl, Mary-Ann. A Traveller, of course. So pretty an' all. Lives on the same site as my sister in Kent,' Evie replied, looking at Sharon. 'We didn't want any more gorgers in the family, did we, Bobby?'

'We must fix Brett up with a nice girl, eh, Kenny? We don't want any more Travellers in our family, do we?' Sharon retaliated.

Kenny and Bobby glanced at one another awkwardly. Both were more than capable of getting into a scrape with any geezer, but when it came to warring women, they'd prefer to keep out of it.

Brett's face fell. His whole world had just fallen apart. Since Jamie's death, his relationship with Sonny and the way he felt about him was the only thing keeping him going. Nothing had happened between them. But they'd become very close. The glances, the long conversations, the way Sonny held his gaze as though he was looking into his soul and trying to tell him something.

Brett had been sure Sonny was the same as him, felt the same connection as he did. He'd even bought him a pair of Dealer boots down the market today. 'I got a nasty headache. You don't mind if I call a cab and shoot off, do you?' he said out loud.

'I've got a headache too,' Sharon said, giving Evie daggers. 'I'll come with you.'

'I've got a headache too, Bobby,' announced Evie. 'A big fuck-off massive one. Must be down to the company.'

'Why don't I drop Evie off, you drop Sharon and Brett off, and we'll meet back 'ere,' suggested Bobby.

Evie stood up. 'You can come with me, Bobby-Joe.'

'Noooo.' Bobby-Joe stamped his feet. 'I wants to stay 'ere with Ricky.'

'I'll look after Bobby-Joe, Mum. I won't bring him back late. I'll have him home in a couple of hours,' Jolene said. 'Dad, can you take all my shopping with yer?'

Bobby did as asked.

'You could've made a bit more effort, love,' Bobby said as he started the brand-new Shogun.

Evie pursed her lips. 'Why should I? Cocky prat, she was. I've come to the conclusion I likes gorger women even less than I likes the men.'

'Bloody hell, Shal. Couldn't you have kept your trap shut, just for once?' Kenny said, as they pulled out the car park.

'What! And be spoken down to by the likes of her? I don't fucking think so. She wants to think herself lucky I never grabbed hold of that silly bun on her head and dragged her round the poxy pub by it.'

'That went well, didn't it?' Jolene rolled her eyes.

Beau burst out laughing. 'There'l be fun and games at our wedding, that's for sure.'

Jolene still missed Tammy immensely. But seeing Beau every day and planning their future together had lessened her grief somewhat. They were both old enough to wed now, couldn't wait to do so. Beau said they should wait a couple of months before telling their parents of their wishes though, give everybody time to deal with their grief first.

'I saw a lovely wedding dress the other day. In a magazine it was. I'm going to show it to Thelma over in Kent. See if she can make it for me.'

'What's it like?'

Jolene playfully punched her boyfriend on the arm. 'I'm not telling you. It'll spoil the surprise on the day.'

Beau smiled. 'Fair enough. How 'bout when we drop Ricky and Bobby-Joe off, we spend a few hours at me dad's bungalow? We can order a pizza or whatever.' Gramps had given him the spare keys, so he and Jolene could spend some quality time together. Not that they got up to much. Jolene was a good girl. Touching her tits was all she'd still let him do.

'Yeah. All right. No trying it on though. I mean it.'

Beau held his hands up, palms outwards. He was desperate to make love to Jolene, couldn't wait until she became his wife and he could do so. But he respected her and her morals. Travelling girls might dress tarty, but they were anything but tarts. 'I won't touch yer, I promise. Well, only your tits.'

Jolene chuckled, then nudged Beau, pointing at her younger brother and Ricky. 'They adores one another. Ain't it lovely to see?'

'It sure is. We'll have to make 'em page boys at our wedding. Give them a special duty, like.'

'That's a great idea. I don't 'arf loves you, Beau Bond.'

Beau leaned across for a kiss. 'Not as much as I love you. You're my girl. Always and forever.'

'Once we're married, no secrets between us, remember? We always tell the truth, even if we do wrong.' Jolene's eldest brother Billy was cheating on his wife Crystal. She'd heard her parents talking about it. No way would she put up with that in a marriage. She knew she could trust Beau, mind.

'No secrets. I promise.' Beau clasped Jolene's hands. There was one secret he hadn't told her. He'd admitted

481

he'd forced Jamie to write those letters. But not that he'd killed him.

That was a secret himself, Brett and Gramps would take to their graves with them.

'Honestly, Kenny, the flowers! I never seen so many beautiful flowers in my lifetime and I been to tons of Traveller funerals. Far and wide they come from to pay their respects. The Highlands in Scotland, the Johnsons travelled from. There were thousands there. Two at least, maybe even three,' slurred Bobby. 'Everybody did my baby proud and at the wake there wasn't even one fight.'

'I'm glad Tammy had a wonderful send-off. We've got Jamie's on Wednesday. That won't be a big turnout. I've booked one side of the Huntsman and Hounds for the wake. Be glad when it's over.' Kenny topped their drinks up. Rather than keep going up the ramp, he'd bought a whole bottle of Scotch.

'I hope it, yer know, goes OK. Between me and you, I worried about my eldest two, Billy especially. I fear he and Johnny might try and do something stupid. I warned 'em if they do, I will cull 'em from my life and chuck 'em off my land, Kenny. I rules the roost. Not them.'

'Whaddya mean exactly? Something stupid to whom?'

'Oh, I dunno. They're still rambling on about revenge for their sister. Take no notice of me. It's the drink talking now. They won't do nothing. I'll make damn sure of it.'

'Good. Because if they do, it'll start a war, and neither of us want that, do we, Bobby?'

'Nope! I actually think you're a good man, Kenny. We got more in common than you think. I know you strayed once, but you regret that now, don't you?'

'Biggest mistake of my life. I love Sharon to the moon and back.'

'And I love my Evie. Me and you are the same. We're family men. Move heaven and earth to protect our loved ones.'

'I make you right, Bobby.'

'Who's that keeps ringing ya?'

'A mate,' Kenny lied, switching his phone off.

It wasn't a mate. It was the second biggest mistake Kenny had ever made, and the way Karen was pushing her luck and his patience of late, chances were she would end up suffering the same fate as his first mistake had.

The two men clinked their glasses: 'To family.'

They were unlikely friends, but they had one thing in common – little did they know what lay in store for their families in the future . . .

EPILOGUE

'A real man never hurts a woman, Kenny. God
made men stronger to protect 'em.'

*That was the only bit of advice me granddad had given
me that I'd ballsed up on. Hand on heart though, it was
an accident. I hadn't meant to kill her. Well, that's what
I like to tell meself.*

*After trashing my marriage, Abigail became even more
unhinged. Three times she rung up the nursery, threatening
to kill Sharon.*

*Divvy Dave had taken all three calls. I begged him not
to tell Shal, told him I'd deal with it. Thankfully, Dave
kept his trap shut.*

*It was a Wednesday evening when I went round to
Abigail's to confront her. Her eyes looked insane, as did
her twisted expression. Lunacy had well and truly taken
over.*

*We argued for what seemed like ages, but was probably
only minutes. Then she pulled a knife on me. A big fucking
meat knife.*

Three times she tried to stab me, catching me in the

chest the last time. Enough was enough – I tussled the knife out of her hands and put me hands around her throat.

That's when things became blurry. Not just for Abigail, but for me an' all. Next thing I recall, she was lying in a crumpled heap on the floor of her hallway. I'd throttled her. To death.

There was no pulse. Nothing. So I rang me old mucker, Bernie O'Callaghan. He waited until dark, then came to pick her up. Abigail was only small, therefore I'd managed to shove her into one of her own king-sized suitcases.

We drove her back to rural Essex to start the usual procedure. I pulled her teeth out while Bernie chopped up the body. Teeth were the only part of her the pigs wouldn't eat.

I'd never seen so much blood and gore spurt out of such a tiny person. But it did and I've had to live with that since.

The following morning, there was no trace of Abigail. She must've tasted nice, 'cause the pigs ate her up for breakfast in no time. I then disposed of the gnashers one by one. All in different places.

I wasn't proud of what I'd done, but I weren't about to beat meself up for it either. Abigail's nuttiness had left me little choice. I'd done what I had to do for all the right reasons. I loved the bones of Sharon, me kids, the grand-kids, and I would move heaven and earth to protect them all. That was my duty as a man.

I might be a cop killer. I might've made numerous mistakes in life. But nobody's perfect, are they? I did what any real man would've done in that position. Protect what meant the most to me: my loved ones.

And I would do the same again, if push came to shove. I got a good heart, but no bastard messes with my clan.

Because I, Kenny Bond, am and always will be, the ultimate family man.

THE FAMILY MAN

is the first in a new series from
The Queen of Gangland Crime

The Bond family

will return in
September 2022

Kimberley CHAMBERS

Discover more from
The Queen of Gangland Crime

For all the latest book news, competitions
and behind-the-scenes exclusives go to:

f **/kimberleychambersofficial**

🐦 **@kimbochambers**

📷 **@kimberley.chambers**

www.kimberleychambers.com